Satan Is a Woman
• • • • • • • • • • • •
13 French Street

GIL BREWER

Introduction
by David Rachels

Stark House Press • Eureka California

SATAN IS A WOMAN / 13 FRENCH STREET

Published by Stark House Press
1315 H Street
Eureka, CA 95501
griffinskye3@sbcglobal.net
www.starkhousepress.com

SATAN IS A WOMAN
Copyright © 1951 by Fawcett Publications, Inc., and published in paperback by Gold Medal Books, New York.

13 FRENCH STREET
Copyright © 1951 by Fawcett Publications, Inc., and published in paperback by Gold Medal Books, New York.

Reprinted by permission of the Estate of Gil Brewer. All rights reserved under International and Pan-American Copyright Conventions.

"Gil Brewer in the Beginning" copyright © 2023 by David Rachels

ISBN: 979-8-88601-033-6

Cover and text design by Jeff Vorzimmer, ¡caliente!design, Austin, Texas
Cover illustration by Bayre Phillips.

PUBLISHER'S NOTE:
This is a work of fiction. Names, characters, places and incidents are either the products of the author's imagination or used fictionally, and any resemblance to actual persons, living or dead, events or locales, is entirely coincidental.

Without limiting the rights under copyright reserved above, no part of this publication may be reproduced, stored, or introduced into a retrieval system or transmitted in any form or by any means (electronic, mechanical, photocopying, recording or otherwise) without the prior written permission of both the copyright owner and the above publisher of the book.

First Stark House Press Edition: July 2023

SATAN IS A WOMAN

Larry Cole's brother Tad is sent up for life for the murder of a couple fellow hoods. Larry has always looked up to Tad, and knows that if he just had enough money, he could buy him a lawyer that could get him out. When he meets Joan, his new neighbor, Larry gets sidetracked by love. He's crazy with it. But Joan is full of surprises, and she has a plan—to rob the Beach Club. This isn't what Larry has in mind to raise cash, but Joan is persistent. If she didn't have her hooks into him so deep, Larry might be able to say no. Because even Hell is more preferable to what Joan has planned for him.

13 FRENCH STREET

"Verne often said you were his best friend, Alex, maybe the only real friend he ever had. Because you disregarded things other men wouldn't put up with. So he never had any real friend, other than you. I'm his wife, yes. But you and me—that's something different again."

"Then why did you push me away?"

"Because—not all at once."

"Petra, this means I'll have to leave. It couldn't possibly go on."

She laughed. Then she threw her head back and laughed still harder. She sobered. "You won't go, Alex. I won't let you."

7
Introduction
by David Rachels

13
Satan Is a Woman

143
13 French Street

265
Gil Brewer Bibliography

Gil Brewer in the Beginning
by David Rachels

On March 26, 1951, Gil Brewer sold his first novel. Brewer had titled the manuscript *Satan's Rib*, but his publisher, Gold Medal Books, chose a more straightforward name for the soon-to-be-published paperback original: *Satan Is a Woman*.

Gold Medal asked their new writer to provide a biography, which Brewer found an awkward business. He reported to his agent, Joseph T. Shaw, "It's a funny thing. When I sit down to write a story, it isn't near the trouble I found when I had to write about myself." Brewer sent Shaw what appears to have been one unusually long paragraph (the middle of it has been lost) and asked him to "delete anything you think shouldn't be there, or whatever" before forwarding the remainder to Gold Medal. Or, if the autobiography were beyond salvaging, Brewer offered to try again. This was his "effort toward the biographical stuff":

> Have been trying to write since I was old enough to peer over the space-bar on a typewriter. For a long period I turned out a short-story a day after coming home from school. Ran the usual gamut of jobs, having been a gas-station attendant, delivered newspapers, ran a carrot-chopping machine in a canning factory—where I quit when told the man who had the job before me lost all the fingers on one hand among the churning blades—was a clerk in a hardware store, tossed crates around and was tossed around by crates, in a warehouse, sold clothes in a department store, washed cars, did a stint as a shipping-clerk in an ordnance depot where I once consigned 11 carloads of 500lb. bombs to Africa minus their arming-wire, without which they were useless. I quit that one day when I had a toothache and because it would only have been a matter of hours before I was fired. There were other jobs, and then the war, with three years in the army, two of them in the E. T. O. Made up for what I lacked in ditch-digging experience. After the war I

skiid [sic] in the Austrian Alps, performing the sport in my own manner, by hurling the skiis [sic] ahead down the side of a mountain, then diving after them. Drink kirsch in Switzerland. Roamed the dank, evil haunts of Marseille and other disenchanting hamlets along the Cote-de-Azure. Started really sweating my guts out in an effort to write in 1947. Literature, it was . . . [here, a manuscript page is missing] . . . standard of high quality entertainment. Like myself, every writer dreams of being read by many; he has something to say, he has a story to tell, he wants it to reach readers. Gold-Medal, it seems to me, confronts and accomplishes that problem. I know that any story of mine published by Gold-Medal is going to be read, not by a handful—but by a country-full of people. This pleases me, and makes me want to write more and better stories, something which I intend to try and do.

Gold Medal also requested a photograph of Brewer, which he was slow to provide.

Three months later, when Gold Medal published *Satan Is a Woman*, they included no information about the author other than his name. Gil Brewer himself was not yet marketable, so the back cover glossed the book's title and teased femme fatale Joan Turner without giving her name:

> There is a legend of olden time that the Devil is not a fallen archangel at all, but a woman with flaxen hair and green eyes—a beautiful creature with an angel face, who can bend innocent young men to her will, and bring them to their doom.
>
> Larry Cole never heard of this legend.
>
> He lived it.

Larry Cole follows the everyman template established by Walter Huff in James M. Cain's *Double Indemnity*. Like Huff

("I loved her like a rabbit loves a rattlesnake"), Cole is an ordinary guy overmatched by a woman ("It's like standing on dynamite, with the fuse sputtering"). Maybe Cole's readers have never experienced a woman so intensely ("If you've never had it like that, then you haven't"), but that's just a matter of chance ("If you don't know what I mean, then you're lucky, or unlucky"). Thus, Cole justifies his irrational, hormonal behavior (it could happen to any man!) while simultaneously heightening the vicarious thrills of his readers (it could happen to me!).

As Brewer predicted, he reached a large audience through Gold Medal Books. The publisher's standard first printing was 200,000 copies, and *Satan Is a Woman* sold well enough to necessitate two additional printings before the end of 1951. This, however, was just a warm-up for the blockbuster that followed later that year: *13 French Street* would sell 1,200,365 copies, by far the most of Brewer's career. Gold Medal's standard advance was $2000, which covered royalties of 1¢ per copy for the first printing. For sales beyond 200,000, authors received 1½¢ per copy, so in the end, Brewer earned just over $17,000 for *13 French Street*, which is roughly $200,000 today (or, more accurately, $180,000 once his agent got his 10% commission).

The packaging of *13 French Street* offers no information about Brewer beyond describing him as "GOLD MEDAL'S discovery." Again, the back cover glosses the book's title and teases femme fatale Petra Lawrence without giving her name:

> Alex came innocently into the house. His friend had a mysterious sickness.
>
> Alex did not know that the sickness was in a woman's soul, and that he would almost die of it, too.

Whereas Larry Cole's last name suggests flammability, Alex is such an everyman that his last name is Bland. And for readers who don't tend to consider why writers choose particular names, Brewer takes pains to spell it out: "Me. Alex Bland. Colorless and common and with a conscience that would keep five people treading the straight and narrow. Nose-to-the-grindstone Bland." And, naturally, even a five-man conscience stands no chance against Petra Lawrence. Bland later notes, "It's a complete helplessness that you feel, knowing all the time that the helplessness is only yourself."

Of course, Larry Cole and Alex Bland are only bit players in their own stories. The starring roles belong to Joan Turner and Petra Lawrence. After Brewer sold the film rights to *13 French Street*, gossip columnist Louella O. Parsons reported that Beverly Michaels, recent star of the film noir *Pick Up*, was slated to play Petra, "a lady who isn't all she ought to be." If Parsons knew which actor would play Alex, she did not deem it worth mentioning. Unfortunately, the film never got made.

Joseph T. Shaw was pleased by the success of *13 French Street*, but he noted that the novel was nothing but "sex angles," and he counseled his client to expand his creative palette. In July 1951, several months before *13 French Street* appeared on newsstands, Shaw had told Brewer that he was capable "of better things, of better stories without sex, for [Shaw felt] confident that [Brewer could] achieve the same emotional effects without it." Over the next year, Shaw urged Brewer to write more slowly and thoughtfully—after the financial success of *13 French Street*, he could take all the time he wanted—but then Shaw died of a heart attack on August 1, 1952. Lacking Shaw's counsel, Brewer continued working too hard and fueling his novels with sex. In February 1953, Gold Medal Books flatly rejected his *Shadow on the Dust* because its plot depended "entirely on sex." But Gold Medal, too, would not stop trying to capitalize on the success of Brewer's million-seller. On the cover of his final Gold Medal paperback, he was still "Gil Brewer, author of *13 French Street*."

—April 2023
Newberry, South Carolina

A Note on Sources
Louella O. Parsons announced the sale and casting of *13 French Street* in her syndicated column of June 9, 1952. The 1.2 million sales figure for *13 French Street* appears in Alice Payne Hackett's *Sixty Years of Bestsellers, 1895-1955*. All other information—including Brewer's early autobiography and his correspondence with Joseph T. Shaw—comes from Gil Brewer's papers, which are housed at the American Heritage Center at the University of Wyoming.

David Rachels is an author, editor, and scholar of noir fiction and poetry. He is a professor of English at Newberry College, where he teaches courses in writing and American literature with a special interest in crime fiction and literary psychopaths. Rachels has edited four short story collections by Gil Brewer for Stark House Press, and is the co-editor of Staccato Crime Classics.

Satan Is a Woman

"The Devil dreamed a dream, and her name is legion."
—Detective Lew Hawley, at the Pink Goat, long after.

Chapter One

It would have been far simpler for her just to kill me. I sometimes wish she had.

A little after seven in the morning, I spotted the light-colored sedan coming down the shell road toward the beach. I was chest-deep in the Gulf, splashing the sleep out of my system, and hadn't noticed the car turn off the main Long Key highway because I'd been watching the girl in the snug two-piece black bathing suit. She was a tall, tight dish with a rugged way of moving, and she was collecting shells. Tourists sometimes do that; then after they've gathered enough to start a business, they dump them in a pile and forget them. Or maybe they take them home in a box, where they stay for the next fifty years. This girl ran true to fashion; she dumped her load on the beach in front of my cottage. Then she glimpsed me thundering out of the water. She turned and strode off toward Pass-a-Grille, her hips bunching the shiny black lastex. I hurried toward the cottage, because I knew that car had to be for me. It was likely, anyway. There were five cabanas in a row along here, shaded by a string of royal palms, and only one was occupied. Mine. I saw the car stop by the owner's office. A tight, wary feeling took hold of me and I knew why.

I padded across the sandy, sunburned porch they call a patio, and yanked the screen door open. The rusty spring screeched like a cat. I stamped the sand off my feet, then went down the hall off the living room toward my room. The screen door slammed behind me and the spring buzzed like an enraged wasp.

The door to Tad's room was closed, so I knew he had seen the car, too. Tad had been in there for three weeks. He only came out long enough to eat, or for an occasional midnight dip in the Gulf. "Sick, Larry," he'd told me when he showed up that day.

"Why don't you let me get a doctor?"

"Not that kind of sick, kid," he'd said.

I took a gander from my window as I stripped off my shorts. The car was approaching rapidly, lurching in the sinkholes. I slipped into a pair of suntans, grass slippers, and a white T shirt.

The car ground to a stop outside. A door slammed. Another door. Feet crunched. Right away somebody pounded on the kitchen door.

I stood there rubbing my salty scalp with a bath towel and let them pound. Finally they stopped and went around to the front. I walked down the hall. Not a sound came from Tad's room. I went on into the living room.

A broad, squatty guy wearing a Panama hat was just getting ready to let the screen door have it.

"All right," I said. "Never mind that."

There were two of them: the squatty one and a tall one, shading his eyes with his hand against the screen, trying to see inside. The squatty one still wanted to make a racket.

"Larry Cole?" the tall one said. "Mr. Larry Cole?"

I shoved through the screen door and stepped outside.

"Yes," I said. "I'm Cole." The squatty one went over and sat on the weathered glider, in the shade. They were cops, both of them. Plain clothes. My heart began to pound. I knew most of the St. Pete crew, but I didn't know them. Business was written all over their faces. I wadded up the towel and pitched it into the glider beside Squatty. He mopped at his face with a dirty handkerchief. "O.K.," I said. "What d'you want?"

The tall one looked at me patiently. There was a kind of patience in the way he moved as he unbuttoned his gray gabardine jacket, shoved it back, and placed his fists on his hips. "So you're Larry Cole?"

"He's Larry Cole," Squatty said. He finished mopping his face, blew his nose loudly, and jammed the handkerchief into his hip pocket.

"I asked you," I said. "What do you want?"

He didn't smile, he just looked. "Shall we go inside?"

I shrugged and yanked the door open. The spring whined. Squatty grunted off the glider. I slammed the door shut and turned to look at them. "No," I said. "We won't go inside. I've changed my mind."

"I'm Fennell," the tall one said. "And this is Malone. We're from Tampa. Police headquarters in Tampa. If it's O.K., we'd like to ask you a few questions."

"About what?"

Malone said, "Ah, Christ!"

"About Tad Cole," the tall one said patiently. "He's your brother, isn't he?"

"How do I know you're from the police?"

Malone said, "Jesus."

"You know, all right," the tall one, Fennell, said. "But here." He held a shield before my eyes, waggled it, and put it back in his pocket.

"All right," I said. "So what d'you want to talk about?"

Malone went back to the glider and flopped down. He sneezed three times in rapid succession, wiped his nose with the back of his chubby hand, and sat there staring wet-eyed at the Gulf of Mexico. "Lord," he said "Oh, Lord."

Fennell jabbed me in the ribs with a rigid thumb. "Seen Tad lately, Larry?"

"No," I told him. Not too fast, not too slow. Just right, I lied, not really knowing why, but damned sure I had better. Tad had told me nothing. But these boys wanted something. They don't act like this unless they really want something.

"Why not?" Fennell said. "Why haven't you seen him?"

"Because he hasn't been around to see," I said.

"Why?"

It was my turn to look now, and I made it as obviously patient as I could.

"O.K.," Fennell said. "You haven't seen him. When did you see him last?"

"What's all this about?"

"When did you see him last?" from Malone, this time. He was still watching the Gulf.

"I don't know exactly," I said, knowing I'd better say something. "Six months ago?"

"Tell me, don't ask me," Fennell said.

"We'll ask the questions," said Malone.

"Listen," I said. "I don't know what this is all about. I haven't seen my brother in at least six months. I only saw him then for a few minutes. He stopped in at the Pink Goat—my place."

"We know," Fennell said patiently.

"I thought he was in California—L.A."

"Sure," from Malone. "Maybe Mexico."

"Maybe," I said. Fennell wasn't fooling me with his attitude of tremendous patience, but I'd rather talk with him than Squatty Malone. "If you'll tell me what it's all about," I said. "Has Tad—my brother, that is—done something, or something?"

"All right," Fennell said. "I believe you. I don't think he'd come around here, anyway. We came on orders. Checkwork, routine investigation. Your brother killed a man, and another guy's dying slowly in the hospital." His patience was painful as panic thrust a choking fist down my throat. "You're clean, of course," Fennell said. "We've checked you straight through."

"Tad's killed some—"

"Lord, oh, Lord," Malone said. He turned his eyes from the Gulf and belabored Fennell with his steady, watchful gaze. "I won't kid you. I don't believe this guy. He's lying. He knows something. He's lying like hell."

"Where?" I said.

"Ybor City—Tampa," Fennell told me. "Three weeks ago. The guy dying in the hospital only began to talk yesterday, last night." He poked two fingers into his throat. "Slugs, here. He thinks that's all, that he's going to get well enough to spend the rest of his life at Raiford."

"Only he ain't," Malone said. "He's bleeding to death inside. Two days at the most."

I was standing there listening to all of this, and not really hearing it, while I figured and planned and schemed and wondered, half crazy with worry. Because now Tad had done it, really done it. "Sick," he'd said. "Sick." And all the time he was inside this very house, probably listening, too. Doing what? He had finally gone and done the big thing.

"Did you know your brother very well?" Fennell asked. He was staring out at the Gulf now, waiting for me to slip. He thrust his hands into his jacket pockets, waiting, patient.

"Yeah," I said. "I know him."

All three of us stared at the Gulf. I said, "Why? What was it all about?"

"Where is he, kid?" Malone said. "Where you got him?"

Fennell ignored Malone and said, "He might be able to run from other stuff, but not this. This is straight murder. Those boys were no good, though. They were holding out on a pay-off, somebody got itchy and the three of them began blasting at each other in the middle of the street in front of Las Novedades."

"Where you got him stashed, kid?" asked Malone.

Fennell said, "Tad Cole is hot. He's a bad egg. He's no good. We've known that, and he's been out of Tampa. But how you going to keep 'em out of Tampa?"

I turned and stared at him.

"Maybe you're keeping him on ice, inside?" Malone said.

Something broke loose inside me. "Sure!" I said. "Go look, damn you!" I grabbed the screen door open and the spring gave a shriek. "Go ahead, damn you! There he is, see him?" I started laughing and I couldn't stop for a minute. Then I quit that and Fennell was watching me patiently, and maybe pityingly. I began to hate him worse than Malone. At least Malone spoke up. Fennell just stood there thinking dirty thoughts, wondering with his scheming brain how he could trip me up; working it the brainy way.

"O.K.," Fennell said. "We've checked, and you know the score now. You know you'd better not keep him on ice if he does come around. You'll be an accessory, kiddo. I think I've got you tabbed. I hope not, but I think so. Two Coles in one family must've played hell with Mamma." He started walking away. Malone shoved up off the glider and started after him. When he got opposite me, he turned fast and said, "Ah-h-h-h!"

"Keep in touch," Fennell said over his shoulder, his heels smacking the cement of the patio. "If you do see him, you know what to do."

"I'll concede this," Malone said, stopping to turn and face me squarely, the sun bright on his Panama. "If I was in your shoes, Mr. Cole, I'd probably lie just like you. We know you know." He looked at me for a long moment with his wet eyes.

"C'mon," Fennell said. He glanced at me. "So long, kiddo." They crunched around the side of the cottage.

I stood there staring at the brightness of the cement. They would watch. It was their job. It was their case. They were on it. Malone was firm in his conviction that I had lied to them. Fennell thought maybe I had lied, but wasn't sure. Neither of them thought for an instant that Tad Cole was inside this very house. If they thought for a split second that Tad was anywhere around here, they would still be waiting, and they would keep on waiting. Or maybe they'd drum up a charge and waft me over to Tampa for a little questioning. That could come, too. I knew about that. Tad told me all about that.

When I lifted my eyes and turned toward the screen door, I saw sun spots just from staring at the reflection of the sun on cement.

Tad had to run, fast. It was his only chance. They were closing in. If there was even a whisper, if somebody saw a curtain move while I was at work, if old man Buck or his wife noticed anything from the office, Tad was cinched. And somebody would notice. I knew Fennell and Malone had tipped people to watch. That was part of the game.

It would have to be quick—now, tonight. Tad had to run. And I had to help him.

Oh, yes. I had known it was something. I'd known Tad was cooling off here at my place, lying low. But I'd never thought for a minute it was this. I'd been scared for him, but I hadn't been able to ask him what it was. Now I knew.

He was whistling in the bathroom. The faucet flicked on and off, on and off, so I knew he was shaving. The big car with Fennell and Malone in it was on the shell road, headed for the highway.

I stood in the bathroom doorway and stared at Tad's back. About my size, medium, only maybe slimmer, neater, with broad shoulders and sandy hair that held a sheen. He scraped at the whiskers on his neck.

"Tad," I said. "Tad."

He dipped his head, winked at me in the mirror, and grinned through the shaving lather. "You know, eh, kid? You know." He swiped the razor at his cheek, a long clean swath. "They told you, hey, kid?" He stretched the skin of his neck on the left, holding his chin high and to the right, and scraped. Then he turned the faucet on hard and swished the razor under the stream of water. Then he started on his chin. "Don't look so sad, Larry. Not so sad. I should have told you." Crisp, neat, his hard face and his hard yellow-flecked eyes.

"Tad, for God's sake! Why didn't you tell me? Why'd you come here saying you had a hangover? Then saying you were sick, a very bad hangover. No clothes, no car, no nothing. I should have known."

He finished shaving, splashed cold water on his face, grabbed a towel, and started drying. "Cut it out, Larry." He tossed the towel into the shower, shoved past me, and walked briskly down the hall into his room. I went after him.

"Don't come around me with that stuff," he said. "Give me a clean shirt."

"There's one on the chair there." I pointed.

He whistled as he turned toward the chair.

"Tad!" I yelled. I grabbed his arm as he reached for the shirt. He stared at my hand, then at me. I let go of his arm. He picked up the shirt, nodded, slipped it on, and started buttoning it.

"What's for breakfast, Larry?"

"Breakfast...."

"A tie, Larry. A real smart, calm, unwrinkled tie. Mine's a mess. Blood on it. My only one, think of it." He picked up the tie he'd worn when he'd come that night three weeks ago. It was torn, and there were brown stains on the light tan expensive weave. "Dry cleaning wouldn't help that."

"By the shirt," I said. I watched him pick up the tie I'd put by the shirt on the chair. He wrinkled his nose at it, then knotted it rapidly, neatly, as he did everything. "Oh, Larry," he said, stepping over to the bureau. He snapped the top drawer open and hauled out a shoulder harness, holster, and gun. "This is for you. Keep it in case of prowlers."

"Tad!" I was sweating and the back of my scalp felt as if it were going to rise like the lid on a teakettle. "What're you doing?"

"Look," he said softly. "I haven't much time, kid. I got only a few minutes to eat some breakfast. Then I got to catch a bus."

"Yeah," I said, relieved. "But not now. Not in daylight. Lay low. They won't be around today, Tad. Tonight. Look. I'll get a car and run you out of the state, anyway. Georgia, maybe. I could close the Pink Goat for a vacation."

He was looking at me with amazement, incredulity.

"Yeah," I said. "Sure, Tad. I'll help you. You've got to run. You killed a man—two men, maybe, if the other one dies. That means—"

"That's right," he snapped. "Exactly." He flipped the gun and harness back into the drawer and slammed it shut. "Remember, it's in there."

"Tad—"

"Breakfast, Larry. Breakfast."

"O.K.," I said. "All right. But will you?"

"Will I what, Larry?" He held his head cocked a little to one side, watching me, tight-lipped. "Will I what?"

"Let me help you? Help you get away?"

His face changed, his eyes brightened. "No. Run? You want me to run? Those guys deserved it, both of them. Punks. They were killers."

"And you?"

"I hope he dies quick. I want it right. Both of them. Run? No, kid. Not run. I'm through waiting, through with running, through with it all." He turned from me and quickly combed his hair in front of the dresser mirror.

"Tad—"

"Shut up!" He turned and his voice was soft, like cotton dragged across a wire screen. "I'm turning myself in."

"No, Tad. Don't do that. They haven't got you yet. Don't be a fool."

He stepped in close and said quietly, "How much have I got to teach you? How much to tell you? How do I have to bash it into your mushy head? I'm through—washed up." He watched me, watched me unable to speak, to do anything. "I've done it all, kid. Nobody has to tell me I'm through. I was going to turn myself in. I just wanted to think, that's all. A little time to go over it all, and find out how I could have been such a dope. I know, of course. Now, be quiet, will you? I'm sorry I came here. Should have stuck it out with a broad someplace. But I wanted to think, nothing but think. Them coming today—well, it was time, it was time. And I don't want you messed in it."

"Tad," I said. "You're talking like a fool."

"I see your broken nose still shows, don't it, kid?"

I looked at the floor between us. I could hear him breathing. "You won't let me help you escape?" I said. "You won't even try? Even when they were just punk killers? When you know they deserved it? You won't let me help?"

"No." I could hear him breathing, and when he spoke his voice was quiet, as it had always been. "Let's have some coffee, Larry. Then you better get over to work."

Chapter Two

There was the time I stole the bicycle light from the hardware store on Ninth Street, in St. Pete. I was fifteen. I came out of the shop with the light clutched in my hand, and ran smack into Tad. He was like that. He'd been in a bar next door.

"What you got there, Larry?" Even then Tad was somehow as old as Satan himself. Wiry, broad-shouldered, hard as sheet steel.

My voice was all guilt. "Nothing," I told him.

"It's a bike light, kid. Where'd you get the money?"

"Saved it up."

"Sure." He took my hand, drew me into an alley. "Take it back."

"Naw!" I was scared. The way he looked at me. His eyes got all flecked with yellow when he was mad, and his mouth quirked at one corner as if it were worked with a string. He hit me, just once, not hard.

I tore back into the store, slammed the light on the counter, said to the man, "Just lookin'," and beat it.

Later that night Tad didn't smile. "Sorry, Larry. Don't do it again. Ever. Here." He handed me five dollars. "Buy yourself a bike light. Try an' get the same one you glommed."

Next time I was seventeen and it was cigarettes. A whole crate from the warehouse off Central. By now I knew Tad was no traveling salesman. With the folks dead and him my guardian, I figured I was hot stuff when he got mixed up in a *bolita* raid at Ybor City. So I lined up the cigarettes with another guy and brought them home. I went out to sell some. When I got back, Tad was sitting on the crate of cigarettes.

"Hello, kid."

I swallowed. "Hi, Tad." He was quiet, but his eyes were yellow-flecked. He stood, stepped up to me slowly, balled his fist, and broke my nose.

I was as big as Tad then. But I didn't dare hit him. He was deadly, somehow. Tad couldn't really be anybody's brother.

When I got up off the floor, he hit me again. I tried to keep away from him, but he beat me till I couldn't move. He was savage about it. Like maybe if he didn't beat me enough it wouldn't be any good.

I wanted to hit back, but I couldn't. And when he got through with me, I really couldn't.

He quit and sat on the crate of cigarettes again. When he lit a cigarette, his hands shook. I lay on the floor.

"That's the last time, Larry. It's supposed to be wrong, I know. But I can't talk so good. If I just talked without busting you first, you wouldn't remember." He flicked the ash off his cigarette. "It's the wrong road, kid."

I swallowed some blood and blurted, "What about you?"

"I'm me, an' you're you. I'm too far on the road to turn back. I'm sunk, kid."

Then he told me all of it. How Pop hadn't really died when I was a few months old. Pop had been shot in the street, in Tampa. Mom had vanished before that. Pop was a paid gunman. Only he finally gunned the wrong guy.

"Way I see it," Tad finished, "it don't run in the blood, like folks say. It's what you see, how you live, how you get to believing, kid. I'm not going to play keeper, Larry. But I'll see you get a chance. You're going to college. You got to live right. The way I couldn't." He frowned and his eyes brightened. "Society's funny. But it won't get to hurt you, Larry. Not if I can help it."

I still couldn't get off the floor, and I was plenty mad about my busted nose. I figured he shouldn't have done that.

"Take the cigarettes back, kid."

"Aw, but Tad!"

He dropped his butt, stepped on it, and walked out of there, hard-heeled, without even looking at me.

I didn't see Tad much after that, but he wrote me a lot. He drove big cars, Caddies mostly, and I went to college. He visited me a few times. His women were with him, one at a time, as sleek as his cars. All beautiful and groomed like race horses. Blonde, smiling, and crisp as new one-hundred-dollar bills.

"Remember, kid. I'm me, you're you. They're just broads. Only they're dangerous broads. Don't get to thinking about champagne and caviar. Stick to beer an' pretzels. It's safer. And, to be honest, it's more fun." His mouth quirked at one corner when he said it.

I understood all of that. Next thing I knew, Tad was in jail. The numbers racket. I was in the war.

When I got out of uniform, I didn't go back to school. With Tad's help I opened a little bar, the Pink Goat, out on the beaches, and took life easy. Tad was out of stir again, and he wrote from Los Angeles. Then Miami. He mentioned a woman he planned to marry. But something went wrong, and he pulled out of Miami with the law after him. From then on he was hot—really hot.

"*Cherchez* the *femme*," he wrote, "then run like hell the other way." But according to Tad, he had fixed this woman's clock in some way or another. Fixed it for good.

Then he went and pulled his gun outside Las Novedades, a Spanish restaurant in Ybor City, and killed two men. Sure, the other one died. He was dead before Tad reached Tampa that day, after he left my cottage to turn himself in.

These two lads had tried to welsh on a large bet of several thousand dollars in some gamble, and they had planned a setup to have Tad knocked off by a hired hood. Only Tad was put wise by a quick tip from an old pal, and he gave the two men just what they planned to give him. He meant it when he did it.

Three weeks later he was in Raiford. He wrote me and told me the chow wasn't half bad. Everything wasn't over with yet, because of the Tampa political mix-up, the bloody whirlpool, but he was quite certain of the chair. Like that, he told me.

Good lawyers, he said—one good lawyer—might be able to save him from the chair.

"But," he wrote, "there's no money by me any more, and good lawyers, hot ones, cost money. Anyway, it's all over. It's all over. I had enough—too much."

So I got to figuring. . . .

Chapter Three

Sentence was imposed on Tad after his trial in Tampa. He was found guilty of second-degree murder, and sentenced to spend the rest of his life in the state pen, at Raiford.

I was there. I watched Tad nod and heard him say, "O.K. Yes. Sure," agreeing and condoning.

So he didn't get the chair, as he had expected.

I spoke to him once before he was sent away. "Isn't there a thing can be done, Tad?"

He cocked his head and watched me. Then he sighed, sitting there on the cot in his cell, flicking ashes on the floor. "Sure," he said. "Lots can be done. But like I told you before the trial, when they were holding me over, it'd cost money. Real money. A lawyer could appeal, and take the case to a higher court. I might get a cut in sentence. Then, later on, in a couple years, maybe lots more could be done if I kept my nose clean."

"You always do," I said.

"Sure. Only I skinned it."

"What?"

"Skinned my nose." He ground the cigarette out on the cell floor with a quick twist of his heel.

"Don't you want that? Don't you want to get it maybe cut?"

"Sure, Larry. Sure I do. Who wouldn't? I thought I'd get the chair. I was ready for it, kid. It really didn't scare me. But now that I'm not getting the chair, the old hope starts rising. Only, what the hell? There's no use. Lawyers cost money. The one I had standing for me at that trial didn't do anything."

"Life instead of death," I put in.

"Nah, Larry. Public sentiment did that. I rid the city of Tampa of a couple of rats. People consider that a gesture of kindness. They can't get it into their heads I would have done the same if those guys had been favorite preachers."

"Then you don't care, really?"

"About them? The ones I killed? No."

"I see. And good lawyers might be able to fix the whole thing?"

"Public sentiment being what it is right now, yes. Maybe later it wouldn't, I don't know. There's all this crime-investigation fuss going on, and I—"

"Fuss?"

"Sure, fuss. Everybody's all hot and bothered. They don't know who to trust, who to believe. Hell, they don't even believe themselves. They get in a locked room and stare at their faces in a mirror and say, 'Good night, am I sane, or what?' Sure, maybe in a couple years, or a bit more, things could be done. Right now, with a really hot lawyer who knows what he's about, my sentence could be sliced if he could get me another trial. The public looks at my picture, seeing my clean-cut face—"

I laughed. It was the first laughter since Tad had left the cottage to turn himself in, weeks before.

"Sure," he went on. "Clean-cut. You know, kid, I got letters at Raiford, while I was waiting trial, when everybody was so damned busy. Letters from folks saying they needed more men like me. They wouldn't believe I was a criminal, a thief, a crook, too. Here in Tampa, folks try to send me food. Apple pies, stuff like that. I don't get it, naturally." He waved his hands at the bars. "The boys out there, they get it. But it comes for me." He leaned back on the cot. "Sure, lots of things could be done. *Could* be. But where is all that dough I used to have? Where are the friends with dough like that? Big dough, kid. That's what it takes, and I haven't got it." He looked at me. "So long, kid. The man with the watch and the lucky key is here." He glanced up at the uniformed cop who stood at the cell door. "Hiya, keeper!" he said. "So long, kid."

I spent a lot of time thinking during the next couple of weeks. I certainly didn't come up with any bomb, either. But there was one thing I was going to do. Every penny I could save, I would. Maybe it wouldn't be much, because the Pink Goat wasn't a large place. But it would be something. Perhaps I could find who a real good lawyer was, and talk him into some deal, where I'd pay him over a period of time, like buying an automobile on credit. It sounded corny to me, but it had to be that way. The best lawyer I could find. And he'd have to listen. But I couldn't even start talking until I saved some money. And money was slow that summer. The tourist season just didn't come the way it usually did.

Tad wrote regularly and told me to take it easy. He was back at Raiford for the long count now and had already wangled a job as trusty. Probably through one of his pals. A tone crept into his letters, a tone of defeat, and I didn't like it. He acted like his spirit was broken. Crime is no good, sure—but I'd rather think of Tad with his Caddies and his racy women than see him up there, not giving a damn any more.

When he talked like that it only made me feel worse, and resolve a little harder to get money some way. I didn't mention any of my ideas to Tad, of course, because it would have made him hot. I'd have liked to ask him about lawyers, because he'd know just exactly who to hunt up. But I couldn't.

And it seemed the more I wanted to make money out of the Pink Goat, the less folks wanted a drink. My liquor sales took a dip. Wine, always a good seller down here in Florida, for some reason wasn't going well at all. Bottled and canned beer fell off, cocktails were demanded so seldom I began to wonder if I'd lost my touch in mixing them. The only thing that held its own was draught beer, and little enough of that. One guy who had always been a regular on wine and beer, taking wine as a shot, and a beer chaser—another peculiarity of drinking down here that I've never noticed to any extent in other parts of the country—saw me drinking a glass of milk one day. So he tried some whisky in milk. Then he cut out the whisky, reformed, and came in about twice a day to dawdle over a quart of milk and talk about his past; his gloriously drunken days. It made me sick, and I even tried drinking beer in front of him, but it didn't take.

It got so bad that I began to really advocate alcohol. I made little signs and hung them on the wall, explaining the benefits of whisky, beer, wine, and the Pink Goat as the best dispensary on the beaches.

It got me exactly nowhere. Some afternoons I'd lean on the bar, wondering what in hell I was going to do, and hardly a soul would wander in. Except Detective Lieutenant Lew Hawley. He was a friend of mine, with homicide, and he ran on bourbon the same as a car runs on gas. There's Marlowe, the fictional sleuth, and Sam Spade, and then there's my friend Hawley. Well, I used to wonder when I read about them drinking like they did. Some of those lads sure guzzled the hard stuff. Hawley was a natural, with his red face and his sleepy blue eyes that looked as if they'd seen too much sunlight, and the way he grabbed a whisky glass with his big hand covered with freckles and sunburned, peeling skin. And the sweat-stained gray felt hat shoved back off his sun-blasted head.

"What you hear from your brother?" Hawley said one afternoon in the middle of June. "He like it where he is?"

"Great," I said.

Hawley finished his drink and motioned for another. He drinks his whisky from a mixing glass; the thick type of glass I use to shake cocktails in. Whisky, ice, with a splash of water on top. I know he's a good drawing card because he makes people thirsty just to watch him drink. Tilting the glass, the ice rattling against his teeth, smacking his lips and saying, "Ah-h-h-h!" very gently. Then a polite belch, and a refill.

"It's too bad about him, Larry. I knew Tad well."

"Yeah, I know."

Then he started humming. It was a habit with him to hum when he was thinking, no special tune, just a continuous noise. He gulped at his drink and the ice rattled. "He used to steer you away from jams, didn't he, Larry?"

"You could call it that, yeah."

"I met a couple lads from Tampa. Malone and Fennell," he said. Hawley's voice was kind of hoarse always; I guess it was all the whisky he drank. "That Malone thinks you were hiding Tad out."

"What do you know?" I said.

"Sure," Hawley grunted. "I know it, too. But that's all right."

I looked at him. He finished his drink and looked at me, then set the glass down with a clink. "Oh, well," he said, "live easy, die easy. What was it the guy said? Everybody'll starve to death when wolves eat wolves?" He grinned, his red face beaded with sweat. Then he said, "Well, Larry, let me know," and stomped out of the bar, his shoulders swinging. His gray sedan swirled off into the sunlight on the highway. I never did find out what he wanted me to let him know about.

On that afternoon, right after Hawley drove away, I saw a maroon convertible Buick slip up in front of the Pink Goat, and a girl stepped out.

Nobody else was in the Pink Goat, so I watched her, because just the way she moved was something. Not that the car was anything special, not new, that is, but just the way that car came in, and stopped. I didn't know it yet, but this was Joan. And my life was due for a change. A big change.

At first, when she came inside, I thought she was just another rich dame on a fling, or maybe just prowling. Or maybe just thirsty. I guess I stared at her as she approached the bar, but she didn't seem to mind. She was smiling, and the way she carried herself was something to see. Light and easy, it was; lithe.

"Hello," she said. "Could you fix me a dry Martini?"

No order, like some of them. Just a nice question, asking me if maybe I might, if I felt like it, or anyway when I got around to it.

"Sure," I told her. "Dry Martini."

She was dressed all in white, a lightweight dress that did all kinds of things for her. Or maybe not. Maybe she didn't need anything to do things for her. At first glance you might think she was just another blonde, only then you'd begin to see that wasn't so. Her hair was this rich, thick, honey-blonde, falling to golden-skinned shoulders that looked warm and made me want to touch them. Nearly as tall as I, she was warm and cool at the same time, with eyes like pale blue diamonds, and soft, moist lips. She carried a long-strapped purse, swung it from one hand.

I fixed her drink and she paid me for it. I rang it up, and as I turned back to the bar she said, "Haven't I seen you somewhere before?" Her voice was liquid, cool.

I reached for the bar rag, dropped it on the floor, stepped on it, and grinned.

"Shouldn't I say that?" She smiled. I kept wiping my foot on the bar rag. And I was dizzy, plain dizzy.

I said, "Probably you've been in here before. But I don't think so. I would have—"

"Noticed?" she put in. We both grinned. I leaned over to pick up the bar rag and bumped my head on the sink. I grinned and looked at her again. All of a sudden I wanted to get drunk. I wanted to talk with her.

"Where do you live?" I asked. I didn't even choke on it.

"Down the beach."

"Me too. How far?"

"Just past that string of royal palms. I came down a week ago from New York. I've been living in town, but today I rented a cottage." She finished her Martini.

There were the five cottages by the royal palms. They were the only royal palms around there. One of the cottages was mine.

"My name is Joan Turner."

"I'm Larry Cole," I said. "I own this joint."

She looked around, even got off the stool and walked around, long-legged, lithe. Then she came back to the bar, and leaned on it. "Larry Cole," she said, "we're neighbors. I live next door to you. I asked that fat fellow—"

"Buck, the owner?"

"That's right, Buck. I asked him who lived there, and he told me about you. So I decided to run over and meet you." She had long, smooth, golden hands. She propped her elbow on the bar, cupped her hand around her chin, and watched me.

I put some ice in the shaker. "Well, I'm certainly glad you did. Now that we're neighbors, I hope you'll make it a habit," I said. "How you like it down here?" I was sure glad nobody else was in the Pink Goat, to break up what was starting out to be a promising conversation.

"It's nice, I guess," she said. "But it's lonely as the dickens if you don't know anybody. And I don't know much of anybody. That's why I moved out here. It's cooler, anyway."

"Well," I said, "now you know me. And I know everybody, almost."

"Why don't you have a drink with me, Larry?"

"We'll let the Goat buy this one." I mixed two double Martinis. "How long you down for?"

"Not long," she said. "I'm a wage slave."

We talked for a while about nothing, like people talk. I knew how I was beginning to feel, but I couldn't tell anything about how she felt.

I figured the Pink Goat needed a chance to graze. There was no business.

"Look," I said. "How about a swim? We could go on home and change."

"But how about the bar?"

"I'll lock up."

"Just like that?"

"Just like that."

So I did. We drove home in her car. She was a good driver, and her hair looked fine blowing in the wind.

Chapter Four

Joan walked slowly across the white sands toward me. She was slipping on her bathing cap, stuffing the thick honey hair beneath the cap, and smiling as she came.

I'll never forget that moment. Never.

There was a soft wind coming in over the Gulf and I felt as though it must have traveled clear from Mexico, maybe bringing some guitar music with it.

"You beat me." She took long strides, her long golden legs gleaming, each hip settling in a wide curving way loaded with grace as she neared me.

"What?"

"Beat me. Maybe you weren't wearing so much."

"I'm thick."

She laughed, throwing her head back, and her teeth were very white between her lips. "My gosh! The undressing, and putting on the bathing suits. You beat me."

"Oh, sure. Did I?"

She frowned, her lips pulling at their corners toward more smiling. "Now I'm the one. You're kidding, hey?" She reached and gave me a push. It felt as if my skin puckered where her hand touched. I staggered back.

"Last one in buys dinner!" She was halfway to the water before I came back to this world and realized what was going on.

I ran. She ran with grace, speed, seeming to skim across the shallows, then flat in a long, low racing dive.

I couldn't catch her. Treading water, she'd look back at me and laugh, kick the water with her feet, then vanish. I swam out near her, in deeper water.

Hands circled my ankles, gripped. I went down, pulled down, knowing Joan was pulling and never realizing a woman had such strength. Down and down. I hadn't had a chance to get my breath. I was dizzy, still dizzy.

Down, down, down. We were on the bottom. The sands sloped brightly away toward the beach. The sun's rays gleamed on white, her white bathing suit, the golden skin. She was still laughing, her teeth white, too, between red lips. Then she was gone—up.

I floated upward and burst the surface at her side.

The sun exploded on her head. We came together. We touched. Her eyes were big and blue. She broke away and swam toward the sun, her arms cleaving the water in long, graceful strokes. Her shoulders gleamed whitely, and again she vanished.

I dove. Sharply. At her.

We came at each other along the bottom, just where the bank of sand tilted abruptly toward the long dark green of depth.

She laughed. Bubbles streamed from her lips. She sprang away in terrific slow motion. I reached, caught her, pulled her to me, and for an instant we came together hard, our lips together. She struggled, then I felt her relax.

We separated. She no longer laughed. There were no bubbles. We swam up into the bright white sun and the same wind coming across the Gulf all the way from Mexico with singing in it now.

"What were you thinking out there?"

I stood on the warm sand, having just come back from my cottage with a blanket. I spread the blanket out, and she knelt on it.

"Maybe I couldn't think," I told her.

She slipped off her bathing cap and her hair belled out around her shoulders as she shook her head. The sun grew in her hair, and her hair was fire.

"Did you ever think, Larry, that you'd like a lot of money? I mean, a real lot?"

I sprawled down beside her and put my face into the blanket, breathed the clean smell of the wool. "Sure. Who hasn't?"

"Did you ever figure to do something about it?"

"How?" I was drowsy in the sun.

"I don't know. I always dreamed of big money." I wasn't watching, but she turned, seated, and faced the sun, the western sky, and added, "Maybe everybody who's poor dreams that."

"Sure, I guess you're right."

"I'd like to go swimming at night. Everybody says it's different. I never have. Is it different?"

"Than daylight?" I turned around and joined her in staring out at the Gulf. I remembered how Malone had stared, too. "I guess it's different. We will. Joan, how long are you going to stay here?"

"In Florida? Here? Two weeks. Then I have to drive back."

"To where?"

"To the little bookstore. I'm a kind of secretary in a bookstore in Manhattan. Didn't I tell you? I push bestsellers, and them that ain't, I shove."

"Two weeks."

"Uh-huh. I wish it could be longer, Larry." She glanced at me, then away. "I think maybe it would be fun. Only I'm not sure yet."

"What do you have to do to be sure?"

She looked at me. She didn't smile. "I lied."

I didn't say anything, my eyes on the curve of her lips, her cheek, her shoulders, her breasts, the flare of her hips, the long graceful arc of thigh and calf.

"I said, I lied."

"Yes?"

"I don't want to go back. I've had a taste of something and I like it." She turned back toward the Gulf, and the wind streamed through her hair, pushing it up thickly so her profile was sharp and clear.

"What have you had a taste of?"

"I don't know, exactly. I'll know better later on maybe. But I don't want to go back. This is my first real vacation. I saved for it, Larry. I saved for that car, too, then saved the car for the vacation. I bought the car through a friend. I was lucky to end up with only a car. He wanted to give me the car, any car—if I'd be understanding. I almost married the guy, too. It took me four years to realize what he was."

"What was he?"

"I'm twenty-seven, Larry. Not young."

"Not old."

"But not young, either. And no dope now."

It seemed to me that the soft line of her cheek hardened, the curve of her mouth straightened. I dug a handful of sand and let it stream down her shin, across her instep.

She looked at me and grinned. "Swimming makes you hungry. Do you handle the Pink Goat all by yourself?"

"I have a guy. Adams—Pete Adams—whom I get to fill in, cheap." I thought of Tad and the hot lawyer I didn't have, and how maybe Pete Adams would be working a bit more regularly now.

"You don't laugh enough, Larry. You don't run around kicking the sand in my eyes." She hesitated, then spoke rapidly. "Larry, what are you thinking about all the time?"

"Like I said, maybe I can't think."

"You're thinking, all right."

"Am I?"

"Yep." Our hands brushed. It was like fire. "So am I."

We were silent for a long while, then. We watched a school of porpoise corkscrewing in the water, not very far out. A fishing launch throbbed through the middle of them and they vanished. I brought four cans of beer down from the house and we drank them. We still didn't say much of anything.

That night I felt reckless. I hadn't taken a vacation of any kind for a long while. I started off maybe a little too well by asking Joan to drop in at the Beach Club for a few drinks and dinner.

The Beach Club is between the cabanas and the Pink Goat. It's a large, sprawling place that takes up a couple of acres.

Two bars, dining, dancing, refreshment bars, beautiful beaches, landscaping; it was money.

I very seldom went there because a bottle of beer cost seventy cents, and that's a hell of a price to pay when I can drink all I want at my place. I drink very little, anyway. But I thought I'd show it to Joan. I didn't ask her if she'd been there before, just took it for granted she hadn't. I was wrong.

"I'd love to go, Larry."

We had Martinis at a buck a throw. We ate steak, both of us, and I noticed she had an excellent appetite. So did I. There was a Hawaiian setup playing Hawaiian music, and a dark-haired girl doing a grass-skirted number, and people said she was good. But I couldn't see anything for Joan.

She seemed partial to white, and was wearing an off-the-shoulder dress that was something between fog and expensive cigarette smoke, and she seemed happy.

"It's all very nice," I said finally, "but let's take off and have us a stroll on the beach. O.K.?"

She hesitated, then said, "Sure, Larry. Whatever you'd like. Maybe we can come here again?"

"Sure," I said. I didn't see why we should, though. I didn't like wearing a tie and jacket. There was too much giddy swirl, false laughter, and sleekly rich noise for me.

Then somebody said, "Well, hi, baby! You startled me," and it was a tall guy with a mahogany tan, too white teeth, oily hair, and dressed in a cream-colored tropical suit that must have set him back a couple of hundred.

Joan glanced at him quickly, smiled, then looked at me.

The man stood there a moment, grunted, shrugged his eyebrows, said, "Didn't mean to butt in, baby," and swaggered off. He wore hard heels.

"I met him here," she told me. "I wasn't going to mention that I'd been here before, Larry, because it's so perfect with just you and me. I—I don't even know his name. That is, I met him at the bar."

"Smooth customer," I said.

She nodded, seemed relieved. "That's just it. Too smooth a customer. He wanted to take me home. I came with a girl I met in town. Practically had to beat him off."

I'd never tell her what had happened inside me when that guy came up to the table. I'd read more in his eyes than a bar conversation. Maybe I'd been wrong. But I'd never tell her, and it was all right, anyway. She had the right to go wherever she chose. I'd only met her today.

"Should have introduced us," I said. Then, "No. That's right. You didn't know his name."

"Better the way I did it, Larry," she told me. "He knew he wasn't wanted."

That night, walking on the beach, I was conscious only of the movement of her body, the secret sounds of something more than woman.

It rained suddenly, as if somebody emptied a pail of water. We were drenched before we'd moved ten feet. It kept on raining and we had several hundred yards to go before we reached our cottages. Halfway there, Joan tripped on her high heels and fell.

"Clumsy!" I said. "Hurt yourself?"

She lay there with her face pale against the pouring rain, her mouth a wide slash, her eyes dark and wide, and the cigarette-smoke dress was a part of her skin as lightning ripped in white staccato flashes across the dark blanket of streaming sky.

I bent to help her. She grabbed my hand and yanked, and I fell beside her on the sand. We came together like a handclasp, and the thrust of her body, the warm pressure of her lips were urgent. When we kissed like that, I felt as if I went right through her into the deep dark ground.

We drew apart.

"Again," she whispered.

We kissed again, with the rain slashing us, feeling the wet sands still warm from the dead sun.

We rose together, and with the same urgency of our kiss. I looked at her, with the rain tearing at her; at the long white column of throat, and I fastened my fingers into the low V of her dress and started to tear.

She shook her head, breath tearing from her throat, too, the wet warm pressure of her breasts against the back of my hand.

"Yes, all right," I said. We didn't speak as we came on along home through the driving rain. She carried her shoes now, and her stocking feet slapped at the gleaming beach.

"Tomorrow," I said, in front of her cottage.

"Yes, Larry." We shook hands, looked at each other. She started to tremble and then she was in my arms. She pushed me away, my fingers clutched at the firm curve beneath her breast. "Tomorrow—good night."

"Good night, Joan."

In my room, I stared at the lights from her cottage. Her bedroom was opposite mine. She came to the window, waved once, and pulled down the shade.

I watched her shadow undress.

Chapter Five

I was worrying plenty now. The days flicked by like the fast pages in a book, and I wasn't saving much money. I couldn't help myself. It got so I tried hard not to think of Tad up there in Raiford, hemmed by four walls, a con.

Joan and I were together a lot. I worked from midmorning till late afternoon, but after that I was with her. Pete Adams had a steady job, and I was out that much more money because of his salary. Joan didn't want to go back to New York. I was in love with her from the start.

I couldn't bring myself to write Tad about her as yet, because I knew that when I described her it would come shining through my words that Joan was a hell of a long way from being beer and pretzels.

It got so I tried hard not to think of Tad up there. . . .

Only it wouldn't work. I couldn't close my mind to it, and right when Joan smiled, when she'd look at me; right when we were happiest, having the most fun, forgetful of everything—right then I'd remember. I'd remember what I had promised myself.

Joan and I fished, picnicked, swam, danced, did all the things we wanted. We got to know each other well. I wanted her so hard I couldn't sleep right and felt like I could swim clear across to Mexico—and would if I didn't have her pretty quick.

She felt it. Knew it. But one of those days, one of those hours, moments, we'd understood without a word that it would all come when it was ready. We waited for it; at least, I did. And it was as if every nerve in my body stood out in a frayed bunch of impatient tips, like the end of a rope.

She was everything I'd ever wanted. Everything. She was the dream, the last word, the hope. She was it.

There'd been plenty of women, girls. But it had always been a little like changing socks, and the real blasting excitement had never been there before. It was now. It was as if I'd been having a good life, fine, getting along, healthy, living as everybody else lived, then waking up to find I'd been stone-cold dead for twenty-nine years.

I finally told her all about Tad.

I had taken off a little early that day, in the early afternoon. She'd been waiting for me at the Pink Goat. She had on her bathing suit and a terry-cloth robe. I picked up a beach umbrella I'd had stuck in the back room at the Pink Goat and a dozen cans of cold beer. Then we ambled down the beach to a spot we liked.

"This umbrella hasn't been open since Tad took a girl—" I stopped, standing there.

"Yes?" She was putting on her rubber bathing cap. "Tad? Tad who?"

I got to wrestling with the umbrella, trying to forget, wishing I'd said nothing. "My brother," I said.

"I didn't know you had a brother, Larry." She quit putting on the cap, pulled it off, and tried to help me yank the damn fool umbrella open. I jammed the spike into the sand, and we both pried at the gadget that slipped up the pole. It was jammed. I found a piece of driftwood and started slamming it with that. "Yeah," I said. "I got a brother."

"Handsome?" She laughed, and I swore because I'd slammed my thumb with the rotten piece of driftwood. I tossed the wood away.

"Yeah, I suppose. Handsome, in his way, maybe."

"Well, you'll have to introduce me."

I quit monkeying with the fool thing. "Sure," I said. "Only right now it'd be kind of difficult."

So she said, "Why?" and I told her. I told her everything. About the family, Mom and Pop and then Tad. And what he'd finally done over in Tampa, and where he was. Then I told her what I was trying to do—going to do. I gave it to her straight.

She looked at me for a long while after I'd stopped talking, then she said, "Here. Let me have a try with that umbrella." So I let her take over.

You guessed it. She opened it as easily as I opened my mouth as I watched. Then she spread out a blanket, and I got the umbrella where we wanted it for the right amount of shade, and jammed it into the sand again. It collapsed, and we began all over. I finally got it up. One side of it was ripped now, but it worked all right.

"Beer?" I said.

"Sure," she said, and I handed her a cold, frosty can with the foam climbing out. "And Larry," she said. "I know you'll find a good lawyer. I know everything'll be O.K."

"Here's to us, then," I said.

"Here's to us."

"At least," she said, "we can always have plenty of cold beer, and stuff."

"At the very least."

So that afternoon we didn't swim. I went back for some more beer and it got warm waiting for us to drink it. But we finally did, warm as it was, and it was good.

The beer maybe got us snarled up. We were sweating, lying there, closer and closer together, until we were twined like fingers in Earth's warm lap. I could feel every muscle, every slight movement in her body.

She whispered, "Larry. Oh, Larry . . ."

I felt a shadow. "Somebody's—"

We sat up. A little girl about seven years old with a sand pail in one hand and the handle of her tin shovel in her mouth stood ten feet away watching with amazed, owlish blue eyes. The world spun—earth, water, sky.

"Two," the little girl said. Then louder, "Two! I t'ought you was one!" She turned and ran up the beach, her tiny bare feet snickering in the sand. "Mamma!"

Joan laughed first, so it was all right.

"We are one, Larry." So we left the umbrella there, picked up the blanket, and went home.

On the way, Joan suddenly looked at me and said, "Larry. I swear, I could drown little brats like that. I hate them."

Her cheeks had colored up and she really meant what she said. She had me puzzled for a while, because of how she'd spoken. But I forgot it soon enough.

Chapter Six

The next day we were in the Pink Goat, alone. Pete Adams was due to take over at three o'clock, and it was two-thirty in the afternoon now. Nobody else was there. I'd been mixing Martinis for Joan, and maybe she was a little high. Maybe I was a little high, too. I got that way from looking at her.

"Gosh, look at that!" Joan said, and I looked up front. A long, sky-blue, custom-built car swerved in off the highway and slammed to a rearing halt. A tall, fairly good-looking bird practically fell out of the car. He was plastered. He wore gray flannels and a white shirt, and was in his bare feet. His black hair hung in his eyes, and he wanted a drink. Joan slipped down to the end of the bar, but she needn't have worried. The guy was interested only in a forthcoming drink.

He reeled sullenly in the door, came over to the bar, propped himself up, tossed a brown wallet on the wood. He'd been carrying it in his shirt pocket.

I knew the type. He wouldn't hang around. He'd gulp his drink and take off. Normally, maybe, I wouldn't have served him. But I had Tad at the back of my mind, and money.

"Whisky," he said hoarsely. "Double. Rye." It took about all of his breath to get it out.

"O.K., brother." I slopped him two shots in a glass and said, "Chaser?"

He leered, grabbed the drink, gulped it down. Then he fumbled a dollar from the wallet and handed it to me. Then he gave me another dollar and said, "Thanksh. Good fella." He turned, jabbed the wallet at his shirt pocket, and practically ran out of the place.

I'd heard a plopping noise, but it hadn't registered. I heard the car roar out of there as I rang up the money in the cash register. And I heard Joan's heels on the floor, and her sudden gasp.

"Larry! Look what I've got!"

I turned. She was holding the brown wallet in one hand, and a bunch of bills in the other. It was the guy's wallet. When he'd jabbed it at his shirt pocket, he'd missed, and it had fallen to the floor.

I left the bar in a hurry and ran outside onto the highway. The drunk and his big custom-built car had vanished. I cursed and ambled back inside. He'd probably be back when he sobered up.

Joan was down at the far end of the bar. The money was on the counter in front of her, I watched her as she counted. Finished, she looked up and said, "Nine hundred and thirty-four dollars." Her eyes were bright. "Larry, think of it!" She was wearing green shorts and a halter. Her face was paler than usual and that made her lips redder. Her long, slim fingers rippled through the money.

"The damn fool," I said. "Well, he'll be back."

She looked at me. "Sure," she said quietly. "The damn fool."

"What's the identification say?"

"There isn't any identification, Larry. Only nine hundred and thirty-four dollars. Nothing else."

"Nothing? That's funny."

"What's so funny?" Her eyes were steady as she looked at me. "It's a break, Larry. For us."

"I've got to hold the money. He'll be back for it when he sobers up."

She folded the money neatly and jammed it into the waistband of her shorts. "No." Her voice was petulant. "It's ours, Larry. We're going to keep it."

I stared at her, not knowing what to say.

"We can flush the wallet down the toilet. Where's some scissors? A knife will do. I'll cut it up."

"You'll cut it out, Joan!" I said loudly. "What the hell's got into you?"

"Nothing, nothing." She came up to me fast, threw her arms around me, and ground her hips into me. She reached up, grabbed my hair, and pulled my mouth down to hers.

I shoved her away, held her away.

She said, "Don't you see, Larry? It's ours!"

"Joan, don't talk like that. You know what you're saying?"

She turned and walked to the end of the bar again. "Sure I know," she tossed back. "And we're not giving it back. It's a natural. He'll never know where he left it." Then turning, she hurried back to me, put her arms around me, pushed in close. "Don't you see? You can't give it back. You can't, Larry!" She looked up at me, and I swear there were tears in her eyes.

All right. I loved her. If you've never felt the way I felt, O.K. It's like standing on dynamite, with the fuse sputtering. It's like nothing in the world. If you've never had it like that, then you haven't. When she looked at me, it was like hitting me over the head with a baseball bat. Like an ice cube on a hot stove. When we touched I felt as if my fingernails were going to curl up and drop off. All right. If you don't know what I mean, then you're lucky, or unlucky. I don't know. But that's how it was with me.

"It isn't much, Larry "

"Only a thousand, is all."

Her whisper was hot. "I mean to him! It isn't much to him. You saw the car he was driving." She smiled and shook me, gripping my arms with her long, tense fingers. "It was probably his week's allowance from Mamma."

"But Joan, he'll be back. It's a lot of money."

"Scratch. It's mad money—nothing. A drop in the bucket." Her breasts rose and fell, rose and fell. She was intense and the smell of her was heady.

"Well . . . maybe we could . . ." And that was that. I fought against it. But I kept remembering Tad up there, and the lawyers he had to have. I kept thinking, Wouldn't Tad do the same for me? Don't I want to get him out of that rat hole? And she remembered Tad, too.

Ten minutes later I was behind the bar, while she cut the wallet up with the scissors I gave her. I listened to the toilet flush in the ladies' room, and stared at the rising points of sweat on the backs of my hands.

"Hi, Larry, m'boy!"

It was Lew Hawley, standing in the doorway. I hadn't even heard his car drive up. He mopped the sweat off his sunburned face and head, then replaced his sweat-stained gray felt hat as he swaggered to the bar.

My throat was like an unswept cellar floor. "Greetings, Lew." My voice was shaky. I grabbed his special mixing glass and poured in the bourbon. As I placed it before him, he winked. I said, "How's the murder business these days?"

"Nary a corpse, Larry. Business is bad." He drank thirstily. I saw the ladies'-room door flinch, and knew Joan was behind it, waiting for Hawley to leave.

Hawley set his glass down empty, with a heavy clink, wiped his mouth with the back of his hand, belched, and said, "Gotta be on the move. See you, kid." He shoved off, his shoulders swaying like a cocky sailor's.

I watched his car leave. He'd only taken one drink. For over a year he'd taken two drinks. I felt bad.

Joan came out and winked at me. I felt better. Then I felt worse because I felt better.

"I'll toddle on home," she said. "See you in a few minutes, Larry? Bring some beer." She came up close and snuggled against me. "Don't think a thing about it," she whispered. "I love you, Larry. We're going to have each other—somehow."

After she left, and just before Pete Adams showed up to take over, I decided I'd better check in the ladies' room, in case the toilet wasn't flushed right.

It was flushed fine. There wasn't a trace of the wallet.

Only on the floor, against the wall, was a torn piece of white cardboard, with printing on it. I picked it up and looked at it. It was part of an identification card. Somebody had written on it with a pen, but only the first markings showed. There was a K, a 3, and a 1. I flushed that down the toilet.

There had been identification. She'd lied to me. I went back into the bar and had a double shot myself, without any water.

I didn't say anything to her about that, though. Because somehow, when we got together, nothing mattered but us. It kept hitting me that it was all wrong, and not like Joan. But the way she laughed about it, I began to feel maybe she was right.

At noon the next day, the sky-blue custom job showed up, and the drunk of yesterday was a very sober-faced, quiet, worried individual today.

"Look," he said. "Was I in here yesterday? Did I maybe leave a wallet in here yesterday?"

I made like I was thinking, while he stood there with bloodshot eyes and fiddled his fingers on the bar.

"You were in, I think," I said. "Yep, you were in here. But I didn't see any wallet. You lose a wallet?"

He massaged the back of his neck. "Did I? I'll say I did. A bunch of money that wasn't even mine."

"Cripes," I said, "that's tough." My insides were going to jelly, and I wanted to yell. "You were a little—well, you know?"

He sighed from the bottoms of the shoes he wore today. "Yeah, I know." He forced himself to smile, brighten up, and I could see it took a hell of an effort. "I'll have a rye and water," he said. "Have one yourself."

I started to hesitate. But maybe it wouldn't look right. We had a drink together, and he left, asking me to keep my ears open. There was a dollar on the bar, and the sky-blue job was gone down the highway in a flash of sunlight.

I was sick, I can tell you that. I'd taken the guy's money, lied to him, and then let him buy me a drink. I was pretty tight when Pete Adams showed up. I was worried plenty as I left to meet Joan, and I kept remembering all the things Tad used to tell me.

Chapter Seven

I tried to keep how I felt from Joan.

"Larry, it's all over now! We'll split the money."

"It's all yours, Joan. I couldn't take any of it." Even her terry-cloth robe couldn't hide the slim, yet lush, contour of her body. Her hair was brushed to a golden sheen. "All right, Larry." She shrugged. "But let's not talk about it any more." Her white teeth fooled with her lower lip, and she half-smiled, then said, "You'll have me worried, first thing you know."

She looked at me, her eyes clear and blue, and I believed her. I had just finished reading a letter from Tad, and still between those off-the-shoulder lines, as he told me everything was O.K., I read his want for freedom.

More clearly, in my mind's eye, I kept seeing three men standing in a night street. I saw the sharp flash, the wink of gunfire. Two men dying, dead. Another running, his eyes cold over his shoulder. I heard no sound.

One day, while we were lying on the beach in front of my cottage, Joan rolled over on her hip and shaded her eyes with her hand.

"Larry, I'm not going back to New York."

For a minute I couldn't speak. I'd been afraid to ask. I'd avoided thinking of her leaving, the same as I avoided thoughts of Tad, and the lawyer I still didn't have, and hadn't tried very hard to find. The same as I avoided the memory of a drunk, a sky-blue custom-built car, and a brown wallet, and a torn piece of cardboard. I'd avoided thinking about Joan's leaving, because her vacation had theoretically ended a week ago. Three weeks we'd been together. I was gone. It was no longer want, it was need, must have, will. We both knew it couldn't stop. I knew it wouldn't.

I finally grinned and we kissed, lying flat out on the blistering sands. Her body was sun-hot, her lips soft, pulsing. Her skin was a dark, golden tan beyond the snug reaches of her white bathing suit.

"Larry," she said, "what you do to me! Look!"

She showed me her arms. They were covered with goose pimples. Her thighs, her legs, her entire body.

"How about beneath this?" I said, snapping the tight waist of her bathing suit.

"You'll see." She hesitated. "You know," she said, "we can't do this much longer."

"I've told you that."

"I wanted to be sure."

"Are you?"

"Yes. Larry, we can't go on lying on beaches under the sun. I'll go mad."

Didn't I know that? Not merely the loving her. The way it was now it might kill us. Three weeks.

"Larry, you don't get much out of the Pink Goat. I don't see how we can marry on that."

I tensed inside, then relaxed. "Season's a little off this year," I told her. "Never can tell. It's usually much better. And I haven't saved. Never thought of saving, until . . ."

"Yes," she said. "There's your brother, Tad, too. It is possible to get good lawyers. It would be possible to spring your brother."

I watched her.

She shook her head, sat up, stared at the rolling blue-green Gulf waters. "No, Larry. When we marry, I've got to have money." She didn't look at me, and I wasn't relaxed any more. "I'm like the little girl in the storybook. I always dreamed of doing things, going to far places. I dreamed of enough money, more than enough. I never planned to go for a guy like you." She turned and glanced at me, the sun bright in the corners of her eyes, her thick golden hair brushing her shoulders. "I came down here to look around. I figured maybe there'd be some money around down here, some man. That's right," she said, as the smile went out of me. "I want money. Lots of it." She was intense. "Got to have it. Life isn't right without it—not today. Anyway, I want it." She paused, her lips parted slightly, her teeth glistening white. "Larry, I love you. I want you. But Larry, the Pink Goat isn't enough."

"Yeah?" I couldn't say anything else. It was getting to me more and more what she was. Not nice. But there was nothing I could do about it.

She brushed sand off her thigh. And just the movement of her hand across that smooth, ripe skin was the same as if she'd taken hold of my heart and squeezed it in her fist.

"The Beach Club takes in a startling amount of money in a week."

I laughed. Maybe it was dry, hollow, but at least it was laughter. "In one day," I agreed. I thought of the money that came into the Beach Club. The drinking class who stood in there from morning till night. The gambling upstairs. Not on a big scale, mind you—discreet, wary, like a secret sin—but just the same, big enough. Yes. The glitter, the Gulf, the rustling palms, the rustling money. "That's out of my class, Joan. The Pink Goat takes in a tidy bit."

"Tidy," she said. "That's the trouble, Larry. Tidy isn't enough."

The hand that clutched inside me clutched tighter. I reached and drew her face around and gripped her chin. "What do you mean, Joan?"

She looked at me, took a deep breath. "Just this, Larry." She was getting excited. "I've been looking around. They hold a week's receipts right at the Beach Club. In a strongbox. It's silly, but they do. They have a night watchman, man named Alfred Lanihan, an old man you could blow over with a weak beer breath. They close on Wednesday at six and don't open until Thursday morning. Thursday is when they take the strongbox to the bank in St. Pete, because Wednesday afternoon the banks are closed."

I looked away, then flopped on my stomach and stared at the red and blue ribs of the blanket we were lying on. I was sick inside. She had no right to talk like this. I heard her speak, and her hand was soft on my shoulder.

"I'm sorry, Larry. But I guess I'll always want things I've never had. Only, unlike the little girl in the storybook, I'll always keep figuring ways and means to get what I want. I can't help it, and I'm sorry. That's why I waited, made us wait. That's why I could never be sure. I love you, Larry. But I want those things, too."

"Forget it. Forget it all, will you?" My voice was ragged. "And for Christ's sake, forget the Beach Club!"

Already I could feel it. The change. Already there was something different between us. I knew I'd take her now; take her when and where I wanted her. I could take her right here under the sun, right now, if I felt like it. But I was sick. A hundred things were thumping around inside my head.

She was silent for a long time. I thought maybe she was mad. Then she said softly, "It'd be easy, Larry. We'd have plenty then. Plenty." There was an undertone to her voice that sent aches through me. "We may as well be frank with each other, Larry. We love each other." Her hand smoothed my back.

I turned over, knocked her hand down, stood, and walked away. I stopped and looked around. She smiled at me. I went back to her and flopped down.

"Joan," I said. "Listen to me. We can't do anything like that. You know we can't."

"Why?"

"Joan, you're thinking all wrong. We couldn't."

"Why?" she said again. "Just why can't we?" She rose slowly and turned her back to me. "You scared, Larry?" she tossed over her shoulder.

Her long shadow lay black against the white sands, and across my feet. In the western sky the sun was a blazing ball of yellow fire, tremendous, and suddenly terrible, because I thought I could see each separate flame.

Chapter Eight

The room was like a cemetery vault.

I was alive. But the man I talked with was dead.

The room was bare, save for two straight-backed chairs.

Through an open door, against the gray wall of an echoing corridor, the grotesque shadow of a prison guard stood motionless. It was as if the shadow's outline had been cut from black tin and pasted there. A gentle reminder to the dead man—my brother.

Tad moved, smiled, smoked, talked. Yet, to me, he was dead. Since that day in Tampa, when he'd flicked ashes on the floor of his cell, sitting there on the edge of his cot, he had changed. Something had gone out of him.

Tad motioned toward the open door. "He's listening, so get used to it, kid. Don't hedge. Speak it up. That's the guy's job. There's nothing you can say he hasn't heard a hundred times. Maybe even today he's heard it."

"Yeah, sure." I'd only been with him for a couple of minutes, and we didn't have all day. I'd taken the train up to see him, just to talk. His letters had been growing empty and I'd decided to tell him I was going to get a lawyer and spring him—somehow.

Only looking at him was bad. His face was gray, like that corridor wall. And his eyes held the same shadow that was on that wall. When he spoke, he sounded like Tad. But somehow, it wasn't right.

"What's on your mind, kid?" He grinned, dropped his butt on the floor, and smashed it with his heel, the way he used to do. Only now I noticed his eyes flicked once over his shoulder at that open door. He saw I noticed, and he banged me on the arm with his fist. "So what?" he said. "I'm used to it, kid."

"Tad, don't you want out?"

His eyes got little flecks of yellow in them, like long ago. My palms were sweaty, and I found I couldn't look Tad in the eye. Ever since Joan had brought up the robbery proposal, I'd been sick. And now, standing here, talking with Tad, it's all I could think of. That, and the wallet, the nine hundred bucks. Suppose he knew? What if he found out?

"Y'know, kid? You're getting like that broken record. Saying the same thing all the time. Don't worry about me!" He turned his back, lit another smoke. When he lit it, I noticed how quick it was, without flourish, without life; like maybe it was his last one. Not the last one in the pack. The last one he'd ever be able to smoke. He whirled and stepped up to me, smoke trailing from his mouth as he talked. "Sure I want to get out. I want out. I told you that."

"Then, why—"

He swore, and the shadow out in the corridor moved. A fat-faced guard peered in, his jaws thrusting stolidly around tobacco or gum, then vanished. The shadow took its place again.

"Kid," Tad said, "if I wanted to get out that bad, I'd just go."

"You mean—escape?"

He nodded, dragged deep on his smoke, and said, "Sure."

"I didn't think they did that any more."

"Nuts. I could walk out of here almost any time. Takes plans, sure. Lots of guys could walk out. I'm a trusty, and it's that much easier."

"Then why don't they?"

"Because, kid. They do. Lots of them. But that isn't all. Take a bird we were gassing about the other day out in the yard. Name of Crunty—Elmo Crunty. Well, Crunty was a killer, a murderer. Like me. Only he killed his wife. Got life, same as me. Only he was a bad one, no trusty—kept locked up all the time. It took him three years, kid. Three years of planning, scheming, conning, waiting, till he got his chance. He sawed through the bars of his cell, and filled the cracks with spit and gobs of chewed bread, imagine!"

"Yeah, sure." He didn't talk like Tad any more. He was trying to make me feel good. Nothing could make me feel good any more. What was Joan doing at this minute? That's what I was thinking. Where was she? Was she alone? Was she planning, too?

"Crunty made his break after three years. It took him seven hours to get outside from the minute he cracked through his cell bars. He was alone. There was no alarm. Everything was rigged right." Tad dragged his cigarette until the hot ember moved an inch, spitting like a Chinese firecracker. "Then," Tad said, "what happens to most all of them happened to Elmo. Folks don't know about that, I guess."

"What happened?"

Tad's voice was soft as he leaned forward. "He got outside, no alarm, he was free. And then he stood there, and he knew he was trapped for good. He had no place to go. He had no money. He was in prison clothes. He didn't know where to start. His plans had ended with the wall."

I watched him.

"It happens, plenty. They plan, they get out, but their plans end with the wall. A con forgets that, kid. Why? I dunno. Out, out, out, that's all they think of. They never stop to wonder what comes after they're out. Friend of mine, Bert Arnold, tried it, too."

"And Crunty?"

Tad shrugged, mashed his second cigarette beneath his heel. "They picked him up in the morning, out on Route Twenty-three, just outside of Sapp. He was sitting in a ditch, bawling his heart out. A sap, headed for Sapp."

Joan, I thought. Joan, Joan, Joan.

"Ones that get out all the way, they make plans. They think. But in here, kid, you get to thinking. Once you're outside, that's all that counts. The wall—the farm. Outside. Past the barrier. The green trees. The crap! If you're punk enough to keep running, keep going, even when you got no place to go, even when you haven't got a nickel in your jeans—if you got moxie, you know what you get?"

"No, Tad, what?"

"The swamps. That's what. This is Florida. Palm trees, Pernod, and pavilions, with plenty of piquant princesses. Crap again. For us, I mean. For the con. Out with the moxie, running. Then the rivers, the swamps. The heat. Spanish moss, so pretty in the moonlight, becomes an old man's bug-infested beard, drooling slime on you!"

"Forget it, Tad." Yeah. He'd changed.

He was bitter. I could see it. There he was, thinking the state was wrong for putting him here, when all he'd done was kill a couple of guys. And if he'd been caught killing those two, then how many others had he knocked off without anybody knowing? Creamed, they call it. I creamed him. Holy Christ, Joan, what are you doing?

He lit another cigarette with that quickly hidden flash of match between cupped hands, eyes sharp to the door where the shadow rested, flung like a black splash of death against the wall.

The shadow melted and the guard looked in, his jaws thrusting stolidly sideways around his cud. He swallowed, blinked, wiped the back of his hand beneath his nose. "You got fi' more minutes, Cole," he said with a soft thick cracker drawl.

"O.K."

"Tad," I said. "I'm going to get you a lawyer. I'm going to see you get out. That's why I'm here. Who do I see? Who do I get?"

His head went over on one side, and his lips thinned out in a gray smile. His shoulders hunched, his eyes brightened. "Screwball Larry, my brother," he said softly. "You damn fool punk!"

I stepped back.

"Get out of here, kid," he said quietly. "Go home and sell your lousy liquor, will you? Leave me alone. I wasn't thinking anything, till you come along putting fancy ideas into my head." He paused. "Ah, forget it. Talk, talk."

"I am, Tad," I insisted. "I'm saving my money. Everything. I'll get a hot lawyer."

He began to laugh. Not with humor. With disdain, almost, maybe with hate. It wasn't good to listen to. His laughter roared and roared in the empty room. It echoed in the corridor.

The shadow on the wall out there melted, and the guard looked in again.

"Tad," I said. "Stop it. I am! I'm saving up. Tell me who to see."

His voice was flat and rapid. "You haven't got that kind of money, kid. You can't get it, either. Hear? I won't tell you. Hands off me, kid. Forget it. I came here under my own power, and if I ever go out, it'll be the same way. No help, understand. Not from you."

"I've already saved a few hundred."

His laughter was mad. It was crazy. He doubled up with it. Tad was sick. The guard stepped into the room, a puzzled expression on his stolidly thrusting face.

"Kid," Tad said, dead quiet again. "Take the money, get drunk, and buy yourself a good hot piece. Now, get the hell out of here and leave me be!"

"Cole!" the guard said. He reached toward Tad.

"Shut up, you cow-faced swamp rat!" Tad blurted. He whirled back to me. "Get the hell out of here, Larry." He quieted again, stepped up, chucked me on the shoulder. "Forget it, will you?" his voice was hoarse. "You can't buy that kind of lawyer."

"I'm going to—"

"Get out!"

"I'm going to, Tad!"

He went off into laughter again. The guard grabbed him from behind. Tad went quiet, still again. "O.K., baby," he told the guard. "It's O.K."

"See that it is," the guard said. They started moving toward the open doorway leading into the corridor.

"So long, Larry," Tad said. "I'm sorry, kid. That's the way it is, believe me. I'll write you all about it."

"Just the same," I told him, "that's what I'm going to do."

He nodded as they stepped into the corridor. "O.K. See you."

I wanted to yell after him to stop. I wanted to tell him what was inside me, what was busting loose inside me. I wanted to tell him about Joan. The robbery. The wallet. The lie.

I didn't, though. I stood there, watching two shadows moving down the gray wall of the corridor until they vanished. Even after they were gone I could still hear the sound of their feet. And then I heard a steely clang as a barred door opened. Tad's quiet laughter, and another grating clang as that door down there closed.

Chapter Nine

A week and a half went by. Things didn't change. They stayed the same, except with every hour it got worse. Worse inside me. Hating the recurrent thought of robbery. Wanting Joan. Knowing I had to have her. Knowing I wanted her, and that I'd do anything to get her.

There were strings tied to my special package. I might fumble and maybe never get those strings untied. Never look at myself in a shaving mirror again. Or I could slice the strings neat, with a knife.

I wrote Tad and told him all about Joan and me. Told him we were going to be married. And with every stroke of the pen I ached to tell him about the robbery, too. Because, I got to thinking, maybe he'd understand. Maybe he *does* want to get out that way.

Only then I knew it was all wrong. It would also mean I'd have to make contact with a guy up on Safety Harbor. Tad told me about that, in case I wanted to write anything to him I figured the prison censor would cut. If I mentioned robbery, it'd be more than just cut. This man at Safety Harbor could work mail through the prison underground. Certain guards could be bought. For a price. It would be a big price, and that was still another catch. The man's name was Walter Pike.

So I told him I loved her. That we were going to be married. I waited for his letters. They didn't come. He hadn't written since I'd been up there to see him. He'd been regular in his correspondence previous to that. But now, nothing.

I went to see two lawyers. One in St. Pete, and one in Tampa. The one in St. Pete clammed up sharp when I mentioned what I was there for.

"I'm sorry, Mr. Cole," he said, flicking through some papers on his desk. "But I couldn't touch anything like that. Frankly, I wouldn't."

I mentioned big money.

He straightened his steel-rimmed glasses, rubbed his thin nose, and said, "I'm sorry. If you'll excuse me, I'm busy."

Now, that was a rotten way for a lawyer to be. The guy was scared.

So I caught a bus for Tampa, and looked up Frank Grenold. Here was a lawyer who was supposed to be hot.

I found his office. He had a plush waiting room. He also had a plush secretary. A redhead in a tight green dress with a shape so ripe it threatened to burst like a sun-hot plum.

"Yes?" She stood at an inner office door. There was no one else in the waiting room.

"I'd like to see Mr. Grenold."

As she walked across the room toward me I could hear the hiss of her nylons brushing together. I held my breath as my gaze touched her breastwork, because the buttons were drawn so tight across her front, I thought if I breathed, she might, and there'd be a free strip show.

"Have you an appointment?" Her voice was mellow, with a tang, like pale ale.

"No."

"I'm sorry, but you'll have to make an appointment."

"I just want to talk with him," I said. "I could tell him quick."

She smiled and ran her thumbs along the inside of the belt around her waist. She also had very white, even teeth. "Truth of the matter is," she said. "Mr. Grenold isn't in right now."

"I'll wait."

She snapped the belt, shrugged, and disappeared into the inner office. The door swung partially closed.

I slumped into a tan-and-chrome chair. A typewriter began to rip like sixty, then stopped.

"What was your name again, please?" She stood in the doorway with a pencil in one hand. Venetian blinds flung barred sunlight upon her, and as she moved the sunlight rippled like water.

I told her my name.

"I'll put it on a card. Probably if you—"

"No," I interrupted. "I'll wait. I've got to see him. It's about quarter to eleven. Won't he be in?"

The tempo of her breathing didn't increase, but I could hear it just the same. It was that kind of breathing.

"I'll just wait," I added, settling in the chair again.

The shrug. The door. The typewriter. And a new addition. A chuckle.

I got up, walked over to the door, and looked in. She was seated at a typewriter desk nearby, with her legs crossed. They were something. I thought of Joan, right away, and knew nothing could compare with Joan. Even now that I knew what Joan was, there was nothing I could do about it.

The redhead looked up at me and said, "I really don't know when he'll be in. It's just a fool waste of time for you to sit there."

"I'm in no hurry."

She slammed the carriage on her machine. I went back into the waiting room and waited, regardless. The typewriter blasted endlessly. At eleven-thirty I stepped to the door again. The only change was that she'd crossed her legs the other way.

"You're still here?" she asked.

"Yeah. Look, d'you get hungry?"

She started thumbing the bell on her machine. *Ding! Ding! Ding!* She was nervous and her hand trembled. She ran her eyes over me. She wet her lips.

"That is," I said, "would you care for some lunch?"

"Very much."

"With me?"

"Not so very much."

"Look," I said. "Maybe he'll stand you up."

"He has already." She hesitated for a long moment and I wondered what she was planning to say. She uncrossed her legs first. She looked a bit perplexed. "All right on the lunch, Mr. Cole. I'm sorry I said that. It was because of the way you looked at me out there."

"You're very frank."

"A necessity."

"I understand."

We went out. She left a note for her boss. It read: "I'll be back. Probably!"

I don't know why I did that. I hadn't meant to ask her. It was hard to know what to expect. It was hard to know what she expected.

My fingers touched wadded bills in my pants pocket, and right away I thought how I was trying to save. And that brought Joan back. It was like having a pail of hot water poured over your head.

All right. I did know. Maybe it was because I was scared down inside. I wanted to talk with somebody who had no connection with what I was going through. Maybe it was a kind of anger at myself; a chance to look inside myself without cringing.

"My car's over here, and my name's Grace Hunter," she said as we crossed the street toward a parking lot.

"Thought I was the hunter."

She stepped onto the curb, looked at me. "We really don't have to have lunch together, Mr. Cole."

"Larry," I said. "And stop it, please."

"I know a place," she said. "If you're hungry."

I wasn't, but I said I was, so we went there. She drove like a demon, and she didn't talk. I knew something was bothering her. The way her hands gripped the wheel, white-knuckled. She drove like she was trying to forget. It was a hell of a thing. I didn't want to talk, right then. It was like sitting in a vacuum. It seemed like some chuckling god was poking me around on a checkerboard.

I glanced at her profile as we screamed around a curve in the highway and cut down toward the bay. Here was potency of a different kind from Joan's. I wondered what was bothering her.

"I suppose you have an in with the cops," I said, "driving like this. Your boss fixes it, huh?"

"I'll be all right."

O.K. I started to say something else. She swung the car into a small lane between tall pines. An instant later we were facing the sun-touched waters of the bay. To the left, jutting out over the water, was a small, rustic structure that looked restaurantish.

She sat there for a minute, staring over the rim of the steering wheel. Then she flicked the engine off, turned in the seat, and faced me. Her chin began to bunch up. She whirled the other way and started to cry.

It was angry, hurt crying. The kind that is uncontrollable. A little savage, maybe.

I sat there feeling embarrassed for a long moment, feeling the movement of the car seat as she sobbed. Her shoulders wrenched and jerked. I reached over and pulled her toward me. It was an instinctive gesture.

She held off for a moment, straining. Then she came over against me, turning at the same time, so her face was buried against my shoulder.

This was great, I thought. The crying ceased. She tried to cut off the sobs, too, but they weren't the kind to be turned off like a faucet.

"I'm sorry!" she said angrily.

"It's all right. It's O.K."

"No—no, it's not."

I pulled her in a little closer and felt the pressure of her breasts against my chest. I fumbled around and found a clean handkerchief and gave it to her. "Blow," I said.

She sniffed and snuffed and said, "Thanks." She snuggled against me. I couldn't help thinking of Joan. Women may be alike in some respects, but there was no comparison here. Even sitting here with Grace, I felt empty and antagonized because I wasn't with Joan. And what was Joan doing?

I looked down, ran my hand up along her throat, shoved her chin up with my fist. Her face touched mine and she looked into my eyes, her own eyes still brimming with tears. Her lips were parted, her breath was sweet and warm.

As we kissed she leaned back against the seat, with her head thrown way back, and then my lips touched her throat. I felt the strong pulse. Her arms came around me, and the warm swelling of her breasts exposed in the flaring V of her dress pushed against my chin.

"I was supposed to go out with Frank—Grenold," she said.

I ran my thumb along the inside of her belt, to see how it felt. It felt nice.

"He didn't show up when he was supposed to. We were going to take the rest of the day off and do things. It was important. I'm a damned fool about that."

"Red hair."

She ignored that. "We were going to have a grand time. So much fun." Her voice was bitter. "We'd planned for a long time. I've been crazy for the bum!" She paused and sank her teeth into her lower lip as I looked at her. "Men are all the time after me. You know. But then a guy like Frank comes along. My boss, no less. And I haven't got it, for him."

My God, I thought. Who's crazy?

"I don't know why I'm telling you this. I'm a damned fool." She laughed. It was a free kind of laughter, like her crying, that bubbled up out of her throat and sounded as creamy as her skin looked. "You looked like a lost pup. I felt like one. Then I got mad, so here we are."

"Yes."

"The bum! Do I look like that kind?" Her hand gripped my arm. "Don't tell me. Yes, I do. I've got a shape that makes men drool. But I'm not that kind, Larry. Just a poor dope. It's easier to talk with somebody you don't know. I can talk with you." She laughed, with the tears mostly gone from her eyes now. "Trouble. I'm trouble. Do I really look like trouble, Larry?"

"Frankly, yes."

"Make believe we've known each other for a long time, Larry. I feel that way, now. I'm sorry I picked on you. You came to Grenold to do the talking, and I'm doing all the talking. None of it makes sense to you, does it?"

"Yes, Grace, it does." And it did. Misery loves company.

"Gee," she said. "Gee whiz!" She flung the door on her side open, climbed out, slammed it loudly. "C'mon, let's go eat something. I'm hungry, darn it!"

So we did. We ate. Pompano papillote, and it was delicious, with some very excellent white wine. What a good chef can do with a hunk of fish and a piece of paper is startling. Of course, a few other things are added. Like crawfish, onions, egg yolks, shrimp, and sherry wine.

We were old friends after the first mouthful, Grace and I. I began to think she was a very wonderful person. It was good to talk with her.

From our table beneath a colored awning, we looked out onto the bay. Fishing boats, a fisherman stringing his nets to dry. The sunlight dancing on the water.

In a far corner of the room a Spaniard fingered his guitar and sang some haunting thing that was repetitive without being boring.

"It's nice here," she said. "I come often, alone. Frank—well, he likes other places."

"Yeah." So I told her. I told her why I wanted Grenold.

"I figured that," she said, after a pause. The sun reflected off the water into her red hair. Her eyes were bright with wine. "You're Tad Cole's brother. Lawyers usually know those things."

"D'you think he'll help me? You think he'd take the case?"

"No, Larry," she said. "I don't think so. But you better try. He's good, Frank is. A walloping lawyer. But if he gets his back up, he's apt not to touch a thing."

I didn't say anything. Even as nice as it was, sitting here with Grace, I began to feel an urgent need for Joan. It was like the slow twisting of a knife blade in an old wound. I knew what I'd be returning to. A sort of hellish heaven. But it was something I had to have.

"You've got a problem," Grace said. "But I can't see why you want to go to all this trouble. Your brother killed two men, Larry. Isn't that bad?"

"You don't know Tad."

"All right. Look. We'll go back. Frank's probably in by now. He'll have some excuse for me, and I'll know it's a lie. He'll know that I know. I won't say anything about that. I'll tell him you were in. I'll tell him you mentioned your brother, Tad. Sort of pave the way. You give me about ten minutes. Then come on and we'll see what he'll do."

The check for the meal was surprisingly small. She saw my puzzled look.

"That's why I brought you here," she said. "Next time I'll do better. Bartenders are the only ones who make money these days."

That's all she knew about it. I didn't enlighten her.

We said, "So long," at the parking lot.

"You sit in the car and gnaw your fingernails, Larry."
"Grace. Thanks. It's been good."
"Me, too."
"We may not see each other again. This is only one of my troubles."

She shrugged. "We all got 'em."

I watched her walk away. With what she had it's no wonder she was discouraged. She probably fought them off by the dozens.

I was nervous now. I wasn't doing anybody any good.

Frank Grenold was big, and he looked steak-fed and smooth in gray gabardine. Grace winked at me as I stepped into the office. She gave no other sign as to outcome. I told Grenold the same old story. He nodded painfully.

"So you're his brother?"

"Yes."

A scowl, a bland smile, and some paper-riffling at his desk. He'd been standing. Now he sat down. The paper-riffling must have been part of the office procedure.

"And you want me? You want to engage me as his lawyer?"

"I thought maybe, if—"

He raised a well-manicured, soft-palmed, ring-bedecked hand, white-cuffed and assured. I could easily see how a girl like Grace could be lost on a guy like Grenold.

I said, "Money's not the question. I'll get—"

His chuckle was throaty, and almost nasty. He glanced under the typewriter desk where Grace had seated herself. He was looking at her legs. She must have been terribly nuts about the guy to endure a look like that. I remembered Joan again, and I wanted to be back with her.

As Grace began banging the typewriter keys with machine-gun intensity, slamming the carriage rhythmically, she glanced up at me. Her head moved a fraction of an inch from side to side. Sitting there, she looked wet-lipped and wanton. Now that I knew her as she really was, the contrast in my mind was sharp.

Grenold coughed. "I'm sorry, Mr. Cole." He looked down, then up. "I've got more than I can handle already."

"But this is—"

"Something I won't touch," he said quietly. He raised his hand. "It won't do you any good to talk. I mean what I say. Not interested."

I said it out flat. "You've been seen?"

He slapped his palms on his desk and rose. The redhead wet her lips. The guy sighed, spread his hands, and shrugged. That was that.

I turned, tried to smile at Grace, and left. I felt like going back into that office and tearing Grenold apart.

Outside, in the hall, I walked slowly toward the stairs. A door opened behind me. Heels clattered. "Larry!"

I looked around. It was Grace. She came up to me, placed one hand on my arm. "I'm terribly sorry."

"You did everything you could."

"It wasn't enough. Don't worry. You'll find a lawyer."

"Sure."

"I want to thank you for—for listening to me out there, Larry." She paused, and I cursed myself silently, because I wanted to break away. Get going. "Maybe we'll meet again, Larry?"

"I doubt it, Grace."

She nibbled her lip. Then suddenly she came up close and kissed me.

"Good luck, Larry."

She'd never know how much I needed it. As she turned to go back to the office, I watched her. Then I felt sick, because Frank Grenold was standing in the office door, watching.

When I got back to the cottage, I checked the mailbox. It was empty, as usual. I walked on over to Joan's. I decided I'd never say anything to her about Grace. I'd leave it the way it was. Forget it. I felt like hell.

Joan was lying on the divan in her living room, staring thoughtfully at the ceiling. I walked right in. She didn't move.

She was wearing black silk panties and a black lacy brassiere. Her left leg was bent at the knee, her right lying flat and still. She had her hands cupped beneath her head, and her full, firm breasts jutted angrily into the flimsy silk, arguing with it. Her belly rose and fell as she breathed.

I stood there, staring at her, and my insides began to buzz.

"Joan," I said. "I saw the lawyers."

"Larry! I didn't hear you come in."

Still she didn't move. Her lips parted, and her eyes were blue with haze. I stood there, chattering inside, and told her what had happened. Grace could never make me feel like Joan did.

"Never mind," she told me. Swinging her legs out, she sat up and ran her palms into the thick tumble of her hair. "It's money they want. Look at you!" She pointed a finger at me and laughed. "Hell's bells, Larry. You look like a tramp. *That* kind of lawyer wants to be assured of money."

My trousers were without a crease. My jacket was baggy. I wore a sweat shirt. "Yeah," I said. "Maybe you're right."

"Sure."

I stepped up to her as she rose.

"Have you made up your mind?" she said.

I could smell her. There was a thin film of sweat across her upper lip, and her thigh brushed against me.

"About what?" I asked, knowing what she meant.

"The robbery, Larry." She was as serious as all hell. "It'll fix us straight. We can get married." She moved away, then turned and looked at me, with her feet planted well apart, her hands on her hips. There was defiance in the way she held her chin, in the bright blue of her eyes. "You'll be able to get your lawyer then. You'll be able to do anything," she said softly. "And we'll be able to do anything. We won't have to worry then."

"Joan, you're crazy!"

"Am I? Crazy because I want you? Because I want you the right way?"

I strode over to her, grabbed her by the waist. For an instant the full length of her touched me, then she spun and moved away.

"You know what'd happen?" she said.

"Yes, but Joan!"

"Well?"

I watched her. Then I went after her. She laughed, ran into her bedroom, slammed the door. I heard the key click in the lock. I heard her laughter, muffled through the thin paneling.

Paneling I could have broken with my fist. But I didn't. I didn't. I stood there, cursing to myself, and waited.

In a moment the key turned, in the lock again, and she came out wearing the white dress she'd worn that first day when she'd walked into the Pink Goat. Only somehow she seemed to fill it better now.

I grabbed her, swung her up to me, and her body was tense. She wasn't wearing a damn thing under that dress. Nothing at all. Her mouth was hot and wet, her breath as sharp as mine.

"C'mon, Larry," she said. "Let's go over to the bar and have a drink. We can talk."

"Joan," I said as we walked along the beach, "did you really work in a bookstore in New York?"

"Yes, Larry, I did." She stopped, holding to my arm. "Not only that, but my grandmother is alive. She's all I have left of my family. A little old lady who thinks I'm the sunshine. I have to pay her way, Larry." She looked into my eyes, and the sun was in hers, twinkling in the corners, and God, how I loved her! I hadn't known her long. I wanted her more than anything in the world. I'd been playing it nice, because she seemed to want it that way. But looking at her now, I knew I'd rape her if this went on.

It was in her, too. In her eyes and her movements, the wanting—just as hard and bad as it was with me.

She said, "I'm sorry if bringing up this idea of mine bothers you. But you've got to see it my way. It'll work. I know it'll work. It's a sure thing."

"Joan, don't you know that's what they all say?"

"Sure, I know it." She paused, and up there, behind her, beyond the white sands of the beach, along the dunes, the palms waved erratic fingers at the sky. "But do you know how many get away with it?"

"No," and I didn't want to hear.

"Plenty! Larry, we only hear about the ones that get caught, that muff it up. We won't do that. I've got it all planned out."

"Shut up, will you!" I started walking. A guy was surfcasting, waist-deep in the Gulf. I could have told him he wouldn't catch anything along here.

She caught up with me, linked her arm in mine. "All right," she said. "I'll shut up. For a while."

Pete Adams was behind the bar, and I left him there. Pete was a short, stocky guy, with a face as round as an orange, not much hair, and he was always smiling. It was in the shape of his mouth. Not unpleasant, and he was a good guy, when he was sober. He never drank much when he worked at the Pink Goat, and that was all right with me.

He gave us the high sign when we came in, then went back to his baseball game, which was coming softly over the radio back of the bar.

At the far end of the bar was one lone customer, and I cursed some more to myself. At this rate, I'd never get anywhere.

Sure, I knew what Joan was now. I knew, and there wasn't a damn thing I could do about it, either. Maybe you could. You, reading about the hell that can grow in a man's soul. Maybe you're stronger—and maybe you're not. Maybe you've never had it this way. If you ever do, then you'll know what I mean when I say there was nothing I could do about anything. She was there, inside me, boiling, seething, and every moment that passed, it grew worse.

Thinking about Tad up there, and the way he'd acted. Wondering why he didn't write. Especially why he didn't write when I told him I'd finally found a girl I really went for. And all the time wondering what he'd say if he knew what she was really like.

Thinking about how I wanted her. Not just for now. Not just for a while.

Thinking about that promise to myself, to get Tad out of there. Thinking about how snarled up inside I was, busting that want of mine against a brown wallet, a lie, and a scheme to rob one of the biggest joints on the coast.

And all the time she was at me, at me, at me. And all the time I kept thinking about those things Tad used to tell me. . . .

We sat at the bar and drank beer. I glanced toward the end of the bar, where the lone customer sat. He was drinking gin, straight, knocking it down out of the shot glass without touching the glass to his lips, then taking a suck at a lime he held in his hand.

He was a rugged-looking bird, tall and very slim, almost skinny, only not quite. Something warned you that beneath the long-sleeved chocolate-colored sports shirt he wore, there were arms like the toughest rope. Maybe it was the way he moved.

His face was thin, too, and fiery red from too much sun on a skin that wasn't used to it. It wasn't the deep, burned red, close to copper, of Hawley, who kept himself well loaded with sunshine at all times. This fellow had a brush cut, and then I noticed something. The lobe on his right ear was missing; in fact, almost a third of that right ear was gone.

And I noticed something else I didn't like. His black eyes were on Joan, and they stayed there. He watched her like a cat, knocking down a shot of gin, then taking a suck at his lime.

"Say, baby," I said to Joan, turning my back to the guy. "Don't look now, but do you know that bird at the end of the bar? Even seen him before?"

She looked right at him, boldly, the way she did everything else.

"No," she said, turning back to me. "I never saw him before, Larry. Honest."

"What you looking so scared about?" There was fright in her eyes.

"The way he looked at me, Larry," she whispered into her beer glass. "And he winked, just then."

Somehow it made me laugh. Maybe it was because I'd been under such a strain. And when I laughed, she blushed. That made me laugh still louder, almost uncontrollably.

I faced the door, laughing, and Joan was trying to quiet me down, when Hawley walked in.

I stopped laughing.

"Hey, don't let me break up the fun!" Hawley grinned broadly.

"Hi, Lew," I said. For some reason my throat felt dry.

He had met Joan. He smiled at her now, nodded, mopped his face, took his hat off, and slapped it on the bar. His thinning hair was all ganged up and sweaty-looking. He banged his big sunburned fist on the bar, and Pete Adams left his baseball game. Pete fixed the big icy bourbon. Hawley hoisted it, drank about three-quarters of it thirstily, then leaned against the bar, holding the glass chest-high, and peered at me. "You know, Larry, I been waiting all afternoon for this. Gonna have me a few today."

"Drink hearty," I said. I wished I could have felt free and easy with Lew, the way I used to. But I couldn't. Not any more. He mopped his face again, and when he tucked his handkerchief away in his hip pocket his coat moved open in front and I saw the strap of his shoulder harness, where he carried his gun. I remembered I had a harness like that back in my bureau drawer. The one Tad had left me.

I began to feel as if I were in a big room with walls of sheet steel. And I felt as if the walls were moving in on me, and as if the floor were moving up toward the ceiling.

I noticed Hawley stare fixedly toward the end of the bar. I glanced down there. The tough gin drinker had his face buried in a lime. Hawley scowled, scratched his head vigorously, finished his drink, and ordered another.

I nudged Joan, and we started out of the Pink Goat. As I reached the door, I heard Hawley belch and say, "Y'know Pete? If it wasn't for the belly, the back might wear gold." He chuckled. Then the ice in his glass tinkled as he drank again.

I wasn't psychic. I didn't know I hadn't even begun to ache.

Chapter Ten

It began to rain a little after midnight.

I lay in bed and listened to it, unable to sleep, only to think. It wasn't raining hard, just a steady, lethargic drizzle. It sounded like hundreds of tiny bats drumming furry wings against the roof and screened windows. The rain hissed on the lawn and on the sand. A warm rain, the kind of rain that is supposed to soothe you. I wasn't soothed. I was tormented.

There was no wind.

I'd left Joan's cottage early, because I couldn't stand listening to her plans for the robbery. I hadn't agreed to it yet. I wanted her so bad the very thought of her pulsed through my veins, along with the blood. Maybe she was a part of the blood, even.

Maybe she was holding that over me. Knowing I'd have to give in, because I wanted her like I did. But she wanted me, too. I tried to talk her out of the idea of robbery, tried to get her to scrape the crazy thought of it away, but she only shut up; she didn't stop thinking.

I smoked half a pack of cigarettes, lying there. Then I got out of bed and went down the hall into the living room and looked through the screen door at the Gulf.

It was calm out there. Calm and black. The water was like a heaving black floor, slick and ponderous. From the southern skies tiny lances of bright white leaped, flickering jaggedly across to the west. The whisper of far thunder roofed the night. Now and again, from the indiscernible horizon, a crackling tree of lightning grew from sprout to flagrant, chittering adulthood, then exploded soundlessly in a white flash.

I stood there in a pair of shorts and stared.

I thought it was thunder. Then I knew it was somebody beating on the back door. Turning, I started toward the hall, then stopped as rapid feet whispered through the sand around the side of the house. Then sobs; short, jerky sobs that came from a woman's throat.

It was Joan, running across the patio, through the rain. She wore white pajamas. I flung the screen door open and she cried, "Larry!"

"What is it? What is it, Joan?"

She was breathless. She clung to me, her body spasmodically tense. She shivered.

"Joan. What is it?"

Still she didn't speak, but took my hand instead, and drew me outside. The screen door slammed, the spring howled.

"Joan, for God's sake! It's raining out here. What d'you want?"

She flung her head from side to side, and I saw her face in a faraway flash of lightning. Her teeth held her lower lip, her eyes were wide with shock. The rain covered us warmly with its damp and gentle hand as we hurried toward her cottage.

She was bent on taking me to her place, and she wasn't talking. We reached her front door, then she flung herself against the door and looked up at me, shaking the thick hair from her face. Her white pajamas clung to her body like wet tissue.

"Larry. I don't know. What'll I—what'll I—?"

She started to shake. I grabbed her, pushed her aside, and opened the door.

"In there, Larry." She ran beside me, her fingers biting into my arm. "In the bedroom—on the bed!"

The bedroom light was lit.

I stopped in the doorway, then walked slowly inside.

There was a man on the bed. His pants were nearly off, dangling bunched about his ankles. He was sprawled face up, one leg halfway to the floor. He wore a chocolate-colored sports shirt, wet from the rain. His hair was wet, glistening. His eyes and mouth were open, and there was an expression of horror, of awful horror, on his face. The man's hands were clutched around the hilt of a knife that jutted from the front of his throat. He had bled a great deal, and the gleaming, fresh, amazingly red blood pooled on the bed at his side and dripped slowly to the white rug on the floor.

It was the same man who had been in the Pink Goat this afternoon. The man with part of his ear missing; the man who had stared at Joan. He was dead.

Chapter Eleven

I must have sensed it because I turned just in time.

Joan stood with her hands clutching the sides of her head, pushing her tangled hair up, and a scream worked in her throat. The scream was in her eyes, her mouth was open, her tongue moving, her throat all ready to give out.

I grabbed her and pushed my palm over her mouth as she writhed, trying to break away from me. I released my hand from her mouth quickly and struck her three times across the face as hard as I dared. That did it. She began crying softly, staring at the dead man. For the first time I noticed that blood had splashed across the front of her pajamas.

She'd have to cry it out for a few moments. My whole body had tightened like wire, every nerve stretched and strained.

Between her crying and the soft warm rain, the sound of dripping blood gradually grew louder. It was forming a puddle on the rug. I toed the rug slightly, and the noise ceased. My action did something to Joan.

She fell to her knees, clinging to my leg, and cried still more loudly. Then abruptly she ceased.

"Larry!" she said. "What'll we do?"

I picked her up and urged her through the door, into the living room. Then for some reason I switched off the wall switch with my elbow—probably thinking of fingerprints—and swung the door closed with my toe.

Joan flopped on the divan and stared at me. But I knew she wasn't seeing me. Her eyes were slightly mad, and I knew she was seeing something else. A dead man, certainly, but what else?

I went out into the kitchen and found a bottle of rye, and I poured two water glasses about half full and splashed a little water in one for her. I went back into the living room. She hadn't moved. Her face was white; her lips, without lipstick, seemed pale. Her eyes reflected things, it seemed to me, like glass.

As I handed her the drink, I knew she didn't see me. But she drank. She drank it down steadily, like medicine, without pausing even to breathe. Then she set the glass on a small end table with great care, still staring.

I drank most of my drink and sat down on the divan, about a foot away from her. She kept staring straight at the bedroom door.

For a moment I thought the screaming was going to start again. But just as it was beginning to build up inside her breast, the rye began to take hold.

Her hand jerked where it lay on her knee, clenched, and grabbed at her knee.

"I killed him," she said. "I did that. I killed him." She said it flatly, without the slightest expression.

I finished my drink and set the glass quickly on the floor before I could shatter it in my fist. I realized that I was making faces and staring a little myself. I began to feel sick; my stomach did a complete turnover and I had to swallow it down. Then the rye caught up with me and that part was all right again.

My eyes watered and I began to tremble, then it faded away into nothing. She had killed him. Sitting there, I suddenly felt terribly tired, as though I would never be able to rise from the divan. I didn't want to talk. I didn't want to move. I didn't want to think.

There was a dead man in there.

Bleeding.

She killed him.

"Stick to beer an' pretzels . . . it's more fun. . . ."

I moved my foot sharply, inadvertently, and my glass leaped across the floor, struck the wall, and shattered with a crash. The broken shards glistened like diamonds along the baseboard.

She started talking. The noise had broken her heavy mood, released her. "He tried to attack me. Oh, God, Larry! He broke in through the screen. He ripped the screen. He'd been watching me. Oh, Larry!"

Her voice was hollow. She was looking at me now, her eyes filled with despair and loathing.

"Yes, go ahead, Joan. Tell me all about it. Get it out of your system," I said. And out of mine, I thought. I moved over next to her and held her close.

She was calming now. "I didn't hear anything. I'd been reading, trying not to worry about you. Because I know how you felt when you left."

"Yes, yes, go on."

"I'd been eating an apple while I read, that's how come the knife. I always peel my apples before I—eat—them." She started to tense up again. I shook her a little and she was all right again.

She went on, "So that's how come the knife."

"It was a big knife."

"I didn't have any small ones. I remember thinking how big it was when I was eating the apple."

"For Christ's sake Joan, please!"

"Yes." She swallowed. "I put the knife on the floor. I was sleeping, and I thought I heard a funny noise, like tearing. Like ripping." She clung to me, her damp hair against my face. "Then there was a big tearing noise, and I woke up." She shuddered. "He was already in the room, standing there, unbuttoning his p-a-a-a-n-ts!"

I left her quick, made it into the kitchen in nothing flat, and came back with the bottle. She was shuddering and staring again. I sloshed some into her glass and helped pour it down her. It did the trick.

"He said awful things, Larry. Oh, God, the things he said! He drooled, Larry, like a dog. He said he'd been watching me, couldn't forget me, he said he had to have me. He said he'd show me something I never saw before!"

I didn't want to listen. It sickened me, but I knew if she didn't get it out of her now, it might pile up inside her later on. Those things happen. So far she was doing all right.

She told me all the things he said, while she lay there scared out of her wits, cringing back into the bed, in the darkness. She said he'd stop talking, and breathe, and the sound of the rain would come to her. And she could smell cigarette smoke clear from my place because of the heavy night air, so she knew I was awake, but she couldn't scream.

"It was good you didn't," I told her.

She said he told her how beautiful she was, how he had dreamed of a girl like her all his life, and that he had saved himself for her. He told her she would grow to love him. He said he'd do anything for her.

"And all the time he was getting ready—to—to—"

"Yes, all right," I said.

And then he'd flung himself on her, tearing at her clothes. She said he was clumsy and fumbling, whispering nutty, mushy things to her, when she remembered the knife.

So she told him all right. That she would. She made him lie still, promising him all the time, while she got out of bed, telling him she had to undress.

She seized the knife from the floor. He saw her and lunged upward.

"He said he'd kill me first," she told me in a fierce whisper. "He said it didn't matter to him, and I swung the knife."

From what she said, he had been starting off the bed as she swung, and it went in easy. In the pale darkness she saw him thrash, grab the hilt, and die.

"He was very drunk, Larry. He died quick. He never said another thing. I switched on the light and watched him. His feet jigged and jigged." She began to laugh. "Like he was trying to dance."

"Joan, stop it!"

"And the blood pumped out of his throat."

We looked at each other. I got up and went in there and turned on the light. He hadn't changed any, and the bleeding was pretty near through. I saw the apple peelings on the floor beside the bed. The screen on the window was ripped out. I went back to Joan. "All right," I said. "You come with me. I'll go over and wake up Mr. Buck and phone the police. We'll—"

She was gripping my hands. "No! No, Larry! Not the police. We can't let anybody know. Not about this. Not this."

Something began to grow inside me and I felt as if I were going to burst.

"We've got to, Joan," I said as calmly as I could.

She shook her head, hanging onto my hands. "No, no. We'll hide him someplace. Not the police, Larry. You've got to help me hide him." Her eyes brightened as she stared at me. "We can—we can take him out in the Gulf. We can take him out there and sink him. Nobody'll ever know!"

Chapter Twelve

I laughed at her.

It was idiotic. She couldn't mean what she said! Yet she did mean it; I saw that in her eyes.

"It's true, Larry," she said. Her voice was hoarse with emotion. "I couldn't possibly turn that—that body over to the police."

"Joan. It's the only thing to do." I tried as hard as possible to retain some sense of right in the matter. I found I was still holding the bottle of whisky. I took a long drink, feeling the warmth bite into my stomach.

"I can't," she said simply. "I can't let you, Larry. You love me, and I love you. We've got to have each other."

"What difference does that make about that in there?"

"There'd be an investigation. There'd be publicity." I nodded. That was true. But I still couldn't see any reason why we shouldn't do the right thing. She had killed in self-defense, that was obvious.

"My grandmother would die," she said simply. "It would kill her, Larry." She looked at me, pulled me down on the divan beside her. "And—and we couldn't stand publicity, not now."

"Why?"

"Our other plans would have to be postponed indefinitely."

I remembered the Beach Club and felt sick, so sick I turned away from her. I knew I should get up and walk out of there; go away and stay away. But even as I thought it, I knew I wouldn't. Her hand fingered my arm, and that touch was enough. Even with this, with what had happened here, and with the way she spoke, I still wanted her, loved her. I cursed myself. I didn't want anything—just Joan. How the hell could I explain it to myself? There was no way.

"Joan," I said. "If we did hide the body, and it were ever found, if we were ever connected with it in any way, it'd be a natural confession of guilt."

She didn't say anything. Just watched me. The tip of her tongue tipped her lips, and she nodded.

I stared back at her, feeling numb and half mad. Actually, she *had* killed in self-defense. I told myself that over and over. The man had been a mental case. If not Joan, then some other woman would have fallen before him. And another might not have been so lucky as to have a knife handy. Another might not have had the courage to use the knife, either. Joan had that courage, or whatever it was. She had something inside her that even I couldn't understand. I could feel it, sense it—it was something I didn't want to know about. Sometimes I believed her not quite right herself, the way her brain worked, the way she schemed and planned.

"Larry, no one must know. Think of the scandal!" Her voice grew very quiet. "And, too, think of your brother, Tad."

"What?"

"If something like this came out, and you were connected with it in any way, they're apt to think anything. Anything at all. You know that. You're a killer's brother. A criminal's brother. Perhaps—perhaps he's even killed before. They'd say it ran in the family." She paused, and I felt sweat trickle down my spine. I rubbed my back against the divan. My chest was covered with sweat.

She went on, "Remember what you told me about your father? He was a gunman. A paid gunman. Do you think they've forgotten that? And your mother—"

"A common prostitute," I said. "Yes. They'd think of those things." I sat there, staring at the bedroom door now. And I knew she was right. But to dispose of a body . . .

"Joan. We don't even know who he is. There'll be a search. He was in the Pink Goat. Somebody'll report him missing."

"So what?" She rose, and I saw assurance in her stance now. She looked down at me, and though her face had regained some of its natural color, there was in her eyes still that slightly glassy look; and it didn't come from what she had drunk. "You'd never be able to get a lawyer to take Tad's case if this came out in the papers."

"Maybe we could keep it out of the papers."

She laughed. "How dumb are you, Larry? Don't be that way. They'd smear this across every front page in the state!" She whirled, stalked to the far wall, then strode back. "I can't let that happen. I won't. If you won't help me, then I'll do it myself. The least you can do is be quiet about it." She suddenly changed, sat quickly beside me, and held my hands. "Don't you see, Larry? We've got a chance to make some money—"

"For Christ's sake, Joan! There's a dead man in there."

"He's better off dead."

I looked at her without astonishment now, without anything. She couldn't see it as I saw it. She couldn't see it as any normal person had to see it. Then she wasn't normal. And the horrible thing about that was that I didn't give a damn.

"If we go ahead, like I say," she told me, "then you will be able to buy a lawyer for your brother. It'll take money, and it'll be hard to find the right one. One who'll take the case, because it'll be touchy. Even I can see that. But you will be able to find one. And you'll have enough money. We'll go into it together, Larry. I'll help you. But if this"—she motioned toward the bedroom—"comes out, we may as well forget everything. I'll just go back to New York—back to the bookstore, back to being a secretary." She hesitated. "Would you want that, Larry? And you would just go on being a bartender. Or you'd be forced to move, because nobody would drink in your place. Would you like that?"

"No!" I shouted it, stood, and walked over to the bedroom door. I kicked it open with my foot and stared into the darkness. "All right. How'll we do it?"

She stood, moved slowly up to me. I didn't look at her, but I could feel her standing there beside me. I could feel the warmth of her. Her voice was very soft. "If you don't want to help me," she said, "I'll do it myself. All I ask is that you say nothing. I killed in self-defense, Larry."

I turned to her. "All right. Never mind. Wait right here. I'm going over and put on some clothes. I'll be right back. We'll work it out."

She looked at me solemnly and said, "Thanks, Larry."

Chapter Thirteen

At my place I stripped down and took a cold shower. As I stood there with the fierce needles of water knifing my skin, it seemed sort of comical. Get all cleaned up to go get rid of a body.

I put on a pair of tennis shoes, khaki trousers, and a sweat shirt. I was sweating already, covered with it.

Outside it was still slowly raining warm rain. The southern sky still flickered with lightning.

"I—I went through all his pockets," Joan told me when I stepped into her bedroom. "He had just three dollars." She held them up. Three limp dollar bills, drooping in her hand like dead leaves from a funeral wreath.

I glanced at the dead man. She had belted his pants around his waist.

"I—I couldn't take the knife—"

"Yeah, O.K.," I said. "Get rid of those dollar bills. Here, let me have them."

She handed them to me. They felt as warmly limp as they looked. I tucked them into the dead man's shirt pocket. "You're sure there was nothing else on him? No wallet? No identification of any kind?"

I stood there while she shook her head at me and I remembered how I had asked that question once before. I think the hair on the back of my neck lifted. I said nothing more about it.

"You'd better go get dressed," I told her. I waited while she went to the closet and took out blue slacks, a red jersey sweater, and a pair of loafers. She walked past me, gave me a pat on the arm, and went on into the other room. I stepped over to the dead man.

This was going to be nasty. Nasty all the way. But somehow it wasn't so bad now that I'd made up my mind to go through with it.

Get this, though—I did go through his pockets. Just to satisfy myself. And there was nothing in them.

Rigor mortis still hadn't set in, and his hands came away from the knife blade without too much trouble. The knife had apparently struck a vital spot in his throat, the jugular vein. I decided Joan must have given him a whale of a smack with the blade. Otherwise, if she had missed that vital spot, and the blade hadn't gone in the way it had, she would have merely had a very mad man on her hands, with a bleeding cut in his throat.

As it was, though, he'd probably died like a stuck pig. I clamped my teeth together, sucked a good deep breath, grabbed hold of the knife hilt, and pulled.

Never mind. I got it out, and that's enough. I walked fast into the kitchen and washed it clean the very first thing. Then I went back to the living room. "Joan," I said, "don't touch a thing. I'll be right back. Just remembered I'd better check on the Bucks."

Joan was brushing her hair. I went out the back door and cut across the lawn toward the office. The Bucks, man and wife, owned the cabanas, and lived in a two-room addition built onto the office. It was all dark. I pussyfooted over to their bedroom window and listened.

The unmistakable sounds of one person snoring emanated from the window. A woman—Mrs. Buck. I stood there, fretting a little, then pressed my forehead against the screen, maybe feeling a little like the dead man had felt. Old Man Buck wasn't in bed with his wife.

I went around to the carport on the other side of the office. His car was gone. That was that. I didn't like it. He never was out at night, even, let alone late at night.

I went back to Joan and the dead man. She was still brushing her hair. It shone like polished gold, with streaks of copper running through it, thick, and all hazed together, like a foggy rainbow.

We looked at each other and she stopped brushing. I went on into the bedroom and stood there, remembering something else.

The damned mattress.

I grabbed the dead man and rolled him over off the bed, onto the floor, onto the rug. He fitted nicely. Then I looked at the bed. I turned to the door and cleared my throat.

She looked at me.

"We've got a hell of a job," I told her. "The sheets, the mattress, and the rug."

She shrugged. "They'll all sink, Larry—won't they?"

"How're you going to sink a mattress? Stand there, out there in the Gulf, and hold it down till it's waterlogged?" I shook my head. "Uh-uh. Besides, it'd probably come floating up in your front yard in a couple of days."

Fright bared its teeth in her eyes for a single second.

"How are we going to get out in the Gulf?"

She swallowed and swatted the brush against her thigh.

"That's an expensive mattress," I said. "After we do figure a way to get rid of it somehow, we've got to replace it."

Her head began to jerk up and down, and she wasn't nodding in agreement.

"And," I went on, "we've got to replace it without the Bucks' knowing anything about it, and it's got to be the same kind. The sheets, too—and the rug." I felt panic begin to elbow around inside me, preparing to give me a few swift kicks.

"But—but—but—"

"And Mr. Buck isn't home. He's out, with the car, and he's never out with the car at night. He doesn't only not like to drive at night, but his wife kicks up a fuss about it because she thinks he'll go on a tear."

"Larry! Stop it!" She composed herself with an effort. "We've got to go through with it somehow. And you know as well as I do that the body'll have to go out in the Gulf." Her chin trembled, and she paused. She was thinking. She said quietly, "I seem to remember that fishes eat—" She swallowed and went back to brushing her hair with much too vigorous strokes.

Suddenly I went flat, like iced tea. "It won't work, Joan."

She ran—yes, ran—up to me, her face all twisted and scared-looking. "It's got to work. It's got to! You hear me?"

"O.K. Go brush your hair. Let me think."

She was right about one thing. We'd better go through with it now. I'd hate to have to stick that knife in there again, call the police, and tell them it happened over an hour ago, but we didn't know what to do about it. We *were* guilty now. We *had* to get rid of the body.

We were guilty. . . .

That's exactly what it was. We had to get rid of the body, because we were guilty.

I leaned against the wall in the bedroom, where she couldn't see me, and stared at the dead man on the floor and cursed him under my breath. Then I cursed myself. I started to curse Joan, but I couldn't.

What choice had she had? She'd had to do it, or maybe lose her own life. But why had I listened to her? Why hadn't I told her to shut up, and gone and called the cops?

I knew why. Because I knew damned well I'd lose her if I did, that's why.

O.K. It had to be the Gulf. Way out. And that meant we had to have a boat. It would be smart to get a motor launch of some kind, and wake up everybody along the beach. Sure. No. It had to be a rowboat. Out there.

It was still raining. If the rain held, with no wind, it would be all right. The water was as smooth as molasses. But would it stay that way? I could manage a boat in it the way it was, a small boat. But we'd have a hell of a time.

I quit thinking like that, went out through the kitchen, and cut over to my place. I found what I wanted. A new coil of clothesline I'd bought a few months before and never used. There were two hundred feet of it. Plenty. I remembered buying it for Mrs. Buck, in town, and how when I got back with it, she already had some. So I'd kept it. That was before Tad came to the cottage to hide out, before Joan, before any of this.

Those days, way back there in memory, seemed peculiarly happy.

It wasn't smart to take a rowboat out into the Gulf. It couldn't be too big a boat, either. I wasn't used to rowing, and it wouldn't be nice to end up down the coast someplace. Or upside down.

A boat. Where? Where could I find a boat?

Excitement had me. My heart pumped heavily. I felt exuberant, ready for action, lightheaded. It was after one o'clock and that meant we had to get going, or find ourselves overrun by daylight with a corpse on our hands.

Then I remembered Jock Hewitt. He lived over on the other side of the highway, on the bay. He had several boats, and one of them was a round-bottomed affair light enough for one man to carry. I also recalled Jock's telling me that boat would stand about anything.

Jock wasn't living out there now, though, and that meant I had to steal the boat. I ran over through the soft rain and told Joan. Then I jogged up the shell road, crossed the highway, and headed for Hewitt's.

It was dark among the cabbage palms that surrounded Hewitt's shack, and the rank smell of dead and living fish hung in the heavy air. I went out on the wooden pier that jutted into the channel and inspected the boats tied up there.

The one I wanted wasn't there. I was glad of that, because it'd only make more trouble taking it out of the water. I spotted two hulls lying upside down back on the bank, but neither was the light, varnished job I was looking for. I began to get panicky, because these other boats were all big cypress-plank babies. Heavy, they were, and it'd take ten men to carry one.

I was about to give up, ready to go hunting in back yards, ready for anything, when I glimpsed a hull resting on top of the shed where Jock Hewitt kept his fishing paraphernalia. I found a box, shoved it close, and climbed up there. It was the one. I slid it down on an angle to the ground, and tried hefting it. It was heavy, cumbersome, but I'd manage all right.

I got it up over my head, teetered around, and started off. Then I remembered—oars. Jock kept the oars locked in that shed. I put the boat down, and I was getting tired already.

There was no waiting now. I went up to the shed door, took hold of the padlock with both hands, braced one foot against the shed, and twisted the hasp off the shed, lock and all.

When I saw Jock, I'd tell him I borrowed his boat, and that somebody had broken into his shed. I got the oars, stuck them beneath the seats in the boat, hoisted the boat on my back, and started for Joan's place.

Light as the boat was, it was exhausting work. I rested once, then decided I'd try to make it clear across the highway. I was coming along the road that branched off the highway when I froze.

A man was walking down the road, whistling. He was staggering. Right then, one of the oars slipped loose from under the seats and rattled out of the boat to the ground.

The man ceased whistling and halted.

I dropped to my knees and slipped the boat off my back as carefully as possible. I was in a slight ditch, and hoped the shadows would cover me.

Then I saw who it was. It was Pete Adams, and he was pretty well slopped up. He reeled around in the road, muttering to himself. Once he looked straight at me, without seeing anything.

"God damn!" he said. Then he began whistling again, and staggered off.

I got my breath, hoisted the boat up, and teetered the rest of the way. That had been close. That was how murderers got caught.

I sat on the beach, rested for a moment, then went back to Joan's cottage.

We put the mattress and sheets into the boot of her convertible. It wouldn't do to bury the stuff near here. Some dog would probably dig everything up. I figured we'd take the stuff to the city dump tomorrow, pour gasoline on it, and burn it.

I got all the tools in Joan's car and hefted them for weight. Too light. I didn't want that body bobbing up in the morning.

Then I recalled a two-cylinder outboard motor I had under my kitchen sink. It was no good. A friend of mine had given it to me because I thought I'd be able to get it working again. I got that and filled the gas tank with sand. It was plenty heavy. It would do fine.

"We'll wrap him in the rug, with the motor tied to it," I told Joan. "He'll stay down then."

We looked at each other.

She said, "Suppose—just suppose the rug comes up."

"Yeah."

So we put the rug with the mattress, and tied the dead man to the motor with the clothesline. It was bulky, but it seemed to be a good tight job. Now. If the body ever did come up, it was a cinch that outboard motor wasn't going to come with him.

We stood there, breathing hard, standing over the thing on the floor.

"Get a bottle," I said. "We'll need a drink. The hardest part's yet to come."

While she went for the bottle out in the kitchen, I tried to keep from thinking. I realized that that's what I'd been doing all along. Not allowing myself to think, because I might go haywire. I thought of Tad now, though, and how he'd always tried hard to keep me out of jams. He had, all right, and I'd saved myself up for a real big one.

All I knew was that this had to be accomplished. There'd be time to think after that. The room with the steel walls was closing in tighter and tighter. For the life of me, I couldn't see why. . . .

Joan came back with a bottle and we had a few, straight off the neck. All the fear was gone from her now, and she looked pretty as the dickens. Both of us were too excited to be sleepy, even though I felt as if I'd been laboring in the salt mines for a week on thin soup.

I couldn't carry it alone. Joan couldn't lift either end, so we had to drag it. I'd put the boat in the water, with the bow on the beach. We were halfway across the beach, dragging the body toward the boat, when car headlights flashed brightly down the shell road. We must have stood out like actors behind the footlights. And the play was a ghastly thing. I dove at Joan and knocked her flat.

The lights rode over us now because of the jutting bank where the sandy beach ended. I snaked my way up to the bank and hung my chin over the edge, peering through sand spurs and grass. The car turned into the long drive behind the cabanas and went up into the carport beside Buck's office.

"Joan," I said. "You wait here, and don't move. I've got to see what it's about."

She said she would, and I took off, keeping well in the raining shadows. The rain hadn't lessened or increased. Just that steady, warm drizzle.

It was Old Man Buck. Drunk as a hoot owl. I took a place by the bedroom window again, and waited. When he came into the bedroom, Mrs. Buck turned on the light and started giving him hell.

It turned out he'd been on a party, nothing more. So I beat it back to Joan.

"It's O.K.," I told her. "Let's go."

Then I saw that the boat was drifting off. I went after it, floundering in the syrupy water, got it, and dragged it back.

Somehow we lifted the corpse into the boat. Joan climbed in and I climbed in after her and shoved off.

Lightning ripped across the southern sky, and I felt a soft wind blow against me.

Chapter Fourteen

The dead man stared at me.

Joan sat in the bow, behind me. The body's head was propped against the back seat in the boat. Its face glistened from salt-water spray, pale in each flash of lightning.

I tried not to look at the body, but there it was, open-eyed and awful. I heaved my shoulders into those oars, let me tell you, and we began to make time. I didn't like the feel of that wind. It was increasing, even though I told myself it wasn't. And the thunder loomed closer now, every rumble a little louder than before.

"Larry?" Joan's voice lifted, cut off sharply by a gust of wind. I saw fine ripples across the smooth surface of the water.

"Yeah, what?"

"You—you aren't worried any more, are you, Larry?"

"No."

"Because it's all right, I'm sure. He was probably just a tramp. Probably doesn't know anyone."

"Sure."

"You see it my way, don't you?"

"Sure, Joan."

"I mean, you understand how the publicity—"

"I understand, yes."

"I'm so glad, Larry. It's an awful thing to have happen. But even if we had told the police, that wouldn't change anything. It would all be exactly the same—basically."

She was right, I suppose. Only she was forgetting what we were doing. That was the tough part.

We hadn't gone far out yet, but all of a sudden I knew we were getting into deep water. And we'd have to go a lot deeper. A little boat like this is pure hell on the sea. You feel the heave and swell, the tremendous surge, the awful power of that water underneath you. You begin to feel pretty damned small. Not like a cork, either. A cork won't sink. You don't feel a bit like a cork.

I knew the Gulf was beginning to break up. We'd ride the crest of a roller now, then slide down into a deeper trough. Without stopping rowing, I looked around, straining my eyes into the night. Here and there, not often, but just beginning, were white-capped waves.

One of those waves lifted the bow, then the whole boat, and we slipped over its back into a dark trough. At the same instant, the wind came up and stayed up, increasing. This was bad, real bad. They weren't little slapping waves; they had swelling power. You could feel the boat give sickeningly, and ride sidewise, then swoop and give again.

"Larry, you think it's all right?" Joan had to raise her voice a little now.

"Yeah, it's all right!" My breath was coming in shorter gasps now, as I strained at the oars. We weren't making much headway now. And I knew we had to go out a long way yet.

The rain quit monkeying around about then. It ceased abruptly, then changed to big drops that began falling faster and faster. Now and then a hand of wind slashed the rain against the boat.

The dead man's head bobbed and bobbed.

"Isn't this far enough, Larry?"

"No."

Salt spray whipped into the boat and lashed across us, making a sound like buckshot flung against a board.

Joan screamed. I quit rowing and twisted to see what was the matter. A mullet had leaped into the boat and was bouncing around by her feet. She was standing up, cringing away from it.

"Sit down!" I shouted. The boat heeled around giddily, and a big one struck us broadside. If Joan hadn't sat down the instant I warned her, she might have gone over.

I struggled with the oars, trying to get the boat headed into the wind again. Finally I managed, but it was tough, and my heart was in my throat.

The mullet jumped down between my feet. I managed to get my toe under it and flipped it over the side.

"Larry, I'm—I think this is far enough."

I swore at her. "You want him to beat us home?"

I turned and looked at her over my shoulder. Her face was white, her lips a dark slash, her hair blowing wetly away from her head. Her clothes were soaked, as were mine, and every slight outline of her body showed in bright relief against dark shadow. She was beautiful, like some goddess sitting up there. She laughed at me, her eyes shining, and yelled, "Heave ho, then!"

And I began to want her more than ever before. . . .

Then another wave knocked that out of my head, and I couldn't get my eyes off the dead man. He seemed to be nodding at me. The look of horror was gone from his face. He seemed peaceful, almost smiling, with his mouth open, and he kept nodding at me, as if he were saying, "Sure, Larry. That's right. Only be careful, you might slip up. And then where would you be?"

I tore my eyes off him and worked on the oars like fury. It kept coming to me what we were doing, until it had me nearly nuts. The wind was growing stronger every minute, and I began to worry plenty now.

I'd seen plenty of dead men, in lots worse shape than this one, during the war. And during the war I'd come to accept death, too. It had never bothered me too much, and I told myself that's why I was able to endure this the way I was. He was dead, and it didn't much matter after a guy was dead. It was all over for him.

Then I got to thinking, O.K., so that's how it is with me. The war numbed me, like, so it doesn't bother me too much.

But how come Joan stands it so good?

Then another wave grabbed hold of the side of the boat and tried to climb in with us. I was ankle-deep in water, and I knew damned well this was it. We weren't going any farther out. I wasn't sure how far out in the Gulf we were, but it had to be far enough.

Already the waves looked like garages swooping down on us, and pretty soon they'd be houses, then skyscrapers. And when they got that large, I knew this little boat wasn't going to climb them. We had to get rid of the body.

But if I let go of the oars now, we were sunk—literally.

"O.K., Joan," I called over my shoulder. "Take it real easy, come on down past me. You'll have to help me."

She didn't answer and I came close to dying. But I whirled around, and she was already working down next to me. I didn't row, just held the oars, keeping us from turning, working first one, then the other, while Joan straddled the seat and wriggled under my arm.

On her knees there beside me, she looked up at me, put her arms around me, and kissed me. It was like being wrapped in fire.

Then she went back by the dead man. All the time the boat was dancing up and down, jabbing viciously from side to side, trying to turn around with the wind and the waves.

Then I knew how hard it was going to be. With the dead man's weight on one side of the boat, we were apt to capsize.

"Wait a minute!" I yelled. "Lemme think."

I kept battling with the growing sea and tried to think. I remembered how we were going to have to turn around, and that solved it.

I told her to get the body ready to go over the side, then I'd turn in the other direction. And when it was just past broadside, with the waves piling at us, I'd ship the oars and we'd both pitch him over. That way we could utilize the weight of the dead man in getting us around without turning over.

It worked. It was close, but we did it. It was all done in such a wild hurry, with my cursing, and shoving, that I hardly remembered what it was like. One minute the corpse was there, balanced on the gunwales, the sea swarming down on us. And the next instant it was gone. The dead man's hand came back, white out of the darkness, and slapped the boat a hell of a whack before it vanished.

I dove for the oars, and the sea picked us up and sent us charging back toward the mainland. I had fought the sea going out, so I could ride it some coming back. Otherwise, I'd have to fight it going in, or we'd land too far down the beach.

Joan stayed where the dead man had been and we stared at each other while I battled against the sea.

Thunder and lightning were right overhead now, and it was like rowing a boat under spotlights. It was that bright. The rain seethed around us, but it was hard to tell whether it was the Gulf or the rain. The boat was filling fast with water.

She sat there staring past my shoulder now, with a hand on either side of the boat, and she looked wild. I was sweating, and I could feel the blood swarming hot into my head, shoulders, and arms. My arms and back were stiff with strain, ready to give out, and the breath burned in my throat as if somebody'd shoved a hot poker down there.

There was no use trying to talk now. We couldn't hear each other. I shouted something at her and she just looked at me. I saw her mouth open, and I knew she'd said something. I heard her voice far away on the wind, but I couldn't make out what it was.

I rowed like hell. Pretty soon, as we crested a wave, I glimpsed a car's headlights over on the main highway. We were still a good way out, but we'd make it. I'd no sooner thought that than the wind roared, and I lost an oar. I made a wild grab for it.

Joan screamed something and started toward me. The boat heeled around, and I crouched there, trying to make headway with the one oar I had. It was no use. It was like jabbing at air, and actually it was mostly jabbing at air.

A mountain of a wave came down at us, and I yelled at Joan, "Dive!"

We both dove. I felt the boat sling over on its beams against my feet as I went into the water. I floundered up and looked around. The boat was upside down and a long way off. Then I didn't see it any more.

Something grabbed me, fingernails ripping into my arm. It was Joan.

We could both swim and the water was warm, so it was all right. Only then I felt the current. It was pulling us out.

"Swim!" I shouted at her. "Swim!"

She broke away from me and we started churning toward the distant beach, which gleamed like a glistening black snake in the savage lightning.

Chapter Fifteen

The water was very warm, almost hot compared to the cold wind and rain. Right away, I went under and took off my trousers. The tennis shoes were light and didn't bother me much at first. But after a little while longer in that wild sea, I went down again and fought it out with the soaked, knotted laces. That was something I'd always remembered until tonight. When out in a small boat on a big sea, leave your shoes untied.

I was underwater more than on the surface, and it seemed to relax me. I swam in a steady crawl. Now and again I'd shove myself chest-high out of the wild churning, and straighten out for the highway that showed beyond the seas. I kept an eye on Joan, too. Once she waved at me from nearby. She seemed to be doing all right.

Underwater I could hear the roaring of the storm; the hiss of the rain and spray, the deep surging boom of cresting waves. I could feel the staccato thrust of palsied white lightning, feel the steady and violent mutter of thunder, then the awful clashing cracks that split right down through the water.

I kept remembering the dead man's hand, white and stiff, as it banged against the side of the boat. And I thought, Now it's done. Now it's done. What happens now?

I shoved myself out of the water and took a quick gander around through the flying scud for Joan. I didn't see her. Again panic clutched at me.

I yelled her name into the wind. And the wind tossed her name back at me. I yelled again. The wind crammed the name right down my open throat.

All I could think was that I'd lost her. A cramp, maybe. Or maybe she'd become tangled in her clothes. I cursed the night, the wind, the sea.

It seemed as if I'd never make the beach. Time was like a staggering old man limping across an eternal treadmill. Lethargy crept through me, but I didn't dare relax. My arms and legs had become huge logs, weighted with iron.

Then, after what seemed hours, a wave, angry-faced and white-bearded, full of mean argument, grabbed me up and hurled me.

I struck hard sand and slid along it on my back for a few feet with shells slicing into my skin as I was tossed and tumbled. Then I was over my head in water again.

But I'd reached the beach.

A few more strokes, and I'd made it, on my hands and knees. I crept along, with the sea thrusting at me, tumbling me, until I was just out of reach of the waves. They hissed and smoked at my feet.

I lay there for a moment with my face toward the violently streaming sky, and drew wind and rain and good air into me. I felt somehow cleansed.

Then I forced myself to my feet. I looked down the beach, thinking, Joan, Joan—praying she hadn't gone down. I had to find her. I shouted her name, heard it whisked away by the wind. I turned up the beach, running, trying to locate her.

The stunted thrust of a haggard slash pine, rooted perversely into the shadowed edge of beach and bank, told me where I was. About five hundred yards down from the cottages, near the Beach Club.

I forced myself to hurry toward the cabanas, knowing that if she had come through, she'd head that way, too.

My foot hit a sinkhole in the sands, and I sprawled flat. At the same instant, I heard her voice. I guess I thanked God, then.

"Larry!"

Still lying there, I looked up, saw her running toward me. Running white and lithe toward me through the rain. Every few steps she'd stumble and fall to her knees. She was naked, with the rain streaming on her.

Lightning ripped white across the sky and she looked like something mad and untame running down out of the savage heavens.

"Larry, Larry, oh, Larry!" she panted.

Then she was there beside me and we came close together as we had on a night long ago. Only now it was different, and I knew why we were here.

"I didn't think you made it," I told her. "God, you scared me."

She couldn't speak, but her lips answered for her. Then as we quieted down, she shook and trembled against me, repeating my name over and over as she clung to me. The Gulf hissed and boiled at our feet. The sand was hard and cold. But gradually a warmth crept through us as we lay there. We stirred to something that the rain and the cold could never take away.

"Larry!"

"It's all right," I said. "It's all right. We made it, that's all that matters."

"Yes, yes, yes . . ."

There was the storm. Then for a long, raging moment, filled with brutal hunger, I heard nothing—nothing until she screamed. . . .

For a while we lay there together, until we both began to shiver with the cold, decreasing rain. The sky in the east was gray with morning. The wind was almost gone now.

We rose and moved slowly off toward the cabanas. We were tired and cold, and we didn't talk. But we were together.

When we reached home, she headed for her cottage, and I for mine.

I watched her enter her door. Then I waved and whispered, "Good-by."

Chapter Sixteen

Run!

That one word stood out like a red danger signal in my mind. I didn't let myself think anything else. Just run!

It had to be that way. If I saw Joan again I'd never be able to break away. I didn't want to, I hated it above everything, but I had to run, and I knew it.

The house was dark, just beginning to get gray, the shadows of the furniture yet indistinct, but beginning to clarify. I stripped off my sweat shirt as I walked down the hall and headed for the shower.

Hot, then cold, and out of that.

Maybe I was a little crazy during those moments when I hurriedly dressed, putting on my best lightweight gray suit, a pair of thick-soled brown shoes, a dark blue sport shirt, without a tie.

I went over to the bureau and looked in the top drawer. There was the gun and holster—Tad's harness. I slammed the drawer shut and glanced out of the window, across the morning, toward Joan's place. A light was lit in the living room, and I saw her walk past the window.

I don't believe I really knew what I was doing. Things were foggy; I was a monomaniac. Run, run, run!

I had to run and forget. In the back of my mind I nursed a hazy dream, something about staying away, hiding, and returning to discover that all of this was dream stuff, and I'd been walking in a dream. No Joan. . . .

I refused to dwell on that, because I knew with my conscious mind that there was a Joan, and that I loved her, and wanted her more than anything in the world.

But I knew this couldn't be. Not if I wished to stay sane; to live the way life was meant to be lived.

No. I had to get away. Out of this. Hide.

I knew that if I saw her once more, if at this instant she walked in that bedroom door, I'd never escape. *Never.*

As I slammed the front door, locked it, and headed for the rear, I wondered if maybe I was running from myself; trying to escape from myself.

I locked the back door, bounced the key in my hands, and finally placed it in the gutter pipe that ran along the edge of the porch roof.

The rain had ceased. The wind was brisk with early morning, and the sky was rapidly achieving a dismal dawn.

For a moment I stood there, glanced once toward Joan's cottage, then turned and ran.

The shell road crunched beneath my feet. I didn't think about that back there; what the night had been filled with. I thought instead of the traffic on the highway, of how at this time in the morning cars would be headed for St. Pete, people going to work.

On the highway I looked back again, panting—back across the windy dunes, brown with sunburned grass; the savage palms, gesticulant and disarrayed, black hands against the sky. Then I turned and began trotting up the highway. Cars breathed by, tires screaming on the still wet pavement.

A man in a battered Chevrolet sedan stopped and flung the side door open. He was smoking a pipe and the car was thick with smoke. I climbed in, slammed the door, and we were off.

"Town?" he said.

"Yeah, town," I said.

He looked at me and I stared straight ahead through the dirty windshield. Neither of us spoke again until we hit Ninth and Central.

"I turn here," he said.

"Thanks," I said, and climbed out. As the car whipped away into the Ninth Street traffic, I realized I didn't even know what the guy looked like. All I knew was that he smoked a pipe.

I turned down Central, walking fast, and in close to the buildings. Here in town there wasn't much wind, and far down Central, over the bay, the sky was a pale blue. The gods were pulling the blanket of night off the heavens. It had been a hell of a filthy blanket.

The stores weren't open yet. I cursed that and kept walking. I didn't know where I was going. I was just walking in a daze. I walked the whole length of Central, clear to the Yacht Basin. A bedraggled woman in brown shorts came out onto the deck of a schooner with a bottle of beer in one hand. She took a swig, spat it over the side, and went back down the companionway. Breakfast.

I turned, walked through the park, then cut across, and started back up Central on the other side. I walked clear back to Ninth Street and stood there.

I went into a restaurant, ordered a cup of coffee at a cold white counter, left a quarter on the counter, and walked out. I didn't want coffee. I didn't know what I wanted. But whatever it was, I'd find it. I had to find it, or go mad.

Every time I thought of Joan it was like a stab in the belly. I crossed Central and started down again.

The next thing I knew, the banks were open, and I was in my bank. I had just drawn three hundred dollars and was putting it into my pocket. I started out of the bank and stepped on the scales by the door. I didn't see how much I weighed, but I saw my face in the mirror and it scared me. The man who stared back at me looked dead.

I went out onto the street.

Love! All I'd ever dreamed of had walked into the Pink Goat that day, and look what it had turned out to be.

As I moved slowly down the street I heard the sound of the sea in my head. I heard Joan crying, and I heard her scream. . . .

The first bar I came to, I went inside. It was empty. The bartender, a young, broad-shouldered fellow, smoking a cigarette, was cleaning up last night's debris. I walked on past the bar to the phone booth in the back.

Pete Adams didn't sound too well, and I remembered last night when I'd seen him weaving along the road, drunk. I remembered how lucky I'd been that he hadn't seen me with the boat. Thank God for that ditch.

"Pete," I said. "Open up today, will you?"

"Cripes, Larry, I—"

"Sure, I know. You got a hangover. So what? Lots of us got hangovers. Open up today. I'm going away for a while. Don't know when I'll be back. Work it out any way you want."

"Larry, I dunno."

"Listen, Pete. Remember the time I—"

"All right, all right. I remember. You kept me out of the can. All right!" I heard him mutter. "All right, I'll open up. When'll you be back?"

I hung up and leaned back against the side of the booth. The bartender went behind the bar and drew a first beer for a customer. I stood there, watching the guy drink his beer. Then I went out and up to the bar.

"Shot."

The bartender grunted and poured the drink. "Chaser?"

I drank the shot. "Yeah, water—and another shot."

He poured the second, and got me a glass of water.

"Another shot," I said.

He poured, then stood there and watched me drink that, holding the bottle ready. He poured another. I drank it.

"Look," he said. "Here's the bottle."

"That's all I want," I said. "No, pour me another, and have one."

"O.K." He poured us both one. He said, "Mud," and I grunted. We drank. I laid a fiver on the bar and left.

I walked diagonally across the street and traffic waited for me. One old geezer laid on his horn to beat hell. I went into the first bar I saw and told the bartender. "Shot of rye."

He poured me a shot. He was moon-faced, wore glasses, and was nearly bald. I laid a five-dollar bill on the bar and stared at the glass of whisky. I could feel what I'd drunk burning in the pit of my empty stomach.

"Can you fix me up with a sandwich?" I said.

He looked at me without smiling or blinking and said, "All right. Take what you get?"

I nodded. He lumbered off toward the back of the room and returned very suddenly with two slices of bread around a slab of cheese. He put it on a plate he fished up from beneath the bar someplace, and clattered it down in front of me. I ate it.

"D'you know what you et just then?" the bartender asked.

I shook my head. "No."

He went back to drying some beer glasses he'd just washed in a vile-looking sink. "I didn't think so," he said. "Just wanted to make sure."

I had another drink there, paid up, and walked out.

The next bar was one of these red plush and chromium joints, with air-conditioning—the works. It was all right, because the sun had really come out, and the streets were growing hotter by the minute.

The bartender was a very slick-looking bird with a pencil-line mustache, and he acted as if he'd done something very bad last night, and wanted to redeem himself in everybody's eyes this morning. He was leaping around there fit to kill himself, and maybe the customers, too.

"Rye," I said

"Rye," he said, and poured it. "Chaser?"

I shook my head. He looked pained. There were two other men drinking in the middle of the bar, and at the far end a woman in a blue dress, with dark blonde hair, was working on a bottle of beer.

Then, with the glass of whisky halfway to my lips, I remembered. The whisky splattered out of the glass, all over the bar. I set the glass down. It rattled on the wood.

The bartender was right there, swabbing it, pouring me another, saying, "Tsk, tsk, do you want a straw?"

The mattress . . . the sheets . . . the rug!

I'd forgotten. They were in the boot of Joan's convertible. The blood-covered memories of last night.

But that wasn't the worst. I remembered Hawley. What brought him to mind I don't know, but I was quite sober, remembering Hawley.

He had been in the Pink Goat that afternoon that seemed long ago and was only yesterday. Hawley had seen the man in the chocolate-colored shirt with part of his ear missing. Hawley had looked at the man, and the man was dead.

I knew that if that body ever came up, Hawley was going to ask questions. He was going to think things.

Suddenly, I knew Hawley was going to connect me with the crime. I knew it as well as I knew my name. Lew Hawley was both bulldog and fox when it came to murder. I'd seen him work. The minute he saw that body he'd connect me with it. And somehow I knew he would see the body.

I drank the drink the bartender had poured me, paid for it, and walked back to where the girl was seated.

"I'm lonely," I said. "I want to talk. Will you—"

She looked at me as if I were a fly on the edge of her beer glass. I turned and walked out of there fast.

I was sick inside, and I felt full of panic. It streamed through me like chills. I was beginning to feel the drinks, and with every passing minute I felt more excited.

It was kind of funny, wasn't it? Last night? I got to thinking it was very funny indeed. So funny I couldn't stop laughing. Hawley would know. I knew he'd know. And right then I'd have bet every cent I had that the body would come up with its finger pointing at me.

I was nearly running now, and the faces of people on the street were a white blur. I found myself in front of the Greyhound Bus Terminal. I went inside and a bus was getting ready to leave for Tampa. I bought a ticket, hurried next door to a liquor store, and bought a pint.

Then I went back and got on the bus, taking a seat by myself, way to the rear. The bus pulled out with a roar.

I realized I was soaking wet with perspiration. I held the bottle in one hand and shook.

Settling down in the seat, I ripped the cap off the pint of whisky and started swallowing. Nothing happened. I kept at it. I had no idea where I was going, but I had to go someplace, do something! I had to run.

Chapter Seventeen

"I'm Larry Cole!"

"I don't give a damn if you're Jesus Christ himself," the lawyer said. "Get out of my office. I told you when you were here before I didn't want to touch it. I mean it." Grenold's overfed face looked plenty mean. The room spun and spun. There was Grace, the redheaded secretary. There she wasn't. She was looking at me, coming toward me. I started for the door, opened it. The sleek lawyer turned and walked toward another door.

"Please leave," Grace said. "He'll do something nasty, I know."

I pushed her aside, went over to the lawyer, and grabbed his arm. He whirled around, his eyes bleak.

"Listen," I said. "Money doesn't mean a damn thing. I told you that."

"You're drunk," he said. "And I'm going to hate hitting a drunk. But I will, so help me."

I staggered all the way across the room and up against the wall. Grace was still by the door leading out of the office. I grinned at her. She tried to smile, I guess, but couldn't. I felt suddenly as if I'd missed her. A long-lost friend. There was plenty about Grace I liked.

"Are you going to leave?" Grenold said.

"I don't know," I told him. I tried hard to pull myself together, but nothing happened. The room continued to spin. I took the pint bottle of whisky out of my pocket and looked at it. It was empty. I flung it at a wastepaper basket by the desk. It missed and slammed against the edge of the desk and smashed. The broken bottle fell into the wastebasket—most of it.

"Wait!" I said, when he started across the office toward me. "Wait a minute." He stopped. "Look," I said. "I'll go. But tell me one thing, just one thing."

Even as drunk as I was, I could see him taking hold of himself, forcing himself to be calm. It got to me through all the whisky fog that maybe he wasn't such a bad guy. Maybe he really didn't want to take the case. I said, "Just tell me why. Explain it. So I can believe it, understand it. Why won't you help me? You're a lawyer, and a good one. I asked around—" I waved my hand, trying to show him that I'd been in many Tampa bars that morning and afternoon; trying to show him that many people knew of him, and that their word was good. "I'm trying hard to like you," I said. "But you're making it extremely difficult."

"I'll tell you this," he said. "You haven't got enough money so I would take the case. Aside from that, I wouldn't touch it. I don't like it. I don't want it. Is that clear? Now get out of here before I break your damned neck!"

"I don't like you," I said. "That does it." I shoved myself off the wall toward him. It was pure luck. I let him have one, and it got by his guard and caught him full on the mouth.

The next few moments were the beginning of the haze—the real haze. He hit me so fast and so hard I can't recall a thing about it. I found myself out in the hall, lying beside the stairs that went down. As I started to get up, I heard rapid heels on the floor, and the red-haired girl was there again.

"Listen to me!" she said sharply. She shook me by the shoulders as I leaned against the railing of the stairs. "Quick. Get out of here." She took me by the arm and led me down the hall. "There," she said. "See those stairs?"

"Yeah, sure." There was a dull pain in my head and my eyes wouldn't focus at all now, but I made out the stairs.

"They're the back stairs," she explained. "Take them quickly and get out of here. He's calling the cops. If they get you, there's no telling what they'll do. They'd probably love to get something on you, anything. You're Tad Cole's brother, and that's about all they'd need."

"I liked you from the very start," I told her.

"Yes, well, do as I say." She gave me a push that started me for the stairs. I had to keep my legs going or I'd have landed on my face. I went right on down the stairs at a stumbling, grabbing run, trying to call back to her. When I reached the bottom and looked up, she was gone.

I stepped through a door and found myself in an alley. It was growing dark and I was very drunk. I started out of the alley and saw I was coming out at the front of the building. So I turned and went toward the back.

"I'm Larry Cole."

"That's nice. My name is Kirkman. It seems to me you're a bit under the weather, old man."

"You're a lawyer, and I got to have a lawyer. My brother is Tad Cole. I need a lawyer."

I couldn't make him out very clearly, but he was in an office somewhat similar to the one I'd been thrown out of and the office was on the second floor of a somewhat similar building.

"I'm sorry," he said. "But you see, I'm not a lawyer. I'm a dentist, just getting ready to close up and go home. I'm afraid you're a little mixed up."

"Then you're not a lawyer?"

"No, Mr. Cole, and I'm sorry." He was grinning. "I'm no lawyer. But I'll offer you some free advice. Go home and go to bed. Because if you need a lawyer now, there's no telling how much more you'll need one if you go on the way you are."

I turned sharply and left him. Somehow I got out of that building, too. What stumped me was it didn't have any back stairs like the other building. I had to take the fire escape, but that was all right with me. I guess I would have flown down if there hadn't been a fire escape.

"I'm Larry Cole!" I shouted, pounding on the door. This one *was* a lawyer. I had made certain of that. I read the name again on the frosted glass of the door. D. Murphy, Attorney at Law. I pounded on the door again and shouted, "Let me in! I'm Larry Cole!"

Somebody took me by the arm. I shook the hand off and beat on the door some more.

"Look, fella—"

"Leave me be," I said. "Why doesn't that damn fool open up?"

"That's what I'm trying to tell you, fella."

I turned around, reeling. A gray-haired man stood there, chewing something. He had a broom in his hand.

"I'm the janitor," he told me. "The reason Murphy don't answer is he ain't to home. He left a half hour ago, and I'm here to clean up. Now, I gotta lock the doors, so would you go on along? You got a hell of a load, fella. You better get to hell someplace fast, before you fall down."

"You mean to say Murphy isn't here?"

"That's right, fella."

"That's a hell of a note. Murphy isn't here." I stared at the broom in the man's hand. "Good old Murphy."

"Yeah. Now look—"

I started off toward the back stairs. There weren't any back stairs. There was no fire escape, either. Not even a window.

"Look, fella," the gray-haired man with the broom said. "Take it easy, now." He took my arm and led me over to a broad door and pushed a button and pretty soon the door opened. He gave me a light shove and I staggered inside.

When I turned around, the door was already nearly closed. I was in an elevator. It went down. It stopped. The door opened and I started walking.

I walked right out of the front door of the building, and realized I wanted a drink. I wanted a drink more than anything in the world. Then I thought of Joan, and I ran across the street toward a bar. Brakes squealed, and a car's headlights spiraled toward me. I paid no attention. I kept running. I ran into the bar and fell on my face beneath a table.

I lay there for a while. Nobody bothered me. I was stunned. We were in the boat, trying to pitch the dead man over the side. I could see his hand reach back out of the night and strike the boat. I tried to get up. A man cursed, and I was yanked to my feet.

"Get out of here!" the man snarled. He dragged me toward the door and I was conscious of faces, staring faces. I fell sprawling out of the door onto the street. I tried to stop myself from falling, but the pavement came up and slapped me. Panic gripped me again, and I was on my feet, running down a long dark street.

Suddenly I stopped and leaned against a building.

Somebody called my name. "Larry! Larry Cole!"

I reeled around, stared along the sidewalk. A girl was running toward me and she kept calling my name.

Chapter Eighteen

"Here, drink this!"

A hand came down toward me with a glass in it. It was a woman's hand.

"Grace," I said. I felt sure it was Grace. But I didn't know where she'd come from, except out of the fog I was lying in.

"That's right. Drink."

I tried to see her, but I couldn't seem to get my eyes past the glass. It was pressed to my lips and I drank. It was whisky and something else and I began to feel better. I realized I was lying in a bed. And then I did see her. It was Grace. The redhead.

"Yes," she said. "It's me. And you're not going to stay drunk any longer."

I sprawled back on the bed, breathing hard, and I felt shattered. My muscles twitched and I kept my feet moving steadily, as if to stop would mean I'd fly apart. I felt like hell.

But the drink was warming me, calming me. I looked up and tried to grin and the grin vanished.

Grace was a very lush September Morn, and she didn't begin to possess the shyness of that slim little girl who has been standing in the water all these years on many calendars.

She was smiling and looked very good, standing there.

"Where did you come in?" I said. Then I made a wild grab for covers, couldn't find them, and sank back with a groan. I wasn't wearing anything, either.

"You get one more drink like that. You want it now or later?"

"Now," I said. "Right now."

She brought it. I drank it. I began to feel better.

"I followed you from the office," she said, sitting on the edge of the bed. "I liked you, Larry." She stared off across the room, holding the empty glass I'd drunk from, and said, "Now I like you still more." Rising, she waggled enchantingly over to a table, set the glass down hard, and said, "Not that it'll do me any damn good!"

I tried to remember an office. Then the picture began to shape up. It shaped up to when she had come running along the street, calling my name. After that things were gray, very gray. Now and then something bright and painful showed through the grayness. Her face. Her warm body. Her eyes, which I'd discovered were green. Several men's faces, all mean-looking. I felt my jaw. It was sore.

"Yes," she said. "Wait'll you look in the mirror." She came back to the bed and sat there, staring at me. I wasn't shaking so badly now. "I followed you from the office," she said. "I wouldn't have interrupted your brief odyssey, but you were running amuck."

"Where are we?"

"At my home. And you've got to get dressed, because my mother will be along and she'll wonder what gives. She's been away for three days."

I sat up quickly, tried to hang on, couldn't make it, sank back. My head let loose like a trip hammer, and my heart gallumphed all over my chest. "How long's it been?"

"Three days," she said. "It is now the evening of the third day."

I reached out and laid my hand on her thigh. It was smooth and soft. "You mean you've been with me all the time?"

She nodded and sighed. "Yes."

"What did I do?"

"What didn't you?"

"Bad, huh?"

"Ghastly." She rose quickly and waggled into what I took for a bathroom. Pretty soon I heard a shower going in there. I lay on my back and stared at the ceiling and Joan came back to me. It was a sledge-hammer blow, and I sank under it, shivering. Everything came back with a sickening rush. The world became a horrible black place, filled with phantoms.

I sat up and swung my feet to the floor. The floor heaved upward, but I hung on, then stood. I reeled all the way across the room and landed in a chair. It was a woman's bedroom, and there'd been some violent carryings-on in it. There were empty bottles on the floor, empty glasses. The ash trays overflowed with butts.

Then I noticed my shoes. They were shining and clean, set neatly side by side under a table. My suit hung on a hanger on the back of a closet door that was open and revealed varicolored dresses within. My shirt was over the back of the chair I sat in.

I stood again, and went to a window shielded by pale blue curtains. Outside it was pale dark and the street lights were on. A car hissed down a suburban street.

The bathroom door opened and Grace came out. She was dressed and looked fresh as a morning flower. She was wearing a fawn-colored suit, and on her it was terrific.

"O.K.," she said. "Get in there." She motioned toward the bathroom.

I went.

"Wait," she said. She came over and handed me something and closed the door on me. It was a tiny razor. One that she probably used to shave her legs with. It was sparkling clean. I went over to the mirror and looked at the guy in it.

I didn't look as bad as I'd suspected I might. My jaw had a lump on it. There was a gouge under my right eye, and the left side of my mouth was puffed a bit. Otherwise I just looked like general hell; eyes bloodshot, hair standing on end, pale and sick.

I shaved, using the tiny razor. It was a job, but I managed. Then I got in the shower.

When I came back into the bedroom, I felt better. Grace was sitting in the chair now, with her legs crossed. She stood. I went over and held her and kissed her; her body was lushly compact, the curve of her hips strong and full.

"No," she said, breaking away. "You don't remember, do you?"

"Yes," I lied. I did want to remember.

She smiled and her lip twisted into a polite sneer. "Yeah, like hell." She motioned to my clothes. "Get dressed, Larry. We've got to get out of here."

"What about your job?"

"I had a vacation coming. I took a few days of it."

"Why?"

She blushed, and that looked good, too. "I liked you," she said. "Leave it at that."

I didn't want to leave it at that, but I did, because Joan was coming back clearer and clearer now. I got my socks, shoes, and trousers on, then inspected the bottles. They were all empty.

"Where were we?" I asked.

"In a lot of joints," she said. "You led me to all kinds of terrible places. You got in a few fights, and I finally got you here. We—we've been here ever since."

I went up to her and she came against me and I thought maybe she was going to cry. But she didn't. "What did we do?" I whispered.

She broke away and went and stood by the window, staring out into the night. "Get dressed," she said.

"Look," I said, pulling on my shirt. It had been freshly washed and ironed. That only made me feel worse. This girl had gone to an awful lot of trouble for me. "Look, Grace," I repeated. "I'll write a check for what I have left in the bank, and we'll go over to St. Pete and cash it. I don't think I could get it cashed here."

"All right," she said. "I have a car." All the life was out of her voice now and she didn't turn around. Her hair was burnished copper in the glow of the bed lamp. It was the first time I realized the bed lamp was lit.

I finished dressing. I felt lousy, but a few drinks would fix that. I was shaky, and my insides felt as if they rested on air.

She said, "You think a lot of your brother, don't you?"

"Yeah."

"I'm going to talk to Grenold and see if he won't reconsider." I remembered that Grenold was the name of the lawyer, her boss.

I went over to her and tried to hold her again. She turned and faced me, looked into my eyes, then broke away and walked to the door. "Let's go," she said.

"Listen, Grace. What about Grenold?"

"What about him?"

"Well, like that day I met you. Remember? You were supposed to have a date and he—"

"Stood me up? Yes. Well, it's all over. He's got his tongue hanging out now. But it's too late." She paused. "He had his chance. I gave him a big chance. I loved him, Larry. I really did. Looking back, I wonder how, but I did. Now . . ." She glanced around the room quickly, nibbled her lip, then moved through the doorway.

Going down the stairway in the peaceful dimness of the house, she said, "Larry, it was terribly wonderful."

I didn't say anything, because Joan was with me again.

She got her car out of the garage. "The neighbors've probably wondered plenty," she said.

"I'm sorry, Grace."

"Don't be. I'm not."

As we left her home behind, I said, "We'll get the money and go to Miami. O.K.?"

"Sure." She didn't look at me and she drove like hell.

Crossing Gandy Bridge, we spoke again.

"Larry. Do you do this often?"

"First time in my life," I told her truthfully.

"I believe you," she told me. "I just wanted to hear you say it, Larry."

I looked across at her. There was something about Grace that was very wonderful, very clean, very honest.

She said, "You have twenty dollars left. When we came to my place the other night, you tried to give the twenty to a cab driver. I wouldn't let you. It's in your watch pocket."

I felt in my watch pocket. A bill was folded into a small square. I left it there.

We stopped on Central in St. Pete and I wrote a check for a thousand dollars, just about all I had left in the bank. I'd had her stop before a bar where I knew I could cash it.

I'd say good-by to St. Pete. Pete Adams would be able to sell the Pink Goat for me. Grace and I could go away someplace. I'd get a better job, and save my money.

I patted her leg. "I'll only be a minute. Then we'll take off, Grace. We'll talk it all over. Let's leave right away, tonight, eh?"

"Sure, tonight." She wasn't looking at me. I opened the door. She turned toward me and she was crying.

"What's up?" I said.

"Nothing. Go ahead. Cash the check. I'm just being silly again."

"Sure nothing's the matter?"

"Nothing at all, Larry. Go on!"

I got out quickly. "I'll only be a minute, baby. Hold the fort. Right with you."

She closed the door. I started off toward the bright lights of the bar. Her voice arrested me.

"Larry," she called. "Say hello to Joan for me. I hope you two have—have fun!"

I turned toward the car, then ran for it. The engine roared, and she was off into traffic. The last I saw of her was the taillight on her car, winking like a sleepy red eye. Then it turned a corner and she was gone.

I stood there with the check in my hand. Then slowly I tore it to bits, watched the pieces blow along the sidewalk, into the gutter. Turning, I walked into the bar, fishing for the twenty in my watch pocket.

Chapter Nineteen

It was an evil night.

I was sick. Not from being drunk. I was sick because I'd never found out anything about Grace. I was sick because I knew now that I had talked about Joan. I was sick because I didn't know what else I'd talked of.

Grace had been a good kid.

I didn't know what to do. From bar to bar I wandered, drinking, and the drinks did nothing. With all my might I tried not to think of Joan, but she was there all the time. And I wanted her, I needed her.

About an hour and a half later, I was walking slowly down First Avenue North when I heard fast swinging footsteps behind me. I turned and stopped.

"Evening, Larry."

It was Lew Hawley. He came up close, pushed his hat back on his head, and stared at me. He nodded slowly.

I didn't know whether to run, or what. Running would have been foolish, because Lew would have probably caught me. All I could think was that the body had come up. It had been identified, and I was it. I couldn't speak for a minute, just tried to look back at him.

"You've been drinking, but you aren't plastered," Hawley said gruffly. "Where you been, Larry?"

I managed a weak "Around."

He nodded. "Sure. Around where?"

"It's personal, Lew."

"Yeah? Two bartenders just let me know they'd seen you. What you trying to do, kill yourself? O.K. So you wanta help your brother. This isn't helping him, Larry. What's got into you?"

"Am I under arrest?"

He grinned. "Yes, suspicion of intoxication." He chuckled. "I got somebody here wants to see you. A friend of yours. Been looking all over hell for you."

I began to shake. He took my arm, scowled down at me, and looked puzzled. Then he led me up to the end of the block and opened the door of a convertible that sat there. He gave me a shove, and I got in. He slammed the door, and Joan said, "Hello, Larry," from the driver's seat.

I stared straight ahead, through the windshield.

Hawley reached in and banged one off my shoulder. "Take care of him, Miss Turner," he said. "These Coles are full of nothing but trouble."

And then Joan said, "I don't know how to thank you, Mr. Hawley."

"Forget it. Take 'im home and feed 'im black coffee. Little rogues easily become big ones, so hold 'im down, miss." He turned and swaggered off, his shoulders swinging.

Then we were kissing each other, and she was shaking in my arms and saying, "Larry, Larry, Larry!"

It was like holding paradise in your arms. I buried my face in her thick hair and thanked God for bringing Joan back to me. I knew now that I'd never let her go, never try to escape.

"Larry," she said. "Where were you?" Her voice was strained, worried, hopeful.

"I was drunk," I told her. "I had to think."

"Did you?"

"Yes. I'm here, aren't I?"

Her body was hot beneath the thin shield of her dress. Her eyes were big and round, her lips warm, demanding. My hand touched her thigh. She stiffened. "I'd better drive away from here!" she whispered.

"Yes. Home. Step on it, Joan."

She started the car, turned to me. She shook her head. "No, Larry. Not yet. We've got to do something else that's important."

"What d'you mean?"

"In the trunk of the car," she said. "The mattress, the rug and sheets. I couldn't do it alone. We've got to burn them, like you said."

She'd saved them for me. We were right back where we'd started. All it needed to do was rain, and it would be the same night, the same everything.

Chapter Twenty

It did rain.

The rain was a fine mist that settled over the city dump. There wasn't enough rain to put out the brilliant pyre caused by gasoline-soaked mattress, sheets, and rug.

We sat in the car a little distance off and watched the dead man's blood burn away.

"Larry," Joan whispered, "hold me tighter."

I held her tighter.

"That fire does something to me, Larry. Just watching it, knowing what it is."

"Sure," I said, and I could feel her body stir against me, and I knew what it was. Then we were trying to get at each other, maybe like animals. I don't know. Want is like that. There had never been much gentleness between Joan and me. There certainly was no gentleness now.

Her lips were fierce, her tongue lashed like a flame itself, and there was no gentleness, only a wire-tight hunger; a vivid, savage want. And through it all, even against the closed lids of my eyes, I could see the red demonic flickerings of the fire out there in the dump.

Moments later she slipped beneath the wheel of the car again, her breath still coming in long, whispered shouts.

"Let's get out of here, Larry."

"No, not yet. You wait here. I'll go check the fire."

I climbed out of the car and walked over across piles of damp ashes, through other smoldering fires, by stacks of wooden crates, until I reached our fire. It was like a wasted hell, there in the dump. Like, a scarred city, demolished by the atom bomb, maybe.

The mattress smoldered. The sheets and rug were gone. The bloody part of the mattress was gone, and the maker's name was burned away. I went back to the car.

"O.K. It's all right. Let's go."

We drove out of there and headed for the beaches. I was still a long way from feeling well, and I knew it would be several days before I felt halfway decent again.

Then I knew maybe there wouldn't come a time when I'd be well again.

"Larry, I nearly died when you didn't come the other morning. I nearly died. I went over to your place, and you didn't answer when I knocked." Her voice caught in her throat and she reached over and squeezed my arm with her long, tense fingers. Her hand was trembling, the way we had both trembled a few moments ago—trembling deep within the bone. "I almost went crazy," she said.

"I'm sorry."

"I've been looking for you ever since. I got Hawley, the cop, there—the detective. He was the only one I could think of might help me. He seemed to understand. He said you were trying to help your brother, and that I shouldn't worry. I told him you might get into trouble, and we've been looking ever since. I nearly died, Larry."

"I love you, Joan. You know that."

"Yes."

"Joan, you mean you had Hawley in this car? Riding around, with *that* in the back there?"

"Sure, why not? He'd never suspect anything."

"But—"

She laughed. "He says I'm a very straightforward young woman. He likes me, Larry."

I didn't say anything. I just sat there while she drove the car over the causeway. Neither of us spoke again until we reached the cabanas.

But all the time I kept feeling worse. Because it was like returning to some hellish dream. My desire for Joan seemed to mount all the time, instead of decreasing. Her leg would touch mine, and I'd want her. I'd want her from the sound of her voice, with my back turned. From the touch of her hand. From the smell of her. I would have wanted her just seeing her shoes sitting on the floor, maybe.

But being with her meant all the rest of the hell. With more of it to come. And if I touched her . . .

"I'm going in and change my clothes. I'll, be right over," I said.

"All right." She turned and smiled. "See that you do, this time. Oh, Larry," she said, "I love you so."

I kissed her and rumpled up her hair, wishing to Christ none of these things had ever happened. Just Joan.

"Oh," she said, as I climbed out of the car. "By the way, you don't have to worry about another mattress."

My breath stopped in my throat.

"I bought one," she told me. "Got it myself, had it stowed in the car, and brought it here at night. It was a devil of a job. I could hardly make it, but I did. Nobody saw me and it was the same kind."

"O.K. Be right over." I slammed the door and headed toward my back porch. The key was still in the gutter pipe where I'd left it. I unlocked the door and went in. The darkness felt good. I didn't turn on any lights. I went in and took a shower and put on clean clothes. Inside I felt better after I'd had a couple of stiff ones from a bottle I kept in the kitchen.

Then I remembered the mailbox. There should be letters from Tad—something. He hadn't written in a long time. I hurried outside and flipped the lid on the metal box nailed to the side of the house.

There were no letters. It was empty.

Joan was waiting for me outside her cottage.

"Thought we'd take a walk, Larry," she said. "Like we used to. It seems you've been away so long."

"Sure." She was right. It did seem that way. We went down along the beach. Slow rollers were coming in off the Gulf, leaving a white froth in a long string as far as the eye could see.

As we walked, Joan got close and bumped me with her hip at each stride. For some reason this got me to thinking of Grace. I wondered what all I'd told her. Maybe plenty, maybe little or nothing. But I wished to God I'd told her nothing.

Grace had gone through plenty for me. Little snatches of the last three days kept coming back into my head, like bright flashes on a moving screen. At a sudden memory of her white body in bed, a memory of impetuous playfulness, my arm jerked.

"What's the matter, Larry?"

"Nervous, I guess."

"You drank too much, I'll bet."

"Yeah." Then Joan started humming. I began to feel relieved and I wondered why. Then I knew. She hadn't mentioned the robbery. Could it be she'd forgotten about it? Maybe she was forcing herself to forget, realizing what it did to me. I didn't dare mention it, but I began to feel good.

"Funny," Joan said. "I'm not much in the mood for swimming at night any more. Remember how I wanted to?"

"We did, all right."

She laughed, and it started me off again. That's all it took. I stopped and grabbed her up close. She moaned a little and said, "Oh, God, Larry—me, too!"

We were right by the water's edge, and as we kissed we both tried to get closer. My foot touched something. I kicked, but it got tangled in our feet. I looked down, then reached.

It was a tennis shoe. It could have been anybody's tennis shoe. It didn't matter whose tennis shoe it was. It was enough to bring the whole business back clearly.

"Good night," Joan said. "Imagine!"

"Yes," I said. "Imagine this, too. Imagine if other things start coming up on the beach."

"Larry, don't talk—"

"For instance, a body."

"Oh, cut it out, Larry!" She pulled herself tight up against me and did an exercise with her hips.

"Let's go back to your place," I said. Turning, I heaved the soggy, sand-filled tennis shoe as far out into the Gulf as I could. When I looked back at Joan, she was pouting. "I'm sorry," I said. "But it gets me. Doesn't it bother you at all?"

"What's done is done."

She was brushing her hair. "I think we should do it right away. I've been giving it a lot of serious thought, Larry. Let's not wait much longer."

The robbery. So there it was. She was on it again.

"You're sure nobody saw you bring in that mattress?"

She put the brush down. "Certainly not." She paused. "Did you hear what I said just before? If we keep waiting, we're going to miss out."

I sat there, staring across her living room at the bedroom door, knowing she slept in there now. Knowing that she had killed a man in there. And already she wanted to go on planning about the robbery. She hadn't forgotten. She'd never forget anything.

"Don't talk about it now," I said.

She looked at me and her—eyes were gleaming. I couldn't tell what her eyes were trying to say. Her hair was brushed to a beautiful golden sheen in the soft lights. What the hell. She wore black lounging pajamas, and we were very close. . . .

Later that night, we were in Joan's bed. The darkness was pale, and lying there, I couldn't get my mind off Tad. I hadn't done any of the things I'd started out to do. I figured I should go see him again. If I could tame him down for long enough, he'd be able to tell me what lawyer to see. He knew. It was just that he rebelled against telling me. He didn't want me mixed up in his troubles. Hell, if he only knew.

"Why are you so quiet?" Joan said. She rolled over, snuggling up against me. Her warm, bare skin was like smooth velvet. She twined her legs in mine, ran her lips along the back of my neck.

"Thinking," I told her.

"About me?"

"Don't be so selfish."

"Aren't I good thinking?"

I reached around and slapped her one on the buttock. She started tickling me. After I got her quieted down again, I said, "I think I'll go see Tad again, Joan. He needs—"

"Oh, Larry, why?"

"Because, Joan. Maybe I can talk some sense into his fool head. He wants to get out. But he's too bitter to help himself. Too bitter to let anybody else help him. No one will, but me."

"But why d'you have to see him?" She was sitting up in bed now, holding her hair away from her head with one hand, staring down at me. "I think that's silly."

"You wouldn't if you were where he is."

"Look, Larry. What good will it do? You saw him once before, and what happened? Nothing. He even told you he didn't want any help. Isn't that right?"

I didn't say anything. Outside I could hear the surf piling up on the beach. It was a lazy surf. Somewhere out there a dead man sat on the bottom of the Gulf and pondered.

"Besides, Larry—" Joan flopped over on me, and her hair sprawled across my face, the rich, sweet smell of it in my nostrils. "I don't want to be away from you again."

"You could come with me, Joan. You could meet Tad."

"What?"

The more I thought of it, the better it sounded. Tad could meet her. Perhaps with both Joan and me there, we'd be able to talk him into some kind of understanding. Joan was persuasive. God knows, I knew that well enough.

"We could go right up in the morning. We could drive, Joan. Take your car. It'd be a nice ride. We wouldn't have to hurry, just take our time. Maybe go over to Daytona for a day. How would you like that?"

"I like it here, Larry. All I need is you. And at a time like this, we shouldn't be traveling around the country. We've got to think. We've got a job ahead of us."

It got me, the way she spoke of that. Matter-of-factly. Just as if we were going to build an addition to the house. I was excited now, though. I sat up and held her with my hands on her arms.

"Don't you see?" I said. "Tad needs help. He hasn't got anybody else. You could talk to him, Joan. You could show him—make him wake up."

She was a little tense, it seemed. "Larry, I have enough trouble trying to show you things."

"Fun, though."

"Sure. And I want it to stay that way." She flung herself against me. "I don't want to go. I don't want you to go, Larry. It seems you've been away so long. You'll get tired of me." She paused, held her head off, and looked at me. Her mouth was a dark slash across her face, her eyes sleepy, her hair tousled. "Are you getting tired of me, Larry?"

God, what a question! "Don't worry about that," I said.

"Because, if you are, I'll start doing something that'll wake you up again."

I drew her close. She writhed in my arms and fell back on the bed, pulling me with her.

"Listen, Joan," I whispered. "Won't you do this for me? Just come on up tomorrow. If you don't want to go over to Daytona, we could be back tomorrow night."

"I think we need a drink." She climbed over me, kneeing me one in the belly, and padded from the room.

I lay there, staring at the ceiling. I wondered if I'd ever sleep again. At least, she hadn't talked too much about the robbery. But that might not last long.

"Here," she said. "We'll have it from the bottle. It'd spill in glasses. You need a drink. Hair of the dog, and all that."

To an extent, she was right. I still felt hollow inside from the drinking over in Tampa, and there was a small matter of a girl named Grace who kept haunting my mind. I took the bottle and Joan climbed over me into the bed again. Her body was like a lushly curved moonbeam in the darkness.

"Take a good one," she said. "You aren't happy enough, Larry. Much too serious."

"Yeah." I took a couple of good ones and felt the liquor creep down inside me, warming me. There was an almost immediate reaction. I felt better. I handed her the bottle and began stroking her thigh.

"That's better," she said. She took a drink. "I'll meet your brother, all in due time, Larry. But first let's get that other bit of business taken care of."

The robbery. I reached for the bottle and had another good one.

"Look at it this way, too," she said. "A few days or weeks won't make any difference to Tad, one way or the other. He's in Raiford for life, Larry. He doesn't expect to get out."

"But, Joan—"

"No buts. It's true. If we go up there, and I start talking—if we do that too much, he'll get his hopes up. Any man would, even if he is bitter. You don't want to do that."

I ran my lips up along her throat, then down into the deep smooth curve between her breasts. The whisky was beginning to take hold.

She said, "We'll find a lawyer who'll help Tad. Then, when we do—and we will, Larry!—we'll go see Tad. We'll surprise him. Maybe take the lawyer right with us. Wouldn't that be better?"

Of course, she was right. For once she was really right.

"Yeah," I said. "I suppose so."

"You know so. He'd be happy then, Larry. You see, Tad thinks, in his heart, that nothing can be done. If you keep seeing him, it'll only make him mad. He's helpless, and he knows it. He doesn't want to think of you outside trying to do something that can't be done. From what you've told me, that's the kind of man he is." She mussed my hair, snarled her fingers into it. "But if we've really been able to do something, then you watch the change in him."

I had another drink from the bottle. Then she had one.

"Am I right, Larry?"

"Yes," I said. "You're right, all right."
"Take one more drink."
I did. "Then what?"

She leaned across me, lying across me, and set the bottle on the floor. Then she said, "I'll show you."

And she did.

Chapter Twenty-one

Two days later the body came up. I stood behind the bar at the Pink Goat and read the headlines, while my hands trembled so hard the paper rattled.

BODY IN THE BAY
UNIDENTIFIED MAN
MURDER SUSPECTED

The story went on to say that the unidentified body of a man had been washed ashore on Shell Island. It had been discovered by a fisherman, C. Brown, who saw the figure sprawled on the white beach. The corpse had been in the water several days. A description was given, including the remark that sent my stomach to the floor: Part of one ear was missing—from an old wound.

Detective Lew Hawley had decided that the body had been weighted down by something and sunk. Lengths of clothesline were still wrapped about the corpse's middle. All efforts were being made to identify the man. People were asked to notify the police immediately if they thought they had any clue from the description.

Nobody was in the bar save myself and Joan that afternoon. I went over to her, laid the paper in front of her, and pointed with a quivering finger. She'd been daydreaming over her third Martini.

"For goodness' sake!" she said, and her lips moved as she hurried through the story.

I stood there wondering just how long it would be before Hawley came with the handcuffs.

One good thing. The body had washed quite a distance from where we had sent it down. But this was it, as far as I was concerned.

"Well, so what?" Joan said with a shrug. She looked up at me, and tipped her lips with her tongue. She was wearing a pale green play suit and looked as if candy would melt in her sight. "So he came up. So what?"

"So what?" My voice was a sad, dry crack.

"Yes, so what? There's nothing to connect this to us, darling. Get over that, will you? Forget it."

"Joan, sometimes you—"

She laughed, interrupting me. "Larry, don't be childish. Look at it from the right angle, will you? You know as well as I that it was necessary—it was something I couldn't help doing. D'you think I like having it on my conscience?"

"I don't know," I said. I went over and drew a short beer and drank it. It's all I was drinking these days. I still felt hollow inside from the binge I'd been on, and Grace hovered over and around me like a ghost.

"Forget it," Joan said. "But listen to me, Larry. We'd better get to work on this other thing. Now's a good time, when everybody's all excited about murder."

"It wasn't murder. I mean, in a way it wasn't. Damn it, Joan, I wish we'd told the police. So there'd have been publicity." I paused as she smiled at me and finished her drink. "Now we can never tell. I mean, and have anybody believe the true story."

She kept right on smiling and nodded her head. "Yes," she said slowly, "we may just as well have done it in cold blood."

"Quiet," I said. "Here it comes."

It was Hawley. His car had ground to a stop out front. The car door slammed, his feet crunched, and then there he was, standing by the bar. He looked just as sweaty and just as sunburned as ever. Only he wasn't smiling.

"Hi, Lew," I said, and Joan nodded to him.

He stood there and looked at me for a long while. I had to look back, right in the eye, or something would show. Maybe something showed anyway, because all I could think was: This is it, this is it, this is it. He knows, and he's here to tell me he knows.

Finally he grunted and said, "Cripes, Larry. I almost switched over to rye just then. But I guess my stomach won't take anything but bourbon."

My insides were like jelly, and they quivered like jelly, too. I nodded and gulped, "That so?" I was drenched with perspiration, and I didn't know which way to turn.

"The usual," he said. "The usual."

I decided it was best I bring it up first. Then I'd at least have that to my advantage. But Joan beat me to it.

She said, "I see you're on a murder case, Mr. Hawley."

"Call me Lew, Miss Turner. Yeah, that's right." He turned to me and said, "You read the story, Larry?"

I tried to pour his drink without spilling it all over the bar and myself. I kept my eyes down. "Uh-huh," I said. "I read it. Not so nice, is it?"

"Nope, it isn't." He cleared his throat and drummed his fingers on the bar. "Notice anything funny about it, Larry?"

I shoved his drink toward him. He didn't pick it up, just stood there looking at me, with his fingers drumming.

I nodded. "Yeah, I did, Lew. Not exactly funny. But from the description in the paper, I think the guy was in here once. I don't remember exactly when—"

"I do," Hawley said. "I remember." He looked at Joan and then at me. Then he took a long drink and wiped his mouth with the back of his thick hand. "Funny thing. I got a peach of a memory. Comes in handy, y'know?"

"I should guess so."

He knew. I felt he knew. I could feel it in the air, like a charge of electricity. Then I forced myself to be calm. How could he know? He couldn't know anything. So all right. The guy had been in the Pink Goat. What did that make me? Nothing. I was letting my worries get the best of me. If I didn't watch out, I'd end up in the bughouse.

Hawley finished his drink, motioned for another. When I set it before him, he started in, without touching the glass.

"Had he been in here before, Larry?"

"Gosh, I don't know. I wouldn't—"

"You'd know. Think back. Was he here before that afternoon not so long ago? The day before you took off on your bender?"

I laid my hands on the bar, palms down, so he wouldn't see them shake. "I don't think so," I said. "No."

"How long was he in here that afternoon?"

"He was here when I came in. Pete was working, then."

Hawley nodded. "That's right," he said. "What was his name?"

"I don't know, Lew. He didn't mention it, that I know of."

"Did he say anything? Did Pete say he said anything?"

"No, he didn't." I could feel the sweat on my face. A drop dripped off the tip of my nose. "Just a second," I said. "Turn on the fan, here." I switched on a fan.

Hawley had his nose in his drink, but his eyes were on Joan.

He said, "Did the guy drink much?"

"I guess. I don't know. Gin, I think—shots."

"He drank a lot," Hawley said. "He poured it down all the time I was in here."

"Yeah, I guess he did, at that."

Joan said, "Why, Larry, you know he was drinking an awful lot."

I almost screamed. Only not quite.

"Did he say anything, do anything out of place?"

I started to shake my head, when Joan interrupted again. "He seemed very moody," she said. "I was watching him, because I couldn't take my eyes off his ear, you know? Maybe he committed suicide."

Hawley finished his drink and blinked. Then he belched. He didn't reply to that.

"Couldn't he have?" Joan said.

"Have what?" Hawley said.

I turned toward her. I wanted to yell at her to stop it, before I blew my top.

"Have committed suicide?" Joan asked.

"No," Hawley said. "He didn't. Somebody stuck him with a knife. Somebody who knew what he was doing, too."

"How's that?" I said.

"Well, the killer could have hit the right spot by accident. But it don't happen often," Hawley said. "In fact, hardly ever. In fact, never." He cleared his throat. "Give me another, Larry. I'm plumb irked today."

"Sure, Lew. On the house."

"You insist, O.K." He wiped his mouth with the back of his hand, and turned and looked out the front door at the bright white sunlight. Then he turned back and looked at me as I set his glass down filled again. "I wonder what the poor guy was tied to. Wonder what they sank him with."

I didn't trust my voice. I just shook my head.

"There was grease on the rope," Hawley said. "It was new rope, too. We're checking the stores around for who bought rope lately. It was clothesline rope, common enough. But you can run a bunch of things down, just by asking questions. You'd be surprised, y'know?"

"I guess you're right," I said. I was ready to die. Willing and able, in fact. I almost would have welcomed death.

"Bet we know who he is in a few days, too," Hawley said. "Something'll turn up. You watch."

"I hope so."

"Yeah." Hawley drank, set the glass down with a clink, belched politely, and shoved his hat back on his head. His eyes were fuzzy with sunlight. "Jock Hewitt had a boat stole that same night. Somebody broke into his shed and latched onto a couple of oars, too."

I thought my heart would burst right through my shirt.

Hawley said, "We found the boat, but not the oars. Couldn't expect to find the oars. Somebody'll find the oars, but they'll keep 'em."

"Cripes," I said. "I saw Jock this morning. He didn't say anything about his boat being stolen."

Hawley grinned and nodded. "That's right. It wouldn't have been very nice if you'd've said Jock's boat had been stolen, either, Larry."

"Why?" I said. My mouth was like flannel. I drew a beer and drank it in three swallows.

"Because I told him not to tell a soul. You see, I found the boat. Nobody knows about it, except you two, because I just told you—and Jock. So if anybody else says to me, 'Say, did you find old Jock's boat? I heard it was stolen?' Well, I'll just say, 'That's right nice.' You get it, Larry?"

I nodded.

"That's very clever of you, Lew," Joan said. I looked at her. Maybe nobody else would have noticed, but she was much paler than usual.

"Thank you," Hawley said.

I tried not to think that he was holding something back. But that's what I felt. As if he knew something he wasn't telling. As if he was waiting to pounce.

"You say," Joan said, "you think the body will be identified soon?"

"Just a matter of time. It'll narrow it down considerable, too." Hawley drank. I sweated. Joan rattled the paper on the bar. The afternoon held its breath. Then Hawley said, "Sure must have been hell for whoever sank that guy. He was killed, then taken out there and sunk on that lousy night we had." He looked at me. "The night before you took off on your bender, Larry."

"Sure was a rotten night," I said. "I didn't even stick my nose outdoors."

"Yeah." Hawley finished his drink. He looked at me. "You know who's wise, Larry? I'll tell you. He who learns from everyone." He nodded to Joan, tossed a two-finger salute off his eyebrow to me, and swaggered out into the sunlight.

Joan and I stood there and looked at each other.

"He acts kind of funny," Joan said.

I looked at my hands. They were shaking like crazy.

Chapter Twenty-two

I closed up, and we went home. Then I wished I hadn't, because all that was on Joan's mind now was the robbery. It seemed nothing I said could make her understand that it was wrong to even think that way. I couldn't really believe that Joan had the mind, the moral standards, of a criminal. It was just that she wanted money; she wanted it the easy way, she wanted it quick. I suppose that's the basic motivation of the criminal mind, but Joan didn't strike me that way.

"Try to understand," I told her as we walked along the beach. "Already we've done something plenty wrong. There's no way of redeeming ourselves there, Joan."

"Who said anything about redemption?"

"All right, so we'll forget that, then. But remember. There's a dead man in this now. People are spending their time trying to find who killed him. They know nothing of the facts."

"And they won't." She got in front of me and held both my arms, searching my eyes. "We can't help what happened, Larry. All I know is we'd better go through with the robbery. It's our one chance to make some money, don't you see? You could sell the Pink Goat, then. And we could leave here."

"Leave?"

"Yes. Suppose they do get wise? Suppose Hawley, there, does find something that'll lead to us. Suppose we get caught. Then what? We'd have no money. We'd have thrown up our chance for happiness. And you'd never be able to do a thing for your brother, because you'd be right where he is. And Larry, think of how he'd feel then."

I pushed her out of the way and started walking. It was a beautiful day. The sky was a pale blue, the Gulf a pale green; and the white sands seemed to stretch endlessly. But I couldn't appreciate it any more.

Joan's voice was soft. "We'd get plenty from the Beach Club, Larry, and it's such a cinch. So easy. It's a wonder it hasn't been done before."

How was I to tell her how I felt? I loved her. She was wrong, and she couldn't see it at all. She was blind to it. It was like talking to a wall. Everything I said she had an answer for. A lopsided answer as far as I was concerned, but to her it was a fine answer.

Her hair glowed like the sunshine, her eyes were bright, and she walked with a healthy stride. I couldn't keep my eyes away from the thrusting curve of her breasts, the movement of her hips, her long curved legs beyond the tight rims of her shorts. Every time I saw her, touched her, talked with her, it became worse for me. I wasn't thinking as clearly as I had. The simplicity of her own wrong thinking wasn't so simple any longer. I had to concentrate to convince myself that she was talking foolishly.

Her voice reached me again. "The way we are now, we'll never have anything," she said. "Nothing."

"Maybe happiness," I said. "If we went to the police and told what we knew about that dead man."

"Oh, Larry! Sometimes you make me sick." Her eyes were hard, and her lips drew down at the corners. "Don't be such a damned baby. All we'd be doing is taking money from somebody who doesn't really need it, and giving it to somebody who does—us."

Later that evening, at her place, I talked to her again. Hard. Tried to show her it was all wrong. Here she was, a secretary, planning robbery. I got damned excited and talked a mile a minute.

"The Pink Goat'll bring in enough, Joan. We'll get married. I'll enlarge. That's right, expand. I'll start up some publicity angle, take out an entertainment license. We'll have dancing there." I must have sounded plenty desperate.

She smiled. "All right, honey. Let's take a walk."

I was so relieved I couldn't see straight. We took a long walk down the beach and I held my breath. We talked about other things, and she seemed to have forgotten all about it. I was grabbing at straws, because I relaxed as we walked back along the beach. Already I was beginning to figure what I could do to enhance the value of the Pink Goat. I tried to keep my mind away from the dead man. It did no good to think about it. I didn't believe Hawley would find the motor. But in the back of my mind, I knew Hawley would eventually find us. Only I wouldn't think about it wouldn't face it, because there was nothing I could do about it.

And as soon as I relaxed, she was at me right away, as if she were psychic.

"Larry. If you don't like the Beach Club idea, let's look someplace else. But the setup's perfect at the Beach Club."

We were in front of her place. "Setup!" I said. "Where do you get that stuff, Joan?"

"Oh, Larry." Her eyes glistened in the moonlight. She looked helpless, almost lost. I wanted to put her in my pocket. It was like that.

"Look," I told her, and something left me when I spoke. "We've got to get this out of our systems. It's wrong. I know it's wrong. But nothing I say will make you see that, Joan." I hesitated and she said nothing. She just stood there, nodding, watching me, and there was an understanding smile on her lips. "I'm going home," I told her. "You do the same. Then, when you get there, sit down and think, Joan. Think it out. Think it out straight. Then, if you still want it . . ." I left it that way. She was getting at me from every angle. I loved her. I knew damned well I'd do anything she asked.

Her voice was almost a whisper. "All right, Larry." She turned quickly and I watched her move away.

Home, I checked the mailbox again to see if I'd missed a letter when I came home from the Pink Goat that afternoon. Empty. I hadn't heard from Tad in weeks, and he always wrote once or twice a week, never missed. I blamed myself. I figured he'd got sick of writing, maybe sick of hearing about Joan.

I was facing something that had me all knotted up inside. There wasn't much I could do about it any more.

Chapter Twenty-three

I was in the kitchen drinking coffee when I heard Joan open the back door. She came in wearing white lounging pajamas with a red sash. She was just plain gorgeous and I knew I was going to hang on, no matter what.

I didn't move. She came to me, gently took the cup from my hand, leaned over, and kissed me. Her lips were soft and warm.

"I've thought it out, Larry."

I could see the answer in her eyes. I pulled her close to me, put my arm around her, felt the curve of her hip. "You really want this thing," I said.

She nodded and her hair brushed my cheek. Her voice was a whisper. "It's the only way we can ever marry. Otherwise"— she shrugged—"it'll be a long wait. Maybe never, Larry."

The battle I was fighting inside was deadly. The coffee sat sour on my stomach. I remembered things Tad had told me. And for some reason I thought of Grace. I wondered what she would think about a thing like this, what she would do. Then something released inside me, and I looked at Joan.

"O.K." The words came as if somebody else were talking. "We'll do it. We'll do it."

"Oh, Larry!"

"But listen, Joan." I took her wrists, looked at her. Then I gripped those wrists tightly. I walked her over beneath the light and stared into her face. "Only this once. It's got to be that way. I've done a lot of thinking. I knew you'd come back with this answer. We'll do it just this once. Just enough to get started. We'll never even think of such a thing again. And after this is over we'll never mention it."

"Yes, Larry. Yes. Only this once."

I let go of her wrists and walked across the room. There was a dull pain at the back of my neck. I rubbed it, but it didn't go away. Nerves. "You're sure about their keeping a whole week's receipts? Kind of foolish."

She hurried up to me, pressed against me, and kissed me. "I'm sure, Larry. Oh, Larry! I knew you'd come around."

"Yeah." The decision made, I relaxed. She was obviously so happy about it all I could never ask her to back out again. I loved her, and that was the answer.

Her words flowed, her eyes were alive. "I've checked everything. That's what I've been doing while you worked, whenever I wasn't with you. It's our big chance. There must be twenty-five thousand, maybe more. I know right where they keep the box, in the office. The night watchman is an old man, older even than I thought." She paused, looked down at the kitchen table. "Of course, you'll have to fix him before you take the money."

I could feel the blood rush to my head. "Fix him?" Now that I had agreed to all of this, things were changed.

She laughed and mussed my hair, went to the refrigerator, brought back a couple of bottles of beer. She moved with that lithe, easy swing that I never tired of watching. "Sure," she said lightly. "You know. Tap him once behind the ear?"

"God." I thought a minute. "Listen, Joan. . . ." I ceased, couldn't go on. There was no use trying to go on.

She uncapped the beer, poured, handed me a glass. "Here's to next week's receipts, Larry, my love." She watched me over the rim of the glass, eyes shining. "C'mon," she said, "drink up."

I drank. It tasted like hell.

It seemed as if, after that, Joan and I were much closer. Up to now she hadn't asked me much about what I did during the three days I was away. I'd only told her I'd been drunk. It wasn't like a woman not to probe into those things, and I'd wondered about it. I shouldn't have. I should have known it would all come in its own time.

"Where were you—when you did all that drinking?" she asked me.

"Here and there," I said.

"That's no answer, Larry. Where did you go?"

"I started in St. Pete, then I went to Tampa."

"Where?"

"Oh, I tried to get a lawyer."

"Oh, I see." She looked worried. "Larry," she said. "Supposing you talked to somebody. I mean, suppose you told them about what we did with the body. You could have, if you were drunk enough."

That had been worrying me plenty. Grace knew of Joan. And if I had talked about Joan to Grace, then I may have said plenty of other things. Because that dead man was topmost in my mind, then and now. It would always be that way, I supposed. Whenever I remembered it, I got the cold sweats. I wondered if such a thing could last a lifetime. But then, I knew it wouldn't have to. Somehow, I knew they'd find us—me. I didn't say anything to Joan about the way I thought, because she not only wouldn't agree, she'd try to argue me out of it. I couldn't stand any more of that.

"Did you meet any girls while you were away?" she asked as she poured the last of her beer into her glass.

"No," I lied. It came out like that.

She didn't say anything for a minute. "The reason I asked," she said, "your clothes were pressed. Your shirt was clean. Your shoes were clean." She paused. "That doesn't usually happen when a man's drunk. He's usually a mess."

"I suppose you're right."

"Then you did meet somebody. And—and you were with her?"

I looked at her and tried to say something, but nothing came out.

"Yes," she said. "You were. I can see it. How was she?" Her words were politely spoken, but they had a sting to them.

"It was nothing, Joan. Believe that. Nothing at all. I met a girl, but she was a secretary to one of the lawyers I talked with.

I only tried to get her to talk to him privately, to see what she could do."

"Did you have to sleep with her to make her come around?"

"No." I said it all right, and I could see she wanted to believe me.

"I believe you, Larry. And it's all right. You're too honest a man to make a mess of things by lying."

"Thanks," I said. It didn't help how I felt about things.

"And I'm glad you answered well enough when I asked you."

"Why?"

"Because I had a letter from her today. I wasn't going to tell you, but it's all right now. It wasn't much. She just told me how lucky I was. She'd got the address from you. She wanted to make certain you reached home. And that was all. I wrote her a line, thanked her, and told her that you were all right."

I stared at her. My God! Grace had written Joan! In that case, I must have told her all kinds of things. Maybe Joan didn't think so. But I knew Grace wasn't the type of woman to talk it around.

"We'll forget it," Joan said, coming up to me. She held herself tight against me, moving her hips slightly, her teeth gleaming whitely between her lips.

"Yes," I said. She kept smiling. I slipped the red sash from around her waist and the top part of her pajamas flared and fell away. She wore nothing beneath. Her nipples were like hard, pink pencil erasers.

The next two days we planned the robbery. She had it outlined pretty well because she'd been thinking of nothing else for a long time.

Ten o'clock Wednesday night. She was to drive away from her place early, so there'd be no suspicion there. Then she'd park in a palmetto thicket off the highway, below the Beach Club. This would take place before ten.

I'd wait at my place until nine-thirty, then go along the beach to the sea wall and along the wall to the spot where Lanihan, the night watchman, sat when he wasn't making his rounds.

This was the part that I didn't like. But I couldn't find any way to get around it. I was supposed to belt him hard enough to knock him unconscious. Then I'd go inside with his keys and take the box of cash. She told me exactly where it would be, in a drawer on the left-hand side of the bar at the north end of the Beach Club. She'd taken care to see that this was where they kept it. The drawer, she said, might be locked.

"So what then?" I asked.

"You'll have to jimmy it."

"Pry it open?"

"It's the only way. The drawer's nothing special. I fooled around with the bartender one day, back of the bar, and made certain about that. You could probably rip it right off the bar, for that matter. It's wooden, and it's flimsy as hell. It hangs from the bottom of the bar, like, on wooden runners."

"All right, I'll take care of that."

After I had taken care of that, I'd return to Lanihan, the night watchman, and put his keys back where I'd found them, taking care to lock the Beach Club doors, too. Then I'd head for Joan's car, parked in the palmettos.

Done this way, things would look queer. I'd give Joan the cashbox. She'd drive to her place, alone. I'd return the way I had come, along the sea wall, and then close in the shallows of the Gull, where there wouldn't be any footprints, just in case. We wouldn't even see each other that night. This was for the Bucks, in case they noticed anything. We'd both go right to bed, me without turning my lights on, which would make it seem as though I'd gone to bed early.

We'd carry on as usual in the morning. I'd open the Pink Goat. Joan would go shopping. We'd wait until things cooled in our own minds, as well as around the Beach Club. Beyond that everything was hazy. I didn't like it, any of it, but it did seem foolproof, I had to admit that. There didn't seem to be any loopholes. Only one. That Lanihan might see me, recognize me, before I had a chance to knock him out.

"They'll think Lanihan is stalling," Joan said. "His story will be pretty darned weak."

"The poor old guy."

"He'd do the same, and don't forget it, Larry. Anybody would, if they thought of a thing like this. It's a natural."

"Yeah," I said. "A natural."

That afternoon we were on the beach again, watching the flagrant beauty of a varicolored sunset. Streaks of red and amber and purple shot off across the sky. The placid Gulf reflected them. The sun was a ball of fire, rimmed on the horizon.

Joan had a towel with her, bunched up. She unwrapped it, watching me. "You've got a gun, Larry," she said. "Remember when you showed it to me, in your bureau drawer?"

"Yeah?"

"Look what I've got."

She had a gun, too. She'd bought it in St. Pete that afternoon, earlier. A .32 Savage automatic. It was a deadly little thing.

I lit a cigarette and looked away and my hands shook.

"Don't you like my gun?" she asked, her lip pouting.

"Sure," I said. "It's a fine gun."

I didn't ask her why she wanted a gun. It was beyond me, as so many things were beyond me these days. The sickness inside me was coming back worse than ever.

"I love you, Larry," she said. "That's all that matters."

She leaned close and kissed me. Then she said, "I'd better take it back to the house, so it won't get dirty."

I didn't say anything. I just watched the lithe grace of her body as she moved away, the easy swing of her shoulders, the bunched towel in her hand with the gun inside.

That night Joan slept in my bed. And it was more savage still than the morning in the storm, out on the beach, after we'd buried the dead man in the Gulf of Mexico.

It seemed as if there was no limit to want. And nothing we did took the edge off. Believe me, we did plenty.

Wednesday. . . .

Lew Hawley was there when I opened up in the morning, and it looked like he wasn't going to leave.

His suit was rumpled, a mess. His hat looked like it had been run over by a truck, and he needed a shave. His eyes were bloodshot and fuzzier than ever. His sunburned skin looked almost sand-blasted, and I wondered if it didn't pain him.

The day was a gray one, with promise of rain. A wind came in off the Gulf that increased slowly hour by hour. It increased, and so did my blood pressure. I was worried, let me tell you.

Hawley was morose, sullen, as he leaned against the bar and drank, rattling the ice cubes, belching, and slamming his fist against the bar.

"How's Joan?" he asked, during one of his talkative moments. I was glad he hadn't much to say. A few early-morning drinkers had come in, but the bar was empty again now.

"She's fine," I said. I cleared my throat. "Guess maybe we'll get married, Lew. Keep it to yourself, though."

He didn't smile, just nodded. "They all do," he said.

"What?"

"Get married. Even me."

"I didn't know you were married."

"My wife says nobody would know it lately, not even her. I haven't been home for two days." He drank, then said, "It's getting me down, Larry."

"What? The case you're on?"

"Yeah. We can't run down a damned thing. Seems like the guy came from no place at all."

I started arranging bottles on the back bar, dusting them off, and putting them straight. Pete Adams had left the place in a mess during the time I'd been away. In three days, Pete could let things go to hell. I hadn't bothered to clean up until now. "Why don't you let somebody else handle it?" I asked Lew. "Put a couple of men on it and forget about it."

He shook his head, took his hat off, ruffled his hair, and slammed the hat down on his head again. "No, by God. This one's got me by the nuts, Larry. I've run into a lot of blank walls, but this is the blankest ever. It just don't add up right."

I tried to whistle and nothing came but a rush of air. That scared me more than anything else. It showed me just what kind of shape my nerves were in. I couldn't even whistle. I lit a cigarette instead.

"If I were you, Lew," I said, "I'd go home and forget it. The guy was probably only a bum."

He looked at me sharply. "Maybe we're all bums," he said. "The guy was somebody, Larry. And don't talk like that, you frighten me."

I stared at him, then closed my mouth.

"The first degree of folly," he said slowly, "is to concede oneself wise. The second to profess it. The third to despise counsel."

I nodded.

"But," Lew said, clinking the ice around in his glass and staring at the amber mixture, "take heed of the vinegar of sweet wine, and the anger of good nature." He looked at me again. "You're a good-natured cuss, Larry. And you serve damn good bourbon, which I could choose to call sweet wine, or any damned thing I want." He drank, motioned for a refill. "So don't talk like that. Especially when I haven't slept for two days, and when I'm drinking too much. Because my mind's clearer then. And besides, I'm suspicious as all hell, Larry. You're a suspect, you know?"

"What?" I almost dropped the bottle I was pouring from. I did spill whisky on the bar.

Lew reached out and swiped a thick finger through the spilled whisky. "Look at that," he said. "Just look at it. If I wasn't sure it was just a yen for that blonde of yours, I'd say you were nervous as a butterfly every time I come in here lately. Especially when I speak about that murder. And it *was* murder, Larry."

I didn't trust my voice, decided it was best to say nothing.

"She's mighty sweet wine, I'll bet, isn't she?"

"Who?"

"You know who, Larry." He drank, long and thirstily. "What d'you hear from Tad?"

"Nothing—nothing at all. I mean, I guess he's busy."

"Sure. Busy as hell. Counting the hairs on his head, and subtracting the gray from the brown."

"Well, you know what I mean."

"No, Larry, I don't." He finished his drink, set the glass down hard, winked at me, and swaggered out to his car.

I stood there and watched his car vanish, then stiffened at a footstep behind me.

"Larry, you're getting jumpy," Joan said. "It won't do. You've got to calm down." She went around and sat at the bar, on a stool. She looked beautiful, and as if she'd never stolen, or thought of stealing, even a penny.

"Yeah, I guess I am." Hereafter I'd keep the back door locked.

"Fix me a Martini, will you, honey?"

"Sure, O.K."

"You better have one, too. Wouldn't hurt us both to get a little tanked up. Dutch courage, y'know? They can make fun of it, but I'll bet it'll work."

I had my back to her, and I was glad she didn't see the way I looked. Because my thoughts must have been written on my face and in my eyes.

I closed up late in the afternoon, and Joan and I separated. We wouldn't see each other again until sometime around ten o'clock that night.

"I'll be waiting," she said. "And don't worry about a thing, Larry. When we go to bed tonight, we'll be rich." She grinned. "I might—I just might even sneak over to see you in the darkness. We'd have a lot to celebrate, wouldn't we?"

"Yes, we would," I agreed. "But don't do it. Keep it just like we've planned. It's the only way, Joan."

"Supposing I get to thinking about you, wanting you?"

"I'll be feeling just the same."

"Yes, but after last night I don't think I want to sleep alone any more." She rubbed against me as we walked down the beach toward the cabanas, and fire leaped between us. "Do I stir you up, pal?"

I grabbed her and kissed her. She moaned a little and said, "Don't let it ever stop, Larry."

Chapter Twenty-four

I turned off the lights and sat in the dark.

It didn't seem possible that Joan could talk me into a thing like this. There was an unavoidable tightness in my throat as the wind lashed through the night off the Gulf, showering sand against the screen door. Time passed too slowly.

Looking back, I tried to find how my mind had come to work this way, to believe like that. But I found no answer.

I heard fat drops of rain splat against the clapboard sides of the cottage. In a few minutes I'd start off along the beach and the sea wall toward the Beach Club. The cold, hard butt of Tad's .38 in my hip pocket reminded me that anything could happen.

If Tad knew, he'd say, "Stay out of it, Larry!" But he was up there at Raiford. And he didn't write any more. He couldn't know how much I loved Joan. Nobody would ever know that, save myself. Or what I'd do to make her my wife. In one hour, if things went right, we'd see each other. In a few days Joan would really be mine.

I left the chair and started pacing the cottage, from one end to the other. I was as tense as a cat, and whatever I'd drunk during the day had done no good. I went from one window to the other, looked out at the night, waited . . . and I tried hard to remember all the things Tad had told me. Things that had never meant much, until now.

We hadn't counted on the wind and the rain. But as I stood there, listening to it, I knew it was to our advantage. Nobody'd be around on a night like this. The only thing was, I'd have to hunt Lanihan down. He wouldn't sit out on the sea wall in this.

I hated to even think of doing such a thing to an old man. Joan was hard about that. And I knew she was right, of course. There was no way to avoid batting him over the head. But I hated it, just the same.

Sure, we'd have money now. And if I sold the Pink Goat, we'd have still more. But that couldn't be for a while, because of suspicion.

It seemed like these last few moments had to be plain hell for me. Everything that had happened entered my mind, and shook me. And through it all ran my want for Joan, the woman who was driving me straight into crime.

The sky-blue custom-built car, with the drunk in it, swept into my mind. I could see him, standing there at the bar, asking if I'd noticed his wallet. See him buying a drink. See us drinking and me lying. It got me. Maybe that got me more than anything else.

And the dead man—sinking him, out there, on a night much like this, only worse.

And Grace.

I tried to close my mind, walked into the living room, and stood there staring at the screen door.

I was scared now, and bitterly sick of the whole business. And standing there in the darkness with the Gulf of Mexico roaring outside, I knew we weren't going to do it.

It was as easy as that. A chill went through me from head to toe. Joan would listen, because I'd make her listen.

"If I just talked without busting you first, you wouldn't remember."

That's what Tad had said. A long, long time ago. Well, she'd listen, because I'd "bust" her.

I don't know why it was, but I suddenly saw it all clearly. The fools Joan and I were making of ourselves. Especially me.

I'd been as weak as they come. I'd been thickheaded and blind to everything. But that was over with now. It wouldn't hurt Joan. I'd tell her first that there wasn't going to be any robbery. Then, if she didn't listen, I'd do something else. All right, she was a woman. But my words hadn't done any good.

I had approached her with every thought I could come through with, and none of them even dented the surface. I knew now how I'd dent the surface. And afterward she would thank me. We loved each other. We needed each other, and we'd have each other. Only it would be the right way. Not the wrong way.

Not only that, but tonight—right now—we'd find Hawley and tell him everything. Give it to him straight, the way I'd thought we should have from the very beginning. And it was the right thing to do. I knew it, and I'd make Joan understand that it was the right thing.

Hawley would see it, too. Because he was a right guy. He'd be mad, plenty mad, and he'd have that right. Things would happen; unpleasant things. But after it was over, Joan and I would be happy. We'd be happy, even if she had to face a court with two black eyes and a split lip.

I felt clean inside now. I felt good. And I hadn't felt like this in a long, long time.

I hurried then, opened the screen door, and stepped out onto the patio. I was happy and I felt like yelling it out loud. I ran off the patio and started through the sandy yard, toward the beach. The wind blasted sand and rain at me. I sensed rather than saw the shadow come at me fast from the side of the porch.

I turned toward the movement and something struck me hard on the side of my head. I blanked on my feet, tried to fight, started to come back when something struck me again. I heard the crack, and my head seemed to explode with pain. I dropped to the hard-packed sand, tasting it in my mouth as something struck yet a third time, and I blacked out.

Chapter Twenty-five

The wind and soaking rain helped bring me around. For a moment I couldn't think, with my face in the sand. Then I remembered Joan and the Beach Club.

I pushed myself up, lurched, and sprawled to my knees again. My clothes were heavy with sand and water. I managed to get to my feet again. It was difficult to focus my eyes because of the pain in my head, and I came near to blanking out again. As I staggered along down the beach, I wondered who in God's name had struck me. How long had I been lying there?

My mouth was filled with sand. I spat it out and every step jarred violent pain through my skull. Something had gone wrong. I knew I had to reach Joan. It was more than just telling her the robbery was off, now. Something else had happened; something I knew nothing about.

I finally made the sea wall and staggered along, leaning into the lashing wind. The Gulf was a raging mass of froth and savage rollers that slammed furiously against the lower part of the wall. I knew they'd come higher and higher. Then I remembered the gun. I grabbed for my hip pocket. The gun was gone.

I kept going. The highway would have been better, but I stuck to the wall. The world was a gray, shifting mass, through which I moved. It would have been an easy thing for me to pass out again, fall from the wall into those wild fingers of water.

The wind grew stronger as the rain let up and the moon broke through a rift in the cloud-torn sky. I kept my eyes intently on the wall as I staggered along, trying not to think of what was happening.

I had to stop for a moment, my sense of direction gone. I knew I had to keep going along that wall, but still my mind was jumbled. Then I forced myself to move on. The footing was treacherous, where the sea had eaten at the wall during the high tides of storms. If I slipped and fell, I'd have been smashed in an instant.

Then the gentle turn and slope in the wall told me I'd reached the Beach Club. I cut sharp right, toward the palmetto thicket over along the highway.

I tripped and sprawled over what I knew instantly was a body.

It was the night watchman, Lanihan, wet and dead. In the wan, windy moonlight I made out the round rain-washed hole in his throat. His old man's mouth was open and the wind cried in it.

I got to my feet, turned, and stumbled on through the knee-high grass clotted with sand spurs until I reached a fence of tall palms, beyond which were the palmettos. I heard laughter. Then I saw Joan, and stopped, hidden behind the palms.

I don't know what I had expected and my mind still wouldn't focus sharply, but I couldn't have moved a muscle right then for anything. It was like being struck over the head again, only much harder.

Joan.... She stood braced against the side of her car in a white dress that clung to her, soaking wet. She waved a gun in the air and shouted at somebody I couldn't see beyond the car.

"Stand still, you crazy bastard! You won't screw this up, damn you!"

Joan.... I couldn't believe what I saw and heard. It couldn't be Joan. Yet, it was. Her face was a contorted mask, her once golden hair lank and dark against her head. I seemed to actually feel it. All the evil in the world radiated from her face and the way she held her shapely body, a thing of twisted angles.

Then my breath ceased. For it was my brother, Tad, who spoke from the shadows where I couldn't see.

His voice was quiet, easy. "You're not going anyplace, baby. Except straight to hell!"

I was still too numb for any reaction beyond blank shock, but as I watched and listened, everything seemed to go out of me; like the air from a balloon, cut with a razor.

Joan leaned half against the car and her teeth gleamed whitely. She held her feet wide apart, and she looked naked, standing there, brandishing the gun. There was something mad in her voice; something I'd never heard before and never wanted to hear again.

"You left me without anything in Miami," she cried. "You turned the dough from that steal over to the law. I swore I'd get you then. In Tampa, you killed the only man I ever really loved. You didn't know that, did you?"

"I knew," Tad said softly from the shadows. "And he was a rat, baby—just like you."

She laughed and it sounded like the obscene cry of a jackal. "Well, I'm paying you back. Your dear little brother you talked so much about will take the rap for murder." Her laughter was touched with hysteria, and I didn't want to hear what she was saying. It was tearing me apart. It was something that could not be, but was.

"You hear, Tad?" she went on. "You escaped to come back and help him. Now they'll get you both. Brothers in crime!" She crouched slightly. "Don't touch your gun, darling!" With the back of her hand, she wiped hair away from her face. I had seen that gesture many times before, but now it was something new and terrible.

"You should never have written me, Joan," Tad said quietly. "You shouldn't have gone to all that trouble, getting letters through to me. You should never have told me your plans."

I saw him then. He stepped out of the shadows toward her, as the palms lashed overhead. He was wearing torn overalls and he looked gaunt and beaten against the big night.

She chuckled in her throat, and the sound of her voice was strident above the deep boom of surf down on the beach. "I had to pay Walt Pike up in Safety Harbor plenty to put my mail through, and to keep mum about it. Larry thought I was sweet and virginal," she said. "And all the time I was only paying back his louse of a brother."

It seemed impossible, but now I remembered Tad's writing in his letters of a woman he'd been going to marry down in Miami. And of something that happened, and of how he had "fixed her clock." Only he hadn't, because she stood here now, and with every word she spoke, another part of me broke away into the darkness.

"Nothing matters now, Joan," Tad said. "I killed once because of you, and you crossed me. They'll get me sooner or later." He stood stiffly. "You killed Bert Arnold, didn't you? How'd you ever manage that?"

Joan's voice was triumphant. The bright curves of her body only stressed her defiance as the wind made her dress a part of her skin. "He didn't do what you told him to, darling. He told me how he'd been released from Raiford—how you got him to come to Larry, so he could tip Larry off to who I was. But he didn't. When he saw me, he figured he'd make it good. He figured on blackmailing me. He knew I've got plenty of money put away." She laughed. "So I lured him on. Even you know how good I am at that, Tad. And so does your brother. I told Bert the hell with blackmail, that I liked him. Told him he could come in with me on a big deal and we'd work together. And I told him to come into my bedroom, too. He was easy, darling. He'd been in prison a long time. All I had to do was show him some thigh. I got him on the bed in the dark, and let him have it. It was hard, but I was lucky. I'd have managed anything to do this to you, Tad!" She went off into wild laughter again, the sound of it cutting down through me, cutting away even hate, now. "Larry, poor Larry! He thought I was defending my virtue! My God, what a joke!"

I couldn't feel anything now, one way or the other. Everything had left me, and she was just some woman I had never known. This wasn't Joan—not the Joan who had laughed and drank and loved with me.

She had worked a mad frame to avenge what Tad had done to her. Whatever it was, it had eaten at her mind until it had destroyed her. Or maybe she had always been the same. I had been right long ago. There was plenty wrong with her mind, and I was glad that there was no small part of the Joan I had known left to see. Nothing. I had that part with me.

I saw them both as they really were. Evil and rotten, clawing at each other like jungle cats. I saw two lives gone irrevocably bad, and there was nothing left to save; no smallest part that might be salvaged. Yet, in its way, there was one life that had some good in it. I didn't want Tad dead.

I leaped forward and yelled, "Don't—Tad!" as he grabbed for a gun in his pocket.

Joan saw me and maybe it spoiled her perfect aim. Her gun flamed twice and Tad twisted sharply as if somebody'd socked his shoulder.

I looked at Joan. She had turned to me, and again her gun flamed and lead slapped the bole of a nearby palm. Then two dark spots blossomed like black flowers on her abdomen. She screamed, clutching. Then her face changed. It fell apart as slug after slug from Tad's gun found their mark. She slumped down, her fingernails screeching on the metal of the car as she tried to hang on. Then she was just a heap of white by the running board.

Somewhere a bird screamed in the night and it sounded like Joan's laughter drifting away on the darkness, mingling with the savage boom of the surf.

Suddenly the place was brighter and I knew it wasn't moonlight. It was a spotlight and there were cars on the highway. The police. They were coming slowly toward us, through the grass.

I went up to Tad. He crouched, tried to push himself up from the ground. His left side and shoulder were torn and he was covered with blood.

"Tad!"

"Hi, kid. Told you it was the wrong road."

"You're hurt, Tad! The law's out there!"

He nodded. His mouth quirked at one corner and his eyes were smiling, but I could see the pain in them, the despair he was still trying to keep to himself, as he had all his life. "Sure," he admitted. "Don't run or they'll cut you down. Joan called 'em just before she shot the night watchman. I was too late to prevent that. You'd have been found here, pawing around in the darkness with an empty cashbox."

"Empty!"

"Sure. Kid, this wasn't your stride." He shook his head, and I heard feet swishing nearer through the grass toward where we crouched. "Nobody'd keep a week's receipts in a place like the Beach Club." He laughed, and seemed startled as blood came with his laughter. But he looked at me and said, "You didn't even have sense enough to check on her story, kid."

We didn't have time for Joan, and I was filled with the urgent hope that Tad might pull through. "Why didn't you write, Tad?"

He was on his knees, his gun hand drooping. He looked tired and blood dripped from the fingers of his left hand. Somebody shouted out there in the darkness, beyond the bright rim of the spotlight. "Drop your gun, Cole. Either of you move, we'll fire!" I recognized Lew Hawley's voice, but it meant nothing, and neither Tad nor I did anything. I don't believe Tad knew he still held a gun.

"I did write," he said. "At first Joan must have swiped your mail every day while you worked. Then I tried passing the letters through the fixed guards. I thought Walt Pike would handle that end, for friendship's sake. I had no dough. Hell, Joan even had that angle tabbed. It cost her plenty. Pike gave her all my mail. There was no way to get to you. She told me about poor old Bert Arnold in her letters. Bert never could keep his mind off a skirt. I had hoped he'd get to you—tip you off. But he didn't. And you, you sucker, you let her talk you straight to hell. You're a dope, Larry. Forget it all."

"You mean, you sent him—this Arnold guy? The one we buried out in the Gulf?"

"Sure. He was getting out of the pen. He promised he'd tell you the score. I'm sorry about the way I acted when you were up to see me, kid. But I wanted to keep you out of everything. A hell of a lot of good it did."

The police made a rush then, but when they really saw what it was like, they weren't in any hurry.

Tad still wasn't dead after I'd explained to several cops. I gave it all to them, straight. Lew Hawley was there, and he kept rubbing his hand across his face and shaking his head as if he couldn't believe it. I told him about the drunk with the wallet, and the clothesline, and Jock Hewitt's boat—everything.

Hawley just gnawed his lip and stared at me, then he looked at Tad, then back at me. And then he'd shake his head some more. "Larry," he said finally. "You were number one on my list, did you know that? Because of a torn screen in Joan Turner's cottage, and some clothes that were washed up on the beach—and because of the way you acted. And Mrs. Buck, there, even told me you bought some clothesline not so long ago. But I couldn't connect it up—I couldn't connect it up." He stared at me, and even in the light from the spot, his eyes were sun-fuzzy. "Maybe I'm glad I didn't know, kid—in a way."

Hawley let me talk to Tad, while he lay there bleeding his life out on the wet grass. He knew he didn't have much time. "I was trusty on the laundry detail at Raiford. I got out with the truck and driver. Slugged 'im and made the break. Like I told you, it wasn't hard to escape. Only, like I said, too, I knew where I was going when I got out. My plans didn't end with the wall." He stopped, his chest laboring. "There won't be another wall, either. I didn't want to tip my hand. Wanted to get her solid. I waited outside your porch and belted you one." Again he paused, and the light was going out of his eyes now. "Was afraid I'd hurt your thick head, so I didn't give you a stiff enough crack those first two times."

"My gun, Tad," I said.

"In your dresser drawer, where it belongs," he told me. "Joan wrote me, through Pike, told me all about everything. She was probably giving Pike something besides money. She was like that. Nobody ever turned her down, except me. I couldn't tip the law without involving you." His face twisted with pain and he closed his lips and eyes tight. I glanced over at the white form that had been Joan and it did nothing to me, nothing at all.

Hawley, other plain-clothes men, and uniformed cops listened attentively to Tad. I guess they knew it was no use trying to move him then.

"She was a witch, Larry. She was bugs, and maybe you couldn't help yourself. Lots of guys couldn't. I only got away from her on luck. And you see what happened?"

"Yeah, Tad. Take it easy."

He shook his head. "Spill it clean to 'em," he said. "You'll get off fair. You get a little time, it won't hurt you. It'll do you good." He closed his eyes again and perspiration glistened all over his face. Without opening his eyes he said, "Leave me be, kid. And stick to beer and pretzels."

They took him away in an ambulance, along with the bodies of Lanihan, the night watchman, and Joan.

Maybe I would remember her, but never as she was tonight. There would be things that would remind me of her, and days, and places, and the way we did things. There would be the touch of her lips down there on the beach and there would be the remembered pleasure of moments that were never real. She might as well have been a dream, I guess, because she was going away like a dream. Already it seemed harder and harder to remember her voice and the thick, golden luster of her hair.

Days come, and with the days come happenings, and time passes into night. And with darkness you sleep and dream and who is to say which is real? Do you live and love and ache and hate under the sun? Or is that the real dream?

I rode into St. Pete with cops on both sides of me. They were decent and kind of quiet. The wind had ceased.

The night was lonely. But it would pass. I tried to think about all the things Tad used to tell me. But somehow I didn't need to remember any more.

THE END

13 French Street

Chapter One

Petra's letters should have warned me. Those secret, smiling letters written in an overbold hand with violet ink on pale green perfumed paper, sealed in green envelopes. They should have been warning enough for anyone. And the house should have warned me. The minute I stepped through the doorway at 13 French Street, I sensed something wrong—something I couldn't nail down. But she closed the door before I had a chance to run. So, you see, it was already too late. Only I should have run anyway. . . .

"Alex. You've come!"

I nodded but I didn't speak. She leaned back against the door, one hand resting on the doorknob, the other fussing with the long V neckline of her black dress.

The long, broad hallway was deeply shadowed, though some of the early-autumn twilight filtered into the house. I could still hear the lazy rattle of leaves outside against the porch. The bite of burning leaves had entered the door with me. I remembered the red winking of the taxi's taillight as it rounded a far corner, left me standing on the flagstone walk before the large, square, red brick house. Verne Lawrence's home, 13 French Street.

Yes. Already I sensed the beginnings of panic. The first hint of futility and hopeless outrage.

"Alex Bland."

"Yes, and you're Petra?"

"What do you think?" She smiled. I knew her lips were very red, but they looked black, there in that hallway. Her right hand left the doorknob, and I took it. It wasn't shaking hands. It was holding hands. No, it was even more than that. Communication, from Petra to me.

"Where's Verne?"

She ignored it. She let go of my hand, stepped closer. The perfume she wore was faint, elusive. I remembered the letters. It was the same stuff. I'd smelled that perfume on her letters at least once a week for three years.

"It's queer," she said. "Never having seen you. Only the snapshot of you and Verne in uniform. The one you had taken in Paris. Your face was all in shadow, you know, so I thought you had dark hair. But you're a regular tow-head. And those gray eyes—" She paused and shook her head slightly. "You're a bigger man now, too. I'll bet . . . Well, never mind. Anyway, Alex, you look like I expected—only better." She smiled. "Well, let me take your coat, Alex."

She helped me with my coat, held it in her hands a moment, then dropped it in a heap on a chair. I hadn't moved from beside my two bags. I could feel the leather of one of them against my leg. It felt substantial, like the beach does after you've been swimming for a mile or so.

We looked at each other some more. I guess we had that much coming. That much of it wasn't wrong.

She was tall, slimly provocative. All in black. Black hair, worn long, tumbling around her shoulders. Black eyes, all pupil, or all iris. Her skin was very white. Her black eyebrows arched slightly, making her eyes seem bolder than ever, and her smile had shock value. Long-legged, full-breasted, and the neckline of her dress reached down. *Down.* She was a bold, beautiful woman.

"All right? I mean, what did you expect, Alex? We know each other, in a way. Of course, not . . ."

I didn't tell her I had expected a white house with a white picket fence. I didn't explain that I had always visualized her in a light cotton dress, maybe watering the flowers. Hell, there weren't any flowers.

I said, "Verne could always pick 'em."

"Yes?"

"He outdid himself. Where is Verne?"

She'd been speaking quietly, the tone of her voice soft, warm, full. Now it lost the softness, the warmth. "Oh, yes, Verne. Upstairs. He'll be down. You didn't tell us you *were* coming, you know. We'd have met you at the station."

"You told me you like surprises," I said.

"You don't surprise me, Alex," she said. "I've known all along."

"Known what?"

She smiled.

Somebody walked softly across the hall at the far end. I turned and saw a staircase leading upward and what looked like a while shawl vanishing through a doorway at the foot of the stairs.

Petra's eyes had gone metallic. Then they were molten again. "Mother," she said.

"Your mother?"

"My husband's."

I wondered how much longer this was going to continue. I didn't sense that something was wrong any more. I knew it for sure. But what?

"How long can you stay?"

"A week."

She smiled. Every time she'd smiled at me it had been like the silent communication of her hand. She was saying, "That's all you know about it." She knew I knew what she meant. But I wasn't bothered too much. Yet.

She acted all wrong. I mean, I figured Verne would be there, pounding me on the back, cracking out a bottle, with Petra saying, "Oh" and "Ah."

It wasn't like that. It wasn't like anything. But it was real as all hell.

"Alex, I feel I know you terribly well."

I chanced a smile. "Me, too."

So that's the way it was. When she said something, you never knew what was going to come out. You never knew.

> ... and Verne would so much like to see you. It's been five years now and he still talks of the good old times. He seldom writes anyone, Alex, so he's left it up to me to keep at you until you visit us. He said you always did work too hard and that your fault is you're too honest. Verne says a man can't get ahead anyplace nowadays if he's like that. You're too serious. I know you don't think I'm too forward in saying these things, Alex. But, Alex—let that museum go hang. You need a good vacation. Please come, Alex. We'll have a grand time. I feel I know you so well, now. We've been writing each other for three years, Alex. . . .

Pages. Page after page, every time. As if all she had to do in the world was write to me. An archaeologist with no place to dig and with no one to give a damn if he did dig—but with a dream. And a philanthropic gentleman in Chicago had the foresight and interest to help me realize this dream. A museum for the future to end all museums. It would take years, probably my whole lifetime, but it was what I wanted now.

> ... so I keep asking you, for Verne, to come and spend some time with us here in Allayne. We have a fine home, just outside of town—nearly a mile—lots of freedom. Alex, really. I simply won't give up, Alex!

It sounded good. But there was the museum, and there was Madge, too. We weren't engaged, but marriage wasn't far off, either. Sure, I wanted that vacation. What the hell? So I finally decided to surprise them. I didn't let them know I was coming till I called from the station. Here I was. Great.

Verne Lawrence hadn't been out of the Army a week before he was married. I'd heard from him occasionally and we'd planned to get together after I finished some digging in Yucatan. But he never said much about his new wife, beyond the fact that she was beautiful and they were happy. After about two years he ceased writing, and Petra took over. I returned to Chicago and my dream.

I wanted to see Verne. He'd been a close friend and a good man—a good soldier, too. He was ten years older than I, making him about forty now. I wondered if he had changed.

I figured to spend a week with them. Verne and I would loaf and talk, while Petra mixed cocktails or opened beer cans. The hell with the museum, for the time being—the hell with everything. And Madge said, "Why, certainly, Alex. I agree. You should do something like that. You've been working much too hard. Then, when you come back, maybe ..."

So here I was. And already I wanted to run. I wanted to get away. It was all wrong.

"Here's Verne now."

I turned toward the stairs again. I felt her hand on my arm and the fingers closed just once, not tentatively, but certain.

Then her hand went away. I watched my old war buddy come toward us down the hall.

He looked as if somebody had machine-gunned his soul.

Chapter Two

"Alex! You old fraud, you!"

"Verne, is that any way to—"

He ignored her, didn't even glance her way. "Yes, by God! Sorry I kept you waiting, old man. Damned headache. Trying to—Well, say! You haven't changed."

"Good to see you, Verne."

The handshake. Flat out, once up, once down, release. He slapped me on the back. I don't know how I sounded; I'll never know. Verne Lawrence looked like hell. He was an old man, trying to suck in his guts and stick out his chest; trying to smile a smile that wasn't there. Obviously.

"You've met my wife?" He did not look at her.

I grinned. "Lucky fellow. She's everything I—"

"Sure, sure."

I was sick of it. I wanted to get out of there.

His eyes were haunted. Once he'd had blond hair; now it was a dirty, streaked gray. His face was lined, his mouth pulled down at the corners no matter how hard he tried to pull it up. His neck was wrinkled and his shirt collar didn't fit. He was wearing a tweed suit and it hung over his frame like burlap over a broomstick; like those scarecrows you see in winter-blasted cornfields.

And Verne Lawrence had once been a big man with broad shoulders, a barrel chest, and a face like a slab of beef. Now his face was like breast of chicken, dried in a very hot sun.

All of this in five years. . . .

"Should've let me come down and pick you up at the depot."

"Already had the cab."

"How long you here for?"

"A week."

"What the hell kind of vacation is that?"

"Best I could do."

She was behind him, staring at me over his shoulder now. She dampened her lips with her tongue and her gaze was steady, patient.

"Five years," he said. "Five years." He shook his head, jammed his hands into his jacket pockets. Then he took one hand out and pulled at his lower lip. "You're tired," he said. "Jenny's got your room ready."

I started to tell him I wasn't tired. But I knew he was. He was tired of having me here already. As tired as I was of being here.

"Here," he said. "I'll show you. Wash up. Change clothes. Feel better. Here, I'll show you."

"It would be best," Petra said. She smiled at me over his shoulder.

Great.

The room was all right. Better than that. It was a corner room, on the left front. Big windows, with the late twilight of autumn blowing in. The breeze was balmy, and I suspected there'd be some warm weather coming. Not like Chicago.

Comfortable bed. Two chairs, a desk, a bookcase full of brightly covered unread books, and a sparkling bathroom in blue tile.

So this was how you met the guys you knew during the war. This was what happened to them.

I went over and leaned out one of the side windows. Fields, trees, hills—and 'way over there was town. Allayne. I could see the road winding through the hills, dipping into the town. The hills were savage with color in the failing twilight. Almost as I watched, night began to creep along the sky, tugging a black blanket in its teeth. The wind began to die. It was very still out there, almost as if the evening were holding its breath.

It had been all Verne could do to carry the lighter of the two suitcases up the stairs. It embarrassed me. I would have carried them both, but that would have done more than embarrass Verne.

I walked around the room and rubbed my knuckles into my scalp. This was great, all right.

Some wife. Petra. Maybe . . .

But I didn't want to think of her. It hadn't begun to occur to me why I didn't want to think of her—yet.

I opened the two suitcases on the bed. Somebody whistled softly and said, "I'm Jenny."

I faced the door. It was partly open. She had genuine apples in her cheeks, a wealth of carrot-colored hair, the hint of a turned-up nose, bright, honest blue eyes, and one of those mouths that like to smile but are a bit hesitant about it. She was dressed in white: white apron, tiny starched white cap. She leaned against the door jamb with her hands in the pockets of her apron, and I liked her right away.

"Mrs. Lawrence says to tell you dinner is served at six-thirty."

"Thanks, Jenny."

"That's all right. My job. You're Mr. Bland, from Chicago, right?"

I sat down on the bed. "That's right."

"Heard your name mentioned." She smiled and her face lit up and laughed all over. Still there was that shy hesitancy about the smile. It was the kind of smile model agencies would break budgets for.

"You've been here a long while?" I asked.

"Six months, Mr. Bland."

"Oh."

"That's all right. You can ask anything you want."

"I see. Thanks."

She cleared her throat. "You have plenty of towels 'n' stuff?"

"Guess so."

"That's good."

We watched each other. She had something to say, but she'd decided not to say it. I wondered what it was. It was in her eyes. Somebody was coming up the stairs. Petra said, "Jenny!" from down the hall.

Jenny winked and closed the door. She opened it quickly, stuck her head in, and whispered, "You'd better keep it locked, Mr. Bland." Then the door was closed and the house was silent.

I wondered if Jenny had finally said what she'd come to say. If she had, it didn't make sense to me.

Without a doubt there was something wrong between Verne and his wife. What it was, I didn't know. Petra was a very beautiful woman. Seated on the bed, I thought it over, and only came to realize more and more how truly beautiful she was.

And Jenny. A housemaid. Not a cook. So there must be a cook, too. And Verne's mother. I'd clean forgot to ask him about that.

The vacation I was supposed to be on was slowly becoming something else. I'm a guy who likes things orderly. If I lay my razor down on a certain part of a shelf, I want it to be there when I reach for it next time. Comes from living so long alone, I suppose.

So I got to thinking about Madge. I went over to the desk and found paper. Using my own pen, I wrote Madge, and lied about how swell everything was. That wasn't good either, because some kinds of lying are all right, but others nag at me. This would nag. Then I told Madge I wished we were together, and that was no lie, so I felt better.

But after the letter was sealed I remembered Petra again. I tucked the letter under the blotter of the desk. Then I got out my shaving kit and shaved in the bathroom. I kept thinking about Petra, wondering what her last name had been before it was Lawrence. So I had to whistle in order to quit thinking about my friend's wife's black hair and the way her eyes got soft when she looked at me. I was finished shaving before I realized I'd been whistling *"Danse Macabre."*

Somebody rapped on the door.

"Yeah, O.K.," I said. The door opened.

"It's me, Jenny, again," she said. "Mrs. Lawrence says not to go an' dress for dinner."

"Thanks, Jenny."

She closed the door. I took a shower and went downstairs in gray flannels and a white shirt. I felt good and not at all tired. When I reached the foot of the stairs I happened to glance up. An old woman in a white shawl was leaning over the railing, staring at me.

I went on down the hall and opened the front door, stepped through the vestibule, opened the door onto the porch. Leaves skittered around the threshold and over my feet. Lights from house windows winked between the flashing branches of trees. Verne's place wasn't so far from town. There were street lights out here. And there were some stretches of sidewalk. I stood there in the doorway. Behind me, the house was very still. As if nobody lived there at all.

A car went by out on the road with the radio playing. Music trailed off into the evening. Then it was quiet again. A cow lowed. It wasn't cold at all. The air was warm and still.

I turned to go inside and I smelled the perfume. She was standing in the vestibule. She didn't move, so I had to stop and stand there. It was dark, but her face was pale and I could see her lips and her eyes shone in the darkness.

"You like it here, Alex?"

"Very much. It's very nice."

"Alex, if—if Verne seems peculiar, please excuse him. He's had rotten luck. Business, business, you know? He's a little worried, because he doesn't know how to tell you he won't be able to spend much time with you. He can't possibly take a week off."

"I see. Well, that's all right."

Her hand touched my arm, went away. Her voice was as soft as the breeze outside. "That's what I told Verne. Don't you worry. I'll see that you have a fine time. We should have lots of things to talk about. And I know plenty of things to do."

I tried to make my voice encouraging, but the panic had mounted another notch. "Great. That's fine. I'm sure we'll—"

"So am I, Alex. Come, dinner's ready. And don't you dare let on I mentioned that about Verne."

Already we were conspirators. Inadvertently I touched her shoulder. It was bare and warm. She was wearing a strapless dress. I jerked my hand away. I said, "Don't you worry. Maybe I can talk him into feeling better."

She whispered, "I won't worry, Alex."

For me there has always been something about the darkness of a house, a large house, of a hallway, just before dinnertime in the autumn. Something about the darkness, with the lights in another part of the house—something that excites me. Perhaps everyone has felt it. I felt it now. And she felt it. We stood there and the faint panic increased a bit.

Her voice remained a whisper, conspiratorial. "And Verne's mother. Don't pay any attention to her, either. She's quite deaf, by the way."

"Yes." I cursed myself because I had whispered.

She took me lightly by the arm. "Come on, Alex. I'm famished. I'll bet you are, too. Nobody eats in this house but me. They're all—" She ceased. We went on down the hallway. I was very conscious of her movements, her lithe grace.

They're all what? I asked myself. There was something so damned secretive about her. In spite of anything I could do, it was getting to me. Right then was when I began to fight.

Dinner was a wake. We sat for three quarters of an hour over a rare roast of beef. And I met Verne's mother. Yes. Really there were three corpses at that table. The old woman, Verne, and the roast of beef. Petra and I faced each other across the table. She still was the only one with an appetite. I'd felt hungry, but a few moments at the table took care of that.

Verne's mother. Verne had doubtless been born into her old age. She was very old now. Like those dried, withered vines clinging grimly to the side of a stone building. At first glance, you think they're dead, but then, 'way up there, you notice a tiny green leaf. You wonder how in hell it ever got there. You know the sap still flows, however frugally.

There wasn't much sap left in this old woman. She wore a gray dress, buttoned around her throat, like those World War I Army tunics, with a round diamond brooch in the middle. And above the collar, a small choker of pearls circled her thin neck. Her face was small, shrunken, and sly. Her eyes glinted and gleamed like the slowly burning tips of two Fourth of July punk sticks. The kind you light firecrackers with, or used to, anyway. One of these days those eyes would turn to ash. I wondered if she would find a fuse; she seemed to be looking for one. Her dress was long, tight-sleeved, and a flower of white lace handkerchief bloomed at her wrist. Her hands and fingers trembled like dried willow wands in a breeze. A white shawl, looking somehow too heavy for her to carry, sagged about her shoulders. She was quite deaf, and beyond a nod to me when we were loudly introduced, she didn't speak.

Petra hated her. I saw that from the first. Petra would glance at the old woman and Verne would glance at Petra.

"She's afraid of the old folks' home," Verne said. "She believes they would kill her if she ever went. Don't know where she picked up the notion. I suppose it's just as well she stays here. She can't last too much longer."

"She'll outlive us all," Petra said. She cut a piece of meat, dipped it in gravy, and chewed with unconcern. "She's in the way here. She's unhappy. She has nothing."

"You take her out for rides," Verne said.

"Yes, it's lovely."

Petra ate for a while. The old woman fussed at her plate, believing that she ate, but actually all she did was play. It wasn't nice to watch. Verne drank water. I creased my napkin, and remembered how the red taillight of the taxi had winked around the corner, leaving me here—with this.

"You've noticed I look like hell, I suppose?" Verne said. His gaze touched mine, drifted away. Petra was watching me. The skin of her shoulders and throat looked soft, unblemished, warm.

I shrugged. "A little tired, maybe."

"No. I look like hell, Alex. Everything's going to hell. My business is shot, what with the government stepping in, taking over supplies. Can't get the things I need, have to be there every minute or I'll lose what I have."

"What is it?"

"Building project on Long Island. Have to leave tomorrow, Alex. Don't know when I'll get home. I'm sorry. That's the way it is. Biggest deal I've ever had, and it's tumbling around my shoulders. I'll stand to lose what I've got. It would have set me—us on Easy Street. Really."

Petra stared at me. Her lips were touched with disdain, her eyes hot and black. "He worries too much," she said to me.

"I never worried before in my life!" Verne's voice was harsh. "Excuse me," he said. "Let's go in the other room and have a drink."

"Haven't you been drinking too much, dear?" Petra said.

He ignored her.

The old lady was trying to carry a forkful of cole slaw to her mouth when she erupted into laughter. It sounded like dry leaves rustling against the basement windows of a house.

Verne stared at her. Petra glanced at Verne, then at me, and she smiled.

"Come on," Verne said. He rose and started around the table. "We'll have coffee in there."

"Sure, fine."

Petra watched me. We rose together and I couldn't tear my eyes away. Then I did and it was all right again. But the sense of panic, of the unknown, kept rising inside me.

Verne walked through an alcove into a small room, and on into the living room. I followed. Petra touched my arm. The lights went on in the living room, gleaming soft and slow and saffron, like a stage set. Verne called, "You coming, Alex?"

"Yes."

Petra leaned close and her breath was warm against my cheek. The faint odor of her perfume—was it jasmine?—mingled with her breath. "Try to cheer him up, Alex," she whispered. Only she didn't mean that.

It seemed as though she had spoken merely as an excuse to be near me, to touch me. My throat thickened and I couldn't speak. I nodded. For a brief moment, perhaps, we understood something between us. Then she sighed.

I went on into the living room.

Behind me the old lady commenced laughing again.

I knew I was going to have to cut the vacation short. It had to be. Maybe it was all right for some people, but not for me. I was born with a deadly conscience; something I detested, but something I couldn't override. If I made a mistake, it lived with me for a long while, and it was too much of a price to pay. Even a little mistake. I had long since avoided mental discomfort.

She was beautiful. Petra. My friend's wife. It was all I could think. My best friend's wife.

And there was Verne, leaning against the fireplace mantel, with his head in his hands.

"He's shot his bolt," Petra said softly behind me. "He's simply shot his bolt, the poor dear."

I heard her quite plainly, but Verne didn't.

Chapter Three

After two brandies I told myself I was a fool.

One thing I did know—it was true that Verne was deeply troubled about his business, but business hadn't marked him. It was something else. Petra? How?

"You'll have a good time, you two," Verne said. He still stood by the fireplace. Petra sat directly across from me with her feet resting on an ottoman, ankles crossed. She watched me across the brim of her brandy glass. The old woman was perched like a stuffed bird on a chair in the corner.

"Sure we will," I said.

Verne drained his glass, picked up the bottle, poured himself another, drained that, and set bottle and glass on the mantel. Petra's eyes followed his movements, then she began watching me again.

"Hell of a thing," Verne said. "Been asking you to come for years, and now you're here, I have to leave. Don't know how long I'll have to stay in town. I've only been coming home week ends." He turned to the mantel and poured himself another drink.

I glanced toward Petra. She raised her glass, watching me, and emptied it.

"Wonder if I could have a little soda," I said. "Maybe brandy should be drunk straight, but I think perhaps I'd better have some soda."

"I'll get it." Petra left her chair and crossed the room. She had to pass my chair. My hand was on the arm of the chair, and as she swung by, her thigh brushed my knuckles. It could have been accidental. It was the merest contact. Yet I knew she'd meant to touch me. We were talking together by touch, by looking at each other. I was saying things to her against my will. I told myself again that I was a fool to think that way. Yet there it was.

All right, you say. Laugh. But I didn't want it that way. Because something was wrong, dead wrong. It was in the house. In the way they spoke. In their actions. And already I was a part of it, without knowing anything about it.

There was a long silence. Then Petra returned. She had mixed me a drink, and as she handed it to me our fingers touched. She crossed the room, placed ice and a syphon on the coffee table. I glanced at the old woman in the corner. She was watching me.

Verne brooded at his empty glass, one arm sprawled across the fireplace mantel.

"Is it good?" Petra asked me with her back turned.

"Fine." Her hips swelled beneath her dress, black again, but not the same one she'd met me at the door in. This one clung.

Her back was bare to the waist. Her waist was slim, supple. She poured a drink of brandy into another glass she'd brought with her, went swiftly to the old woman, handed it to her.

"Thank you, darling," the old woman said. It was the first time she'd said anything. Her voice was flat, dusty.

Verne's voice was low-pitched, but harsh. "Damn it, you shouldn't have done that! I've told you."

Petra faced him, brushed a heavy wave of black hair away from her cheek with her wrist. "Don't be tiresome," she said. "The old girl doesn't have any fun these days. Let her have her little kick."

Verne's face was red. The red deepened. He looked at me, tried to smile. I drank from my glass.

Petra settled in her chair again, flipped her feet onto the ottoman, and, glass in hand, watched me. It was nothing, perhaps. She didn't alter her expression; she didn't try to show her legs; she made no movement that wasn't entirely accepted and proper. But she said what she said, all the same. And I got it and I answered right back, because I couldn't help myself. I answered without speaking, just by looking at her. I answered, Yes, you're beautiful. But stop it, cut it out!

She smiled and sipped.

Verne said, "I don't like to have Mother drink anything. It goes to her head. But if I reach for that glass now, she'll knock it down like a scared drunk."

There wasn't anything to say.

"Wish you could see the job I'm working on," he resumed. "It sure is something—would have been. No, damn it! Will be!"

I grabbed at the straw. "Maybe I could go in with you. Maybe we could—"

"No. Wouldn't hear of it. You're on vacation. Petra will take you around, show you the country. I've got a million things to do, Alex. Hell, it's a mess. I wanted to sit and talk. But either I go tomorrow morning, and try straightening things up, or I'm flattened." He paused, gestured with his glass as I didn't look at Petra. He said, "How's the new museum coming along?"

"It's all right. Coming along."

"That's the trouble with you, Alex. You'll never get ahead. You'll go on from year to year, wasting your time. You won't get ahead because you're too damned honest." He drank. "Enough to make a man sick. Don't get me wrong, now. Just that in business today, you got to grab, you got to lie, you got to be there one jump ahead of the next guy. If you aren't—" He snapped his fingers. "Like that. You want to get ahead, don't you?"

"Well—"

"Yeah, 'well.' What good is *well?* What good is a museum? What good is digging up bones all over the damned world? And now you've quit that to build a fool museum, and the man putting up the money must be a fool, too. Ye gods, Alex! Get into something hot!"

"Like you? You're into something hot, from what you say."

"You're right. But listen, it *is* hot. No, damn it—it isn't. Not now. Damn it!" He drank.

Something bumped on the floor. We all looked. The old woman had dropped her glass. It rolled across the rug and onto the hardwood floor, *clink, clink, clink, clink.* . . .

"You're a sweet boy," the old woman said. She was leaning awry in her chair and as drunk as a lord.

"I told you!" Verne snapped.

Petra didn't look at him. She smiled at me.

"Is she all right?" I asked.

"You're a sweet boy."

I'd thought she was speaking to her son, Verne. But she was looking at me. There was a silly grin on her lips, and she nodded toward the right side of her chair, catching herself each time at the very instant of collapse.

"It hits her more quickly than it used to," Petra said.

"He's a good man," the old woman said. She pointed a quivering finger at me. "Yes, you, sonny. Take care of yourself." She went off into laughter. The dry leaves again, rustling against the side of a basement window, maybe with mice playing in the leaves.

"It's a vile thing!" Verne said. He faced Petra. His voice turned from ruggedness to pleading. "Good Lord, don't you know she's an old woman? Don't you know the very smell of alcohol sends her balmy? You do know. You do it deliberately."

"Oh, snap out of it," Petra said. "Stop and think. What's she got? Nothing. It won't hurt her. So she's drunk. So are you drunk."

"Yes, but I—"

"It's no different."

"You know damned well it's different."

The old woman said, "They're talking about me." Only she didn't say it that clearly. It was thick, sickly, bad. "But don't you worry," she went on. "I know what I know."

Petra looked at her.

Verne said, "Take her upstairs, will you?"

Petra rose, placed her glass on the coffee table. "Will you excuse me?" she said, looking at me. She went over to the old lady. "C'mon, Maw," she said, "let's go."

The old woman couldn't stand. Her eyes were mere glinting slits, her mouth a tight clamp of chin to nose, and she kept saying over and over, "I know what I know."

As Petra half carried, half walked the old woman past me, she halted. "Tell Mr. Bland good night."

"Oh, God!" Verne said. Petra was shouting as loud as she could; shouting into the old woman's ear.

"Tell Mr. Bland good night."

"Good night, Mr. Man," Verne's mother said. "I know what I know, but you're a good boy." They reeled off into the hallway. I listened to them going up the stairs. The old woman was muttering.

"I'm sorry about this," Verne said. "Damn it. Seems like everything's going wrong. Naturally Petra doesn't like Mother. She says Mother's malicious, evil." He ran his fingers through his hair and paced the room. "I don't know, Alex. Sometimes I think I'd be better off dead."

"Everything'll be all right."

"Easy to say."

"Don't let things get you down."

He paused before me. I was trying to relax. My muscles ached from being held rigid. It was like waiting patiently for some terrific explosion—waiting until the second of the explosion you know for certain will occur; then, no explosion. But it would come—it had to come.

Verne's mouth sagged at the corners. "A bad evening. But you'll feel better tomorrow. Get Petra to take you for a drive around the lake. It'll do her good, too. Hell's fire, have some fun—somehow!" He strode to the mantel, poured himself a drink, drank it. His eyes were glassy, beneath heavy lids. I wanted to ask him what was wrong. Once I would have asked. Now there was something about Verne Lawrence that hadn't been there when I'd known him five years before. Some added something that prevented you from asking anything personal.

"Well, you have a beautiful wife," I said. "And a fine home. You have money socked away, I'll bet."

"Yes." Nothing more. Just "Yes."

"Look, Verne," I said. "I know something's bothering you. Everything's in an uproar. Why don't I go back to Chicago and you let me know when you get things ironed out?"

"No. Wouldn't hear of it. Never see you again. An evening like this is enough to scare anybody away."

"I know you don't feel much like talking about the old days now."

He looked straight at me, let his shoulders sag. "Alex, I'm tired. I'm dead rotten dog-head tired. In the morning I've got to go into New York and start fires under a bunch of fat behinds. I stand to clear over two hundred thousand dollars if this thing goes through on time."

"Why don't you get some sleep?" I hesitated, and the brandy talked. "Maybe I *could* manage to stay over a couple of extra days. We could get together, drink some beer, go fishing. Might even get in some hunting. O.K.?"

"Alex, there's nothing in the world I'd rather do. Maybe we can—maybe we can work out something. If I can just build hot enough fires."

"This damn business—it's really got you down."

"It's got me nuts."

I looked at him and I knew it wasn't business at all. No. Verne was lying. He was afraid of something.

I heard movements in the doorway and turned. Petra stood there. Her left hand fussed with the waist of her dress. "Well," she said. "The old girl's snoring fit to kill." She looked sharply at her husband. "Why, Verne! Do you know you're plastered?"

Then she looked at me and laughed.

Chapter Four

I sat there on the edge of my bed with one shoe off. I took off the sock and wriggled my toes. It felt good, so I did the same with the other foot. Then I just sat there, wriggling my toes, contemplating my bare feet.

It had always been Verne's creed, I guess. From what I knew of him, anyway. And from what he'd told me of his early life, before the Army. Dig, dig, dig. Well, that much was all right. But he believed in elbowing the other guy out of the way. A little judicious lying got a fellow places. Be fast. Get in there and sock. Sock the other guy out of the way. Everything was business with Verne. There are millions of Vernes, and they don't honestly mean to hurt anyone, either.

He'd always kidded me about not wanting to do enough, go far enough ahead. Well, that was all right, too. Some of us don't. Some of us just want the satisfaction of an accomplished dream, enough money, a good home, and a loving wife.

Yes, wife. He was cutthroat about that, too. Find her—find the one that's right and marry her. She's got to have push and power, too. Yeah. Well, he'd sure made a discovery. Petra.

I finished undressing, flung all the windows up, and climbed into the shower again. I got it just off cold and stood there with it blasting my back.

He'd socked his way out of a family of fifteen and finagled his way from a Nebraska farm to a possible two hundred thousand dollars. With God only knows how much in the bank now. Only maybe he'd used that. Could be. He'd gamble, too. Anything. All the way.

Petra of the long black hair . . .

I shoved my face into the needles of water with my eyes closed. When I tipped my head, it sounded like rain on a roof. Tin roof, maybe.

Well, I wasn't going to get snarled up in his mess. The museum looked good from here and it looked good from the museum, too. And Madge looked good. Now, take Madge and Petra.

I stood there. Then I turned off the water. I found a heavy towel and tried to rub myself pink like they say in the magazines. No luck. Never did have. I padded into the bedroom, finished unpacking my suitcases, and looked at the new pair of pajamas I'd bought special for my vacation.

Hell, I always sleep in the raw. I wasn't going to stop now. I tossed the pajamas on the bureau and sat down at the desk.

Take Madge and Petra, for instance.

Well, I loved Madge. We were going to be married. Chicago was a long way off. Seven hundred miles? Nearly.

I closed my eyes and saw the red taillight of the taxi winking around the corner.

Take Madge. I had, twice. Take Petra. . . .

I slammed my fist on the desk. The blotter moved, and there was the letter I'd written Madge earlier in the evening. I ripped the envelope open and read the letter. Then I went and got my pen and wrote a postscript. I wrote four lines about how nice it was here, addressed another envelope, sealed up the letter, and stuck it beneath the blotter.

His old man couldn't even write, Verne had told me. He died standing between the handles of a plow. The horse was so old it didn't even move when the buzzards came. That's the way they found him. Standing upright between the plow handles, leaning back against the reins. There was a buzzard on each shoulder, plucking at his ears.

Verne said his mother found his old man like that. She shooed the birds away, unhitched the plow, loaded his father on the horse. When she got the body back to the house, she dug a grave. Then she waited till the kids got home from school and she read from the Bible. Verne said he threw the first shovelful of dirt. It landed on his father's face. It made him so mad he walked off the farm in his bare feet and hopped a freight into St. Louis. He never went home again.

"Don't you ever wonder how they made out?" I asked him.

"Yes," he said. "Yes, Alex. Sometimes I do wonder."

I went over and turned off the bedroom light. There was a moon. I stood at the open window, the side window. This autumn was still in the hands of the Indians.

Petra of the hot dark eyes . . .

Another man's wife.

Why in all hell did I have to be born with a conscience?

So, then, maybe I was a fool all the way. I began to wonder. Maybe I was overtired. Imagining things. She probably hadn't meant a thing. I'd read what I'd wanted to read. Maybe it was me, not Petra.

Only none of this did any good. I could still feel it and the house was quiet. I went over and locked the door, like Jenny said. In my friend's home? I unlocked the door, and went to bed.

What was the matter with Verne? What kind of beast was gnawing at the already frayed edges of his being? What was eating away at him? He looked like an old oil painting that someone had carelessly spilled a small amount of acid on. It eroded and bit and gnawed away, making small traceries of lines, curlicues. . . .

The house was very still. Night and moonlight sighed in the windows, billowing the curtains. Somebody walked quietly down the hall. Whoever it was wasn't tiptoeing, wasn't trying to be especially quiet. But the footsteps paused at my door.

Then they went on down the hall. I realized I'd been holding my breath. I got out of bed and opened the door.

I'd recognize that perfume anywhere.

Plenty was wrong, cockeyed wrong. I had to get back to Chicago.

I went back to bed. The footsteps came back along the hall and paused at my door again. I held my breath again. She waited longer this time. Then she went on.

Chicago. Chicago. It was like the wild beating of surf against rocks. *Chi—ca—go . . . Chi—ca—go. . . .*

My door opened. "Is everything all right, Alex?"

"Yes. Fine."

"Just wanted to make sure." Her voice was a whisper. She closed the door very quietly. Some of the perfume remained in the room.

Chapter Five

"Verne? Oh, he's gone long ago. I drove him into town at six-thirty. He caught the seven-o'clock train for New York."

We were alone in the large kitchen. Petra was seated on a high stool at the lunch bar, drinking coffee. The red shorts and halter she wore were very tight and her skin was very white. Creamy, because it was not a sickly white. It was lush, warm, solid. I noticed how long, how perfectly formed her legs were. Her lips were dark red in daylight, and she looked fresh, wide-awake. In the bright morning, there were traces of midnight in her hair. It foamed about her shoulders, seemed so full of life I expected it to sparkle. It did, when she moved.

She sipped coffee. "Verne said to tell you again that he was sorry he couldn't stay. He felt real bad about it."

I wasn't really awake yet. I was in that blank, staring stage.

"Did you sleep well?"

"Fine, Petra."

"Reason I asked, strange bed and all that, y'know?"

"Slept perfect."

"Hope I didn't disturb you when I opened your door." She wasn't looking at me. She rose, swung over to the electric range, took up the coffeepot, poured herself another cup, returned to the stool. All the time, I couldn't keep my eyes off her. Like a magnet, a deadly magnet, even when I tried not to watch.

"You didn't disturb me." I was tardy with that. She drank her coffee black. I suddenly had a strong desire to touch her hair. "What's for breakfast?"

She smiled. "I was waiting for you to ask that. Cook's day off." Her eyes were black. Jet black.

"Oh?"

"But I can cook, my friend."

Ten minutes later I was at the kitchen table eating scrambled eggs, country sausage, toast, and coffee. I'd managed to avoid the stool beside her at the lunch bar by saying I liked my feet on the floor when I ate. But it only made matters worse, because she was above me, looking down. She was perched on the stool, her legs crossed, leaning back against the bar, with a cup in her hand. Her breasts filled that red halter like nothing I'd ever seen before.

The food was perfect. The kitchen was as neat as a pin.

"Where's Jenny?" I asked.

"Gave her the day off."

"And Verne's mother?"

She glanced at me and chuckled. "Not up yet." She drank some more coffee. "We're all alone. Just you and me. But not for long. The old girl will be down shortly."

I managed a weak grin. She grinned back.

"How long has Verne's mother been with you?"

"Ever since we were married, right after Verne left the Army."

I finished off the last of the sausage. Petra poured me another cup of coffee, returned to her stool. I tried to imagine that old woman unhitching a plow, digging a grave, reading from a Bible. "What happened to the rest of Verne's family? I mean, couldn't she sort of shuttle around? It'd make it easier."

She stared at me, thinking. "There were two sisters. The rest were brothers. Two killed in the war. One sister vanished. The other married, but doesn't want the dear old girl around. Husband won't have it. One brother's in the penitentiary for arson. Verne says he was a pyromaniac, a fire bug, but nobody'd believe it." She lifted her hands, let them drop loosely to her thighs. "Others just gone." Petra motioned with her thumb toward the ceiling. "She sold the farm, Verne discovered. Then one morning the people who bought it found her sitting against a fence in the cornfield, and they contacted him. He took her in." She shrugged.

Neither of us said anything for a few moments.

"Alex."

"Yes?"

"You'll never know how glad I am to see you." She got off the stool, stepped over to the table, and leaned against it with the front of her thighs. The table came to just below the rim of her red shorts. She laid her palms flat on the table top, then slowly moved them together until they touched. I smelled that perfume and my heart rocked.

"Wonder how the coffee's holding out," I said.

"Plenty where that came from." She moved away. "I'll heat it up." Her back was to me. "Alex."

"Yes?"

"Did you hear what I said?"

"Yes."

She whirled, shouted, "Good morning, Mother!"

The old woman entered the kitchen. She carried a cane. She said, "Good morning, Mr. Bland."

"She'll never say good morning to me," Petra said. "She's a witch. I wish to God—" She stopped, went and looked out one of the rear kitchen windows with her hands clenched before her. I couldn't see her face. Her voice was low, throaty. "She must be a hundred years old."

Verne's mother staggered in a meandering line over to the breakfast nook at the far side of the kitchen. She wore the same gray dress, I thought at first. Then I saw it was fresh, unwrinkled. A different one of the same style and color. Her white shawl. On her feet were carpet slippers that folded out at her ankles. The only sound as she walked was a faint shuffle and the light rap of the cane.

"Petra, I'm hungry." The old woman's voice was full of wavers; it trembled and it was very faint. "I'll just have a little tea. Some soda crackers in milk."

Petra watched her without expression.

"Warm the milk."

I said, "Petra, d'you get a paper?"

"It's on the front porch. I didn't bring it in yet." As she looked at me, her eyes spoke, trying to say something. "Go look around, Alex. I'll be with you in a few minutes."

As I left the kitchen I heard the old woman say, "Bet you gave Jenny the day off."

"Shut up!" Petra said. But she didn't say it loud enough for Verne's mother to hear.

I found the paper and settled down in what looked like Verne's study, across the hall from the living room. He had a large desk, so I sat there and spread the paper out on the desk. The books in the bookcases looked somehow too neatly arranged to have been read lately.

I wondered what spot on the wall Verne beat his head against after he'd locked the door.

Beyond large windows, autumn was violent with color. A red maple stood close beside the study and its leaves looked as if they had been sprayed with blood. I tried to read the paper. It was no go.

The desk was clear save for a large, unstained blotter, a single pencil, and a framed picture lying face down. I looked at the picture and it was of Petra. A full-length shot. She was lying in a hammock, with one leg dangling, her hands behind her head. Without thinking, without realizing it for a moment, I suddenly knew I wanted the picture. She smiled out at me. I had to have the picture. It was a strong, abrupt desire, and for an instant conscience, will, everything vanished. Then I laid it carefully face down again and stepped away from the desk.

"Did you like it, Alex?"

I whirled. Petra was standing in the door, leaning against the jamb. She held her arms up, tying a white ribbon around her hair, so it bunched at the back of her head.

"Yes. It's a fine shot of you."

"Verne took it. The hammock's still there, too. Only nobody uses it any more. It stayed out there all last winter. It's faded now, but it used to be very bright."

"I'm afraid the hammock doesn't count much in that picture."

She knew what I meant, but she said, "How do you mean?"

I smiled and she smiled. Her hair looked fine tied up that way and we stood that way staring at each other for a long moment.

I heard nothing, but I saw the listening in Petra's eyes. She turned slowly. The old woman's voice reached me thinly from the hall. "That milk was sour, Petra. I don't like sour milk."

"She spies," Petra said. "Oh, God, Alex. She's a witch."

As she moved out into the hall, I noticed for the first time that she wore a red wrap-around skirt over her shorts. It swung at the hem, pendulous, as she strode off.

I went over to the desk and looked at the picture again. I had an overpowering desire to steal it, but I laid it back down on the desk and left the room quickly.

The hallway was dim. Madge Collins. A nice name. Chicago. Madge had blonde hair, dark blonde hair. Her eyes sometimes were blue, sometimes gray. Slim, she was always neat, crisp, quick-moving. She had thousands of sisters, in all parts of the world. Lined up, they would possibly be hard to tell apart. But she was mine and I wanted her always to be mine. Because I knew the woman beneath the crisp exterior. I remembered the letter I'd written to her, and headed for the stairs.

Petra. She stood alone. There was nobody like Petra. One image was made, then the gods shattered the cast. Why?

Halfway up the stairs, I glanced at my watch. Ten-thirty. I wanted a drink. Well, I was on a vacation, so why shouldn't I have a drink if I wanted one? I'd intended to see about mailing the letter to Madge. It could wait. I went back downstairs into Verne's study, because I'd remembered seeing a decanter of whisky on a shelf beside one of the bookcases.

There was no glass. For the first time since I'd left the Army, I drank straight from a bottle. It warmed me and I felt better. Some of the panic that had started growing with morning subsided.

The picture was not on the desk.

My hand shook as I replaced the glass stopper in the decanter and returned it to the shelf. Verne's study was directly beneath my bedroom. Somebody was moving around up there.

Now that I'd drunk the straight whisky, I wanted some water. There was another door in the study. I went over and opened it, expecting a closet. Beyond was a music room, with a baby grand piano, a large leather couch, a record player, and a case stacked with records. There was one window hung with crisp white curtains. The air was stale. I opened the window and autumn breathed on me. It was like summer, only the smell was autumn and blue skies and beyond the edge of an apple orchard colorfully splotched hills rose to a sharp horizon. There was dust on the window sill.

Dust powdered against my fingers when I touched the piano keys. The record player had been shut off halfway through a now dusty record, the arm and needle somehow evocative of a contented past abruptly severed. The record was Debussy's Abrabesque Number 1 in E Major. That was not Verne. It might once have been Petra; it might still be. Yes. It was possible. It was not haphazard selection; not with the library of records in this room.

I went on through the door leading from the music room. A small alcove with a small couch in it led into the main hallway beneath the stairs. I felt myself wishing my own record collection was one tenth as large as the one in this house. I knew I was trying to force my thoughts into other channels— anything so I would not think of that woman.

It was all foolishness. Less than a day ago I would have laughed at anyone who had said he felt as I did.

Once, when I was very young, I had wanted to play the piano; wanted to learn how very much. I saved money and took lessons. But I knew my folks wouldn't hear of such a thing. As I accomplished each lesson and sought out pianos to play on—because we didn't have one—I knew eventually I'd be found out. It would end. Something would happen.

That's how I felt now, only much worse, much more strongly. It had been the same when I tried to paint. I painted anyway, but my family talked me out of that, too. Consequently, I never learned to do anything I really wanted to do. Because I thought there was nothing left. And then it was too late; I felt it was too late. My father died and surprised me by leaving me some money. I'd always had a slight interest in old relics and Indian mounds, so I went and studied archaeology. It was, I decided at first, my way of escaping the knowledge that I had failed to do what I wanted. By taking an opposite. Picks, shovels, brushes, maps, mules, bones, and rusty iron. But I had fun, too, and then I had my dream about the museum and now that was my life. So I had really found what I really wanted.

As I started up the stairs again, Petra called to me as she came along the hall. "Alex. Come on. We'll take a ride." She paused, smiling, and her knee parted the slit in her red skirt. She was wearing red sandals. She painted neither her toenails nor her fingernails.

"I'd like to mail a letter," I said.

"Yes. Well, we'll ride into town, how's that? Have to take the old gal along. Hope you don't mind."

"Sure." I could feel myself relax.

"Yes. Then we'll come back here and eat. I'd like to show you around. Tomorrow we'll go to the lake."

"Be right with you." I hurried upstairs and into my room to get Madge's letter from beneath the blotter.

The picture of Petra lay face up on the center of the desk. Something tense and slow tightened inside my chest, like black thread slowly winding on a spool.

I got the letter to Madge, found my pipe and tobacco pouch, and went on downstairs.

Petra and the old lady waited in the hall. "Ready?" Petra asked.

"Yes," I told her. "I'm ready."

The old woman watched Petra, and her eyes glowed in the daytime just as they did at night.

Chapter Six

We drove between hills through autumn. Petra had insisted that I sit in front with her. Verne's mother was perched in the middle of the back seat. Twice I looked around at her expressionless yet sly face. I wanted to mention the picture. Several times I nearly did, but I couldn't, quite. I felt she knew. It was a large car, black, a Buick. Petra drove at a steady sixty.

"We couldn't talk so well with her up here, you see?"

"I guess that's right. If she doesn't mind."

"She put up a fuss. But what the hell?" She glanced at me. Each time she moved her right leg, the skirt parted a bit more. I avoided looking toward her, but I felt compelled to.

"It's so nice to ride," Verne's mother said. "We take one every day, hey, Petra?" The laugh. The dry rustling of leaves with chipmunks or mice skittering among them. "Hey, Petra?"

"Yes!" Petra shouted. She was biting her lip and the car's speed increased. Then we were in the small town of Allayne. A long, elm-shrouded main street. The business section was about four or five blocks long. We went to the post office and I mailed the letter to Madge. Allayne seemed a quiet, peaceful town. There was a courthouse with a silver dome and the sun gleamed on it. The clock on the city hall read eleven-thirty as we headed back out of town.

"Wonder how Verne's making out," I said.

"Don't bother," Petra said. "I mean, don't trouble yourself about him. You're on a vacation, remember? Verne's had bad luck. He'll have to work it out himself."

"I wish there were something I could do."

"There's nothing. There's the lake, over there—see?" She nodded toward the left. A faint patch of blue water showed momentarily between two hills, like a sliver of glass. "We'll go there tomorrow. We'll have to take her with us." The car's speed increased.

"Probably her only pleasure."

"No, Alex. Her pleasure is spying on me. She follows me around. She hates me."

"Why?"

"I don't know why. She's bad, evil, Alex. I wish to God she'd die—die!"

"She will," I said.

"Now, though, now."

"She's just a harmless old woman, Petra. Sometimes old people become dominant, like that." I wasn't saying exactly what I meant. I wasn't saying that I wanted to reach out and touch her hair. . . .

"She's vicious. I'm a nurse, that's all, a nurse. Left out here with that harridan." She laughed and we didn't speak again until she parked the car behind the house by the garage. Then she said, "You'll see what I mean about her. You can't help but see."

We both helped the old woman out of the car. Petra leaned close to me with her arm outstretched, and for one long moment her right breast pressed full, round, and hard against my arm. At the instant of contact she looked straight at me and her eyes said, Yes, yes, yes!

I turned, went into the house. I wanted to run. I went into the study and had a drink and closed my eyes and saw the red taillight of the taxi winking around the corner.

"She saw that."

I turned. Standing in the doorway, Petra watched me.

"Who saw what?"

"Mother. She saw that at the car." Her eyes were bold. She was too bold, yet at the same time oversecretive. All wrong. "You'll see now," she went on. "There'll be no rest."

"I don't know what you mean," I lied. She was making something out of nothing.

"Yes. We touched and she saw it."

"Oh, that. It was—"

She smiled. "You *do* know, don't you? I was beginning to think you were immune." She unhooked her red skirt, ripped it off savagely. "It's too hot for this. Yes, you know, and she saw it all. She's got eyes like a cat. There'll be trouble now."

"But, Petra!"

"You don't know her, I tell you. She makes mountains out of molehills."

"Aren't you doing just that, Petra?"

She dampened her lips with her tongue, shook her head slowly. "I'm afraid not, Alex." Turning, she vanished from the study doorway. I heard her walking down the hall.

> ... and Alex, it's almost like writing to a lover. Because I have no lover, you see. But then, I shouldn't talk like that, should I? Verne says you embarrass easily.

> ... feel lonely? I mean, among trees, like, when even others are around? Chicago can't be lonely, though, can it? Funny you aren't married. Verne says you're quite a guy with the gals! That why? I mean, I'll bet you have some time!

> ... mind my writing so often? It's really nice here, but it's rather quiet, though I like the quiet. There's a big old apple orchard behind the house where I walk. Let you in on a secret, Alex. I talk to you there. I mean, you know what I mean. Verne isn't much for talking—much for doing some of the things I like to do. We do wish you'd come, Alex.

And that afternoon I saw the apple orchard.
"Take my hand."
"What?"
"Take my hand, I say."
Her fingers were tense, her palm slightly damp, warm.
"We'll cross the creek here, on these stones. We can both go at once. Come on, Alex."
It was a small creek, twisting below a knoll at the edge of the orchard. Beyond was a grassy knoll sparse with hickory trees and, from where we stood, three pines.
"I thought you wanted to show me the orchard."
"Come on, Alex. Cross the creek."
We did. Twice our bodies brushed.
We started through the trees over the knoll. There were more pines and a large sycamore.

"We'll go on the other side of that knoll," she said. There was something abrupt, terse, in the tone of her voice. "It's cooler there. See? It's cooler already. A breeze comes down off the hills. Always that way. Hurry."

"But Petra—"

She didn't release my hand. We reached the top of the knoll. From where we stood the house showed only in red-bricked tiny patches of distance between trees. It was cool and shady, which was good, because the afternoon sun was very hot as it sometimes is in Indian summer.

We paused and she turned to me and said, "Kiss me, Alex." Her hair streamed to one side of her head, thick and full of vagrant sunlight. Her lips glistened, her eyes were molten black.

"Petra . . ."

"Please, Alex. Don't wait now. Talk later, if you must, but kiss me. Don't lie. You want to and I want you to. Don't wait, I couldn't bear that now, Alex!"

"Petra!"

She rushed against me. I stepped back, but I was against the trunk of the sycamore. She pressed against me, her hands moving slowly along my throat, her head flung far back, eyes wide, lips parted.

"Alex!"

Her lips were all-yielding, her body strained, tense, hot with nervousness; her fingers bit into my shoulders. I felt the moving curve of her back and the whole vibrant length of her as my mouth closed over hers.

Then I had her against the tree. Her mouth slid away from mine along my cheek as she pushed away from me, her hands pushing against my chest, and she moaned.

I stepped back. "Petra, good Lord!"

She watched me, leaning back against the trunk of the tree. Her lips were parted as she breathed, her eyes heavy-lidded. Her hands lay on either side of her against the tree trunk, trembling. "It's as I thought," she said. "Just as I thought. As I knew it would be."

I should have struck her then. I should have struck her and run. Because the fuse was lit now—the long hot fuse that would blow me straight to hell.

Chapter Seven

She did not move from against the trunk of the sycamore. My own breathing was as sharp as hers. "Petra," I said. "Why? What happened to you?"

"It was the waiting, I guess. That's all."

"The waiting?" She was making too much of a kiss. But perhaps I was, too.

"Yes, the waiting. We both wanted that, we both want more. It's been silly to waste so much time. Time is too precious."

"But you're Verne's wife."

"Yes. Verne often said you were his best friend, maybe the only real friend he ever had. Because you disregarded things other men wouldn't put up with. So he never had any real friend, other than you. I'm his wife, yes. But you and me—that's something different again."

"Then why did you push me away?"

"Because—not all at once."

"Petra, this means I'll have to leave. It couldn't possibly go on."

She laughed. Shortly. Then she threw her head back and laughed still harder. She sobered. "You won't go, Alex. I won't let you."

"Petra—"

"You wanted that. You want more—you want me, and you know it. Why be childish?"

We stared at each other. The sharp shadows of leaves lay across her bare legs, her red halter and shorts, her arms, and sunlight still sought and found her hair.

"You're very bold."

"Am I? Listen, Alex. I've felt like this for over two years and you tell me I'm bold. Why did you come here? To play checkers with that shell of a man? With what actually never was, never will be? He's shot, Verne is." She smiled. "Don't tell me that. You read my letters, you aren't blind."

She stepped up to me and took my hand, lifted it, laid my palm in her hair. My fingers clutched instinctively, but I jerked my hand away.

"There," she said. "You wanted that, didn't you?"

"Petra. That picture. Why did you put that picture on the desk in my room?"

"Because you wanted that, too." She moved closer to me, stared at me, and the faint, elusive odor of her perfume recalled three years of jasmine-scented mail. "I watched you," she said. "You ate it up with your eyes, Alex. It was all you could do to put that picture of me down on the desk—where Verne laid it face down after he picked it up from the floor, where he'd thrown it." She paused. "You know," she said, glancing away, "I think you really wanted to steal it."

I grabbed her waist and she chuckled. "Really, Alex. I mean that. You were like a small boy all alone in a candy store."

I flung her arm down, turned, and started down the knoll toward the creek.

"Wait!"

I waited. She reached me. "Admit it."

"I won't admit anything."

"Verne told me about you—about how honest you are, to the point of mania, almost. All right, you're like that. You're too serious and you're overhonest. Then you're probably being tortured right now. You admit it!"

I hit her. Across the face with the back of my hand. She moved with the blow like a boxer. I hit her again, the heel of my hand bouncing off her cheek.

"Yes," she said. "I was right. Do you see now why it was silly to wait? I was going to wait. Take my time. Because I didn't want to frighten you off. Verne being your friend, and all that rot. Go ahead, hit me again. It won't change anything."

"Only one day," I said.

"No. That's just it, Alex. It isn't one day. It's over three years. Two years, anyway, and that's long enough. Too long." Something came into her eyes, something like tears, only they couldn't be tears, and she walked rapidly away down the knoll.

I watched her cross the creek, then I crossed. She didn't wait for me until she was nearly through the orchard. Then she waited and we walked through the ankle-deep grass together.

"Will you take my hand again?" she said softly.

"No. I won't take your hand. Now or ever."

She looked at me and smiled. "O.K. Straighten out now, Alex. I told you she had eyes like a cat. We're in sight of the house."

I closed and locked the door to my room and sat on the bed. I could still taste her lips, feel them, tremulous, surrendering, and offering and giving all at the same time.

But this wasn't all of it. I felt this wasn't all. A kiss—a mere single afternoon kiss. Nothing more?

God, yes. Too much more always. The all-impending more that lay even beyond imagination.

As I stripped my clothes off, I realized I was soaked with perspiration. And I knew with a sensation of conscious guilt that the only reason I hadn't taken Petra out there this afternoon was because she was Verne's wife. I had wanted her, I wanted her now.

I had come that close to taking her—beneath the sycamore, on the knoll.

It was bad enough now. I had to leave. I couldn't stay on, not with that . . . And yet, she pushed me away from her.

"Because—not all at once."

I went in and took a shower and shaved and came back to the bedroom. I dressed. I put on a pair of crepe-soled shoes, the same gray flannels, and a clean white shirt. I looked through my shirts. They were all white. I wasn't a very colorful fellow. Just a guy who had damn near attacked his best friend's wife. No, not attacked. It wouldn't have been that. Or would it?

I was combing my hair when somebody knocked at the door. I opened the door.

"Hello, Alex. This came for you. It was in the mailbox. I guess nobody looked this morning."

It was from Madge. In a white envelope. There was no perfume. Only a faint trace of powder, and a very faint smudge of lipstick where she had dampened the flap with her tongue.

I felt her hand on my arm.

"Don't," I said.

"All right." Her hand went away. She wore a white dress and it fitted like a white glove. With the black of her hair and eyes, and the dark red of her lips, and everything, she was a very beautiful woman.

"I'm sorry I hit you."

"It's all right. Only swollen a little. See?"

"I don't want to see."

"All right."

"But I'm sorry. I shouldn't have done it."

"You were talking to me that way, that's all. It was the only way you could tell me without committing yourself by voice."

"Look out, or I'll hit you again." I didn't smile and neither did she. We looked at each other, then I looked down at the envelope in my hand. I tapped it against my other hand.

"So her name's Madge?"

"Yes."

"How nice. Is it too bad you had to meet me?"

"No. It's not too bad."

"You're still trying not to admit it."

"I'm not trying not to do anything."

She smiled now and she was a bold, beautiful woman.

"I'll have to leave," I said. "I'm trying to be honest."

"You don't have to try, darling."

"Don't call me that. I mean it. I'd better leave now, tonight." I really meant it. Just holding the letter from Madge was enough, and with Verne, too. "Verne is my friend," I said. "I know you don't understand. I don't ask you to. I wouldn't have understood myself once. But I do now. Maybe it's wrong, but it's how I feel."

"You have the most peculiar way of admitting things."

"I told you I wasn't admitting anything."

"Well, for the very reason that Verne is your friend—for the very reason that you two went through a war together, and saved each other's lives, and all that—that's why you can't leave, Alex."

"Can't I?"

"No. Don't be thick as well as honest, damn you!" She wiped her palms on her hips, then pushed her hair back. When she released her hair, it flowed around her shoulders like black smoke. Something was happening inside me; something I couldn't control.

"What do you mean, 'thick'?"

"What would Verne think if you left now? What would that old witch tell him? He's suspicious, Alex, as it is. He's kept me cooped up here. I've never been able to go anyplace. If you left now, he'd know. How would you feel then? Your bloody conscience would knock you dead."

She kept jamming that knife home. But all the time, I knew it wasn't that alone. I knew there was something else. But she was right about Verne—what he might think about us.

I said, "I told Verne I should go back home."

"But he said not to, didn't he?"

"You're crazy to try something like this."

"I'm not trying anything. It's there, that's all."

"What's the matter with Verne?"

"His business has got him down. He's knocked himself out. Listen, you don't know what I've been through. I'm watched by that old woman. Watched all the time. I never see anybody. I'm all alone in this lousy house with that crawling old woman!"

"Take it easy. Why don't you go out?"

"Because Verne says I have to be with her." She placed both palms against the sides of her face and sucked in her cheeks. Her voice was very low; she was obviously keeping it under control with effort. "Wherever I go, whatever I do, have done, for years, she's with me. I'll go mad, Alex. Oh, God, I'll go mad!"

"You must have done something to—"

Petra turned. The old woman was slowly climbing the stairs. Just the top of her head showed, ascending into our line of vision with an almost awesome slowness.

"Quick," Petra said. "Close the door. And for God's sake, forget about leaving!" She went off down the hall. I closed the door on her perfume, but some of it oozed in with me. A funny thing. She wore so little of it that if you tried to smell it, you couldn't. Yet it was always there, faint, elusive.

So now we were both hiding from the old woman.

I ripped open Madge's letter. There were two blank sheets of paper. No. At the bottom of the second sheet in very small handwriting she had written:

> Dearest Alex,
> Fill these pages in with all the things you'd like to have me say and write often. I will, too.
>
> > All my love,
> > MADGE

Great. The one time I needed every word she could possibly send and she played jokes. But I knew the letter had been mailed probably at the same time I left Chicago. It was just her way of saying, "Have a good time."

And she would write every day. So if I left now, letters would start arriving and keep arriving for three days after I reached Chicago. Probably. And Petra would read them. And Petra might reply to Madge. Yes, the return address was on the envelope. So there I was figuring myself into a mess, as usual.

I went over to the desk and wrote a two-page lie to Madge about how wonderful everything was and how grand she was, sealed it in an envelope, and stuck it under the blotter.

All the time I'd been writing the letter, Petra smiled at me from the hammock with her leg dangling.

She was right about Verne. If he'd been the way she said, then he'd be certain something had happened if I left now.

I went over and stood by the front window at the corner of the house and looked at the failing afternoon. It still wasn't late. A truck went by with some crates of chickens rattling in the back. Then two girls rode by on bicycles with one of them waving her hand and talking loudly. Then two closed cars went by. Then there was a roar and a hot rod fogged past and leaves rushed in wild eddies on the black-top road. As this last one faded away, the countryside seemed unduly quiet, like the sudden stillness after an explosion. The sky was clear and then somebody fired a rifle. The sound rattled around for a few seconds among the hills, then vanished.

I couldn't leave now. Outside, the red maple was very bloody.

All right, then why did Verne act like that, what had she done?

Cut it out, I told myself. All the excuses keep popping up and all of them are the ones you want because they'll make you stay. You want to go but you want to stay. You know it's not the right thing, but you make excuses so it *will* be the right thing. Then when it's all right, you'll believe it and your conscience will almost believe it. But not quite.

I put my hands on the window sill and leaned my forehead against the wooden bottom of the open window. It rattled slightly but it was cool and the pressure was good.

Once many years ago—many years as the leaves are crisped by time and the price of butter rises and other wars lurk in global focus—once many years ago, in a town in France, there were two men. Verne and Alex. The town was Argentan, wasn't it?

Yes. We had stumbled across this bomb-shattered hospital while other bombs burst beyond and around. We were tired of it. There had been nuns there attending the wounded, I could still see all the black cloth and white and the beads. Bloody bandages and a table piled with arms and legs and things and knives and odors. But one ward hadn't been ruined; it had two walls and part of a ceiling and some iron cots in a double row. The syphilitic ward, it was. Because we were tired, the beds looked good at the time.

Only we didn't stay there long, as it kept coming to us what the room had been, was. And whether or not the odor was that, it seemed to be that, and so you didn't want to stay there long even if you could hardly walk for being tired.

Verne called as he ran into the ward where I had fallen asleep, "Roll out, man. C'mon. I struck oil!"

So I dragged myself out of the ward and down the stairs, where I just missed stepping on a hand, and around back of the remains of the hospital.

"Through here." Verne said. He climbed through a shell hole in the side of the building and dropped out of sight into blackness. I walked around and into the cellar door, down a dirt embankment, and found him sitting in mud, drinking from his helmet.

"They missed this one." he said. "They shot the others full of holes, but they missed this one."

There were about eight of them. Barrels that held thousands of gallons. The mud was wine mud, ankle-deep. As he said, they had missed one barrel. Some of the wine was still coming from a couple of the broken barrels, so it hadn't been long ago.

I turned the spigot and filled my canteen cup. It was good wine and I said, "This will hold us for a time." We drank heartily.

It was red wine. We tried to figure out how they got the barrels down there, but gave up. Either they built the hospital without a wall, then brought in the barrels and sealed the wall, or they dug a cellar, placed the barrels in, and built a hospital around them.

"It's better than an emergency dynamo in case the lights fail," Verne said.

"Yes. There'd be no need for lights."

"Hell. I'm rubbing it in my hair, see? Imagine!"

"Very wasteful."

"I suppose you're right."

It was red wine and it was aged just right.

"Maybe they left this one barrel for a reason," I said, taking a long drink from the cup. My cup was a plastic one so the wine didn't taste bad. It wouldn't have tasted bad anyway.

We looked at each other. "You mean," Verne said, "maybe they put something into it, like Borgia?"

"Thou wert once too august for adoration," I quoted.

I refilled my cup and Verne drank from his helmet.

We mused above the wine. It was an aromatic drinking place. After a while we were drunk. We were brothers. Sharing was wonderful.

"We share the wine," Verne said. "If I have a wife, we'll share her, too. Do you have a wife, Alex?"

"No."

"Well, we'll share her, won't we?"

"Certainly. Are many wives better than one?"

"I think one wife is best."

"One at a time."

"Yes."

"On a share basis."

A piece of the hospital that we couldn't see went away with a loud noise and the empty barrels rocked. Plaster and dust fell into my cup. Verne dumped his helmetful over his feet and refilled the helmet from the wooden spigot. He couldn't stand very well. Whenever he got really drunk he fell all the time. It was bad when there was snow on the ground. Once I saw him crawl on his hands and knees for quite a distance along the Champs Elysées. He said the air felt cold, and since it was raining he'd take no chances.

We had been through a long war and there was still more to come and we were tired and drunk and we were brothers.

"You'll see," Verne said. "I will marry a beautiful wife. You'll visit with me and she will warm your bed."

"Thank you, brother," I said.

But he hadn't meant that, really. And he hadn't remembered, and here I was. I glanced over at the picture of Petra in the hammock on the desk.

How very much Verne had changed! He wasn't the same man now. Something terrible had happened to him. I didn't know him at all as he was now.

She smiled out at me from the hammock with her leg dangling. I went over and turned the picture face down. Then I went out into the hall.

I walked around the stair well and down the upstairs hall toward a door at the far front of the house. This room would be opposite mine, but where my door opened just beyond the top of the stairs, this one opened next to the end of the hall. The door was open.

It was a large room, and the moment I hesitated by the door, I knew whose room it was. Hers. The perfume, among other intangibles, told me. Excitement and panic both crowded my chest. It was a feeling I had never experienced before. The room was empty. She wasn't there. I didn't want to enter, I forced myself against it. It seemed, as I stepped inside, that I was invading the privacy of her flesh itself. Everything in that room read Petra. To the left, along the whole front wall of the house, were huge windows, reaching from ceiling to floor, casement windows. They were screened on the outside, and their inside surface was hung with draped curtains of a peculiar red-and-black color conglomerate. The walls were a deep shade of red-violet, the ceiling a rich, allusive midnight conventionalized by neither stars nor moon. A large room, made to order—ordered by a woman laden with sensuality.

I stared down at the rug's thick nap. It snuggled against the baseboards of all four walls, a heady, unbelievable auburn glinting in errant light like the coat of a freshly slain animal.

I was drawn into the room as I was being drawn to Petra. It was like standing in a vacuum that had become feverish, the airless air writhing against itself in a kind of savage, futile bewilderment, like two newly awakened lovers in the dark.

The bed was large, half again normal size, with thick brown leather headboard and footboard, the spread of the same deep red-violet as the walls. All the furnishings—a table, a desk, three chairs, a small couch to the right of the door, and an immense dressing table—were of the same glowing brown leather. Not masculine, either; feminine. Delicate and heady, like the fine-beaded whisky of the last century. The sprawling mirror over the dressing table was auburn-tinted and as clear as a tropical summer's twilight.

An exciting room. A sensuous and sensual room. A room of wantonness and lurking sin.

I turned and left, rapidly, and as I approached the stairs I found myself wanting more air, wanting above all to escape. But I knew then that I would not escape.

I had seen my face in that huge tinted mirror and it had been the face of a stranger—a stranger who was already running backward on a forward-racing treadmill; a stranger afraid.

We had supper that evening at a table on the flag-stoned patio in front of the house, directly beneath Petra's room. The patio was surrounded by tall hedges. Petra and I talked mechanically, but her eyes—and probably mine, too—spoke a different tongue.

She said only one disrupting thing, and that was as we rose from the table. Her arm brushed mine. She turned and said, "I wonder what Madge would think, Alex." Then she walked away.

I followed, and behind us both I heard the light, rapid shuffle of the old woman's carpet slippers and the abrupt tap, tap of her cane. I wondered about that cane. She didn't always have it with her, obviously didn't really need it. I began to feel watched, as Petra said *she* was.

Again, as Petra and I walked down the inside hall, she turned and said, "Oh, God. I wish that old crow was dead!"

That night she came to my room.

Chapter Eight

I had been in bed about an hour wondering why I hadn't locked the door when the door opened. I knew then why I hadn't locked it.

Moonlight sprayed in the windows on the side of the room where the head of my bed was. As she entered, she said nothing. She simply closed the door. And I lay stiffly beneath a single sheet.

She turned. "Hello, Alex."

I didn't answer. She wore a thigh-length nightgown as thin as gauze. I later found out the color of it was red; you couldn't tell in the moonlight. She was the most gorgeous thing I'd ever seen as I watched her long white legs gleam toward me and the bed.

"I had to see you," she said.

"Get out, Petra!"

The short nightgown folded inward beneath her thrusting breasts and fell to a rustling caress against her hips. She sank slowly to the bed, crossed her legs, and smiled at me. The moonlight was over my shoulder, full on her. The bed sank with her weight, and the full warmth of her hip pushed against my leg. There was that sheet between us. I hauled myself back against the head of the bed, pulling the sheet with me.

Her hand snagged the sheet, tore it down to my waist. She chuckled. "I sleep that way too," she said. "I only put this on for you."

"Go away." It seemed to me I could hear the shuffle of carpet slippers, the rap, rap, rap of a cane.

"No."

"Petra."

"No."

She laid her hand on my arm. I didn't move. I could see her breasts clearly through the thin gown. Her thighs gleamed in an ivory curve. She later told me she liked the length of the short nightgown, that it felt like feathers tickling the tops of her legs.

"I didn't come to cause any trouble. I wouldn't worry you for the world, Alex."

"Liar." Her every breath was tantalization.

"You've got to listen," she said, and for the first time tonight I noticed the strain in her face and eyes. She wasn't smiling now, and she seemed to draw her breath in almost fiercely. She wheeled on the bed, facing me, uncrossed her legs. It only made things worse. The hem of her gown was up as far as it could go without refuting gravity. I had a sensation of being completely trapped. I tried to think of Madge, to concentrate on her.

"It's about Verne," she said quietly.

"Suppose his mother finds us here."

Her fingers bit into my arm. "Don't say it!"

I listened to her breathe.

"I want to tell you this. There's nothing wrong with me, only I'm too much for him."

"Too much?"

"Yes." She didn't say it, she breathed it. "He couldn't keep me—happy. Now he doesn't even try."

"You mean—" I tried to move away from her on the bed, but every movement only brought her closer. "You mean Verne's like that because of you?"

"Yes. He's sapped. He's dead weight. He can't do anything any more."

I thought of tales of the succubus.

"He keeps me cooped up here. Yet he offers me nothing—nothing of what I need. Must have. I'm not crazy."

"Why are you telling me this?"

"Because I love you, Alex. I want you to know. And you love me, you know you do."

"My God, woman, you're off your rocker."

"Don't say that!" Her fingers bit into my arm again. "It's not what you think. Verne tried—hard. But he didn't really love me, ever."

My voice was hoarse; I hardly recognized it. The smell of her perfume, the warmth of her body . . . "Why don't you divorce him?"

"And lose all this? His money? He's going to die. I could kill him myself, I think. Merely by—His heart is weak. He—"

I tore her hand off me, started up in the bed, grabbed the sheet, began to sweat. "Get out, Petra!"

"Listen! You've got to listen. He wouldn't let me divorce him anyway. He wants me here, he wants to torture me." Her voice was a shrill whisper now, her hands against my chest. She leaned closer. I felt her thick hair brush my shoulder as her face neared mine. "I watched him fade away. Bad business lately has helped. He's losing weight steadily. I love you, Alex! Don't you see? Are you blind? I've loved you for months."

"You've never—We never saw each other till yesterday, Petra."

"We didn't have to. My letters told you."

My hand brushed her thigh. I jerked it away and it struck her breasts. She grabbed it and held it there in the soft dark valley between her breasts. I could feel her breath, taste the odor of her perfume, hear the sound of our bodies touching.

"You wrote me regularly," she whispered. "You must have known. Don't pretend you didn't know. Don't pretend anything. I can't bear it, Alex. We've got to face this thing. We can't escape."

"Good Lord, Petra!"

"Yes."

She came down against me then and my arms circled her, pulling her to me. Her lips brushed mine, then she tugged savagely away, her knee on the bed, pushing.

"Petra!"

"Not now. We can't. That old hag!"

My fingers clutched at her nightgown. She slapped my hand away. I had to have her now.

"We must wait for that!"

She was up, standing beside the bed, her breasts rising and falling in the moonlight.

"Petra. Is this true?"

"Yes. You saw my husband. He's a dead man already."

I stared at her, wanting her, frightened, wanting her, wanting to run, escape.

She bent over the bed, over me, and her hair fell across my face as her mouth met mine. She fell away from the bed, started for the door. "There," she said. "You may leave now, if you wish. If you can." She stood by the door. "But don't forget what I said about Verne. There have been no other men, though I tried once. I was desperate. Nothing happened, but Verne caught me. Now, leave, if you can."

She was gone. The door was closed. The air was full of her presence. The sheets were damp and cold.

An instant later I heard her talking loudly in the hall. I went to the door. "Get to bed, Mother!" she shouted. "What are you doing?"

"Harlot! Harlot!" the old woman shrieked.

I opened the door a crack.

"I shan't tell him. Not yet," the old woman said.

Petra was walking swiftly toward her room. Her door slammed. The old woman stood in a flannel nightgown in the hallway, her thin gray hair wisping about her tiny, sly face. Her arms quivered like reeds. She turned and shuffled off. I closed the door and returned to my bed.

I didn't sleep until the first faint gray feelers of dawn touched the floor through the front windows. And I had discovered that I no longer wanted to leave this house.

She was torturing me, but I'd have her. Somehow. If I had to take her by force. Perhaps that's what she wanted. I knew it was wrong. My conscience was like a rasping steel file sawing back and forth inside me. But I refused to listen. And I would refuse. I had to.

When I woke I felt different. I remembered, but I felt wrong. I decided to fight. I'd stay and fight. And though I knew it was the right thing to shut up about everything, I figured I'd have a talk with Verne.

But Verne might not be home for days.

Chapter Nine

Verne called at ten. Petra spoke with him a few moments, then turned to me in the hallway. "He wants to talk to you, Alex."

The old woman was eating breakfast in the kitchen.

"All right," I said. I took the receiver from her hand. She didn't move from beside me, pressed against me. Her hand smoothed my back. She smiled, then moved away.

"Alex! How's everything?"

I was startled at the tone of his voice. He seemed full of life, very different from the way he'd been when he'd left.

"Fine," I said. "Everything's fine. Only I wish to God you were here."

"That's what I'm calling about. Sorry to hell and gone, but I won't be able to make it till sometime Saturday."

Saturday! This was Wednesday. No, Tuesday. Not until Saturday. Petra was standing down the hall, nodding at me. She wore a black skirt, a tight white blouse, and a yellow ribbon in her hair. As I stared at her, she tucked the blouse more securely into the waist of her skirt, smoothed it out.

"I'm sorry, old man," Verne said. "But that's the way it is. Things are bad down here. I had a minor strike on my hands, had to increase wages. Got ten truckloads of lumber not fit to build an outhouse with. Had to return that. Found out my head man was knocking down. Had to fire him and hire another, and the government's got some damned new clause . . ."

"Cripes," I said. Then I realized this was my chance. My chance to leave and to explain at the same time. It would be bad enough that way, but it would be lots easier than staying and standing what might come. I looked straight at Petra and showed her my teeth. She sensed something. "Look, Verne," I said. "It's great here and everything, but why don't I go on back home and wait till you get things—"

He interrupted sharply. His voice seemed snappy, full of power, aggressive. "Wouldn't hear of it. Don't suggest it again. If anything, you're going to stay over longer!"

Petra was watching me. At first her eyes had narrowed, but now she saw my face fall and she smiled again.

I knew I couldn't insist. I felt I couldn't. I didn't want to make him suspicious in any way. So now I was thinking like that.

"All right, Verne. Get home as soon as you can. We haven't even got drunk together yet."

"Yeah. Well, I've got to scram now, Alex. Keep the ball rolling. You get Petra to show you around."

"Sure, I will."

"How's Mother?"

"Fine. She's fine."

"Say. I forgot to pay Jenny and the cook. Will you tell Petra we owe them two weeks?"

"Sure."

"Thanks. See you Saturday."

He was gone. The line was dead.

"You see, Alex?" Petra said. "You wouldn't leave now, anyway, would you—really?"

We drove around the far side of the lake, a good twenty-five miles, ate lunch at a drive-in near Canyonville, and came up the near side of the lake.

We didn't talk much. The old woman perched as usual in the center of the rear seat. She gabbled about the scenery until it began to get me down. But just being beside Petra, watching her from the corner of my eye, and listening to the stirring tones of her voice kept me still.

"I forgot to tell you," I said. "Verne told me to tell you to pay Jenny and the cook two weeks' pay."

She didn't look at me. "Yes. All right. See, we'll park here a while. I'll take you down and show you the lake."

There were pines, and a glen that fed shallowly across the road, but showed great depth on the hillside. The lake flashed blue in the sun beyond the treetops.

"All right."

Petra turned and shouted to the old woman, "I'm going to show Mr. Bland the lake. We'll only be a minute."

The old woman moved her mouth in what looked like some kind of secret smile.

Petra's chin trembled. She opened the door on her side, ran around the car and down the slope into the trees. She ran toward the lake. Her skirt furled around her legs and her legs flashed in the early-afternoon sunlight.

She vanished into the shadows of the trees, whirled, and called, "Come on, slowpoke!"

"Be right with you." I turned to the old woman. "Excuse me," I said. "We won't be a moment." I had forgotten that she was deaf. She didn't hear me. She was watching the darker shadow of the woods where Petra had disappeared.

I went on down, following Petra's course. It was very cool. As I neared the water the air was still cooler and I could smell the water. It was a spring-fed lake, Petra had told me, and very clear and cold. Very fine for swimming if you like fresh, clear, icy water.

"It's a little late for swimming, isn't it?" I'd said.

"It's always whatever you make it."

I went into the trees along the glen with the stream of water from the glen running over black slate to my right. I came out on the shore of the lake. It was about a mile and a half wide. The larger of the three hills on the other side looked like some huge green monster, like a buffalo, perhaps, hunched over, asleep.

I didn't see Petra at first. Then she called to me from nearby, "Hurry, Alex. Hurry!"

She was standing naked on the shore of the lake.

I stood still for a long moment because I couldn't move and couldn't think. The sun shone on her back over the tops of the trees.

She faced me.

"Come here, Alex."

I took two steps, halted. "The old woman!" I said. "She'll—Petra!"

I stepped back as she ran gingerly toward me over the pebbled shore. Her hair streamed back on both sides of her head and she was beautiful, too damned beautiful. Her beauty struck me very hard without release.

"Petra!" The old woman's voice reached us from the highway, just beyond the trees.

"Oh, God!" Petra said.

I turned and ran back to the car. I stumbled and slipped over the water-black slate in the glen and once went in clear to my knee. Scrambling up the slight rise onto the highway, I reached the car. I looked back but Petra wasn't in sight. I'd never forget the way she had looked standing there on the shore of the lake with the sun gleaming like liquid gold on her white skin and her black hair flowing around her shoulders and throat like a dense, fiery fog.

Standing there by the car, I heard splashing sounds beyond the pines and other trees surrounding the lake. And standing there I cursed the old woman silently. Then I cursed her aloud, knowing she couldn't hear. I cursed her until I could think of nothing else to say. Then I climbed inside the car. The old woman was still watching the patch of shadowed woods where Petra had vanished.

Pretty soon Petra came back to the car. She was breathing hard. "Wasn't it fine!" she said.

"Yes."

I looked at her, my hand brushed her leg. Her skirt was damp. Her hair was damp. She'd been in the water.

"I went for a swim," she said. "You should have, Alex." She turned to the old woman and shouted, "I went for a swim. Don't you wish you could go swimming, Mother?"

The old woman didn't answer.

The days flicked by like the shadow from a sundial's finger as you glance at it from hour to hour. Petra put me through hell and there was no way to combat it.

If we were near the old woman, she lured me with eyes of promise and surreptitious caresses. But the instant we were alone it was all I could do to hold her in my arms.

"You want me now, don't you?"

"I'll have you."

"Stop. Here she comes."

"Petra, let's go someplace."

"We can't leave Mother alone. She'd try to follow. She's suspicious now. She's saying awful things to me."

Wednesday, Thursday, Friday—Saturday. It was the longest day, Saturday. And it was that day I realized I hadn't written Madge, nor had I mailed the other letter I had written. I went to the mailbox on the front of the house. Above it in brass scroll I read the number 13; 13 French Street. How many times had I addressed letters here?

There were three letters from Madge. I took them upstairs and laid them on the desk in my room, unopened.

The old woman was everywhere. She had become a shadow. She carried the cane always now and she hardly ever spoke in my hearing.

I wanted Petra now. I didn't understand what she was doing, why she was acting this way, when she said she loved me. She told me that all the time. "I love you, Alex," her lips and her hands speaking too, but when we were alone she became an eel.

I couldn't sleep. I suddenly realized the decanter of whisky in Verne's study was empty. On Saturday morning it was full again. I hadn't seen Jenny or the cook since the day I'd come. I asked Petra.

"I gave them some time off."

I knew I was a little out of my head now, and I looked forward to Verne's home-coming sometimes with distaste, but always a little later with the last bit of hope within me.

I didn't know what was going to happen, but I knew something was going to happen. I was slowly losing all control. Propinquity, whatever, I could not combat it. I wanted her. The gods could have thrown me women from on high, of all shapes and sizes, and they wouldn't have meant a thing. Only Petra.

When I thought of Madge, it was like another day, another year, a bygone something that had never occurred. Chicago was someplace without existence. Only Petra.

Save when my conscience ate at me. That was when I started for the bottle. Not much. Only a bit. Just enough to stave off the sudden touch of the knife edge of despair.

Once I tore Petra's blouse off. Once I fastened my fingers in her hair and told her I wouldn't let her get away.

"I'll scream, Alex. She's only in the next room. I'll scream!"

And, of course, she would have screamed, I think. I thought so then. We did not leave the house after Wednesday. The old woman wanted to take rides. Petra refused.

She seemed to be trying to work Verne's mother into a rage, also.

She was succeeding. No matter what I said now, she would only smile and say, "Wait, my friend."

I felt cowardly. I told myself I should take her.

I didn't. I waited. And I couldn't stand being alone any more. I searched her out wherever she was. I was in love with her. As much in love as a man can get.

"I think you're weak, Alex. You'll never leave now, and you can't leave, of course."

"No. I won't leave now." I looked at her. "I don't want to hurt you, Petra. But I'm going to."

"It's only been a few days. You said so yourself."

"It's been too long. Something's happened inside me."

"You must want me as much as I want you."

I grabbed her close and breathed the warmth of her hair, felt her hot red lips, and most of the time I was with her, I didn't know what I was saying. I watched her like a cat, and the old woman watched us both.

Verne came home at six o'clock on Saturday evening.

He was a changed man. He showed vitality, and some of the color had returned to his face. He would never be the man I had once known, but he didn't look wrecked now. He showed energy. His eyes were bright.

"Things went good?" I asked.

"Terrible, Alex. I only came home because you were here. Got to leave again Sunday night."

A kind of hot rage of triumphant satisfaction hit me.

We went into the living room and Petra fixed drinks. She smiled at me from behind his back and touched me whenever she passed. I wanted to hit her, smash her. But I knew I wouldn't. To me she was becoming a woman who had been denied the things she wanted; a woman of great life and laughter who had been cooped up here, where she didn't want to be. Some of this feeling gradually died as I talked with Verne.

"The whisky's good," he said. "I want a lot of it tonight. And a good dinner."

"I'm going to fix it myself," Petra said. "Steak. You like that?"

"How come?" Verne asked. He seemed slightly suspicious, and his eyes looked queer.

I said, "Petra gave Jenny and the cook some time off."

"Oh," he said. "Why, Petra? Did you pay them?"

"I paid them Monday morning."

"They haven't been here since?"

"No." She became defiant; her eyes darkened. "If you must know, Verne, I fired them. Both of them."

He said nothing. But from that moment on I watched him sag again. Inside of an hour he was a shell again, gray-faced and forlorn.

I tried to talk with him after we ate.

"I'm bushed," he said finally. "We'll make a day of it tomorrow."

Tomorrow . . .

He went to bed, a tired, unhappy man.

"Why did you fire the help?" I asked Petra. We were in the hallway.

She put her arms around my waist. "Why do you think?" she said.

Tomorrow...

Chapter Ten

Verne wasn't up yet at ten-thirty Sunday morning. I had spent another night thinking of Petra. After breakfast I went into his study and began hitting his bottle of whisky. I got a little drunk, I think.

"Alex, come here. She's out in the kitchen."

Petra stood in the study doorway. She wore white rayon shorts and a flimsy halter and her red sandals.

"You've been drinking," she said softly as I took her in my arms. "He's leaving tonight."

"Did he come near you last night?"

She laughed. "No. Goodness, no."

My hands strayed along her hips; I held her tightly against me. Then she whirled away and ran up the stairs. I knew this was it. I started after her, the whisky pounding in my head. It was all right now. I'd found an escape. I would tell Verne the truth, tell him I was in love with his wife. That she no longer wanted him. It had to be that way.

She moved into her room along the upstairs hallway. I followed, and closed the door. The windows were open and a cool breeze blew in, billowing the curtains.

As she looked at me, something like fright came into her eyes. "Go ahead and scream," I said, as I came up to her. The whisky swarmed in my blood.

"I don't want to scream, Alex. Alex!"

Reaching out, I ripped the halter away from her breasts, baring them. She backed away, tripped on the leather couch, and sat down. I pulled her up against me. At first she tried to yank away, twisting in my arms. Then abruptly she was with me, helping me. We went wild.

"You see!" she gasped. "The waiting. It's best!"

Her lips were against mine she was talking around a kiss, and I didn't hear the door open, I heard nothing, wanted to hear nothing until the old woman said, "I caught you! I knew I would!"

We sprang apart. Petra didn't try to cover her breasts.

"I'm going to tell my son," the old woman said in her dry voice. "Harlot—sinners!" She came farther into the room, and shook her cane in the air. I wondered crazily how she managed to hold such a heavy cane in her vine-like arm.

"No, you won't!" Petra whispered. She rushed from my side across the room.

I watched, rooted to the floor—feet sunk in the thick, soft rug.

Petra grabbed the old woman by the front of her dress and they scrambled at each other. Verne's mother beat at Petra with the cane, her sly face twisted, eager. They tore at each other before the open casement window, then the old woman's body sprawled out toward the screen.

"Damn you, damn you!" Petra whispered savagely, striking at her again.

Verne's mother moaned and moaned. The cane fell, drummed against the rug. I moved then, fast, but I moved too late.

"Catch her!" I said. Petra's moving figure was between me and the old woman. The screen ripped, sang out. I heard Petra's breath indrawn on a gasp. A dry noise, almost like wind in an alley, reached us, followed by a faint thud.

Petra whirled and leaned against the window, wide-eyed, her breasts heaving. "Alex!" she said. "Alex!"

I grabbed her arm, hurled her across the room, looked out and down through the torn hole in the screen. The screen was rusted, old. Verne's mother was sprawled out in a mass of gray on the flagstones of the patio, two stories below.

A quiet wind rustled in the curtains.

"She's surely dead," I said.

As I turned, Petra began to scream. She screamed three times. Then she stopped and looked at me.

Tomorrow and tomorrow and . . . tomorrow.

Chapter Eleven

"What's the matter?" It was Verne. I heard him running down the hall, his bare feet pounding.

"Quick," I said to Petra. "Cover yourself!" I started for the door. Verne burst into the room in his pajamas, white ones. I whirled toward Petra. She was on the other side of her unmade bed with a flame-colored robe wrapped about her.

"What's the matter?" Verne repeated. "Who screamed?" His hair was mussed, his face haggard.

I started to say something, but Petra interrupted.

She pointed toward the window. "I was just getting up when she came in," she lied. Her hands went to her head. "Oh, God, Verne! She reeled against the window. Alex beat you here."

"What? What window? Who?" He stepped farther into the room and his mother's cane rolled beneath his foot. He stared at it, slowly awakening. His gaze moved to the window to his left, to the torn screen. He leaped over, stuck his head through the rent. I saw his shoulders shake.

Petra looked at me with genuine fright in her eyes.

Verne kept on looking down at the patio.

Petra said, "She just went all of a sudden, Verne. She just fell, she just reeled toward the window. I don't know what she wanted. She didn't say anything. She just—she just—she just—"

It was a great act. She sat on the bed and began sobbing uncontrollably.

Verne turned slowly, stared at me, then at Petra. He suddenly ran from the room. I heard his feet pounding on the stairs.

Petra wheeled on the bed. "Go with him, Alex!" she whispered. "Hurry! It will look bad if you don't!"

"You pushed her," I said. "You murdered her."

"No, no, no, don't be a fool. Hurry downstairs with him, Alex. Hurry, I say!"

I stared a moment longer at her beautiful face and felt the flames creeping up around my legs. Then I went after Verne.

He stood in the patio staring down at his mother. It took but a glance to know she was dead. Her head was shattered like an orange. She had landed flat on her back. Her face was in repose. Her right leg had flapped beneath her, and the toe of her right shoe projected over her right shoulder.

Neither of us spoke. Verne seemed unable to tear his gaze away, then finally he went over and sat at the round luncheon table and bit his lower lip. He ceased biting, looked up at the torn screen. Then he commenced biting his lip again.

I heard Petra behind me. She walked past me, without glancing toward the body, and stood by Verne. He didn't look at her, either.

"Verne," she said. "I don't know what to say."

"Don't say it, then."

I hadn't moved. She glanced at me, her face still, her eyes jetty and unamazed.

A fly came from nowhere, lit on the old woman's nose, crawled across her half-opened left eye on to her cheek. It stopped then. Faint wind fingered the gray dress. The fly did not move.

Verne rose, stepped around the body, started toward the front door of the house. "Phone," he said. "Phone." He looked very forlorn in his bare feet and his haggard hair and his wrinkled white pajamas.

When I glanced down again the fly was gone.

I closed my eyes. The red tail light of a taxi winked around the corner.

"You killed her."

She watched me.

"You killed her. You pushed her out of that window."

She held her hair bunched at the back of her neck and watched me, unblinking, serene. She had on a soft black dress now, and a cloud-thin white scarf was tied around her throat. "Don't be silly, Alex," she said. "You don't know what you're saying."

She was denying it. "You saw your chance," I said. "A natural. You took that chance."

We talked across the corpse. The old woman's body was between us. I was numb inside; rigid, like a plank, like a sheet of cast iron. Then somebody struck the iron with a maul. I stepped over the body toward Petra.

She whirled, pushed through some hedges, and retreated around the side of the house. I followed her, caught up, flung her against the side of the house.

"You're a bitch!" I said. "A murderous bitch!"

I held her back against the red brick side of the house. Her feet were in a flower bed, but this was fall, and things were dying. Flowers crisped beneath her feet.

"He mustn't catch us out here, Alex. Not like this."

I tightened my grip on her arms. She didn't wince. That old bold quality was there in her eyes and the turn of her lips, and it seemed then that nothing could destroy it.

"I'm going to tell him," I said. "I'll have him phone the police instead of just the doctor. What good will a doctor do? She's dead, and you killed her."

Her tongue tipped her lips and for an instant her eyes dropped. But then she looked at me more strongly than before. "No, you won't, Alex. You want me too much."

"A proud bitch, too."

"Yes, Alex. And not only that. If you started anything by telling such a story, what would they think? What would the police think?"

"You black beautiful bitch, you!"

"You love it!" She brought her hands up to my arms. I flung them down. She said, "You're as implicated as I am in this. Don't you see that? She's better off dead. But if you say anything, you'll go where I go. If it could be proved. Which I doubt. And we've waited too long already. We've told Verne one thing—we can't change it."

"Where do you get this 'we' stuff?"

"Alex, if you don't let go of me and stop acting like a fool, I'll tell Verne something. I'll tell him you did it. Because she caught you trying to attack me."

I grinned at her. Then I let go and stepped away. I started laughing. Bitter laughter. There was a defenseless old woman lying dead out there just because I'd decided to pay a visit to an old Army pal. I ceased laughing and stared at her.

Petra's fingers closed over my arm and she said, "Use your head, lover." Then she turned and walked rapidly toward the rear of the house.

I stood there and stared at the woodpecker-notched trunk of a tall pine tree in the yard. I knew I should leave now. Madge was waiting; a life that was becoming very remote was waiting. I'd been here a week, I should be planning to leave anyway. Only anyway I couldn't leave now, and I felt the stir of that inside me, too. Excuses. Reasons. Somethings. Put it off. It was easy.

I went on around toward the front again. Petra was all I'd called her and she had been right in everything she'd told me.

Verne was sitting on a chair by the circular luncheon table staring at the body of his mother. As I broke through the hedge, he glanced up, then stood and started toward the house. I followed. On the doorstep he paused and turned.

"I phoned the doctor," he said. "A hell of a lot of good it'll do to have a doctor."

"Yes. Of course. . . ."

"God," he said. "This is great for you, isn't it?"

"Good Lord, man, don't think of me." The wind blew. "I'm sorry."

The dry leaves skittered about our feet. A maple leaf crawled humpbacked with burry noise across the flagstone walk and tipped over in the grass. It reminded me of a crab scuttling.

"Did you see her fall?"

"No," I lied. He was still in his pajamas. This lie would pile on top of everything else.

"Do you think we should bring her in?" He meant his mother's body.

I didn't answer.

"I guess not. They'll—" He paused. "Alex, will you do something for me? We'll need some help out here. Take the car and run into town. Pick up Jenny, will you? She was our maid. Jenny Carson. In Allayne." He told me her address. "Will you do that, Alex? Then hurry back?"

"Sure," I said. "Can't you phone?"

"No phone." He went inside the house. "Petra's got the car keys." He called her. She'd been in the living room. As she entered the hall, she didn't look at me, only at him. He told her what he wanted. He seemed very haggard, worn out.

"Why, I'll go," Petra said. "There's no need sending—I mean, why should Alex have to go?"

"Because I asked him. Give me the keys."

Petra's eyes turned my way. She was a beautiful black bitch. "Well," she said. "I'll just run in along with Alex, then."

"I'll need you here," Verne said. "The keys!"

She got them and handed them to me. Verne started up the stairs. I headed for the front door. She ran ahead of me, got in front of me. I tried to pass her.

"Kiss me good-by," she said. "And hurry, hurry." Her eyes were a little wild and then I had her in my arms. God, oh, God, I said to myself. Her lips were hot and good, her body something I wanted to crush up against the wall. I held her so tightly she moaned. Then I flung her away.

"Lord, Alex!"

I went on out to the car and drove to Allayne. I wondered whether we were praying or cursing. Both of us. Every minute that passed snarled me up in this thing a little more. I was wading in deadly quicksand. Already it was too late to back out. Death. Murder. Sure as God.

Me. Alex Bland. Colorless and common and with a conscience that would keep five people treading the straight and narrow. Nose-to-the-grindstone Bland.

She was a sickness. I was filled with the insidious sickness of her and the only doctor was time and I wasn't sure Doc Time would do so hot with this case. Pulled one way, yanked the other. She'd waited, all right—she'd held me off, and now this. . . .

I passed a couple of cars on the road to Allayne and wondered if one of them might be carrying the doctor Verne had phoned.

The black-top road dipped and Allayne spread out before me; gray-roofed buildings beneath a roof of gray sky, church spires, the courthouse dome, and all the rust-red-green autumnal trees.

Chapter Twelve

Church bells tolled a solemn recollection of timeless Sundays spent in an apathy of occasional prayer tokening an afterward of roast chicken and mashed potatoes, stuffed stomachs and shirts, groaning couches and the geometric disarray of thick newspapers among the wailing havoc of snores, wet diapers, clanking kitchen sinks, or the shade-drawn sedate parlors where through rich cigar smoke they mumbled ritualistic weekly histories of business and how Oscar got drunk last night at the hotel bar. As I drove up Main Street people were congregating in front of the churches and it was a nice autumn Sunday for death.

The elms were disrobing now and seemed slightly ashamed of it, clutching to the last minute browning remnants of their wardrobe. I found Chapman Lane, where Jenny Carson lived, and turned down.

It was a tiny house with two tiny front windows and a very small door. There was a second story, but it looked as if you'd have to bend over to walk around up there. The house was tightly enclosed by an artificial cement-stone fence, which only made the house seem smaller still. There was a gate. The house dated 'way back, the broad, white-painted boards running vertical. There was a brass bellpull. I pulled. It tinkled.

I half expected a little old lady dressed in blue with a teacup rattling in her hand. Instead, I got Jenny. She was a different Jenny from the Jenny I'd thought I'd met out at Verne's.

"I kind of expected you'd come, Mr. Bland," she said. "Don't stand there, come in."

I followed her inside and she closed the door. A radio played quiet melodies from somewhere.

"In here," she said, leading me into a small living room. It was decked out like a studio, very clean and neat. A broad studio couch up against the far wall, with a tired but colorful blanket sleeping on it, a couple of easy chairs, a large bookcase, filled, and in one corner an easel with a painting of a nude woman partly completed on it. There was a table by the easel cluttered with paints, brushes, rags, and bottles. There was a faint odor of turpentine. Jenny went immediately to the painting and tossed a piece of cloth over it.

She turned, smiling that hesitant smile. "Simply because it's not finished," she said. "Please sit down. Why did you come?"

I stared at her, groping for a chair, and sat. Her carrot-colored hair was sort of all flung over to one side and her eyes were filled with patient questioning laughter. She wore a fawn-colored skirt and a white blouse, short-sleeved, that buttoned close around her throat. Turning, she moved over to the studio couch and sat down, crossed her legs, put her elbow on her knee, and cupped her chin in her hand. She had very broad hips and a very thin waist. One of her soft red slippers had a hole in the toe.

"Well, for goodness' sake, Mr. Bland. Don't sit there like that. What's the matter?"

"I came because of Verne, Jenny."

"Oh?"

"He wants you back." I told her about Verne's mother. I told her how she had died, only I didn't mention that Petra had pushed her. And I didn't tell her what Petra and I were trying to do at the time.

"I see," Jenny said. "Is Mr. Lawrence broken up?"

"Seems to be."

"I'm sorry, of course. That was a horrible way for the old lady to die, but—"

"But what, Jenny?"

She glanced down at the floor, then up at me again. "I rather expected it would be something like that."

"How do you mean?"

"Did Petra push her?"

"What!"

"Did Petra push her out of the window?"

"Listen," I said. "Will you come with me?"

Jenny shook her head slowly. "No," she said. "No, I wouldn't go out there again. I've had enough of that place. It was bad enough, just knowing—"

"Knowing what?"

"Mr. Bland, you know what I mean."

"Please call me Alex, and I don't know what you mean."

"All right, Alex. Yes, you do. She's got you, hasn't she?" She rose quickly, moved across the room to the corner by the windows. The radio—a small set—was on the floor. She turned it off, then stood there with her back to me, staring out the window. "You're—you're stuck like a fly in the glue," she said.

"Verne's waiting," I said. "Will you please come?"

The thought of Petra was like a cold knife getting red hot. I suddenly wanted to burst these walls and be with her. Jenny turned and looked at me.

"I'm not going with you, no. He'll have to wait."

"He needs help."

She tipped her head and smiled at me. "Yes," she said simply, "he surely needs help. A pail of arsenic would do the trick."

"Jenny!"

"I'm sorry."

I rose and something went loose inside me as I found myself staring at a telephone on the studio couch. It was a dull ache.

"Verne said you had no phone."

"Just had it installed. I have a new job now. I can afford one."

"Could I use it?"

"Sure." She didn't move. The couch was broad, as I said, so I had to crawl over after the phone and unsnarl the wires. I placed a call with long-distance for Madge Collins, at her home in Chicago. Then I hung up and sat there, waiting.

"You're sweating," Jenny said. "Running around in your shirt sleeves, sweating. I'll go get you a drink of water." She turned in front of me. "Don't peek at that painting." She turned and left the room. I watched the sway of her hips and thought of Petra. Water. I needed something stronger than water.

Murder didn't lie. I looked at my hands and they were trembling. I was in it right up to here; and "here" was a long way up. Jenny wouldn't return with me to 13 French Street. What would Verne say about that? The phone rang. I grabbed it up. And all the time I was thinking how I wanted to be back there with Petra.

Madge's slightly puzzled voice finally reached me.

"But why haven't you written? Only one letter, Al."

"That's why I'm phoning."

"But Al, I've worried."

"I know, I know. Something's come up." The couch sank beside me as Jenny sat down. She handed me a cool glass of water and I drank it down, all of it. Jenny took the glass, watching me openly, and smiling a little.

Here I was, thinking of Petra, sitting beside a very pretty girl called Jenny, talking to the girl I intended to marry, Madge. And through it all I kept seeing a gray something smashed against stone, like a broken rag doll.

"Al—Al, say something!"

"I'm sorry." I tried to think of nothing but Madge. It wouldn't work. I could taste Petra's lips. . . .

"Al—"

"Madge, darling," I said, and I didn't want to talk with her. She was too far away, too far removed from me and the things that were happening. I told her about the death of Verne's mother. "Madge. That'll mean I'll have to stay here a bit longer."

"Oh, Al! It's been long enough already. My gosh, maybe they don't want you around there—with that going on, and all."

"No, Madge. He asked me to stay." Jenny's fingers touched my arm. I glanced at her. She shook her head and clucked her tongue. She looked somehow very clean and fresh.

In my mind's eye I could see Madge standing by the phone in her hallway, looking crisp and efficient and blonde. She was Madge and right now her eyes were gray, sure as anything. She'd never act like Jenny, of the country, of hay and summer and sunshine, or like Petra, of . . . She was Madge. Jenny quietly inspected the hole in her red slipper.

"I think you should come home," Madge said.

"I can't, darling."

"You can, Al. There's no sense in your staying on. Besides, what about me? What should *I* do all this time? Just sit around and stare at walls?"

"Madge, I can't help it. I don't know how soon I'll be able to make it."

Jenny rose, went over to the paint table, and began fussing with her brushes.

"Well, all right." Madge's voice was a bit crisp. "Stay, if you must. When you can make it, let me know." She hung up. I slapped the phone in its cradle.

Jenny and I looked at each other.

"She's a fine girl," I said. "You'd like her."

"I'm sure. But she hung up on you, didn't she?"

I rose and said, "I'll leave five dollars for the phone call. If there's anything left, buy a new paintbrush."

"It's not necessary," she said.

I found a five-dollar bill and put it on the table by her easel.

"You coming with me?" I said.

"I'm afraid not, Alex. I'm sorry, but, as I said, I've got a new job, beginning in a week or so. Meanwhile I'm just going to loaf. And I don't want any more of *them*." She kept trying to smile at me. "Why don't you stay and have lunch with me? This is supposed to be your vacation, isn't it?"

"Yes. But I can't stay."

She watched me a moment, soberly. Then she smiled again. "All right. Maybe some other time?"

"Maybe."

We walked to the door. I opened it. She leaned against the wall, watching me. There were pockets in her skirt and she had her hands jammed in them.

"Good-by, Jenny."

She smiled. She didn't move. I went out and closed the door with her still standing that way, watching me.

Then all of the terrible parts of my world fell on me with a silent bang.

As I drove out of Allayne the streets were very still. Everybody was at church. Everybody except Jenny. She'd been a very easy person to get along with, to know, to feel free with. She had accepted my coming as a fact. Why? I'd forgotten to ask.

The downtown section was completely deserted except for three parked cars, looking strangely alone. The sidewalks and street looked dusty and autumnal. Then, pretty soon, I was between the hills again, on French Street, and Allayne was out of sight and mind. I was thinking of Petra, when suddenly I remembered Madge. The phone call, talking with her, seemed to mean absolutely nothing. Yet I knew I should feel good, having spoken to her.

Then I knew something else. I was driving back toward trouble. But every bit of distance covered carried me closer and closer to the hell I wanted more than anything on earth.

Chapter Thirteen

I nearly missed seeing the man in the middle of the road. The house was just a short way around another bend. The man stood nonchalantly in the middle of the road and flagged me down. I started to drive past slowly on his right, but he leaped in front of the car.

"What do you want?" I shouted out the window, stopping the car.

He grinned, lounged quietly up to the side of the car, and stood there. He was chewing tobacco, a man of perhaps thirty or so, raw-boned almost to the extent of cadaverousness. He turned, spat a long string of brown juice, then fastened slitted, bloodshot eyes on me. "Mr. Bland," he said.

"Yes."

He grinned again. His lips were loose, his mouth broad, his teeth very square and outlined in black. His mouth trembled when he grinned. He wore ragged blue jeans, a pale-washed blue denim shirt, and a battered, sweat-stained felt hat of no color.

"Mister," he said, "drive the car in them bushes." He pointed to some bushes off the side of the road.

"What the hell's the matter with you?" I said. "Get out of the way."

One big dirt-grimed hand, knuckle bones nearly showing through the skin, grasped the window ledge. He shook his head. "Nope. I seen it. I seen it all. Now, ram your damn car in them bushes like I say." He ceased chewing and stared at me with his mouth open, then he grinned again. "Come on," he said, slapping my shoulder. He hitched his own shoulders. His arms hung loose at his sides. He chewed and spat on the left front fender of the car.

We watched each other for a while.

"What was it you say you saw?"

He grinned. "Hell, mister. The old lady. I seen that dame push the old lady out that there window. I seen plenty." He winked grotesquely and hitched his shoulders. "Hurry up, 'fore I get a wind up, damn it."

I drove the car into the bushes. He came in after me. I got out of the car and faced him. He was about my height, with a slouch. He carried himself with a slouch. He smelled strongly of the barnyard, and of wet tobacco.

"Played a mite too far, hey?"

"You'd better explain yourself," I said. He looked wise and jumpy, overexcitable. He scrubbed a hand across the dirty stubble on his face and spat again. Some of it splashed on my shoes. "Who are you?" I asked. I could feel everything tightening up, like when you swim down into very deep water and begin to want air in a hurry.

"She wouldn't never come across for me," he said. He mused on it for a while.

I turned and started to get back into the car. He grabbed my shoulder, whirled me around. I slammed at his arm. He stepped off, blinked at me, and grinned. "Wouldn't if I were you, mister."

"All right. What do you want?"

"I'm the hired hand down to Corey's."

"Corey's?"

He gestured. "Next farm, down there a piece." He chewed and spat. A car went by out on the road. The bushes moved and a fine settling of dust formed in the air. "I seen it," he said again. "They's a bunch of trouble at that there house, mister. Constable's there now. They taken the corpse off to town. It ain't no mind, though. I seen it all. I seen you rip the front offen her." I stepped toward him. He stepped back, holding a hand up. "Easy, now. 'At won't get you no place. She got nice big ones, ain't she?"

I stepped in close, let him have one at the stomach. He caught my fist and wrenched, and I landed on my back. I looked up at him. He seemed very proud of himself, grinning, chewing, spitting, and hitching his shoulders. I knew I could take him; it had been a lucky grab.

"Get up," he said. "I'll finish what I got to say."

I got up. "I don't know what you're talking about," I said. How could he have seen anything? Where had he been? "But I'll listen. Talk and talk fast."

He threw his head back and said, "Humph!" Then he squinted at me. "All right, mister. You're gettin' at that bitch in the red brick house. I been watchin' her for months from a little hill across the road. Watch her undress, watch what she does after that, too. Quite somethin', sometimes." He winked. I sweated and waited.

He said, "Like I say, I seen plenty all along. Caught 'er down the road once at night. Tried to take 'er, but she wouldn't have me. She called me a pig. Hell, she's the pig."

"You'd better get to the point in a damned hurry."

He spat. "This mornin' I milked an' fed the stock, then I kind of wandered over on my little hill just to look an' think about that sweet piece across the way. They's a shade tree in the front yard, an' I could see plumb in them big windows. Just like at night. I seen you an' her havin' it good. All ready for the ride, you was, when the old lady come in." He cursed obscenely. "Seen what happened. The gal fought the old lady, an' she pushed her out the window. You was there, an' you seen it too. You know, mister."

"You're lying," I said as calmly as I could. "You didn't see anything like that. You couldn't."

He blew air through his nose. "I'll show you shortly. Anyways, after you went off in the car, the rest of the folks come. The cor'ner, he comes, an' ol' Herk Williams, newspaperman, he come. An' Constable Sturge. So I went on over, to sort of see what they's sayin'. 'She fell out the window,' they said. 'Poor old lady, fell out the window.' Well," he said slowly, "I know she was pushed."

"You're a liar," I said. I was soaked to the skin and I had to see Petra. But first I had to know if he was telling the truth. Yet he must be telling the truth. Because how else could he know?

"Come on, then," he said. I followed him. We crossed the road, then a stubbled cornfield, a small creek, and started climbing a low hill from the near side. Pretty soon we reached the top. Brambles grew on the hill. Directly opposite us, across the road, sat the house. Three cars were parked in the driveway. Two men were talking in the front yard.

"Now, just squat down," the man said, "an' take these." He fished a pair of small field glasses from inside his shirt. "See? Fiel' glasses, hah!" He pointed with a broken-nailed finger. "Look in the big window of her room. See? At night mebbe it's better, but it's good right now, ain't it?"

He was right. If the big casement windows had been closed, it would have been impossible to see much. But with them open, and the field glasses, the screen seemed to vanish and I was looking straight into Petra's bedroom. I saw the couch where we'd been sprawled when the old lady caught us. A man was bending over by the torn screen, looking at it. I rose, handed him his glasses, and started quickly back down the hill.

"Ain't I right?" the man cried behind me, his feet crashing through the brush. "Ain't I right?"

I didn't say anything. We reached the car.

"Well," I said, "what about it?"

He grinned. "Figure I might's well be plain. Them little fiel' glasses, yes, *sir!* You pay me, an' I'll shut up. You see I get what I ask you for, see? Otherwise I go to Verne Lawrence and tell 'im what I seen, or mebbe the police, or Constable Sturge. All the same. You'd be a cooked goose an' so would she." He paused. "I sure would miss seein' 'er undress, an' all."

"That's blackmail," I said. "Do you know what they do to people for blackmail?"

He spat. "D'you figure you can give a damn? You think mebbe they wouldn't believe me if I told 'em? Huh. Listen, man, everybody in the county knows about her, an' how she had to tote that old woman wherever she went. A pretty dame like that." He shook his head. "If the money don't agree with you, then look at it this way. Talk with the gal, there. Tell 'er if she'll shack up with me one, two nights a week, O.K. I'll work it that way, too." He faced me, and tobacco sprayed from his lips. "But by God, it'll damn well be one or the other!" He spat at the ground. "An' mister, you better look out it ain't both!"

I hit him with everything I had, flush in the face. I felt my knuckles bite and blood spurted as he flailed backwards into the bushes. I stood, staring down at him.

He brushed his hand across his face, where he lay, and looked at the blood. Then he propped himself on his elbows and grinned up at me. "It ain't no matter," he said. "You can't hurt me. An' mister, you best show up right here tomorrow night, say about nine. Don't bring no money, just bring a yes or no. We'll see about the money later on." He spat his entire cud to the ground beside him. He lay there, grinning up at me, his lips trembling.

I climbed into the car, backed onto the road, and drove ahead. My knuckles were sore, but they didn't bother me at all. It was too late to worry now. It was too late to back out. It was all piling up and I knew it hadn't finished. There was more to come, a hell of a lot more, because through it all, through all this rotten hell, I still wanted her. I still wouldn't give her up. And I was in it now, in it all the way. . . .

There was only one car parked in the driveway when I reached the house. I drew up behind it.

Petra's voice reached me from the house and I glimpsed her at the doorway. "Oh, here he is now. Alex! Alex! Hurry up. Sheriff Reynolds wants to see you!"

Yes. There was a sheriff's star on the rear bumper of the car up ahead, and it looked as big as a Ferris wheel.

Chapter Fourteen

For a minute I couldn't move from the car.

Petra ran down toward me across the lawn. I watched the movement of her body, the way her hair swung out behind her, the anxious light in her eyes. Behind her, standing in the doorway, I saw a large man in a gray suit wearing a blue tie and a gray hat.

Petra's hands gripped the window ledge. "It's the sheriff. He just wants to talk. It's all right."

"I'm going to tell him. I've made up my mind. I mean, after the sheriff goes, I'm going to tell Verne. He can do what he wants." I didn't know when I'd decided, but I had, suddenly.

Her hand reached in and briefly touched my face. "No, Alex. Don't talk that way. We have much too much in store for us."

"Just the same—He's watching us."

"I know, I know. Now, come on. Get out of the car and meet the sheriff. He says it's just routine, that's all."

"Was the constable here?"

She opened the car door. "Yes. Just a damned hick fat fool, that's all. He just wanted to look at me, that's the only reason he came. They've already taken the body into town."

"I know."

"How? Never mind now. Come on."

I got out of the car and we walked toward the house. She talked loudly enough so anybody could hear now. She was very beautiful and I wanted to feel her against me. But I knew I had to tell Verne. I couldn't weaken. My God, was there nothing left to me?

"Where's Jenny?" she asked. "I thought you went in for Jenny." We approached the porch and the man stood there, watching. "Verne feels terrible. Where is Jenny?"

"She couldn't come just now," I said. I didn't want to tell her now because the sheriff might think anything. Sometimes these country sheriffs were something to deal with—lots of times.

"This is Mr. Bland, Sheriff Reynolds." She went on inside. His hand was cold and hard.

"Pleased to meet you," the sheriff said.

I nodded.

"Let's go inside," he said.

We went in and the door closed again. The hall was cool and dim, and in the living room Verne was seated drinking brandy. He was dressed in shirt and pants, but his hair was still uncombed.

Petra stood by Verne's chair, one hand on the back of the chair. Whenever her gaze touched mine it was like a current passing between us. I'd never had it like this before. And now it was all mixed up with murder and blackmail; hired hands who sat humped in the cool darkness of brambled hills staring bug-eyed at a bedroom window.

The sheriff was a plain man, from head to toe. His face was something like a wad of dough with mouth, nose, ears, and eyes carved in it. But his eyes were little black oily beads and they watched.

"Just wanted to asked a few questions," he said, "then I'll run along."

Verne glanced at me. "Where's Jenny?"

I started to answer, but Petra spoke up. "She couldn't come just now."

"Oh," Verne said. He drank from his glass and stared at his shoes.

"Reason is," the sheriff said, "in a case of this kind, and all. Routine. Did you happen to see Mrs. Lawrence fall?" He turned to Verne. "Verne, why don't you go into the—"

"No, it's all right," Verne said.

"No," I said. "I didn't."

"Well," the sheriff said. He sighed. He was holding his hat in his hands now and his hair was very sparse, plastered tight to his skull. It was straw-colored hair. "Well," he said again, "would you tell me what happened, so far's you know, Mr. Bland?"

I hated it. Every word was like yanking a tooth out of my head with a pair of pliers. Because it was all lies, and I was saying it before Verne and she was standing there watching me and knowing with whatever it was in her eyes telling me, Yes, yes, yes, yes.

"I heard a scream," I said.

"A scream?"

"Several. Two or three, maybe. I don't know. I was in my room. I ran down toward Petra's, Mrs. Lawrence's room, and went in. The door was open. Petra was standing over on the other side of the room, by the bed, and she—well, she was rather troubled."

"I see. Yes, certainly," Sheriff Reynolds said.

"She told me Verne's mother had fallen out of the window and right then Verne came into the room." I spread my hands. "That's all, Sheriff, that's all."

"Yes. Well, thank you." He turned to Verne. "Now, Verne, you get some rest. You take it easy. I had to do this, you understand? Routine and all. Not many window fallings. . . ." He glanced at Petra. She smiled. He looked at me, jammed his hat on, and went out.

A moment later he returned. "Pardon me," he said. "But if you could move your car, so I could get out of the drive?"

"Sure." I went out and moved the car and he drove off. As I walked back to the house across the lawn, I glanced over at the hill beyond the road. Then I looked down the road. It was the man, the hired hand from Corey's; he was leaning against a tree just beyond Verne's home, watching. He saw me looking and waved. I went into the house.

I wanted to tell Verne everything, the whole stinking business. I wanted to tell him, and yet I was pulled the other way, too. I wondered if I'd be able to tell him. If she would just stay away from me long enough, maybe I would tell him.

Chapter Fifteen

She didn't stay away from me.

It was like relighting a fire that had guttered down some, refeeding it with fresh dry fuel, the way she looked at me and spoke to me between normal conversation. And Verne sitting there in the chair in the living room staring at the floor. Now and then he'd shake his head.

"She had to go," Verne said. "It was time she died. She'd expected it herself, and I know I did. It was the way. The way she died. That's what gets me. She never had a damned thing. Never had any rest, any peace, until she came here. She didn't know what rest was, or peace. She'd never known."

"Buck up, now," Petra said. "Take it easy, Verne." And while she said it, she looked at me, standing there by Verne's chair, with one hand by his head, looking at me with her eyes, her lips, her whole body.

I didn't say anything, just waited.

"And then, when she did come," Verne said, "when at last she had a chance at some rest, she went deaf. Not that it mattered much. She didn't seem to mind that. It isn't that I feel so bad about her dying. Death isn't much, not to an old person, anyway. It isn't that. It's the way. The way she died."

"Darling," Petra said, "you better have a drink."

"I don't want one."

"It might help."

"I said I don't want a drink."

She shrugged, standing there behind him, where he couldn't see. I had been standing. Now I found a chair across from Verne and settled down.

"I should have left her sitting in that damned cornfield," Verne said. "Leaning against the fence, like they found her that morning. She was nearly dead then. It would have been best."

Petra said, "Are you going to—are you going to bring Mother back here?"

"I was, but not now. Only the funeral will start from here. The funeral procession will start from this house. Where she at least found a remote hint of happiness."

I watched Verne. There was something wrong with him. Some men would dwell on a thing like this, but it wasn't in Verne's make-up to sit there talking about it the way he was. It seemed almost a kind of morbidity.

"Should have left her in the cornfield," Verne said. "It was winter, too. Dead winter with the snow piling up against the fence. Nobody knows how she got there, either." His eyes looked burned out.

I tried to catch Petra's eye, so she'd pour him a drink of brandy, but she only smiled at me.

"She was wearing a straw hat," Verne said. "The kind you wear in the summertime—pitching hay, too."

"Where will she be buried?" Petra asked. She went over and sat in the chair the old woman had been sitting in that first night when she got drunk. Verne stared at the floor. There was no sunshine outside and the room was gray and still.

Verne glanced at me. "I wanted to bury her with Pa, out at the farm. Where she buried Pa."

Petra said, "Oh, but *Verne!*"

"In Nebraska, you mean?" I said.

He nodded. "But I don't think so. It's too far, and when you get down to it, one piece of ground is as good as another." He poured himself a small drink and drank it, then said, "Or maybe not."

There was a long silence. Petra drummed her fingers on her knee. Then she said, "Well, then you're going to bury her in town? In the cemetery in town?"

"No. I don't know yet," he said. "The funeral procession will start here, though."

"There won't be any procession," Petra said.

I glanced at her sharply.

Verne saw me. He said, "That's all right. She's right, Alex. There'll only be us. Nobody else knew her."

"But Verne," Petra said. "Where will you bury her?"

"I think I'll bury her out on that knoll, the other side of the orchard. You know, up by that sycamore. It's a nice spot."

"Aren't you being a little—well, I mean—" Petra stared at me.

"I know," Verne said. "No, I'm all right."

"But no hearse—" Petra said.

"That's right. We'll have to carry her. Damn it," he said. "I'm all right. I don't know why I think this way, but I do."

"But who will you get for pallbearers?"

She was watching him as she spoke, a little apprehensive, maybe. She had a right to be. My insides were knotted up like a tangle of barbed wire, and I kept wanting to tell him. But how could I tell him?

"There should be six," Petra said.

"Four will do," Verne said.

"Won't people talk?"

"What do you care how they talk?" He turned in his chair and looked at her without any expression. Then he turned back and stared at the floor some more. I decided the best thing to do was to let him get rid of whatever was inside him. Then maybe he'd be all right.

"I ordered a light casket," Verne said. "She'd almost fit in a child's casket. So four will do."

"Verne, if you don't stop it!" Petra said.

"Stop what?" He seemed slightly startled.

"Nothing."

I couldn't seem to get comfortable in my chair. It was hard, bumpy all over. I knew it wasn't, actually, but it seemed that way.

"Yes," Verne said. "Up on that knoll." He rose and walked into the hall. I heard him at the telephone. Petra rose quickly and came over by me.

"He acts funny," she said.

"He's been working too hard. Any kind of shock might make him act this way. He'll be all right in a little while."

She stood very close to me. She leaned over, and without volition I put my arms around her, felt the firm swelling of her hips. Her lips descended. I shoved her away. "Look out," I said.

"Yes." She went back to her chair. "You're excited, aren't you?" she said. "I am, too. I wish it were over."

My hands were gripping the arms of the chair so hard the tendons and muscles in my wrists ached. It seemed as if little voices were shrieking and screaming in the back of my head. When I looked at Petra, her eyes were like black holes. They were pointed at me, but I don't believe they really saw me. It was all going on in her head, behind the eyes. I began to perspire.

Verne returned. He stood in the center of the room and ran both clawed hands through his hair three or four times, briskly. "I talked with them," he said. "Two men will be out to dig the grave up on the knoll."

I sat rigid with my hands gripped around the ends of the chair arms.

"You can hire professional pallbearers," Petra said. Her voice was little more than a whisper.

"Listen," Verne said. "Don't think anything's the matter with me, for God's sake!" He turned to me. "I'm sorry, Alex. It's just the way I want to do it, is all. No. I'll get old Herb Corey and his hired hand to help. You and I will make up the other two. She knew them; they're the only ones she knew around here. The only ones ever spoke to her. They'll be glad. You'll help, won't you, Alex?"

"Sure, Verne." My voice was a raven's croak.

Corey's hired hand. . . .

I wanted a drink, but I couldn't trust myself to pour one because my hands would have trembled too much. Corey's hired hand. God. Up there on that brambled hill in the quiet nights of passing seasons, squatting, with those damned field glasses sweating against his eyeballs.

It was murder, that's what it was. And I was in on it. It was hard to believe, to comprehend. It always is, I guess, when things get close to you, like this.

Just after a lunch of sandwiches and coffee prepared by Petra, and during which no one spoke, I met Verne in the hallway by the stairs. Petra was in the kitchen.

"Alex, what about Jenny?" He tried to hold himself straight, to act all right, when he looked like death itself.

"She said she couldn't come, Verne. She has a new job. She was very sorry to let you down. Sorry, too, about your mother."

"Oh." His mouth twisted down at the corners.

"She has a phone now. You could talk with her if you like."

"No," he said. "I understand, Alex. I don't blame Jenny, either. Hell with it all. Let Petra take care of things."

I said nothing. Just stood there looking at the man who had been my comrade through a lot of hell-roaring days. A man I'd been able to depend on, as he'd been able to depend on me. We'd drunk together, and fought together, and raised hell together. Once we'd been brothers. And now I had seen his own mother murdered—yes, been a party to that murder. But I didn't have the guts to tell him. I didn't have the guts because his wife had her hot hands snarled up in my brain. Too late. It's always too late.

"Going up and take a nap," Verne said. "Sorry about all this, Alex." His smile was ghastly.

"Sure. Take it easy."

I watched him climb the stairs. He looked very, very old.

Chapter Sixteen

The picture. Petra in the hammock. She had returned it to Verne's study, laid it face down on his desk, the way I had first seen it.

"Only while he's around, darling," she said. "He might notice it was missing. No use taking chances. Not that it means much."

She was standing close to me when she said it and the faint odor of her perfume seemed to choke me. I agreed with her, without speaking. And that afternoon the gravediggers came.

I walked out into the orchard and watched them up there on the knoll. Two men. Their shovels scraped and flashed in the gray, cooling light of autumn. The sky was a tent of gray and their voices joked upon the air between the rasps of earth against steel.

The sun was dead.

"Boy, will I be glad when this is done!"

"Ain't it a fact?"

"They buryin' a dog? Hell of a big dog."

"Naw. Old woman kicked off."

"Wish my old woman'd kick off."

"Damn that root. Hand me the ax. What in hell anybody'd wanta dig a grave up here . . . What they make graveyards for?"

"Nutty. Went to Buffalo last week."

"Hot dog!"

"Did somethin' I'd always wanted to do."

"What's that?"

"Had two of 'em in bed with me the same time."

"Hell, man. Ain't you ever done that before?"

I left the orchard and walked around the front of the house. Somebody rapped on a window. It was Petra. She motioned for me to come in. I went on inside the house.

"He's asleep."

"Good," I said. "Petra . . ." I had to tell her about Corey's hired hand and what he knew, but I didn't know how to begin. It seemed I wasn't able to tell anybody much of anything these days.

"Never mind," she said. "Just hold me."

"No." We were in the hall. "Stay away from me, Petra. We were seen."

She still wore the thin black dress and the white scarf knotted about her throat. Her eyes were very black. "What do you mean?"

"Somebody saw you push her out of the window, Petra. Not only that, but he saw us—what we were doing when she came into the room."

She was very quiet. She stared at me for a long moment. "You're serious, aren't you? But you can't be. How could—"

"He did, I tell you. Corey's hired man. He's been sitting on top of that hill across the road with a pair of field glasses watching you for God knows how long. He stopped me on the way back from town and told me. He wants money, or—"

Her lips had parted, but otherwise her face hadn't altered expression. "Go on," she said. "Or—what?"

"Oh, God. Or you—once in a while, twice a week—nights. Or—or both," I said.

She was wearing a thin silver bracelet. She took it off one arm and put it on the other.

She said, "And the funeral's tomorrow and he's going to help. He's going to be here."

"Yes. So the funeral's tomorrow."

"Well, how much does he want?"

"I don't know. I have to see him tomorrow night."

She became bold again, the way she always was. With both hands she bunched her hair behind her head, then let it sprawl out over her shoulders again. "Well, we'll pay him something. I can just about figure his price. He'll be dirt cheap."

"My God," I said. "Don't you see?"

"Of course I see. I'll think of something. Meanwhile, we'll pay him. You say he was watching from across the hill?"

"That's right."

"He couldn't prove a thing."

"Sure. All right," I said "Maybe he couldn't. But if he said anything, it might start the ball rolling. What if he spoke to Verne?"

She socked me with it. "What if Verne were dead, Alex?"

"What?"

"Oh, nothing." She moved in close and it all came in on me like a kind of white heat, dry and stifling. She moved in my arms and brushed her lips across mine. "Alex, Alex," she said, "I love you so much."

"What did you mean—what you said, there?"

"What?"

"About Verne."

She leaned away from me, from the waist up. "Nothing, darling, honest. Nothing at all."

"You're lying."

"All right, I'm lying. Kiss me, damn you! Come on, darling, kiss me!"

"Don't call me that. You'll slip."

"You're getting to think right, aren't you? You're admitting it to yourself at last."

I grabbed her close and pushed my mouth down on hers. My hand was fumbling at her dress when I heard footsteps in the upstairs hall. It was Verne. I let go and pushed her away from me.

She headed for the kitchen. I went into Verne's study and drank from the whisky decanter. I choked the stuff down. But it didn't help. It didn't stop my heart from whacking in there and it didn't stop that sense of being stifled, of being wound tighter and tighter and tighter.

Chapter Seventeen

The funeral was at ten o'clock the next morning.

Sometime during the night it had started raining and it didn't let up with morning. A slow, cold drizzle that seeped into you, into your bones. The sky was a gray pall, splotched with black, as if it had some kind of disease that was spreading. And the rain kept slowly coming down, whispering in a steady hush over the cold country.

The Reverend Mr. Waugh was the first to appear at the house. He was a small, tight man in a tight-fitting suit, with tight eyes and a close-lipped mouth. He walked as if he were strapped together with leather, and when he turned, he turned his whole body. Maybe there was something the matter with his neck.

He had been talking with Verne in the living room after we'd been introduced. I had gone into the study. Petra was with Verne.

The Reverend Mr. Waugh's voice went on and on, droning monotonously from the living room. I kept sampling the whisky. It was the only thing that would help pull me through. I tried not to think. But all I could think of was Petra and that our time was a little closer.

The Reverend cleared his throat in the doorway and walked tightly up to me.

"This is highly irregular," he said. "Highly, you know. I don't mean to—of course, Mr. Bland—friends and all. But the officials won't like it. Burying out here when there's a cemetery in Allayne. There's an ordinance, you know."

"We're outside its jurisdiction," I said.

"Yes, but it's highly irregular."

"Would you care for a drink?"

He looked startled, blinked tightly at me, with his small eyes. "No."

I heard a rustle at the door. Petra glanced in, blew a kiss at me, and vanished. Inside I began to tremble. You don't fool around with death like this. I kept telling myself that. Only it didn't do any good.

The Reverend Mr. Waugh went to the study window. "Here comes the hearse." He turned, looking at me. He seemed happy.

I heard Petra call to Verne, "Here comes the hearse, dear."

I didn't move. The Reverend Mr. Waugh scurried tightly from the room.

A funeral service was held in the house and after that we started with the casket for the knoll.

Verne had the left side and I was behind him. Herb Corey—a red-faced, embarrassed, stout farmer—was opposite Verne. Behind him, across from me, was Corey's hired hand. I'd been more or less forced to shake his hand when we were introduced, watching the loose smile play across his lips. His name was Cecil Emmetts.

Petra followed behind us, walking with the Reverend Mr. Waugh through the dripping orchard. All of us wore raincoats. Petra carried an umbrella, beneath which the Reverend Mr. Waugh leaned tightly.

The coffin was not in the least heavy. The rain dripped and we walked slowly through it, through the wet grass and across a makeshift board platform bridging the creek.

Then we climbed the knoll. There were two other men from town up there to help lower the casket into the ground. As yet there was no headstone, but I'd heard Verne speak of getting one.

I refused to look toward Emmetts. But I knew he was watching me.

Herb Corey and Emmetts had come just after the arrival of the hearse, and Emmetts' eyes stayed on Petra, watching her with a kind of harsh amusement. He was chewing tobacco, and as we trudged along, he occasionally spat.

I wondered if the old woman moved much inside the casket. We were very careful. Verne's back was straight and he walked stiffly. Climbing the knoll was bad, though, because the grass was slippery. Once Herb Corey, rather ungainly to begin with, dropped to one knee. He wrenched himself erect with a gasp and an embarrassed word of apology.

The Reverend Mr. Waugh muttered something to Petra behind us.

I heard Petra say, "It can't be helped."

We reached the top of the knoll by the sycamore, where the dark grave yawned. It was all I could do to keep from jabbering like an idiot. The whole business was horrible, and it was ripping me apart inside.

The rain struck the freshly wounded earth at the sides of the grave and, diamond-bright for a brief instant, vanished.

They whispered and mumbled while the casket was arranged on the slings over the grave.

Then Verne stood on one side with Petra and her umbrella. I was on the other side, facing her. Herb Corey and Emmetts and the other two men from town stood off to one side while the minister began praying.

It rained slowly, the fine mist of rain drifting down straight and almost as if a cloud were descending over the earth. Water dripped from the sycamore and fingered the shiny black surface of the casket. I didn't hear a word the minister said.

I looked into her eyes and she looked into mine.

I couldn't tear my gaze away. I felt Emmetts' eyes on us and panic knotted nauseously inside me and the Reverend Mr. Waugh's voice rambled on and on in prayer.

My friend, I thought. My friend's wife.

We looked at and into each other. I saw her lips part, and her breasts rose and fell more quickly beneath her coat and the umbrella's filmy shadow.

I wanted her. I wanted to leap straight across the grave and take her, bend her body to mine. She wanted me to.

We were both damned. . . .

Beneath us in that glistening black casket lay a murdered woman, and I'd been a partner to her death.

Returning to the house, Emmetts suddenly elbowed my side. His shoulders hitched and hunched beneath his raincoat and he smiled broadly, lips trembling. "Body's buried, but the truth lingers, hey, Mr. Bland?" he whispered.

I turned on him, close to flying apart.

"Easy, now," he whispered. "See you tonight, hey? You ain't forgot, have you?"

"Get the hell away from me before I kill you."

He chuckled quietly. "Figure you done enough killin' for a time." He spat. "Only thing you'll be killin' now is yourself, on her!" He nodded toward Petra's back, where she was walking beside Verne. Just then she turned and glanced at me. For an instant her gaze locked with Emmetts'. He nodded and grinned at her. She turned away quickly.

His voice was low. "'Pig,' she says. We'll see who's the pig."

None of them stayed at the house for long. They all seemed in a hurry to get away. And then we three were alone in the house and the slow rain continued to sift along the eaves.

Ten minutes later, Verne said, "I'm going into town. Try and pick out a headstone for the grave. I feel better now all this is over with."

I glanced at Petra. I couldn't help it. She was staring at me and her face was pale.

She said, "I'll go see if I can't fix something good for dinner."

I knew I had to say something. I knew I had to say what I said. I was shaking all over inside and was afraid my voice would tremble, but it didn't. I just sounded a bit hoarse. "You want me to go in with you, Verne?"

He hesitated, put on his hat, shrugged into his coat. "No, I guess not. You stay here." He smiled, the first smile in quite a while, but I wasn't seeing it, wasn't interested. "Keep Petra company."

He strode down the hall and the door slammed behind him.

Petra had started for the kitchen. She whirled.

"Keep me company, he said!"

The car wasn't even out of the driveway before we were at each other like two crazy animals.

I fastened my hands in her hair, jammed my mouth down on hers. She writhed away.

"Upstairs!"

I let her go. She ran for the stairs, undressing as she went. By the time we reached the door to her room, her dress was off.

I grabbed her in the doorway and we fought against each other, staggering wildly toward the bed. She was moaning now and beginning to cry a little.

We never made the bed. We fell to the floor and the house shook and her jetty hair spread out like a broad black fan on that thick auburn rug.

Chapter Eighteen

We finally did reach her bed, and, lying there now, Petra suddenly sat up. Then she leaped to the floor and hurriedly dressed.

"He may be home any time. I've got to fix something to eat, like I said. Good Lord, it's been almost two hours."

"Yes." I didn't look at her. Then I felt her hair fold heavily across my face and her lips brushed mine.

"See you later," she said, and I listened to her feet hurrying down the hall, down the stairs.

There was only sickness inside me now, sickness over what had happened. I tried to fight it off, but it wouldn't go away. Lying there, I stared up at the dark midnight ceiling, and it seemed I was lying at the bottom of that grave with the damp walls pushing in on either side and with the dripping coffin slung above me. There was Verne's haggard face. A trusting guy. Why didn't he know better?

And then the pile of broken gray on the stone of the patio. . . .

Dressed, I went over and looked at the window. The torn screen was still the same. It would always be the same, too, in my mind. It wouldn't change; the jagged edges, and down there on the bare stone the broken gray mass.

I turned and went down the hall into my room and closed the door. Even closing the door didn't help, but it did start the thought, I've got to stop now. It can't go on. Something's got to be done.

I stripped and stood in the shower with the needles of cold water blasting on me, and I kept thinking of that grave out there on the knoll by the sycamore. And the pines were dripping beneath the forlorn gray half-light of an autumn sky. And when we had returned down the knoll to cross the creek, the creek was filling slowly, the grass along its edges soggy with an ability to draw more water from that mist than seemed probable. And the boards the men had put across the creek were swamped slightly, and in the orchard the mist jeweled brightly among thick spider webs.

Wild, she had been, wild, there on that auburn rug.

Rubbed down with a thick towel, I went back into my room and stood staring at the front window, beyond which the shank of the hill leaned against the road. Squatting among the brambles . . .

Madge was in Chicago, wondering what was the matter, or maybe with a chip on her shoulder. And there would never be any way of explaining to her. If I wanted to explain.

Murder.

The sound of a car turning in the drive told me Verne was back. A moment later the front door slammed and I heard him going down the hall. Then voices very faint, from the kitchen, probably.

There had been no rules. Just an acceptance of what was to come. She'd resisted, put up a barrier of sorts, held me off.

She'd held me off until the old woman was in the ground. Then she'd exploded. And it hadn't been sane, either. And me without guts enough to go to Verne, or at least to run. Yes. Without guts enough to run.

There was a rapid tattoo of knuckles on the door. I turned. The racket ceased sharply, then commenced again. I slipped into a pair of pants and hurried to open the door.

"Alex, Alex! He's had an attack!"

She stood there momentarily in the doorway, then sprang at me, not touching me, but standing there with her hands out and her face dead pale with passion. She wore a black housecoat, belted tightly at the waist.

"What?"

"A heart attack. Verne. When he was in town. He said it happened in the car, just as he started out of town. He stopped the car and waited, then drove on in."

I started past her. She clamped her hands on my arms, shoved her body in my way. "No. Let him be. He's lying down. Don't you see?"

I tried to shove by. For a moment we pushed at each other and she began to curse. One look in her eyes was enough. I stopped.

"Don't you see?"

"Did you call a doctor?"

"He won't have a doctor. Simply won't have one."

"Call one anyway, Petra. For God's sake. The man may be bad off. He might die."

"That's right. Don't you see?" She flung herself against me. I grabbed her and swung her around at the bed. She sprawled to her knees beside the bed, still talking, gesticulating with her hands. "Don't you see, Alex? This is our chance. I told you his heart was bad. He'll never admit it's as bad as it is. The doctor told him he can't smoke or drink, but he doesn't care. He's down there now, with a bottle of brandy." She paused. She spoke so rapidly that her voice seemed to run over itself, as if she were talking against time. "All that money, Alex. He's worth plenty. It would be mine—ours."

I stared at her without comprehension really, not even believing I heard straight. "Petra. His mother's just buried this morning."

She rose to one knee, imploring, her mouth a bloody gash almost as black as her eyes and hair against the pallor of her face. "Yes. Yes. That's right. The shock of his mother's death. It could kill him. We could see to it. Don't you understand? I can't bear it any longer, it's been too much. We could . . ."

I stepped in close, brought the flat of my hand, the heel, sharply against her jaw. She lifted backward against the bed. I wanted to hit her again but I couldn't. It was like striking water, because when you drew your hand away nothing had changed. She lay there watching me, breathing harshly. The housecoat was half off her, her legs spraddled out, her breasts bared, with only the dark belt holding the flaring housecoat around her.

She watched and watched while little beads of bright scarlet purled from the corner of her mouth.

"You love me," she whispered. She nodded slowly as she spoke. "You love me and it's hard for you to prove it, but you say it when you do things like that. You can't stand hearing me tell what's true; what's in your own mind. You can't stand it because you know I'm right and you love me."

I couldn't answer.

"It's you. You're still fighting against yourself," she said. "Why don't you stop, let yourself go? Admit it to yourself, why don't you? Because you struck me now you'll want me more than ever. You won't sleep, because you can't stand it. I've heard you pacing the floor at night. You keep thinking about that girl in Chicago. Was she as good as I am, Alex? No. I can see it in your eyes, she wasn't. She couldn't be. She doesn't know what love it—the need. Even to kill for it, how better to prove it? How could you—"

I walked out of the room and hurried down the stairs. At the foot of the stairs I glanced back. She was leaning in the doorway of my room, looking down at me.

Verne lay on the couch in the living room with a bottle of brandy cradled in his arm. He was extremely pale and his face and shirt were bathed with sweat. He didn't move as I stepped up, but his eyes followed me.

"How do you feel?" I asked.

"Fine. I'm fine." His voice was hollow, and when he smiled it wasn't a smile at all, just a torturing of the muscles around his mouth. There was something like fright in his eyes. But that went away as I stood there.

"Let me call a doctor, Verne. Petra said you had a heart attack."

"No doctor, Alex. I'm all right. Had these damned things before."

"Hadn't you better lay off the bottle?"

"No. It's good for me." He grinned. "Hell. You know how I always drank cognac."

"Yes."

"Well, this is cognac."

"Fine. How do you really feel?" I kicked the ottoman over by the couch and sat on it.

"Tired. Outside of being tired, I feel fine."

"Did it hurt much?"

He grinned this time, took a swallow from the bottle. "No. It's not bad. You just wonder how many more you can stand. Or if this is the one, or what. Have some?" He offered me the bottle.

I took it and had a couple of good swallows. It was really good. I hadn't drunk any in a long while, and the flavor of it brought back flashing memories of times and of lots worse cognac.

As I sat there beside my friend, it began to get very bad. The realization of what had happened and of the things I had done in this house began to eat at me. It was the beginning of the really bad time ahead. No matter what I said to Verne, it was shaded on some side by a lie.

"I think I'd better call a doctor," I said.

He looked at me. "No. Give me the bottle."

I took another drink and handed him the bottle. I knew I should phone the doctor anyway. But I didn't. It was a minor thing, but maybe there was that much trust he could place in me.

"Petra's had a bad time of it with my mother," he said. He closed his eyes. The beads of sweat stood out on his forehead as large as field peas. "What will I do now?"

"What do you mean?"

"Nothing." His eyes stayed closed. "Alex, will you stay on a while yet?"

"Yes."

I heard the piano from the other side of the house. It was exact, brilliant, passionate playing. At first I didn't catch the music, then I did, and glanced quickly at Verne. His eyes were still closed.

"Petra," he said. "She certainly can play. It's been a long time since she's touched the piano."

I stared at him, wondering how he could have such a small knowledge of music as not to know what she was playing. It was patent that he didn't know.

It was Saint-Saëns' *"Danse Macabre";* the very well-known Dance of Death. I wondered if she had taken time to dust the keys. I remembered how I'd caught myself whistling the melody the first night I'd been in the house. The way she played sounded a little mad, and a chill touched my shoulders. It was foolish and maybe melodramatic, but I felt that this was a house of death, of evil. Standing away from it, I wondered if it would be possible to detect any humor in it. All I could feel was horror at my own faults.

And I knew that I couldn't leave without telling Verne everything. I wondered how much he knew, how much he guessed.

Cecil Emmetts. The afternoon would go fast, and then the evening, and he would wait beside the bushes on the highway.

I could tell him only one answer. There was only one.

The piano ceased. I looked at Verne. He was asleep, the bottle beginning to slide from his arm. I took the bottle and drank deeply. As I set it on the floor by the couch I knew it was taking hold and it helped. But not much.

I went to the music room. The door was closed. I opened it, went in, and shut the door.

"Hello, darling."

She was seated at the piano. She still wore the black housecoat, but she also wore stockings now and high-heeled shoes. As she turned and looked at me there was an instant when I couldn't believe all that had happened. Then I could.

I sat in the chair by the window. The window sill was damp from the rain, but she had closed the window. She rose and came over to me.

"Look," she said. "I forgot to show you." She smiled. "Guess you were too busy to notice."

She undid the belt of the housecoat and, lifting her left leg, placed her foot on the left side of the chair cushion. She unhooked the garters from her stocking and peeled the stocking down her full thigh. "Here," she said. "See what you did when you grabbed me yesterday?"

There was a large black-and-blue mark on her thigh.

She took my hand and ran the palm across the mark.

"You're getting excited," she said. "I can tell."

I stood quickly and walking over to the piano, felt of the keys. Most of them were still partially gritty with dust. "Why did you play that?" I asked.

"Because I felt like it. It was suitable. Why do you *fight* yourself?" She was fixing the garter on the stocking. Her legs, all of her body was white, voluptuous, and like fire to my heart and blood—just watching. Her eyes gleamed darkly and as yet the fighting within me was no good.

The brandy had gone to my head completely. "Damn you."

She put her leg down from the chair. The housecoat draped open. She wore nothing beneath it but the garter belt.

She smiled and her scarlet lips glistened. "You love me," she said. "Why deny it?"

My voice said it. It wasn't me, yet it was me. "Damn you. Lock that door."

She did.

"Come here," I said.

She did. The smile had changed from a smile of amusement to sudden passion.

"Why can't we forget it all? You, I mean," she said. "Why can't you forget it? We could have fun then. We could be like we should."

I was sitting in the chair again. She was perched on the arm of the chair, one hip against my shoulder. The housecoat was in a heap on the floor.

"Dress," I said. I rose and unlocked the door, peered into Verne's study. The house was silent. I closed the door but didn't lock it and watched her as she slipped on the housecoat. She did it carelessly. Her breasts were large, perfectly formed, upthrusting, and firm. Her body was flawless, as if she had been carved with some lusty godlike precision from a warm, utterly unblemished slab of pure alabaster.

She drew the black belt tight around her slim waist. "Why can't we?" she asked again. "We never joke, it's just fire. Of course, I like the fire, too."

"Shut up," I said.

"I won't. You're still fighting yourself. How long will it go on? How long before you'll admit it?"

I didn't answer aloud but I said, Never, to myself.

"It's him—it's Verne, isn't it? You keep thinking about a foolish friendship that no longer exists. About a man who is no longer a man, but a machine. A machine with a broken part, at that—one that'll quit any time."

I rubbed my hand across my face and the smell of her was on my hand like some acid eating into the skin, burning, until it could not be removed—ever.

I left the room, walked through the study, and looked in at Verne on the couch. He was awake. He blinked at me.

"What'd you do with my bottle?" he asked.

"I drank it."

His hand had dropped down beside the couch. He grinned as his fingers touched the bottle. He took a drink. Then he sat up on the couch.

"Feel a lot better," he said.

I stood in the doorway.

"Since you've been here," he went on, "I've felt better, somehow. A lot has happened, but maybe it'll calm down now. Maybe everything's ironed out."

I didn't answer right away. Calmed down, ironed out. "It's been fine," I said. "Only don't let anything get you down." He looked better, all right.

"I feel good with you here," he said. "Like old times. It's good to know you can depend on somebody."

His words slashed me, cut into me, dug at me. And he didn't know. There was nothing I could say or do. If I'd never met despair before, I had now. And what in hell was I to do? You weak-willed coward, I told myself. You gutless wonder. Not alone taking your friend's wife, but murder, too, and now blackmail, and all that wonderful clean world of yours gone.

"Alex, is something troubling you? You don't look right, the past couple of days. Somehow."

"Nothing. I'm all right. A little tired, maybe." A little tired, I thought. A little tired.

"I know it's been rough. I'll make it up to you."

I laughed. It sounded like the last note of a funeral dirge. "Forget all of that, will you? I'm going up and take a nap."

He didn't say anything this time, just stared at me, puzzled, maybe.

I went on upstairs to my room and closed the door and stared at the bed.

Panic was nothing to what I began feeling now. Panic was like a mosquito bite on a dying leper.

I went and washed my hands, then smelled of them. The odor of her wouldn't go away. I poured rubbing alcohol on them, then suddenly looked at myself in the mirror on the medicine cabinet. Something lurked in my eyes that I'd never seen there before.

"You're going crazy, you damned fool!" I said. "You're out of your head."

But the smell was gone from my hands.

Chapter Nineteen

I was well on the way to being good and drunk by eight-forty-five. It was the first time I'd seen Petra slightly worried. The more she frowned and watched me, the more I drank.

We were in the living room. Verne was still resting on the couch. He had drunk some, but sparingly, and was quite sober.

"Alex," Petra said, "you're getting pie-eyed."

Verne said, "He's on vacation. He ought to stay drunk all the time."

Only it wasn't that kind of drunk. Things kept getting clearer and I knew I'd have to drink a lot before I reached the stage where I could forget, or become careless enough not to give a damn about what I thought.

Petra said, "It's ten to nine already," and threw me a meaningful glance.

"So what?" Verne said. "I'm not going to work tomorrow. Let the damned job take care of itself for a few days. I'll handle it by telephone. Least I can do for Alex."

"Thanks," I said. "It'll be good for you, too." I rose a bit unsteadily. "Think I'll get some air, take a walk."

"Sure," Verne said. "I'm lazy, myself. Go ahead with him, Petra."

I cut her a look that said, No!

"No," she said. "But don't get lost and don't be long, Alex. It's still drizzling. Verne's raincoat is in the hall."

I was already in the hall with the raincoat half on. I walked toward the rear of the house and found an unopened pint of whisky on the liquor shelf in the kitchen. I put it in the deep raincoat pocket and went out the back door.

In the back yard I opened the pint and took a good drink, capped it, and put it away again. Then I went out to the highway and started walking down toward the bend. The rain was still a mist, but slightly heavier, and it felt good on my face and on my bare head. It was clean. It came straight down from the sky without touching anything at all.

I kept thinking, Maybe it will wash out my brain, get the smell off my brain. That had been bothering me. My hands didn't smell of her right now, but how could I wash my brain? I decided the rain couldn't do it because it couldn't get inside.

It was very dark and the hills blended into the dark but the trees didn't. The trees were like flat deformed black hands against the streaming sky. Actually the sky was not black but more of an extremely dark violet, and somewhere there was a radiance because the vibrant puddles in the road gleamed. A single bird piped fitfully up in the brambles on the hill.

Cecil Emmetts. It didn't bother her at all. It didn't reach her. Murder didn't. So nothing would. That's what I knew now.

I was waiting for something. Every day. What was it? Strength? Will? The driving will that had always kept me on the straight and narrow, forsaking me like a lost hat when I most needed it? I was waiting.

Something was going to happen. It had to. Because it kept on mounting and getting worse all the time. Something had to break. I had a feeling it would be me.

It was getting a lot colder now. This was the coldest night since I'd been here. I got out the bottle and had a good one. Then I was by the bushes.

I walked around the bushes on the soggy pasture grass. He wasn't here yet. I went and stood on the shoulder of the road. A car hissed by, whipping a spray of rain and exhaust into my face. I thought of Chicago. I wrote a letter in my mind to Madge.

> Dearest Madge:
>
> I am an accessory to murder, or maybe in some eyes an accomplice. I am sleeping regularly with my best friend's wife. We are being blackmailed for the murder of my best friend's mother. Right now I am drunk. I am also wet, and believe me, sick with despair. Whenever I see her I want her. I am rotten with desire for her. Yet I am certain that I love you. I will always love you, no matter what happens, and it probably will.

I began to laugh. Finally I stopped and had another long drink from the bottle. I looked at my watch and it was nine-fifteen. I laughed at nine-fifteen.

It began to rain harder, hissing on the highway.

All I wanted was to get away, back to Madge. Get away from the house and Petra. But now there was more to it than just that. Whatever way the dice turned, I had to stand up to their reading. It wasn't enough now just to get away and exhibit some bones and relics in Chicago. And not only murder, either. Somehow I had to face Verne and tell him. It was the only way for my own freedom.

I had another drink.

When I next glanced at my watch, it was nine-thirty and I was pacing in the rain. "Hell with Cecil Emmetts," I said aloud. I started off down the highway.

"All right, mister. Stay put."

I stopped, turning. Emmetts came out from behind the bushes. He lounged up to where I stood and snorted through his nose. "Been watchin'," he said, punctuating his words with a stream of tobacco juice from the side of his mouth.

"You've been here all the time?"

"Not quite. Just thought I'd figure to give you a worry."

I started walking off again. He grabbed my arm. "Set tight," he said. He wore a poncho and his hat, and he was very wet, but his eyes and mouth laughed. His shoulders hitched and hunched beneath the poncho.

In my left raincoat pocket I had one hundred dollars, just in case. I kept crumpling the money between my fingers.

"Give me a drink," he said. "I seen the bottle."

I didn't move.

"Y'hear?"

I handed him the bottle. He uncapped it. "Beggars can't be choosers," he said. "You ain't holdin' out nothin' from now on." He drank and smacked his lips, then he threw the bottle cap away.

"You're worried, ain't you?"

"This will be the last time you ever pull a stunt like this," I said.

"Think so? I don't figure you got much to say 'bout that, mister."

"What if I go to the police?"

He grinned. His teeth gleamed. He tilted the bottle.

"Bet you must've felt funny carryin' the old woman to her grave, hey?" He blew air through his nose and slapped rain from his hat brim with his left hand. His eyes were like wet agates.

"Well," I said.

"Must feel dandy," he said. "Your friend's wife, too. Figure mebbe I'm doin' him a turn, this way. Trusts ya like a brother, don't he? Ol' Herb says Verne told 'im you're th' one man in the world he can depend on." He made a noise through his nose.

"You better shut up," I said. I wasn't going to be able to stand much more of this. It was hell. Every bit of it was hell and inside me I was cramped up.

"Ain't ya got no shame? Figure mebbe the gal had reason, plenty reason, t' shove the ol' gal out the window. Cooped up like she was. Had t' carry the ol' woman ever' place she went. I seen it comin' in her eyes. Could tell what would happen someday. You show up an' things pop, hey? Bet she's red hot, hey?"

The whisky had worn off. I trembled beneath the raincoat and my guts knotted and writhed like a nest of snakes. Nobody could ever know how it was. It was something you read about in the old novels, where the hero crawled white-faced and weak back to his mistress' bed—throwing honor and pride and courage in the gutter, then crawling in after them, not even trying to find them again. You laughed at it today, because things had changed. You laughed if there was laughter with it. Only when it turned sour and you saw it was really evil, you were scared stiff. But you still crawled back toward those wanton gleaming eyes.

And maybe she was like the gatekeeper Milton wrote about, with the scales and the hell hounds running in and out of her womb, snarling and snapping, and you didn't care. Maybe that was it. Maybe you were subduing the hell hounds.

I began to laugh.

"Startin' to get you, hey?"

I ceased. I wanted Madge. God, how I wanted to see Madge, to be with her with all this done and over with. No matter what happened, and anyway, I'd have to take whatever came my way. And it would come—it had to. I knew that.

And now she wanted to kill Verne. I couldn't think clearly any more and it wasn't the whisky now. My mind felt like a smudge of smoke. She wanted to kill Verne, so we could have his money.

She had already nearly killed Verne. There wasn't much left now.

He finished the bottle, tossed it to the side of the road. It struck a stone and the glass shattered.

"All right," he said. "Make up your mind?"

"What do you want?" I said. I said it from the front of my mouth without thinking at all, trying to hold myself away from the thought.

"Figure to tread easy for a spell. Later on, I'll clamp down. Fifty dollars now. Told you no money tonight, but I figure you got fifty on you. Next Sunday you bring the gal. Same time, right here. I want to see her face."

"Fifty dollars?" I said. "You're scared, aren't you?"

He shook his head. But he was scared. It was in his eyes. He was lousy cheap.

"No," he said. "I ain't scared. I figure to have me a regular income from now on. Easy at first, so nobody suspicions." He paused and grinned. "Sunday bring the gal. I'd kind of like to see her close up."

He had asked for the money now. When I gave it to him he was in all the way. It might have been five thousand. It was all the same. And he knew it. That's why he was scared. But he was fairly sure of himself.

I gave him the money. He put it away beneath the poncho and spat. "I'll be watchin'," he said. "You step outa line, or don't show up with the gal, I'll make my move. Count on it."

"You haven't got any guts," I said. "Why don't you make a big haul and leave?"

He snorted, thrust his face close to mine. I smelled the wet barnyard and tobacco and his eyes gleamed. "You're a fine one to talk about guts," he said.

I turned and walked away before I hit him again, because what good would it do? Maybe I'd feel a little better, but it wouldn't change anything.

"Don't forget to bring the heifer Sunday night."

I walked faster. The rain had stopped.

My God, she wanted to kill Verne. It was just getting to me. So much had happened I was getting numb to shock.

I turned, looked back. He was standing in the road, watching after me.

"Sleep easy, mister," he called. "Thanks for the drink."

Fifty dollars. Fifty lousy dollars' worth of silence. Silence I didn't want. That was it.

But the closer I got to the house, the more I thought about her, and when I reached the house I wanted a drink. Because as the alcohol wore off, it was much worse.

In the kitchen I found a bottle and drank it down like water. There wasn't a sound in the house, although a light was lit in the living room. As I drank I thought of Petra, and with every drink I wanted her a little more.

I draped the soaking raincoat over the lunch bar and dried my hair on a towel. I knew then I was quite drunk. The panic didn't go away, but neither did thoughts of her. It was like hot iron, being jammed between dry hot iron flanks—stuck to them with the skin searing without odor but with a kind of exquisite pain. Not love, even. If there had only been love with it, real love, or whatever it is—maybe like Madge and me—then it would have been all right. I could have killed then, maybe. No, not killed. That wouldn't have happened, none of this would have. Because it would have been all right then. We would have gone to Verne and told him. It would have been complete because it would have been right.

And whatever sorrow there would have been would be honest sorrow, not secret or hidden. And the despair wouldn't have been there.

But it was not love. Not lust, even. Something else. I was unable to fight back because there was nothing to get a grip on. All the sharp edges were worn round and smooth. But there was hope. There had to be hope, and all through this I knew there was hope. Without that subconscious realization of eventual hope after the blowup that had to come . . . but to kill Verne. Even the thought. In my friend's home I stood drunk in the kitchen wanting his wife, knowing she had murdered his mother.

There was nobody in the living room. I turned off the light and felt my way upstairs. Taking a chance didn't matter now, nothing mattered. In the back of my head I wanted him to find us, so it would be finished.

I went directly to her room and she was waiting.

"He's asleep," she whispered. "We'll have to be quiet."

We stood there in the cool darkness and she closed her bedroom door. Her bare feet hissed on the thick nap of the rug.

"I paid off our keeper," I said, and my voice not only sounded bitter, it tasted bitter. I told her what silence cost.

"I knew it," she said. "He's that cheap." She stepped closer and her perfume struck me like a blow.

"He's cheap," I said. "But he'll get expensive."

"Let him," she said. "My God, you stink of whisky."

"Do you care?"

"No. I don't care."

The room was dark, which was a shame for anyone who lingered across the road up on the brambled hill. . . .

It was three-forty-five when I dressed to return to my room. I don't know why I dressed, but I did. Petra pleaded with me to stay until dawn, but the whisky had worn off and I felt rotten. Her passion didn't cool with time, it grew hotter.

"Stay with me, Alex. Stay. Verne's asleep. He'll never know." She was lying spread out on the bed, her hair black against the pillow.

Without the whisky to hold me up, it was hell, plain hell. I was living in a fire and she was the one who kept hurling gasoline on the flame. Being with her had been a kind of hellish heaven. It was maybe like trying to drown yourself in pleasure, hoping to God that you would drown, but hoping that the pleasure would continue and in the back of your mind hating every second of it, but never wanting to let up, either.

We hadn't talked much. I had nothing to say to her. When she mentioned Verne's heart, I told her to shut up.

She had chuckled.

We'd been talking enough without using vocal cords. I didn't reply now, but left the room.

The house was still and dark. I went quietly on down to my room and opened the door. Moonlight flayed the shadows into soft light.

"Hello, Alex."

It was Verne, seated on my bed.

Chapter Twenty

I went all to pieces. I shook like crazy. I couldn't control any part of me, just stood there shaking, unable to speak. Somehow I managed to close the door.

Then suddenly it was all right. He knew and it was all right. The relief was so great I wanted to laugh.

"You took a hell of a long walk," Verne said. He was in his pajamas on the bed. "But I don't blame you. I would too. This must have been hell for you these past few days. I just woke up a few minutes ago. Thought I'd see if you were awake. Felt like talking."

He didn't know. He didn't even suspect. There wasn't a tinge of suspicion in his voice.

"I brought a bottle," he said. "Have a couple with me?"

"Yes," I said. "Sure. I'll have a couple with you." Then the lies came out. It was simple, and my voice was calm even though the old torture was worse than ever inside. "Been sitting downstairs," I said. "Turned off the light when I came in a couple of hours ago. I didn't feel very sleepy."

"Yeah. That's the way I feel. This has been a rotten vacation for you."

I went into the bathroom, closed the door, and lit the light. I looked as if somebody had squeezed me through a sieve and then tried halfheartedly to put the strings together again. I washed, then went back into the bedroom and turned on the light.

"You do look kind of tired," he said.

"Yes."

"We'll just have a couple of short ones. Then I'll let you get some sleep."

"I'm not sleepy."

He handed me the bottle. It was cognac again. When I drank, it again went down like water. It seemed weak.

"I'm worried about Petra," Verne said.

I glanced at him. He looked as sick as you can get.

"There's something the matter with her, Alex."

"I hadn't noticed anything."

"Well, that's natural. You wouldn't, not knowing her, and all. But there's something the matter."

"What seems to be the trouble?"

It was easy, a cinch. You just talked along with a kind of savage politeness, not knowing half of what you said. But you knew you must be saying the right things. Because convention had taught you that long ago. So you didn't have to think and you could see her all the time lying on her bed in there. And none of the pain inside you showed, either. None of the conscious guilt showed while you stood there and lied like hell to a man who obviously trusted you completely. You were just like one of those talking machines, robots, where somebody pressed the keys and the voice came out.

"She's not happy, Alex. She hasn't been for a long while. I can tell. Of course, Mother, and all that... But like now. Suddenly she wants to run the house all by herself. It's a big house and she's never taken any interest before. But suddenly she doesn't want any help. Wants to cook all the meals—everything else."

"Sounds good to me."

"Yes. Only you don't know her like I do."

"Maybe you're right."

"Firing Jenny like that. And the cook. All right about the cook, but Jenny was swell—a swell girl."

I knew what he meant. But I didn't know how much longer I'd be able to stand there facing him and lying, even with the help of the bottle.

It wasn't anything you could just escape from, it was something that held you until it was done and you couldn't be free until the time came. God. To think. That beautiful goddamned bitch in there with the black hair not even knowing enough to know that she didn't know what was anyway partly the matter with her, or that she was cockeyed crazy and headed for doom.

All she knew was Get in bed with me, I love you. Kill. And money. And her husband suspected that something was the matter with her. I took a long drink from the bottle, glad that I was getting drunk again.

"I met her in a bar in New York," he said. "She played the piano there. You know what her last name was? It was Jones. Billed Pet Jones, and she sure could play."

Jones. It rocked me. Petra Jones.

"And she was so damned beautiful, Alex."

"Sure."

"We got married and bought this place and we were happy, too. For a while. Anyway, until Mother . . . I didn't mean to—" He stopped. "Give me the bottle."

He took a good drink.

"I'm going back to bed," he said. "Good night."

I watched him leave the room. He left the bottle on top of the bureau in my room. He had tried hard to tell me something but he'd found himself unable to. Maybe it was something he couldn't even tell himself and believe it at the same time. Or just tell, it even; maybe he couldn't even do that.

I got undressed and took the bottle to bed with me and by five o'clock I was really soused and not a bit sleepy.

The next day I stayed that way. Every time I felt myself beginning to sober up I'd take a couple of good drinks. Not staggering drunk, just brain-helpless drunk, not-care drunk, hell-with-it drunk.

I kept trying to tell myself that it was just that Verne had kept Petra cooped up too much and running around with his mother, and now she was blowing her top. Only it was no good.

At noon Verne went up to look at his mother's grave. The headstone was supposed to be ready in a day or so, he told me.

Petra was washing the dishes from lunch. She was a good cook. Almost as good in the kitchen as she was in bed.

I went upstairs and into her room and started going through the drawers in her dresser. Then I went over to her dressing table. There hadn't been anything. That's the way it would be with her. Only in the top right-hand drawer of her dressing table there was a .32 Savage automatic. A deadly little thing. I stared at it. There was a full clip in it.

Lots of people keep a gun around.

"It's just like you," she said from the doorway. "Especially the way you've been drinking."

I dropped the gun back into the drawer and closed the drawer. "What have you got that for?"

"What do you think?"

"What difference does it make?" I said.

"That's right."

She was close to me. She had her hair tied up with a ribbon in back and she wore a white apron over a black dress. Her eyes were clear and her smile was something you could watch for a long time—if you didn't know her.

"We won't have time now," she said. "He might come back."

"I wasn't thinking of that."

"Like hell you weren't."

"Suppose I beat it and leave you with this mess in your lap?"

"You won't," she said. "But, Alex, if you do try anything, I swear I'll go to Verne and tell him you killed his mother. I'll tell him you've been making love to me. I'll tell him anything, you hear? I mean it, Alex."

We watched each other. She was quite serious.

"He'll believe me, Alex. You may be his friend, and all that rot, but he'll believe me. Because I've never told him how I felt." She smiled slowly and her eyes glistened. "I just sort of worked on him."

He would believe her.

"He kept me cooped up here, I tell you. With that damned . . . And I want that money. He's no good any more. It's us now, Alex—us, you hear?"

"Yeah. Us." I started past her, but I didn't get by. It was like passing a magnet, one of these huge electromagnets they use to hoist junk. Like trying to pass one of those with twenty pounds of steel buttoned inside your shirt.

Holding her tight against you with her moaning a little. Then both of you tearing, trying to get away, because you knew he might come back any minute from up there on the knoll by the sycamore.

I made it and got downstairs and found a bottle.

The next day the headstone came. And while Verne was up there on the knoll with the men and the headstone, Petra and I were on the living-room couch.

And the days went on like that. Wednesday, Thursday, Friday, until Saturday I was still drunk and maybe a little out of my head. Verne was concerned about me. He well might be.

But he suspected things now. I knew he did; it was in the way he looked at me. He suspected but I couldn't allow myself to think of it.

I locked myself in my room and paced the floor and wrote letters to Madge that I tore up. I couldn't get away from Petra.

She was everywhere. It was a mad hot hell from which I couldn't escape even by crawling into a bottle. And through it all Verne strolled, amiable, smiling, saying, "Couple more days and I'll be feeling tops. You stay on, Alex. Then we'll get out and do things. I just want to be feeling right."

Saturday night at six o'clock I got up from the dinner table.

"I'm going to take a walk," I said. Neither of them paid any attention. I'd walked out into the orchard or along the road several times. This time I took a pint of whisky and my topcoat and started down the road toward Allayne. There was one way left. Hair of the dog. The antidote. Bounce one woman out of your mind with another. If I could do that, if I could stay drunk enough so I wouldn't turn around before I got to Allayne . . .

It was a windy fall night and the sky was black and moonless but with a million lazy stars blinking up there.

Hell was nearby, all right. But I only thought I knew what it was like. I hadn't seen any of it yet.

Chapter Twenty-one

Saturday night in Allayne was the big night. It was the night when those from the surrounding country came to town and when those in town went to town. The main street was jam-packed with cars and trucks, parked diagonally in toward the curb, fender to fender. The stream of traffic up and down the street was continuous and erratic in movement. Farmers and townspeople mingled in a bobbling, elbowing stream on the sidewalks, and the brisk autumnal wind blew dust in their eyes. The cheaper bars were loud with booming jukebox songs, loud red-faced laughter, the tinkle and clash of glass.

This was everywhere:

"Feller Lawrence. Out on French Street, there. Dug himself a hole in the ground an' stuck his old mother in it."

"So I hear. Guess she was dead, anyways."

"Dead, all right. Know what I think? Think she committed sewerside, by damn. Taken it into her head an' jumped plumb outen the danged winder."

"Seen 'im on the street the other day. Looked peaked. Walked like he was in a trance, like."

"Mebbe you'd look dangle-eared with a wife like her."

"She sure is a whingding, ain't she?"

"Give us another beer, Charley. Say, I'd pay to get peaked over that."

"It wouldn't take long, neither. But you ain't got enough."

"Feller stayin' out there now. Cece Emmetts says he met up with 'im at the funeral. Says he packs a pint ever'where he goes."

"Say, you don't suppose . . ."

In three different bars where I stopped for a beer, such conversations reached my ears. Verne Lawrence was literally the talk of the town, and Petra was the added spice. Doubtless the exact truth was spoken more than once, all unknowing.

Without drinking too much during the past few days, I had managed to keep myself in a light haze. There was no sign of its catching up with me. I'd eaten regularly and I hadn't overdone it. But now I felt like blotting it out. The haze was all right, but every day I had to increase the dosage to prevent descending clarity of mind.

There were two hotels in Allayne, one a rather rundown establishment with a loud, roaring bar, on the main street. The other, Allayne Hotel, was more imposing, a block off the main drag on an elm-shrouded street.

I drifted that way and found the cocktail lounge. There was a jukebox here, too, but it wasn't quite so loud and the selection of recordings was of the syrupy rather than the bang-slap-bam type. It was cool, rustic, and obviously frequented by some part of the town's elite. Men and women conversed over highballs and cocktails rather than beer and wine. They dressed differently and the men had haircuts. They probably said the same things as in the other places, and they certainly got just as drunk—or drunker.

I had a bottle of beer at the bar. In another room off the bar there were tables with chatting couples beneath a low-beamed ceiling.

I stared at her for perhaps a full minute before I knew who it was. Jenny. She didn't see me. She was with a broad-shouldered man who sported a hand-painted tie but very little chin.

Turning, I went out the side door of the bar into the parking lot and tilted my pint. I drank as much as I could without retching, pocketed the bottle, and returned to the bar. The whisky was taking hold fine now. I had a glass of water at the bar, then went in and approached Jenny's table. I didn't know whether it would work, but I was going to try. I didn't feel bad about it, either, because the guy with Jenny didn't look like her type. Besides, the whisky was taking hold fine.

I came up to them from behind the man's back and winked at her. "Miss Carson," I said. "Something important's come up, and—" I turned to him and said, "No, sit still," although he hadn't moved. "You'll have to come with me."

Jenny frowned, her eyes puzzled. She looked fine with her carrot-colored hair and gray dress with a thick silver chain around the waist. "What do you mean?" she asked.

"I mean, something's come up. Very important. I'm sorry, but—"

"Say," the man said. "What is this?"

"It's nothing at all," I said. "Merely something Miss Carson has to attend to."

Jenny looked from the man to me, then back again. She was obviously puzzled. She started to say something and I shook my head slightly. She began to play along.

"You mean the house?" she said.

I nodded. "Yes, and you'll have to come along right away. Can't afford to lose any time."

I reeled slightly.

The man said, "But Jenny—" What chin he had positively vanished.

Jenny said, "I'm terribly sorry, Tom. I didn't know this would come up."

Her coat, also gray and light, was over the back of her chair. I held it up. The guy looked at me, I looked at him and nodded.

He stood. Jenny stood. I slipped the coat over Jenny's shoulder and took her arm.

"I know it's tough," I said. "But you know you'd better see about it right away."

"But, Jenny—" the guy said. "Listen here," he said to me. "What is this?"

"You're spoiling the record," I told him. I guided Jenny carefully away from the table. The guy took three steps.

"Will you be back?" he said. "Jenny!"

"Tom, I don't know," she said. "I'll try. I'm terribly sorry. You can have my drink, I didn't touch it."

He stared at her drink. We left by the door into the hotel lobby and a moment later we were in the street. I wondered if he enjoyed her drink.

I glanced back through the large glass doors. The guy was coming down the length of the lobby with a determined stride.

"Now, listen," Jenny said. "What's so important?"

"Me," I said. "Me." There was a taxi stand and two minutes later we were turning onto the main street of Allayne.

I looked back toward the hotel. The guy was standing out in front, lighting a cigarette.

"You're drunk," Jenny said.

"Yes."

"Why did you do that?"

"You looked unhappy."

"That was a mean thing to do, Alex."

"You went along with it."

"Well, I—"

"Sure. Never mind. But you weren't happy, were you?"

"No."

"All right. How'd you like to take a walk? It's a beautiful fall night and we could take a walk."

She sighed and stared at the back of the cab driver's head. He had a fat neck that bulged over his shirt collar.

"All right," she said. "We'll take a walk. Is something the matter?"

"Not something. Everything."

"I didn't think you drank like this?"

"I don't." We were coming near the end of the main street, and traffic was thinning out. "Look," I said. "We'll get out here. Can you drink warm Martinis?"

"I never tried."

"I'll get a bottle of it already mixed," I told her. "And some paper cups. We can drink it that way. It may not be fine and there won't be any olives, if you've got to have olives, but it will be something."

She watched me and broke into a grin. "All right."

When I paid the driver I slipped him what was left of the pint of whisky. He said he didn't drink. I told him not to be foolish.

After we bought the bottle and the paper cups, we started off down the street. I felt fine. I knew there was Petra and the house out there and murder and that I was impaled on a hook, but I didn't care so much. I knew that when it wore off I would be in a complete hell, but right now it was all right.

"Where will we walk?" I asked.

She hesitated. "Let me carry the cups," she said. "Well. We can walk to the end of this street and then cross the park to the lake. Will that be all right? It'll be chilly, but the lake will be nice tonight."

"The lake it is."

We stopped. It was a dark corner. I drew her close and she looked up at me and she was fresh and clean like a summer's wind. Her lips were warm and sweet and for a single moment she responded, then I felt her stiffen.

We walked on. "Jenny kissed me," I said.

"All right."

We went on through the dark shadows of the park to the edge of the lake. She was right. The lake was something to see beneath the star-freckled night with the dark hills humped and leaning over against the living mirror of slowly broken water. The water was very cold, so I put the bottle between two rocks in the water and we sat on a bench close by.

The wind smelled of pure clean autumn and pine and water. We sat very close together now because it was rather cold.

"We could have gone to your house," I said.

"Yes. I guess so."

"But it's nicer here." I took her hand. I started to put my arm around her but then I remembered the bottle. "We'll try a drink," I said. "It won't be cold but it'll be cooler."

She smiled hesitantly but her eyes were bright and I told myself I must be very drunk because I thought her eyes reminded me of the stars. I did need a drink. She sort of reminded me of Madge, too.

"I have the cups," she called to me.

I thought for a minute I'd lost the bottle, but I found it. It felt cool. The water was so cold my hand ached just reaching for the bottle. I remembered how only a short while ago Petra had gone in swimming. It certainly hadn't cooled her.

"It tastes good," she said. "Really." She was lying.

"After the first few swallows it'll taste all right." Then I noticed something and remembered. "We'll have to drink each drink quickly."

"Why?"

"The gin softens the bottom of the cup. See?"

"Oh," She stared at me for a minute, holding the hair away from the side of her face with her hand. "It's a fine way to get a girl plastered, isn't it?"

"Yes." I touched my cup to hers. "Drink up."

We had another.

"What's troubling you, Alex? What is it?"

"It's nothing," I said. "Kiss me."

"No."

"Why not? We know each other, Jenny. You know we do."

"Yes, I do know you, Alex. Maybe better than you think."

"Then come on."

"You really want to?"

"The other one doesn't count."

She moved closer to me and her body felt warm even through both our coats. Maybe it was something more than just warmth. I kept thinking of Madge and Madge was all mixed up with Petra when we kissed. She drew away. "Please," she said.

I poured us each another drink. She drank hers fast. "The bottom of the cup," she said. "It's come out."

I started to hand her another cup. "It's getting colder," I said. There was a large thick clump of bushes beside the bench, and a few feet beyond the bushes was a large tree trunk with thick well-mowed grass between. "Wait." I got up and took off my coat, spread it out between the bushes and the tree.

She sat there looking at the coat. The park and the lake seemed very still but the wind blew stronger.

"Alex," she said.

"Come here," I said. "We'll sit on the coat." I put the bottle and cups down. "It's warmer here, very good here." She didn't move. I walked over by her and took her hands. She stood up against me, watching me, not smiling.

"Please," I said.

"All right."

We went over and sat on the coat. For a while we sat quite still and with perhaps a foot between us. The bushes did break the wind and on the ground it was much warmer. I was very warm. I was drunker now but doing O.K.

Every now and then I'd remember Petra and it was like a black sack dropped over my head. I wanted to yell. Because there was no release. The sensation of despair and panic cropped up inside me. And when I thought, Tomorrow is Sunday; Sunday night we have to meet Emmetts by the road. I wanted to get up and run. It's that way sometimes. It's a complete helplessness that you feel, knowing all the time that the helplessness is only yourself. That you should be able to stand up to it—act. So you take another drink sometimes.

I looked at Jenny and for a moment I thought she was going to cry. I felt bad about tonight. Then I saw she wasn't going to cry and I felt all right.

I was kissing her and we lay down on my coat.

"I think I'm a little tight," she said. "Alex, don't."

My hand moved down across her hip beneath her coat, down across her thigh.

"Let's take your coat off. We could put it over us."

She didn't say anything. I helped her out of her coat and we lay there with her coat over us. We lay on our sides, facing each other, pressed tight.

"Alex," she said. "This isn't right."

"Why not?"

She didn't answer. But I knew she was right, too, and something inside me began to draw away. She burrowed her face into my neck. I moved my hand along her leg across the hollow in back of her knee, and suddenly she moved against me, reached up, and unbuttoned the front of her dress.

"You don't love me, though," she said. "It's nothing like that."

I couldn't answer.

"The coat doesn't cover us very well," she said rapidly.

"There is one way it will."

"Yes, Alex, only—" she stopped. Her arms were tight around my neck.

"Only what?"

"Only hurry up!"

I held her very tight, then, very tight, and it was perhaps the most difficult thing I ever said in my life when I whispered, "I'm sorry, Jenny. We've made a mistake." I kissed her and rose. She lay quite still, her face pale.

Jenny sat on a large boulder beside the lake and stared at the dark water with errant starlight moving in it. I had thought wrong. I didn't want and wouldn't have anyone but Petra.

I went over by Jenny. I was still drunk, but I didn't want any more to drink right now and I felt bad about everything.

"It's all right," Jenny said. "I understand. You didn't love me or anything, really. I suppose I should curse you, or kick you. Anyway, it's all right. There's nothing you can do and you don't want anybody but her. I'm not sorry." She turned and looked at me. She smiled.

I didn't say anything.

"Tell me about it, Alex. You can tell me."

I tried to tell her something about how I felt. But not about the murder. I didn't tell it to her straight, but I knew she understood. Then for a minute I busted loose and said, "I can't get away!" My voice was loud.

"What about Madge?"

"Oh, God."

"I'm glad you love her, really."

"If I could only see her, be with her for a little while, it might help. But everything's all messed up now."

"You're shaking all over, Alex."

"I can't help it." I wanted to tell her I was scared, really scared. But sometimes you don't speak of that.

Then it all piled on me hard. I couldn't wait to get away from the lake, from Jenny. I knew it was the liquor wearing off. But that didn't help, the knowing. I had to see Petra, had to get back there to the house. What was she thinking?

"I'm frightened, Alex, the way you act."

I touched her shoulder.

"You really love this Madge? What's her last name?"

"Collins."

"You really love her, but Petra's got you stuck?"

"Yes."

"Only there's more to it than that. More you're not telling me."

"Yes, there's more. Let's go, Jenny."

We walked to her house and we walked fast. I kissed her. "I've got to go," I said.

"I know. Don't worry. It's all right about tonight." She didn't smile. She seemed almost as worried as I felt.

I squeezed her hand. Ten minutes later I was on French Street in a taxi. Then we had stopped in front of the house.

My hands shook so I dropped change on the floor of the taxi. Then I was out, running toward the house. A light was lit in the living room.

I went in the front door. Right away her perfume struck me and she was there in the hallway.

"He's upstairs," she said. "Where have you been, Alex?"

"In town. I walked into town."

Then she was against me and I breathed against the thickness of her hair.

"You wouldn't try to run away from me, would you?"

"No, no."

"I didn't think so."

I broke away from her, ran for the stairs. Reaching my bedroom, I locked the door. I heard her coming up the stairs.

I barely made it to the toilet. I blacked out in an agony of retching, tearing the stuff up, trying to vomit all the crazy hell out of the bottom of my guts.

Chapter Twenty-two

She rapped on my door several times during the night. Softly. She whispered my name. I knew she waited for me just beyond that thin panel. I kept the door locked. I didn't answer. Somehow I stayed in bed, cold with perspiration, staring through the dark at the filmy outline of the door.

"Alex, Alex, are you all right? Alex!"

Was Verne deaf? Was he blind not to realize what was going on in his own home?

Finally she went away.

This was my first victory. Then I knew how small, how truly petty a victory it was. Because I kept seeing her in her room. Maybe pacing the floor. Waiting, waiting. . . .

The pulse of my emotions ran up and down a crazy scale. I wondered if I were thinking right any more—if I could think at all. I couldn't sleep. I was exhausted but I couldn't sleep.

Thinking of Jenny, I knew that consciously or unconsciously I'd got her drunk and tried to take her in a vain effort to knock the rot out of me. The clash of her sweetness against Petra's savage evil kept reminding me that I'd done Jenny a wrong, even though I'd stopped short of the wrong I'd intended.

Instead of helping matters, it only made everything worse. It added another bit to my own personal agony of mind.

The mental torture was something I would never have believed possible. To be any kind of criminal one had to be conscienceless. The ones who had a conscience, the ones who went through despair afterward, were those who did the screwy things. Like running out on the street, shooting up the town, going hog wild.

I could never do it. But it would be a pleasure to kill her. Not with a gun—not even with a knife. With my bare hands. Choke her, strangle the putrid life out of her, watch her writhe, make her scream for release.

It was like being chained. Better than that. That would be something you could fight, knowing what it was. It wouldn't be something in your head, in your body, uncontrollable.

I'd read someplace that there was one woman like this for every man. One evil bitch, or not evil, but one that could scar your soul, shred it to a bloody pulp, just with a glance. With a thought, even. Snare, trap you, talk you into anything. One you'd do anything for, knowing you didn't even love her. Knowing it was only want, desire. One that could drive you into black madness, into a deathless, grinning glassy-eyed hell.

Madge. It was like a name mentioned in some cool beyond I couldn't reach.

My hand lying on the sheet clenched. I yanked and the cloth ripped, stuttering in a violent agony of sound.

Getting out of bed, I went over by the window and stared at the black outline of the brambled hill and waited for the dawn.

Anything to stay away from her.

At noon I was standing in front of the house watching the dirty sky piling up in the east. I was sick in every way a man can be sick. All morning Verne had watched me, puzzled. I had avoided Petra as much as possible.

Deep in thought, I didn't hear the approaching horses until they were almost opposite me on the road.

"Whoa!" It was Emmetts. He was driving a team dragging an empty stone boat along the shoulder of the road. Standing on the boards of the stone boat, he spat and watched me. His mouth loosed itself in a grin, but he appeared nervous. His shoulders hunched beneath a threadbare jacket. "Nice day," he said.

I didn't answer. It seemed as if every way I turned I ran against a hot iron wall.

"Don't you think? Don't you think it's a nice day?"

I still didn't reply.

"Ain't talkin', hey? They're talkin' in town," he said. He glanced quickly toward the house. There was something in his eyes now that hadn't been there before. His hands were nervous, fussing thickly with the leather reins. "C'mere," he said quietly.

I stepped closer.

"They's talk in town," he said. "Plenty."

One of the horses jerked forward, the other pulled back. "Whoa, you walleyed sons-o'-bitches!" The horses ceased, ears twitching. "Listen," he said, "Bring five hundred tonight." His mouth jerked loosely.

"Scared?" I said.

"Y'heard me." His voice went loud for an instant, then quiet again. Turning, he spat a wad of yellow tobacco into the road. "Five hundred. An' bring her. Don't forget, damn it. Bring the gal!" He lashed the horses, ran beside the stone boat a few paces, then leaped on.

I watched him go along the road. He didn't look back. His shoulders were hunched and there was something about him that had changed. He was nervous and he was overanxious.

Five hundred dollars? Five hundred dollars. . . .

"Verne's going up to the grave. We'll have time."
"No," I said. "Watch out. Watch out, damn you!"
"Alex, what's got into you?"
"Nothing. Stay away, that's all."

She reached up and opened the front of her dress. She wore no brassiere. Her face was full of defiance. "There," she said. "Come here, Alex!"

The kitchen door slammed.

"Oh, God!" she said. She ran upstairs. I watched her go and something went through me that I didn't recognize as yet.

Verne came into the hallway.

"I thought I heard Petra," he said.
"No. I don't think so. She's upstairs."
"Oh." He came up to me. "Alex, you look like hell. What's up?" He wore a gray sweater that once probably fitted him, but it hung on him now, like the rest of his clothes. His face was gaunt, his eyes unclear and sunken.

"Nothing," I said. "Guess I hit the bottle too hard."
"Go into Allayne last night?"
"Thought I'd look the town over."

We watched each other for a while. He frowned. He shook his head. "Alex," he said, "things have changed, haven't they? Those days back there in the war—it's all sort of unbelievable, isn't it?"

"Yes."
"Alex, you sure you feel all right?"
"Just hung over."

He stared, frankly puzzled. "It hasn't been such a hot vacation for you, has it?"

"It's been fine. It'll be O.K. Think I'd better have a little drink. Hair of the dog."

"Sure."

I turned and walked toward the kitchen. I could feel his eyes boring into my back.

Chapter Twenty-three

She tried to corner me.

I stuck by Verne. I stayed out of her way. I didn't know what was happening. She had changed somehow. She acted different. She was still excited, but not excited in the way she had been.

Verne didn't talk much and he watched me a lot. I began to wonder if I were coming apart.

It went on like that all day. It was the worst day I ever spent in my life. Late in the afternoon it started to rain again. It rained softly at first, but hour by hour it increased, until by eight o'clock it was a steady downpour.

"We could all go to a movie," Petra said in the living room.

I grinned at her. Verne glanced at me and said, "Would you like to?"

I shook my head. "Let's save it for another night." I wasn't sure what was going on in my mind, but it was something.

The minutes marched along to the round of rain.

The silence that descended was horrible. All three of us tried to break it, but it was like howling in the wilderness, shouting into a hurricane.

At ten to nine Verne went into his study.

"How are we going to leave?" Petra said.

I watched the faint tightness around her eyes and wanted to laugh. She came toward me as I got out of my chair.

"Don't," I said. I stared at her, at her body, at the gleaming black eyes and the thick jetty hair. I let my gaze linger on the rounded thrust of her thighs against her black skirt and the full curve of her breasts.

"Alex—"

I didn't say anything. But I knew—I knew. . . .

"Stay here," I said I went through the back of the house, picked up a raincoat, and left by the rear door. As I glanced toward the house, a light came on in the kitchen. The curtains parted and I saw her face pressed against the glass.

Then I heard Verne call, "Petra. Petra."

Her face vanished from the window. I sloshed through the driveway that had become a river until I reached the road. Then I started down toward the bend. The rain gusted in blinding sheets, driving in a vicious splattering across the road.

Already I was soaked to the skin. The raincoat was no help in this weather. As I neared the bend in the road I began to run.

This time he was waiting.

He stepped back as I reached him. "Where's the gal?"

I laughed and rain washed into my mouth. "Here," I said. "Here she is, damn you!" I feinted with my left, then slashed him with my right. He stumbled back into the bushes.

"Did you feel her?" I yelled. I dived at him, dived into the running mud and the streaming bushes. He sprang aside with a curse, then leaped at me.

As he leaped I kicked. My foot caught him squarely in the face. I felt his nose crumble and he let out a yell. Blood spurted from his face. He groped blindly for me.

"Go ahead," I said. "Go ahead. Here's your five hundred dollars!" I grabbed him by the front of his poncho at the throat, and put everything I had into the blows. Five of them, straight to his face, feeling the bone grit. He was senseless before I finished.

I helped him up. It wasn't only the bone of his face; the bones in my hand were broken. Pain lanced up my arm. Still I hit him with a kind of blind, groping despair.

Then I let go. He sprawled at my feet. For a long moment I stood over him with the rain tearing at us. He began to moan. His face was covered with blood. He tried to push himself up, moaning and trying to talk. Only he couldn't talk very well, with the blood streaming from his mouth.

I gripped my right arm around the wrist with my left hand, but it didn't stop the pain. Then I whirled and ran back toward the house along the highway. A tearing brilliant white streak of lightning slashed through the sheeted rain. Thunder cracked and slammed overhead and the world rocked. And all the time I ran I was laughing, laughing like hell.

I dropped the raincoat on the back stoop and entered the house as quietly as possible. My shoes squished water, but I walked softly into the living room. Nobody was there. I headed for the stairs. As I passed the study, I saw Verne hunched over his desk.

I hurried quietly on up the stairs, still gripping my right arm. My whole hand was smashed. Two white, crimson-flecked spears of knucklebone jutted through the skin, and at the slightest movement of my hand they gritted with bright-iced pain.

I had to keep choking back laughter. It burst in my throat and I gagged with it, choking it back, my chest filled and heaving with laughter.

She was in her room. I entered and closed the door.

She came at me from the other side of the bed, wearing white lounging pajamas. A beautiful black-eyed devil straight from the fires of hell. Then she stopped, clapped one hand across her mouth. Her eyes widened, staring at my hand. I held it up, clenched before her eyes, and blood dripped to the floor, mingling with the thick auburn-tinted rug.

My voice was little more than a hoarse whisper and I sounded mad, even to myself.

"It's done. It's all over with, Petra. It's finished."

"Alex. Alex! What's happened?"

I looked at her, wanting to laugh, but not wanting to make any noise yet. Stepping in close, I lashed out with my left hand, snagged the front of her flimsy pajamas, and tore the cloth away from her breasts.

And it *was* done. I could look at her now. I could be near her and nothing happened. It was done. Something had snapped inside me and she was nothing but a painting: a picture of a frightened woman. She began to talk rapidly.

"Alex, what have you done? Did you see Emmetts? Did you see him? Tell me what happened, Alex. You know I love you. You're acting foolish, Alex. What's happened?" Her voice was getting shrill.

"Shut up! I just wanted one last look at you before I go down and tell Verne. Tell him everything."

"Alex—" she stepped toward me.

"Don't," I said quietly.

She stopped, both hands half raised, her fingers trembling. "Alex," she said weakly.

"Yes. You killed her. And you damned near had me help you kill him. Only not quite, not quite."

"Alex, we could. We could have it all—all his money. The house, even. The house is in my name. He's nothing but a—"

"Shut up!" I watched the scheming behind her eyes. "You killed his mother," I said. "You murdered her."

"What if I did? Sure I did. I hated her. She was in the way. Oh, Alex." Her voice dropped a key, scheming, planning. "You don't know what you're saying. You've hurt yourself. Here, let me see your hand."

"Get back, you bitch!"

Her head began to jerk a little, out of control, and her eyes were very bright. Her breasts stood out firm and thrusting beyond the shreds of the torn pajama top. They lifted and fell with her erratic breathing.

"You almost had me," I said. I was dazed, weak. "Almost. You were so damned beautiful I couldn't tear myself loose. But I'm all right now. It had to come, didn't you know that? Didn't you know it had to stop someplace? I waited. I didn't think I'd make it—but I did."

She didn't answer. There was something going on behind her eyes.

Her voice was low. "Yes. Do you know I planned it all, darling? Do you know I planned it so that old hag would catch us doing that? Here, in this room. I planned it, knowing it would come that way. I left the windows open. I knew she'd follow us in here, if not the first time, then some other time. I aroused her suspicions until she was certain to follow us—break in on us. I planned it so I could shove her out of that window, somehow. I wanted it just to look like a fight. But it didn't come off, did it? It was too much to expect."

I stared at her. She was crazy, all the way. It had been a good scheme, but it was going to kill her.

"Going to Verne now," I said. I didn't wait, but left the room. She didn't move, still stood there, with her breasts going up and down.

I went down the hall, then stumbled down the stairs. My hand was a swollen cluster of pain now and my head throbbed. I thought I heard the front door close.

Verne was behind his desk, in the study. I staggered into the room. He watched me without speaking. He seemed very calm.

"Verne," I said. "Verne, there's something—"

"You don't have to tell me," he said. His voice was hollow and empty of expression. "I know all about it, Alex. I've known about you and Petra. I tried not to believe—I've been helpless." He motioned toward the door. "Emmetts was just here. He told me the rest."

"Verne," I said. "You don't understand!"

"I understand everything. And I'm going to kill her, Alex. You hear me?"

"Verne, for God's sake!"

He watched me very quietly. Then his gaze snapped to the study doorway and he smiled. "Well, good evening," he said.

I turned slowly, then rested partially against the desk. Something inside me clenched up tight like a fist, a fist of blank despair. And suddenly I saw how it all was going to end.

It was Petra. She still wore her torn pajamas, and clutched in her steady white hand was the .32 automatic. She stood with her legs apart in the doorway, her black eyes glistening like wet glass beads.

Chapter Twenty-four

"Well," Verne said. "We're all together again. All the important ones, that is. Emmets doesn't count."

"Verne," I said. "Believe—" I stopped.

He didn't take his eyes off Petra. "You killed my mother," he said. "Didn't you?"

"Yes," Petra said. "And I'm going to kill you." Her voice was edged with hysteria.

He did not smile. "Well. You're going to fix everything all up proper, eh?" He glanced at me. "You certainly messed Emmetts up, Alex. He was pretty mad about that. I think he'd have come to me anyway. Folks beginning to get nosy. Too many peculiar things going on."

Verne sounded almost under control, but I knew better. I could see something in his eyes.

He said, "You hurt your hand on Emmetts, Alex?"

"Yes."

"Too bad."

The silence dragged out. Then he said, "Tell me about it, Alex."

Petra didn't move from the doorway. There was a half-smile across her lips. I told him everything I knew, and tried to tell him something of what I'd gone through.

"I guess I wasn't right for her," Verne said.

"Yes," Petra interrupted. "Yes. You dried-up old—you husk!"

Verne recoiled with each word, but his expression didn't change. Only the look in his eyes became worse. The haunted, stricken, awful look in his eyes.

"Yes," Petra said softly. "Yes. Only you don't know it all. Neither of you know." She didn't move. Her voice was so quiet I had to almost strain to hear. She leaned slightly forward, the gun in her hand quite steady. "I've waited over a year, Alex. Trying to get you here. I had it all planned, all of it."

Rain drummed against the windows, slashed in wild gusts across the eaves.

"You were just the type," she went on. "Verne told me all about you. A man of truth, honest, dependable." She laughed. "Didn't take me long to break you down, did it?"

I stared at her.

"I want Verne's money and I'm going to get it. I planned the old woman's death—just as I've planned yours. I'm going to kill you both. Both of you. You hear?"

I didn't move. Verne said nothing.

She looked at me. "I knew you'd come to Verne eventually. You had to. It took you long enough, damn you! You liked it, didn't you? I was good, wasn't I?"

"I'm sure you were," Verne said.

"Yes. Well, they'll find you both dead. You'll have killed Verne because he saw what was going on between us. Because he's jealous, as everybody knows. So you'll have killed him." She paused, her lips working. "And I tried to save him, but it was too late. Except in the struggle, you, Alex, got shot."

"You're a fool," I told her. "It'll never work. They'll see right through it."

"You think so?" she said. "You should know by now I'm a pretty good actress, Alex."

"What about Emmetts?"

"I'll take care of him—don't worry. I know how to shut him up."

"It may be too late," I said. "Verne, say something. Tell her it's nutty. She'll never get away with it."

"It's worth a try," Verne said.

"Yes," she said. "You forget, I'm a woman. A beautiful woman. I'll get away with it." She paused. "Which of you will be first?"

I couldn't move from the desk. There was nothing to do. She was on the verge of squeezing the trigger and she looked as if she were familiar with the gun. I watched the small black muzzle poise for an instant on Verne, then swivel toward me. It was very steady and she was smiling. I saw her knuckles whiten faintly with pressure.

The room erupted with thunder. A steady, reverberating, monotonous crash, crash, crash. I fell back against the desk, staring at Petra.

The gun leaped from her hand, spiraled to the floor. Her mouth was a sudden gaping hole through which gouts of blood spurted. Then her right eye vanished in a blob of crimson.

She took three wavering steps into the room, hands groping. Between her breasts another hole appeared, then the tight front of her pajamas across her belly splashed scarlet. Her right leg buckled. She danced for a brief moment like a crazy doll, then crumpled into a grotesque heap on the floor, one knee raised, both arms outflung to embrace her last, her final lover—Death.

I turned slowly toward Verne. He still sat quietly behind the desk. In his right hand was an Army Colt .45. As I looked, a faint, nearly indiscernible wisp of smoke vanished above the gun barrel.

"I still hit what I aim at," he said. "I always did. Even with a lousy pistol. You remember, Alex?"

My voice seemed to come from someplace far away. "I remember, Verne."

He kept staring at Petra's body on the floor.

"She was truly beautiful," he said.

"Yes."

"But only on the outside. On the inside she was evil. All evil. I've waited for this moment. Knowing what she and you have done in my home."

"Verne, I—"

He whirled. "Get out! Get out, Alex. Quick—before I kill you, too. Alex, get out!"

"Verne!" I shouted.

He rose behind the desk and the muzzle of the gun jerked toward my stomach. My bowels writhed and I leaped for the study door.

"Don't come back!" he yelled. His voice was shrill.

Outside, I ran across the rain-soaked lawn to the road.

A single muffled shot sounded from the house.

I didn't need to be told what it was; I didn't need to see. I knew there were two dead bodies in there now.

Wind and rain lashed at me as I turned down the road toward Allayne. I walked fast, then I broke into a run between the dark hills and the slowly moving shadows of the trees.

It was all over now. I knew I would have to pay for my part in it. First I had to see the police, then get back to Madge. Returning to Madge was all that mattered.

So there was hope. Without it you couldn't live. Because hope and tomorrow are the two things that keep you going. And you can always keep reaching out beyond, until that one final tomorrow. Then you don't need hope any more.

Petra and Verne were dead. I wondered if Verne had found peace. It was hard to believe that I had lived through those long days of hell with Petra. She was gone, but there would be many tomorrows before I could forget.

But I tried to forget. And then I knew I would forget. Because I'd never again address another letter to the big red-brick house at 13 French Street.

THE END

Gil Brewer Bibliography

NOVELS:
Love Me and Die (1951; w/Day Keene, published as by Day Keene)
Satan is a Woman (1951)
So Rich, So Dead (1951)
13 French Street (1951)
Flight to Darkness (1952)
Hell's Our Destination (1953)
A Killer is Loose (1954)
Some Must Die (1954)
77 Rue Paradis (1954)
The Squeeze (1955)
The Red Scarf (1955)
—And the Girl Screamed (1956)
The Angry Dream (1957; reprinted as The Girl from Hateville, 1958)
The Brat (1957)
Little Tramp (1958)
The Bitch (1958)
Wild (1958)
The Vengeful Virgin (1958)
Sugar (1959)
Wild to Possess (1959)
Angel (1960)
Nude on Thin Ice (1960)
Backwoods Teaser (1960)
The Three-Way Split (1960)
Play it Hard (1960)
Appointment in Hell (1961)
A Taste for Sin (1961)
Memory of Passion (1962)
The Hungry One (1966)
The Tease (1967)
Sin for Me (1967)
It Takes a Thief #1: The Devil in Davos (1969)
It Takes a Thief #2: Mediterranean Caper (1969)
It Takes a Thief #3: Appointment in Cairo (1970)
A Devil for O'Shaugnessy (2008)

The Erotics (2015)
Gun the Dame Down (2015)
Angry Arnold (2015)

As Harry Arvay
Eleven Bullets for Mohammed (1975)
Operation Kuwait (1975)
The Moscow Intercept (1975)
The Piraeus Plot (1975)
Togo Commando (1976)

As Mark Bailey
Mouth Magic (1972)

As Al Conroy
Soldato #3: Strangle Hold! (1973)
Soldato #4: Murder Mission! (1973)

As Hal Ellson
Blood on the Ivy (1970)

As Elaine Evans
Shadowland (1970)
A Dark and Deadly Love (1972)
Black Autumn (1973)
Wintershade (1974)

As Luke Morgann
More Than a Handful (1972)
Ladies in Heat (1972)
Gamecock (1972)
Tongue Tricks! (1972)

As Ellery Queen
The Campus Murders (1969)
The Japanese Golden Dozen (1978; rewrites by Brewer)

STORY COLLECTIONS:

Redheads Die Quickly and Other Stories (2012, revised 2019; edited by David Rachels)
Death is a Private Eye: Unpublished Stories (2019; edited by David Rachels)
Die Once—Die Twice: More Unpublished Stories (2020; edited by David Rachels)
Death Comes Last: The Rest of the 1950s (2021; edited by David Rachels)

UNPUBLISHED NOVELS

House of the Potato (autobiographical novel, late 1940s)
Firebase Seattle (Executioner novel, 1975)
The Paper Coffin (spy novel, 1970s)

From the Master of Obsessive Noir. . . .

Gil Brewer

1-933586-10-9 Wild to Possess / A Taste for Sin $19.95
"Permeated with sweaty desperation."—James Reasoner, *Rough Edges*

1-933586-20-6 A Devil for O'Shaugnessy / The Three-Way Split $14.95
"Brewer's insights into the psychology of sexual enthrallment and obsession still resonate."—David Rachels, *Punk Noir Magazine*

1-933586-53-2 Nude on Thin Ice / Memory of Passion $19.95
"His entire livelihood came from writing works in which lurid narratives were rendered in a punchy, unadorned prose style."— Chris Morgan, *Los Angeles Review of Books*

1-933586-88-5 The Erotics / Gun the Dame Down / Angry Arnold $20.95
"Showcases the impressive storytelling talents of Gil Brewer, a true master of the noir mystery genre . . . strongly recommended."—*Midwest Book Review*

978-1-944520-58-8 Flight to Darkness / 77 Rue Paradis $19.95
"Murder, madness, swamps, gators, a savagely beautiful woman . . . it doesn't get much better than this for noir fans . . . crazed and breakneck."—James Reasoner, *Rough Edges*

978-1-944520-55-7 The Red Scarf / A Killer is Loose $19.95
"There are some neat plot turns, the various components mesh smoothly, the characterization is flawless, and the prose is Brewer's sharpest and most controlled."—Bill Pronzini, *Big Book of Noir*

978-1-944520-76-2 Redheads Die Quickly and Other Stories: Expanded Ed. $19.95
Edited and introduced by David Rachels. A reprint of the 2012 edition with five new stories, including the novelette "Meet Me in the Dark."

978-1-944520-77-9 Death is a Private Eye: Unpublished Stories $17.95
Editor David Rachels has assembled another essential noir collection, 22 previously unpublished stories, including two classic novellas from the early 1950s.

978-1-951473-61-7 Death Comes Last: The Rest of the 1950s $17.95
Taken together, *Death Comes Last* and the expanded *Redheads Die Quickly* contain all of Brewer's short fiction published between 1951 and 1959.

978-1-944520-88-5 Die Once—Die Twice: More Unpublished Stories $15.95
Twenty-four previously unpublished stories from the noir master, including some of his 1970s erotic fiction. Edited and with a new introduction by David Rachels.

978-1-951473-04-4 The Tease / Sin for Me $19.95
"Brewer packs each novel with plenty of unexpected twists to keep the suspense taut and our interest maintained to the very end . . ."—Alan Cranis, *Bookgasm*

Stark House Press, 1315 H Street, Eureka, CA 95501
griffinskye3@sbcglobal.net / www.StarkHousePress.com
Available from your local bookstore, or order direct or via our website.

www.ingramcontent.com/pod-product-compliance
Lightning Source LLC
LaVergne TN
LVHW021804060526
838201LV00058B/3237